# Ghost Target

# GHOST TARGET

## WILL JORDAN

CANELO

First published in the United Kingdom in 2016 by Canelo

This edition published in Great Britain in 2019 by

Canelo Digital Publishing Limited
57 Shepherds Lane
Beaconsfield, Bucks HP9 2DU
United Kingdom

A CIP catalogue record for this book is available from the British Library.

Print ISBN 978 1 78863 461 8
Ebook ISBN 978 1 910859 71 1

This book is a work of fiction. Names, characters, businesses, organizations, places and events are either the product of the author's imagination or are used fictitiously. Any resemblance to actual persons, living or dead, events or locales is entirely coincidental.

Look for more great books at www.canelo.co

# Prologue

*Forward Operating Base Chapman, Afghanistan – 30 December 2009*

It was a cold December afternoon in Khost province, the low winter sun already slanting down towards the clouds gathering on the western horizon. The small group of CIA intelligence operatives who had congregated in the centre of the lonely outpost pulled their jackets a little tighter as a chill wind whipped in from the desolate mountains to the north.

Intelligence analyst Abigail Page could think of about a thousand other places she would rather be at that moment, most of which involved tropical beaches and umbrella drinks, but she gave no thought to returning indoors. Not now. The events that were about to play out here in this isolated base at the edge of civilization could well change the course of the War on Terror forever. Here, today, they were about to make history.

Her radio earpiece crackled as a transmission sounded over the secure comms net. 'Checkpoint Bravo. Principal is confirmed. He's coming through.'

Page watched as the barrier at the base's inner security checkpoint was raised, and a beaten-up red station wagon trundled beneath, threading its way through the concrete chicanes.

She could feel her heart stepping up a gear as the vehicle slowly approached the waiting group. Two men were just visible through the dust covered windshield. The driver was an Afghan man named Arghawan who served as the chief of external security for Camp Chapman. He was the only local they trusted to make such a dangerous trip all the way from the Pakistan border with a high profile asset on board.

His passenger was the one they had gathered here to receive. A 32-year-old doctor from Jordan, Humam al-Balawi had been a vocal al-Qaeda supporter until the Jordanian intelligence service caught up with him and turned him about a year ago. Their offer had been simple enough – become a double agent for the CIA, or we'll throw you and your entire family in jail for the rest of your lives. Needless to say, al-Balawi had accepted.

Since then he'd been feeding the Jordanians and the Agency a steady stream of actionable intel, resulting in a number of confirmed al-Qaeda kills through drone strikes and targeted assaults.

He'd earned his stripes, but such minor victories were of little consequence compared with what he now claimed to have for them. The location of Ayman al-Zawahiri – the second most powerful commander in al-Qaeda, and Osama Bin Laden's right hand man. An asset whose capture could well result in the destruction of the terrorist network's entire command structure.

It was easy to see now why so many of the Agency's senior intelligence experts were on site for this meeting. Even a cursory glance at the assembled group read like a who's who of the Agency's anti-terrorist elite.

First up was Jennifer Matthews, the chief of the base, and a 20-year veteran of CIA field ops. She'd been tracking al-Qaeda since well before the 9/11 attacks, and was one of their foremost experts on the ground.

Hovering close to her was Don Livermore, the deputy chief of the Kabul station, and the Agency's second highest ranking officer in Afghanistan. Livermore had been around since the dark days of the Cold War, and had managed agents everywhere from Eastern Europe to Africa, Iraq and Afghanistan.

Also present was al-Balawi's Jordanian handler. Page knew little of the man, though it was rumoured he was the cousin of King Abdullah II of Jordan. Even the royal family wanted a piece of this action, not that she could blame him. If al-Balawi did indeed hold intel that could lead to the destruction of al-Qaeda, he would want his name stamped all over it. This was a moment that could make or break careers.

Keeping her eyes on the approaching station wagon, Page raised the encrypted satellite phone to her ear. 'He's inside the perimeter,' she reported, speaking in hushed tones. 'Approaching now.'

–

A hundred and fifty miles away in a secure conference room at the US embassy in Kabul, CIA Station Chief Hayden Quinn leaned in closer to his laptop. Laid out before him was a grainy overhead video feed of Camp Chapman that was being beamed from a Predator drone orbiting the site of the meeting. The unmanned vehicle had been tracking al-Balawi's vehicle all the way from Pakistan to ensure it wasn't interfered with.

Quinn had desperately wanted to be there for the meeting himself, having pulled more strings and circumvented more protocols than he cared to remember to make this thing work. But having the Agency's most senior commander and his deputy at the same forward operating base was a risk nobody was willing to take.

'Roger that,' he replied, connected to her via an encrypted satellite uplink. 'How's he look?'

'Hard to say,' she replied, trying to keep her tension from showing. What a dumb question. How does he look? She didn't know the man, could barely see him through the grimy windshield, and certainly wasn't in a position to gauge his mood. 'The car's stopping now.'

Bringing the dust-covered station wagon to a halt, the driver killed the engine. A moment of tense, fraught silence passed, broken only by the sighing of the winter wind. Page held her breath, knowing this was a crucial moment.

Then, just like that, the passenger door creaked open and a man stepped out. All eyes were on him in an instant, comparing him with the face they had memorized from his intelligence dossier. Medium height and build, even features, his still-youthful face mostly hidden behind a thick beard that hadn't yet started to grey. He was dressed in a long, padded overcoat, no doubt to ward off the late December chill.

'It's him,' Page confirmed over the encrypted line, unable to disguise her relief or her excitement. 'He's really here.'

Indeed, the sense of exultation and burgeoning elation amongst the gathering was almost palpable. At a nod from Matthews, the base commander, one of the private security contractors flanking the group moved forward to give al-Balawi a pat-down search.

He had been untouched thus far on Quinn's orders, his unimpeded entry to Camp Chapman intended as a sign of respect and mutual trust, but even this goodwill gesture only extended so far, with some of the Agency's top personnel only yards away. A simple frisking would ensure he hadn't brought anything that could be used as a weapon.

Al-Balawi's hands were thrust deep into the pockets of his overcoat and remained that way as the private security contractor approached. The man hadn't drawn his weapon, but his hand hovered instinctively close to it.

'Please raise your hands, sir,' the operative instructed, speaking in an uncharacteristically deferential manner. He was under strict orders to treat the Jordanian double agent as an honoured guest.

Watching the man closely, Page caught something she hadn't expected. A momentary flicker in his eyes, a sudden tension in his body as if he were readying himself for some great exertion. He raised his hands from his pockets as requested.

'Oh fuck,' Page gasped when she saw the plastic detonator in his left hand, a wire trailing back in through his sleeve.

She saw the operative go for his gun, saw his hands close around the weapon, then there was a sudden flash and the world around her was engulfed in darkness.

–

Quinn started in shock as the video feed suddenly turned pure white, the drone's infra-red cameras temporarily blinded by an intense flash of light and heat in the centre of the compound.

'What the fuck was that?' he demanded, a sudden knot of fear and concern twisting his stomach. 'Page, come in. What's your situation?'

Slowly the image swam back into focus as the flash receded, revealing a scene of utter carnage and devastation in the centre of the small encampment. Fires burned in every corner of the screen, particularly around the shattered remnants of the car and the building that had been set aside for al-Balawi's debriefing, while other thermal sources that conformed roughly to the shape of human bodies lay scattered around the area.

Some were less recognizable now.

'Oh God,' Quinn gasped, staring at the screen in horror. 'Oh Christ, no.'

The base commander, the deputy chief of operations, the Jordanian liaison… nearly all of the Agency's major players in Afghanistan had been on hand for that meeting, had been standing just yards away from the centre of the blast.

Realizing the satellite phone was still active, he leaned closer to the speaker. 'Page, talk to me. Are you there? Page!'

–

Abigail Page couldn't hear the tinny buzz of his voice through the damaged satellite phone lying several yards away. Her eardrums had been shattered by the concussive force of the blast.

Dizzy and confused, unsure what had happened, she opened her eyes and looked around. She was lying on her side some distance from where she'd last been standing, and couldn't understand why she'd suddenly moved. But she could smell something in the air: smoke, burning fuel and melted plastic.

In some vaguely understood corner of her mind, the pieces seemed to come together. She remembered al-Balawi in the instant before the explosion, remembered seeing the flicker in his eyes, the trailing wire leading into his bulky overcoat.

A suicide bomber. He had betrayed their trust, using their eagerness, their desperation against them. Blowing himself up right in the heart of the base, with some of the Agency's top brass just feet away.

That thought was enough to galvanize her.

You need to get up now, she told herself. There could be secondary explosions. The others might need your help. Get up and find out who's hurt.

She tried to pull herself up, tried to move, but her body wouldn't obey her commands. Her legs felt like lumps of lead, weighing her down but transmitting no sensation back to her brain. There was a moment of fright, of panic, then the realization that something warm and wet was spreading outwards from various points across her torso. It meant something, she knew, but her thoughts were growing hazy and confused.

Surprisingly, there was no pain. Or maybe there was, and she simply hadn't recognized it yet. Her mind was dimming, like a flashlight slowly running out of power, and it was becoming hard just to keep her eyes open.

Someone else was lying on the ground near her, she realized then. A man. She recognized him as the Jordanian intelligence operative who had come to oversee the meeting. With an odd sense of detachment, she noted that his right arm was missing at the shoulder, ending in a torn mass of bloody flesh and jagged bone. His deep brown eyes stared lifelessly into space, seeing nothing.

The cousin of a king, she thought with an incongruous flash of humour as a gust of frozen wind swept across the devastated base, stirring the fire and smoke, and darkness encroached on her vision.

I'm going to die beside the cousin of a king.

# Part I

# Reunion

In 2010, a declassified document from the National Security Archive asserted that the ISI, Pakistan's external intelligence agency, covertly used $200,000 of US aid contributions to fund the suicide attack on Camp Chapman.
The ISI denies all involvement.

# Chapter 1

*Marseille, France – three months later*

Philippe Giroux hung back in the shadowy recess of the shop doorway, pretending to be texting someone on his phone as his target passed by on the opposite side of the street.

It was a quiet morning, the air just starting to warm up as the morning sun rose above the horizon. A light breeze wafted inland, carrying with it the salty tang of the Mediterranean Sea and the distant squawks of gulls circling the harbour. On a nearby road, he heard the rhythmic chug of a small van engine, perhaps a baker making his morning deliveries.

Aside from these minor distractions, the streets were almost deserted at such an early hour. Perfect for what he had in mind.

The secret of a good takedown was preparation. Most men in his profession were opportunists, taking action as soon as chance allowed, but Giroux was better than that. He took his time, observing his targets until he built up a picture of their habits, their awareness of the world around them, the possibility of them fighting back.

After patiently following and watching this one for the past few days, Giroux now felt confident enough to draw a few conclusions about him.

In his late-thirties, standing an inch or two over six feet by Giroux's estimation, his target had the trim, athletic physique of someone with plenty of spare time to exercise. The hard, uncompromising muscles of real physical strength were visible beneath his tanned forearms, and his casual white shirt sat comfortably across his broad shoulders and firm chest.

His face was lean and sharp-featured, his hair dark brown, cut in a short and practical style, his jaw coated with several days' growth of beard. Doubtless women found him attractive, especially his eyes. They were green; deep, vivid and piercing. The kind of eyes that saw much and gave away little.

But more than his appearance, it was the way he moved that marked him out as a man of means. It wasn't quite an arrogant swagger, but rather the confident, measured tread of a man sure of his abilities and his place in the world.

His clothes did not speak of great wealth – just plain grey cargo trousers, a loose shirt with the sleeves rolled up, and inexpensive but practical walking shoes. But as Giroux knew well enough, rich men were often to be found in simple attire. They were confident enough to dress down, unlike those of lesser stature, who bought expensive clothes to feign the appearance of wealth.

This man belonged in the former category.

Each morning he walked into town early, before most people were up and about, and bought food from the same bakery. He never followed the same route through the old town, which spoke of a certain awareness, and an understanding that predictability and routine could lead to vulnerability.

But there were only so many different ways to reach the same destination, and even this man was constrained by the geographical layout of the city.

For the most part his route took him along La Canebière, the main thoroughfare leading from the old port, with its big luxury yachts moored side by side, all the way to the Reformes quarter to the east. But Giroux knew that at one point he would have to cut to the right, taking one of the narrow side streets that led uphill towards Notre Dame de la Garde cathedral.

That was where it would happen. That was where Giroux would take him down.

His contract hadn't specified the manner or the location in which his target was to be killed, which was all to the good as far as he was concerned. Some people could be annoyingly particular, demanding a certain kind of weapon or a specific fatal injury, but this one had given him all the latitude he wanted. All he'd been asked to provide was photographic evidence of the kill.

Waiting until his target was a good distance ahead, Giroux pushed himself away from the doorway and followed him, still pretending to be absorbed in his phone just in case the man glanced back. His well-worn trainers made no sound on the cobbled road as he walked.

The key to following people was to look confident and relaxed, as if you had every right to be going where you were. Like an actor playing a role, you had to assume the identity of someone who was just out for a casual stroll, a man who had no interest in what was going on around him.

His appearance helped. Of average height and build, with a rounded and unthreatening face, Giroux had always found it easy to blend in. Few noticed him, and even fewer saw him as a threat. More fool them.

His target gave no hint that he was aware of being followed. He continued to walk with the same relaxed, measured pace, glancing occasionally left or right at things of interest, but for the most part just enjoying his morning stroll without a care in the world.

Keep walking, my friend, Giroux thought. That will change soon enough.

About a hundred yards further on, the side street came into view, and sure enough his target angled across the road to make for it. Giroux followed, still keeping his distance, waiting until his target had disappeared around a corner before picking up his pace. He would close the distance as quickly as he could now.

The side street was mostly used as a service entrance for the line of shops and restaurants that backed onto it. Flanked by three-storey buildings on both sides, it was nearly always in shadow. The road itself was littered with big steel bins set beside the rear doors of kitchens and other work places, many overflowing with plastic bags.

The place reeked of spoiled food. Still, it was a perfect place for a takedown. The unsavoury odours meant that few pedestrians came this way, the shops and restaurants were still closed, and the shadows and big steel bins meant that he would be hidden from prying eyes on the main road. Not that he expected anyone to be passing so early in the day anyway.

As Giroux approached the corner, his hand reached inside his jacket and gripped the moulded handle of the police baton hidden within. It was an old-fashioned wooden weapon, the kind that had long since been superseded by the lightweight telescopic night sticks used by today's police officers. But it was simple and reliable, and he knew from experience that a good solid blow to the base of the skull would drop a man like a brick. And if that failed, he also had a knife concealed in a sheath at the small of his back.

Some men in his profession carried guns, but what was the point? Guns were expensive, not always reliable, and needed to be carefully looked after. Most importantly, guns made noise, and noise attracted attention. Takedowns were supposed to be quick and quiet, and in that regard he'd yet to find a better tool than this sturdy wooden baton.

He was almost there now. He removed the baton from his coat pocket and pushed it up into his sleeve so that it was hidden from casual view. His target wouldn't even know what had hit him. He took a deep breath, ready for another profitable day.

He never expected what happened next.

Rounding the corner, he suddenly found himself face to face with his target. The man was just standing there, hands by his sides, staring at him with those vivid green eyes.

'Why are you following me?' he demanded, speaking in accented but perfectly understandable French.

Shit.

Giroux had been wrong. This man wasn't as blissfully unaware as he'd thought. Maybe he'd heard something during the approach, maybe he had noticed him before and grown suspicious of his reappearance today. Either way, he had lost the element of surprise. But Giroux still had the baton, his opponent was unarmed, and he was already psyched up for what he was about to do.

No way was he losing this contract.

Reacting instinctively, he loosened his grip on the baton, allowing it to fall down into his hand. At the same moment, he launched himself forward, swinging the club around to strike his opponent a sharp, vicious blow across the jaw. Perhaps this takedown wouldn't be as quick or clean as he'd planned, but the end result would be the same.

But the man was no longer there. Moving with frightening speed, he had ducked aside just as Giroux swung, throwing him off balance. He tried to adjust his posture for another swing, but even as he did so he felt the baton yanked out of his hand. Turning right to face his opponent once more, he was just in time to see a clenched fist coming right at him.

There was a sickening crunch and an explosion of white light as the punch connected. The impact sent Giroux, already off balance, sprawling on the ground in a heap, stars flashing across his vision and blood streaming from a broken nose. He had landed in a pool of fetid water, strewn with discarded trash. Within moments it had soaked into his jeans and jacket.

Snorting and coughing the blood out of his throat, tears streaming from his eyes, Giroux looked up at the man who only moments before had seemed like such an easy mark. He was standing a few yards away, looking as calm and relaxed as when he'd strolled out of the bakery.

This was a new and very unwelcome experience. Giroux was no stranger to violence, but he was used to inflicting it, not receiving it. He was used to ambushing people, catching them unawares and subduing them before they knew what was happening. He wasn't used to his targets fighting back. But this one was.

Anger and fear flared up in him, the former magnified by the latter. He wasn't used to being afraid of people, and he didn't like it.

Clenching his teeth, he scrambled to his feet and reached for the knife at his back.

'You've already made one mistake today,' his enemy warned. 'Don't make another.'

But Giroux wasn't hearing him. His hand went for the knife, fingers closing around the haft. Just as he yanked it out and swiped in a wide arc to catch his opponent across the midriff, the man took a step backward, swung the police baton down and knocked the blade right out of his hand, breaking a couple of Giroux's fingers in the process.

Giroux had no time to register the injury. Before he could recover, his opponent closed in, placed one foot behind his and gave him a single powerful shove in the middle of his chest. He tripped and went down a second time, hitting his head on the rough cobbled road as he fell.

A moment later, he gasped as he felt the blade of his own knife pressed against his throat. His vision was blurred by blood and tears, but he knew his fearsome opponent was kneeling on top of him, one knee pressed into his chest. He could kill him whenever he wanted. Fear, sheer and absolute, charged through him.

'Now you've made two big mistakes. You tried to kill me, and you tried to do it alone,' he said, his voice low and menacing. 'Don't make another mistake by forcing me to ask a third time. Why have you been following me?'

'T-to steal from you,' Giroux stammered.

He gasped as the knife was pressed in harder, causing blood to well up.

'Are you working for someone? Think carefully before you answer, my friend.'

'It is the truth! I swear it!' Giroux pleaded. There was no pretext of playing tough now; he was begging for his life, and he knew it. 'You s- seemed like an easy mark. I thought you were just a rich tourist.'

The man's intense green eyes were locked with his own, seeming to penetrate his very soul. Finally, with some reluctance, the pressure of the blade eased.

Keeping him pinned to the dirty ground, the man rifled through his pockets until he found Giroux's creased, grubby and disappointingly empty wallet. Still, even he possessed a few cards and scraps of identification that his erstwhile victim had no problem rooting out.

'Philippe Giroux, right?' he remarked, comparing the battered and bleeding face before him with the far more youthful one on his expired driver's licence.

'Yes.'

'Right then, Philippe. Obviously you're not the brightest guy, so I'll keep this simple. If you try something like this again, I'll kill you. If you follow me, I'll kill you. In fact, if I ever see your face again in Marseille, or anywhere else for that matter, I'll kill you. If you understand what I've just said, say yes.'

Giroux stared at him. The look in his eyes told him this was a man who had made good on such threats before, and wouldn't hesitate to do it again.

'Yes,' he said at last.

'Good.' The knife was removed from his throat and tossed into a walled courtyard nearby. 'Don't forget to wash up.'

Without saying another word, the man stood up, picked up his bag of goods from the bakery, and walked off as if nothing had happened.

# Chapter 2

Set halfway up a gentle hill a couple of miles east of Marseille, overlooking a sheltered bay and the vast swathe of the Mediterranean beyond, the old French villa enjoyed views that would have made most estate agents green with envy. Unfortunately for Ryan Drake, the view was just about the only thing this place had going for it.

In need of a place to lay low after being forced to go on the run from the Agency last year, Drake had chanced upon the old, dilapidated villa about six months ago. Clearly the building had suffered from decades of neglect, but for him it had seemed ideal. A cheap, isolated, easily defensible building in an elevated position, with only a dusty single-track road leading up to it.

Nobody could approach closer than half a mile without his knowledge. And given that the nearest house was on the far side of the bay, he had little concerns about his neighbours spying on him. In short, it was a perfect safe house.

Posing as a foreign property investor looking for a restoration project, he'd put in a cash bid the very next day. Needless to say, his offer had been accepted almost immediately.

He hardly considered himself a rich man, but like any deniable CIA operative with an ounce of foresight and pragmatism, he'd set up a pretty comprehensive security blanket during his time with the Agency – false identities, travel documents, passports and a decent financial reserve that he could tap into. A man like him never knew when he might have to disappear in a hurry, and last year in Libya that fear had proven all too real.

*Some modernization required*, the property listing had said. That was a euphemistic way of looking at it, he'd soon realized.

The previous owner had obviously been a bit of a hoarder, because the place had been packed with junk of all descriptions – everything from old newspapers, magazines and pictures to ancient television sets, radios, ornaments, broken furniture and a hundred other things he hadn't bothered to look at. There had even been an artificial leg hidden away in a corner of the basement. Drake had been tempted to put an ad in the local Lost and Found, since its owner was sure to be missing it by now.

Still, six months down the line, things had improved marginally. The plumbing worked, when it felt like it. The boiler, like a moody teenager, would alternate between being cooperative and useful, to not wanting anything to do with him. And the electrical system, installed in 1936 as the yellowed sticker on the fuse box proudly proclaimed, couldn't be counted on if more than three lights were turned on at once. He'd done what he could to get it back into working order, but his modest electrical expertise was no match for the madness of 1930s French building practices.

Swinging the big oak door closed behind him, Drake walked through the wide tiled hallway to the kitchen, set his bag of bread and pastries down on the counter and started the kettle boiling.

Glancing at his hand, he frowned when he noticed a trace of dried blood on his grazed knuckles. He had barely thought about the fight on his long walk home; he'd just carried on with his morning routine as if nothing had happened.

For a while after he'd noticed the man observing him, it had crossed his mind that the guy might be a real player – a professional hit man sent by the Agency to hunt him down and kill him. There were plenty such men on the payroll.

But their brief scuffle earlier had taught Drake otherwise. The man's attack had been clumsy and stupid. He was a street thug; nothing more. There were a lot of them in Marseille these days, ready to prey on the rich Brits, Russians and Americans who flocked here every summer.

As he ran his hand under the cold tap at the sink, watching another man's blood wash away and disappear down the plug hole, he felt a familiar throb of pain radiating out from his knuckles. He'd broken his hand in a boxing match many years earlier, the damage forestalling whatever aspirations he'd had as a professional fighter. It had healed well enough, but the old injury still troubled him now and again.

He hadn't felt the pain at the time; the adrenaline had been pumping and he had been too intent on not getting clubbed or knifed to death to worry about it, but now that he'd had a chance to calm down, it was starting to catch up with him.

It had been a while since he'd found himself in a situation like that. More than a while, actually. Living a simple life, the past six months had been deceptively quiet and uneventful. A man could almost forget his past if he spent enough time in a place like this.

Almost.

Standing by the sink, he paused for a moment, playing over the events again in his mind. Street thugs he could handle, but not if the situation escalated into something more. Even if his actions today had been necessary for self-defence, he had called attention to himself by beating that man down.

There was a chance of course that Philippe Giroux would heed his warning and steer well clear of Marseille, perhaps finding a new town in which to prey on unwary travellers. A chance, but Drake sensed it was unlikely. Street criminals were as territorial as a pack of wolves, and just as vicious when provoked. There was no telling who Giroux might talk to about the mysterious foreigner who had nearly killed him this morning, no telling where the rumours might end up.

Perhaps it was time to move on, find a new place to lay low. That would be the smart thing, the prudent thing to do to ensure his survival. Why then was he so reluctant to contemplate it?

The click of the kettle snapped him out of his dark musings. Turning off the tap, he shook his hand a few times to get most of the water off, then emptied the boiling water into a waiting coffee pot. As he made for the fridge to get some cheese and jam, he decided to put his earlier thoughts on hold, at least until after breakfast.

Making decisions on an empty stomach was never a wise move.

A short while later Drake was sitting at a weathered old wooden table – one of the few items salvaged from the original owner – on the villa's outdoor terrace, staring at the clear blue waters of the Mediterranean as he waited for his laptop to boot up. It was already shaping up to be a warm day, the sun rising slowly into an almost cloudless sky.

He took a sip of coffee, watching as a big motor boat powered through the light swell about a hundred yards offshore, waves and foam churning in its wake. Even from this distance he could make out the young women in bikinis sunning themselves on the stern deck, while a couple of older guys in garish shirts messed around in the wheelhouse. The sort of people that Giroux would have an easy time relieving of some not-very-hard-earned cash.

'Enjoying the view, huh?' a voice chided him.

Drake felt a pair of slender hands slide across his shoulders, pausing to tighten their grip a little as they reached his neck.

'I see you eyeing up those bikinis, you know.'

He glanced up as Samantha McKnight walked into view, barefoot on the stone terrace, dressed only in briefs and a white tank top. Her dark hair was tousled from sleep – or lack of it, given what they'd been up to last night – and her face untouched by make-up. Not that she needed it. Already an attractive woman, life in the Mediterranean sun had tanned her naturally pale skin, endowing her with a glow that he found most pleasantly diverting.

Drake grinned. 'Wouldn't dream of it.'

'Sure you wouldn't. Not when I've got a gun in my bedside drawer.'

'Yeah, but I've seen your shooting,' Drake teased her. 'Anyway, what's with the Rip Van Winkle routine? I've been up for hours already.'

'I spent ten years in the army, getting woken up by asshole drill instructors at 5 a.m. The way I see it, I've earned some downtime.' She grinned playfully, her eyes glinting like the sea behind her. 'Plus I lost a couple of hours last night.'

14

'Play your cards right and you might lose a couple more today,' he said, eyeing her over the rim of his coffee cup. The sea breeze had stirred up, flattening the tank top against the contours of her body, giving the momentary impression that she was wearing nothing at all.

It was an impression that wasn't lost on him.

'Keep dreaming.' Reaching down, she snatched up his plate of untouched croissants, leaping nimbly beyond his reach before he could stop her. 'Especially when you hog all the food.'

'Hey! I had to walk four bloody miles for those!' Drake protested.

'And I truly appreciate such a noble sacrifice for your helpless maiden.' McKnight gave him a look of mock seriousness, before tearing off a chunk of pastry, dipping it in the jam and popping it in her mouth.

*Helpless* and *maiden* were not words Drake would choose to describe Samantha McKnight. Nonetheless, eyeing the graceful lines of her body, the soft curve of her breasts that her minimal clothing did little to hide, he felt less inclined to argue the point.

She settled herself on a chair beside him, her long legs stretched out before her, and for a few moments seemed to lose herself in the view. She was smiling; the kind of smile that came so easy to her now.

'You know something? I don't think I'll ever get tired of being by the sea. The sound of the waves, the smell of salt in the air, the endless horizon...' she said wistfully. 'No matter how many times I wake up to it, it still feels new every time.'

Drake decided not to dwell on that last statement. 'Beats a rainy Monday morning in Croydon, that's for sure.'

She glanced sidelong at him. 'Hey, give me a break. I'm a Kansas girl – didn't even *see* the ocean for the first time until I was nineteen. Couldn't believe there was so much water in the world.'

Drake cocked an eyebrow, resisting the obvious joke about her not being in Kansas any more. 'Parents not big travellers, then?' he asked instead.

At this, her smile faded a little. 'Mom didn't stick around too long, so it was just me and Dad. And no, he wasn't big on travelling.'

He felt bad for dredging up unhappy memories. 'I'm sorry.'

She looked at him, and there was a sadness in her eyes that seemed quite out of sync with her usually buoyant personality. Then, with a single blink, the dark cloud seemed to pass and she was herself again.

'Don't be. He was a great father.'

As she resumed her breakfast, Drake turned his attention back to the laptop and opened his email to check for messages from his former team-mates Cole Mason and Keira Frost. Once part of an elite group known as a Shepherd team, tasked with finding and rescuing lost Agency personnel, their attempts at exposing the secrets of the Agency's corrupt Deputy Director Marcus Cain had led to them being branded as criminals and traitors. Now they were on the run like Drake and McKnight, maintaining loose contact via anonymous email accounts.

There was the usual round of spam offering Rolex watches to 'Gentleman with high ambition but low moneys', and another effort by the deposed king of Nigeria to get Drake's bank details. The guy really must have been desperate; this was his third email in the past month.

But there was one message in the inbox that most definitely wasn't a waste of time. There was no subject, but the sender was one J. Doe. Hardly an original name, but Drake knew what it meant. J. Doe wasn't the kind of person to send 'How are you?' emails. If she contacted him, it was for a reason.

Putting down his coffee, he opened the email.

*We need to talk. Can we meet?*

Drake frowned. As far as missives went, this one was about as short and to the point as it could be. Still, he knew the sender well enough by now to understand she wouldn't give anything away over an unsecured email server. Whatever she had to tell him would be delivered face to face.

The question was, what did she want?

'Everything okay?' McKnight asked, noticing his change in expression.

'Hmm?' he said, stirred from his thoughts. 'Yeah, nothing I can't handle.'

'Sounds ominous.'

'Try tedious.'

Despite his evasive words, he knew he would have to send some kind of reply. For one thing, J. Doe wasn't someone you ignored. For another, whatever she wanted to discuss would likely find its way to him sooner or later anyway. Better to meet it on his own terms.

A moment later, he started typing.

*Marseille, tonight. Bar Mele, 8 p.m.*

If she wanted to be brief and blunt, he was happy to respond in kind.

His simple missive complete, he sent it winging off through cyberspace to wherever the sender happened to be. Depending on the vagaries of server cross-links and how many budget Rolex watches were being touted that day, the message should take anywhere from ten seconds to two minutes to arrive.

He had set the meeting for tonight partly because he wanted to get it over with, but mostly to gauge how badly she wanted to meet with him. If she agreed, it meant something serious was going down.

Three minutes later, the reply came.

*I'll be there. Don't be late.*

Drake leaned back in his chair and took another sip of coffee. Well, that confirmed his theory at least. Whatever she wanted to discuss, it was important.

It didn't make him feel any better.

# Chapter 3

*Langley, Virginia – 30 April 1985*

'Morning, Tom,' Marcus Cain said, striding down the corridor with a coffee in hand. 'Ready to save the world?'

It was barely 9 a.m., but he'd already managed to fit in a five-mile run through central DC before work. Rather than leaving him tired and worn out, the early morning exercise had served to focus his mind and body. He felt alert, energized, ready to take on anything.

Tall, lean and ruggedly handsome, Marcus Cain cut a striking figure amongst the slumped shoulders and middle-aged beer guts that populated Langley. At just 30 years old, and bright and ambitious, he'd only recently been promoted to full case officer, giving him command over both field operatives and the authority to recruit his own intelligence sources. It was both an honour for a man of his age, and a challenge that he was determined to rise to.

His colleague, Tom McBride, was clutching a set of sealed brown file folders that represented their combined workload for the day ahead. Instinctively he fell into step beside Cain to match his strides; no easy task when McBride was several inches shorter, ten years older and a good deal heavier. Still, he'd never have admitted to having difficulty keeping up.

'You're annoyingly cheerful today,' he remarked with good natured mockery. 'You get laid last night or something?'

Cain gave him a sidelong glance. 'Your jealousy smells worse than your aftershave, Tom. And that's saying something.'

'I like this aftershave.'

'Someone has to, I guess,' Cain acknowledged. 'So hit me with it. What's the good word?'

'Latest intel reports from Afghanistan,' McBride began, holding out the first folder. His expression said it all. The Soviets were winning, and the CIA-backed Mujahedeen were losing. Same old story.

Cain accepted it reluctantly. 'That good, huh?'

'Worse. I'll leave you to pick through the gory details later. The short version is that the Divisional heads want you to spin your usual bullshit. Full work-up and high-level summary, along with operational recommendations by tomorrow morning.'

'Why? So they can ignore it like my last two reports?' Cain asked, a measure of his good humour departing. 'Maybe I should record it and play it on loop for them.'

McBride smiled faintly. 'This one's different. There's a briefing scheduled later this week with one William Carpenter; a colonel with army special operations. I don't know many of the details yet, but a lot of heavy hitters will be there, and they've asked you to present your findings. Draw your own conclusions on that.'

Even Cain was taken aback by this. Perhaps, just perhaps, his pleas for direct US involvement in Afghanistan hadn't fallen on deaf ears after all. Of course, there was always a downside to stepping into the limelight. If you screwed up or failed to deliver after people had put their faith in you, it could land your career on the fast track to nowhere.

Still, Cain wasn't afraid to take risks. He hadn't made it this far by playing safe. And if he could actually sell them on this plan and make it work, he could quickly find himself a rising star.

'Well, shit. That just makes me feel warm and fuzzy inside,' he said, tucking the briefing folders under his arm. He was just about to make a right and head to the relative quiet of his cubicle office when McBride called after him. 'Oh, just one other thing.'

Cain paused in his stride. 'Yeah?'

'Something that came in from our colleagues in Norwegian Intelligence.'

He feigned surprise. 'There is such a thing?'

'I'll be sure to pass those remarks along,' McBride chided him. 'Anyway, bit of a curve ball, but it looks like they caught themselves a Soviet defector.'

That was enough to pique his interest. 'Military?'

'Nope.'

'Government?'

'Civilian. Nineteen years old. She presented herself to the Norwegians and requested asylum in the US.'

Cain's enthusiasm faded. 'Then she wants the State Department, not the CIA,' he decided, turning away, his mind already on the upcoming briefing.

'Wait, here's where it gets interesting. According to their debriefing, she hiked through a hundred miles of Arctic terrain to cross the border. Nearly died of exposure in the process.'

'So she's tough but dumb.' If true, hers was an impressive feat of survival, though not terribly smart. There were far easier ways to defect. 'Why should we care?'

'Because she requested to work for us against the Soviets. Well, demanded would probably be more accurate. She said she was willing to do anything to work against them.'

Cain wasn't impressed. Normally intelligence agents were recruited through a careful process of trust building, training, bribery or, in some cases, coercion. They didn't just show up on the Agency's doorstep asking for a job.

'Forget her,' he advised, having made his assessment already. 'She's probably just some messed-up kid looking for attention.'

'You're not taking her seriously. Neither did the Norwegians. They had some junior analyst try to debrief her, but she saw right through it, refused to speak until they sent a case officer in.'

Cain frowned. 'She knew their chain of command?'

'No, you don't understand. She knew they were lying,' McBride explained. 'According to their debriefing document, they knowingly fed her false information on six different occasions, and she caught them out every time. For whatever reason, it seems she's almost impossible to deceive.'

Cain was tempted to laugh at the notion. He still didn't believe it, but he had to admit he was intrigued. 'So what do you want from me?'

'You're a case officer. Recruiting agents is your job,' McBride reminded him. 'Look, give her a quick evaluation. If you think there's something we can use, we'll put it through the usual channels. If not, we ditch her. Fair enough?'

Cain glanced down the corridor to his office, where he knew he should be heading right now to prepare his briefing. And yet, the notion of meeting this mysterious young woman who had trekked through a hundred miles of ice and snow just for a chance to work for the Agency had kindled a spark of curiosity in him.

'Fine,' he conceded reluctantly. 'Where are they holding her?'

He would spare her five minutes before making his decision. After that, he would consider his duty done. He didn't imagine he'd be seeing her again either way.

–

*Langley, Virginia – 14 March 2010*

Removing his reading glasses, Marcus Cain closed his eyes and rubbed his temples, trying his best to ignore the headache that was pounding away inside his skull and focus on the briefing documents laid out before him. It was a silent, if painful reminder of the bottle of whisky he'd done his best to get through last night.

He couldn't remember the last time he'd finished up a day without a drink.

Reaching into his desk drawer, he fished out a strip of aspirin, popped two in his mouth and washed them down with the tepid remains of his cup of coffee.

The contents of his daily briefing certainly gave him no reason to feel better. Everywhere the Agency was fighting the War on Terror, they were losing. In Iraq and Syria, ISIS were on the move once more, regrouping their scattered forces for another major offensive. The pre-emptive drone strikes he'd ordered in Libya might have killed some of their commanders and dealt their cause a blow, but such attacks were only delaying the inevitable. Without American support, the fledgling Iraqi army wouldn't stand, and after nine years of costly and fruitless warfare, neither Congress nor the public had the stomach to send troops in again.

Things were even worse in Afghanistan, where a resurgent al-Qaeda was striking with increasing impunity from the lawless mountain regions that remained well outside government control. Afghan military forces barely had the manpower to hold the ground they already had, and their capabilities were diminishing as desertion and battlefield casualties took their toll.

The Afghans weren't the only ones taking casualties either. The suicide bombing at Camp Chapman three months ago had dealt the Agency a crippling blow from which it was still struggling to recover. With nine of their most capable and experienced personnel dead and another six severely injured, it had been their worst single loss of life in a quarter of a century.

But the effects had gone far deeper than that. Every aspect of the Agency, from their procedures to their operational outlook to their leadership, had been under scrutiny since news of the blast had begun to filter through. Even the public had become aware of what had happened, the scope of the disaster simply too big to conceal, and as a result confidence in them was at an all-time low.

The world's most formidable and secretive organisation had been exposed to the world as fallible, vulnerable and desperate. And never had they been more needed.

He glanced up from the depressing briefing documents as his door opened and an older man strode in without so much as knocking. Not many men could walk right into Marcus Cain's office without warning or permission, but unfortunately CIA Director Robert Wallace was one of them.

One of the new crop of top-level replacements that had arrived in the wake of Barack Obama's march to the White House, Wallace's appointment as director was unusual in that he hadn't come from either a military or intelligence background. Instead the Agency had been lumbered with a serial politician; a man whose career had been based around drawn-out hearings, dusty subcommittees, small-minded party bickering. A man with little understanding of the work that went on at Langley.

It was obvious that a man with a blank slate in the intelligence game had been chosen specifically to clean up the Agency's image, which had been well and truly tarnished after eight years under the Bush administration. Some of his first acts as director had been to start official investigations into the enhanced interrogation techniques the Agency had been using successfully for years, to curtail funding for human intel and pump ever increasing resources into unmanned aircraft.

Cain had never had much time for the man, and he was quite certain the feeling was mutual. And judging by the look on Wallace's face as he approached, it wasn't about to change today.

'Have you seen this?' he demanded, slapping down a copy of the *Washington Post* on Cain's desk, open several pages from the front to expose a full-page article headlined: *CIA in Crisis – Have They Already Lost Afghanistan?*

Cain leaned over, briefly surveying it. He'd read the article already, but he didn't want Wallace to know that. 'I'd say it's a valid question, Bob.'

Wallace shot him an angry glare. 'This is no time for your smart-assed remarks, Marcus. Don't you get it? We're not just fighting a war in Afghanistan and Iraq; we're fighting one right here in DC. And we're losing all of them.'

Cain leaned back in his chair, scrutinizing the Director. He'd barely been in the job a year, yet his hair was noticeably greyer now, his forehead already etched with deep frown lines. There was a reason most Directors only stuck around for a few years, and it wasn't just for political reasons – the constant stress and pressure simply burned men out.

Cain would be surprised if Wallace made it another year.

'Then I guess it depends how you want to fight those wars,' he said at length. 'As a politician, or an intelligence operative. Because you can't be both. Sooner or later you have to choose.'

The not-so-subtle barb wasn't lost on the Director. 'Watch your tone, Marcus. My predecessor might have had a hard-on for you because of what you did in Afghanistan twenty years ago, but this is now, and I'm not him,' he warned. 'The President's looking for results. He wants an exit strategy, and we can't give him one as long as al-Qaeda are still in the fight. All we've got to show him are some new stars on the wall downstairs.'

That remark was enough to make even Cain wince. The Wall of Remembrance in the building's main lobby had a new star added each time a CIA employee was lost in the line of duty. There were a lot more of them now than there had been when Cain started his career.

'What would you have us do?'

Wallace jerked a finger at the newspaper on his desk. 'Get our dicks out of our hands and take charge of this situation. You're still in this job because you're supposed to be our expert on all things Afghanistan, so find me a solution. Or I'll find someone who will.'

Cain's eyes hardened then. He could feel the headache that had lingered with him all morning growing in intensity. Hidden from view, his hands curled into fists.

'All right, Bob. I'll see what I can do,' he said, his voice flat, devoid of emotion.

Wallace's weak jaw clenched as if he were biting back another scathing rebuke. Nonetheless, he turned to leave. 'Keep the article. You might find it interesting,' he called back over his shoulder.

'This solution you're looking for,' Cain said just as he was opening the door. 'You want me to find it as a politician, or an intelligence operative?'

The Director hesitated a moment, his grip on the door tightening. Without saying another word, he walked out, closing the door firmly behind him.

Cain sat there in silence for a few moments, pondering the exchange. Wallace was an asshole politician, more interested in embellishing his own reputation than making tangible intelligence gains, but he was still a powerful asshole. If it came to it, he could have Cain removed as Deputy Director.

A position he'd sacrificed so much to attain.

'Goddamn it,' he mumbled, pushing himself away from his expensive desk and striding across his office to the windows overlooking the parkland that surrounded the Agency's headquarters.

It was a dark, sombre kind of day in Virginia, characteristic of this time of year. The sky overhead was a mass of slow-moving clouds, heavy with rain. Whatever possessed the founding fathers to build the nation's capital in a fucking swamp, he'd never know.

Staring out towards the distant spire of the Washington Monument, he caught a momentary glimpse of his reflection in the polished glass. It was the reflection of a man he wouldn't have recognized a few years ago. An old man before his time, his face worn and lined by years of care and worry, his hair greying, his shoulders stooped and his eyes showing the pain that came from watching everything he'd worked so hard to build slowly crumbling.

And to think he'd scoffed at Wallace for showing the stress of his job.

It was time to act, he knew now. Not as a politician or an intelligence operative, but as a man worthy of the enemy they now faced.

Turning away from the brooding sky, he crossed the office to his desk phone and dialled a number he'd been using more often than he would have liked lately. The line clicked and buzzed a few times as the phone's encryption software worked to establish a secure satellite connection, then it started ringing.

It didn't take long for the recipient to answer. 'Station Chief.'

'Quinn, it's Marcus.'

Hayden Quinn was his station chief at the US embassy in Pakistan, overseeing all Agency operations in the country. A competent enough man that Cain had believed ideal for leading the hunt for al-Qaeda's most senior leadership. But competence meant little without results, and after nearly a year in the position Cain was starting to doubt the wisdom of his choice.

'Give me good news,' Cain prompted, wasting no time on greetings.

There was a pause, which told him pretty much what he needed to know. 'I'm afraid the Pakistanis aren't playing ball, sir,' Quinn said at last, his trepidation obvious. 'They claim they're already extending us their fullest cooperation. Usual BS, but they're stonewalling us. We can't get in.'

Cain could practically feel the muscles across his shoulders tightening, while his headache seemed to grow more insistent. 'What about back-channelling?'

'We've tried every channel that's open to us, sir,' Quinn apologized. 'I'm afraid if we push much harder, they'll turn against us.'

Cain had long suspected that elements of the Pakistani military and intelligence community were sympathetic to al-Qaeda's cause. Unfortunately, one couldn't simply accuse America's only tenuous ally in the region of double-dealing. Not without starting another war.

Cain closed his eyes as the pain in his head threatened to overwhelm him, blood pounding like some great drum inside his skull.

'Sir, are you okay?' he heard Quinn's tinny voice echo down the line. 'Did you hear my last?'

It was at that moment that Cain made his decision. A decision there would be no coming back from. One way or another, he was going to break the stalemate.

'Yeah, I hear you, Quinn. Don't worry, I'm sending someone to help you out.'

'Sir?' There was outright fear in his voice now. The fear of a man watching his career dissolve before his eyes, as he was quietly moved aside and a replacement brought in.

'Trust me, he'll get the Pakistanis to play ball. But I want you to extend him your fullest cooperation. No matter what he needs, you make it happen. And you do it quietly. Do you understand?'

'Yes, but—'

Without waiting for Quinn's stunned response, he killed the line, reached for his private cell phone and dialled another number from memory. A number known only to a select few.

If Quinn couldn't get results, Cain knew of one man who could. The kind of man who wasn't bound by the same rules as Quinn and his contemporaries. The kind who was ready to do what others weren't, without question.

'Yeah?' came a low-pitched, gravelly voice after the third ring.

'Hawkins,' Cain began. 'Get yourself ready to travel. I'm sending you on a little errand to Pakistan.'

# Chapter 4

*Marseille, France*

As far as food and drink went, there were worse places to spend an evening than Bar Mele. An outdoor café specializing in seafood and local delicacies, it was situated right on the waterfront of the ancient trading port that had long been the heart of Marseille.

The port itself was still as busy as it had been a few hundred years ago, but these days the wide harbour was home to luxury yachts, speedboats and other pleasure craft instead of the traditional fishing fleet and cargo ships.

Many of these yachts were now strung with decorations and lights, music from a dozen different cultures drifting across the water. Smaller craft moved constantly between the big ships, carrying passengers and cases of booze to keep the festivities going.

Further out near the northern end of the harbour mouth, huge and indomitable, lay the ancient fortress of Fort Saint-Jean. It was joined on the southern side by Fort Saint-Nicolas, their towering walls and gun ports lit by floodlights in a dazzling display of colour. Two hundred years ago they had protected the vital trading port from the Royal Navy. Today they were just tourist traps.

Sitting at a table with only a bottle of Corona for company, Drake stared out across the harbour, watching as light from the moored yachts and crowded buildings glittered across the waves. The air had cooled with the onset of evening, and lamps had been lit along the perimeter of the seating area, providing both heat and light for the small groups of patrons that were slowly filling the place up.

He had chosen this particular bar for a couple of reasons. For a start, it was situated on one of the old piers, so there was only one way to approach it on foot. His seat faced towards the main concourse, allowing him a good view of anyone coming his way.

Another less dramatic but more practical reason for meeting here was simply because he was hungry, and he saw no reason he couldn't kill two birds with one stone.

If he'd been on an actual op, he never would have arrived here first. It was always best to hang back and let your contact get there first, allowing you to observe their body language, looking for the subtle indications that something might be wrong. But he knew J. Doe was likewise trained and far more paranoid than himself, and he was in no mood to waste half the night in a pointless stand-off.

He took another sip of his beer and allowed the noises of the busy city at night to wash over him, mingling with the gentle lapping of the waves and the distant music from the party boats. Up until today, the storm that had beset his life for the past couple of years had seemed far away indeed, hidden beyond the horizon and almost forgotten.

Almost.

As it turned out, he didn't have long to wait. A couple of minutes past eight, he spotted his contact coming towards the bar, moving with the unhurried pace of a trained field agent pretending to be out for an evening stroll. Drake felt himself tense involuntarily.

Anya had always elicited that reaction in him.

Tall, tanned, athletically built and with finely sculpted but indescribably exotic features, Anya cut a strikingly attractive figure that neither men nor women could fail to notice, somehow embodying everything vital about her gender all at once. Now in her mid-forties, she nonetheless possessed the toned physique and youthful energy of a woman half her age, though the subtle grace and quiet confidence of her movements spoke of the experience that only age could impart.

But what set her apart in Drake's eyes went far deeper than mere physical appearance. He had always thought that anyone who doubted whether women had the killer instinct, the resourcefulness or the sheer ruthless determination needed to make it in the world of covert operations, need only spend an hour in Anya's company.

Actually, ten minutes would probably do the trick.

Once a decorated field operative with the Agency, he'd first encountered her nearly three years ago when he'd been tasked with breaking her out of a maximum security Russian prison. That had been the easy part, as it turned out. At the time, he never could have imagined the web of conspiracies, betrayals, murders and cover-ups his actions would unleash.

He'd never known much about Anya's private life, or her time before joining the Agency, which seemed to suit her. But gradually, through his own experiences and her reluctant admissions, he'd begun to fill in the blanks on a life that was as shocking and tragic as it was remarkable and mysterious.

Part of him wondered if he truly wanted to know the full story.

Her sharp, icy-blue eyes were on him already. Giving him the kind of look that he suspected lions gave antelopes just before they pounced, she angled towards his table and slipped into the seat opposite without saying anything. Once there, she stared at him for a long moment, as if comparing him with the mental picture she had stored in her memory.

He couldn't help but do the same.

It had been nearly a year since their last meeting, and it didn't seem like a great deal had changed about her since then. Her light blonde hair, once cut short for practicality rather than style, was longer now, and styled differently. Perhaps in an effort to blend in better amongst civilians, she had opted for a pair of white trousers, grey tank top and a fitted dark blue jacket.

It was warm enough to not need one, but Drake knew she wouldn't take it off. Doing so would expose the network of scars that criss-crossed her back; mementos of an ordeal many years earlier she would no doubt rather forget. She never made an issue of them, but he sensed they made her feel self-conscious all the same.

Apparently satisfied with what she saw, Anya nodded in greeting. 'It's good to see you again, Ryan. You look… rested.'

By her standards, that was the equivalent of a tearful, joyous embrace.

Drake flicked his eyes towards a group of young men and women walking past on their way to one of the party boats. All tall, slim, tanned, well dressed and well groomed, they looked like they had strolled right off the set of a French tourism commercial.

'Just keeping up with the Kardashians.'

Uninterested in his attempt at humour, Anya glanced around, taking in the lines of moored yachts, the medieval fortresses, the bustling bars and cafés. She looked like an astronaut surveying the surface of some alien world.

'I did not picture Marseille as your kind of place,' she said at length.

He managed to stifle a grim laugh. Where the hell had she expected him to wash up? New York? London? Washington? It wasn't as if the world was one of boundless opportunities for a disgraced former CIA operative wanted for treason.

'Any port in a storm, matey. Besides, I think it's growing on me.'

'So I see. Tell me, what have you been doing these past six months?'

'Keeping busy,' he retorted, raising his beer to take another drink before laying it down a little harder than he'd intended. 'Listen, all this how-you-doing stuff is great, but let's be honest, small talk's not exactly your style. So can we skip to the part where you tell me why you're actually here?'

She tilted her head, eyeing him thoughtfully. 'Why do you think I'm here?'

'Well, I'm hoping you came to thank me for rescuing that woman Mitchell from federal custody for you. As far as favours go, that one was stretching it a little. Did I ever mention that my team and I almost lost our lives pulling that one off?'

He hadn't known it at the time, but the woman Anya had asked him to recover from a hospital in Istanbul had been a fellow CIA operative. Badly injured and in intensive care following a gunshot wound to the abdomen, she must have done something to piss off the wrong people, because getting her out of the country alive had proven challenging even for Drake and his team. A fact he'd made sure to impress upon Anya once it was over.

'Repeatedly,' she assured him. 'And for that, you have my gratitude.'

It was hardly gushing praise, but at least it was honest.

'But we both know that's not why you're here,' he continued. 'So thrill me.'

Glancing down at the hand that was clutching his beer, she noticed the bloodied grazes along his knuckles. 'If I'm not mistaken, those are the kind of injuries a man picks up from fighting. Run into trouble?'

'Depends what you define as trouble,' he evaded. 'Why do you ask?'

Anya leaned back a little in her chair, those pale blue eyes shimmering in the light of the fire lamps as she watched him. 'Because I was the one who sent him after you.'

Drake didn't react immediately, because he thought it best not to voice his most immediate thoughts in such a public place. Instead he raised the bottle to his lips and took a slow, thoughtful pull, marshalling his thoughts and his composure before taking on this particular conversation.

'If there's some kind of explanation waiting in the wings, now would be a good time to bring it centre stage, Anya,' he said, his voice now carrying a dangerous undercurrent of hostility. 'And for both our sakes, it had better be good.'

Another person might have been intimidated by his hostile tone, by the thinly veiled anger boiling away beneath the surface, just waiting for an excuse to explode. Another person, but not Anya.

'It was a test.'

His brows drew together in a frown. 'A test of what, exactly?'

'*You*, Ryan. I was testing you.'

Drake could feel the muscles in his jaw tightening. It was well for Anya that she had been born a woman, otherwise his knuckles would have a few more grazes after tonight.

'The man tried to kill me,' he said icily. 'Suppose he'd succeeded. What then?'

'Then I would have known there was nothing left of you worth saving,' she decided. 'The Ryan Drake I once knew would never have been in danger from a simple street thug... assuming he is still in there somewhere.'

'What the fuck is that supposed to mean?'

Once more Anya's cool gaze took in their surroundings. The bars, restaurants, party boats, the young couples out for an evening stroll and the groups of friends on their way to dinner. Normal scenes in a normal enough city.

'This is a... comfortable place for a man to lay low, yes?' she went on. 'Good weather, good food, good wine. The sort of place a man like you could disappear for a long time, if he chose. Maybe for ever.'

'I'm still waiting for that point.'

Anya laid her arms on the table and leaned forward, her gaze one of accusation. 'You're becoming *soft*, Ryan. Soft and complacent. Too much

28

sun, too much drink… too much rest. You are losing your focus, forgetting the mission. Before you know it, this false life will swallow you up, and you'll forget who you really are.'

Drake could feel the anger and indignation rising within him as her words sank in. How dare she accuse him of growing soft? How dare she put his life at risk just to prove a point? What fucking right did she have to invade his life and start telling him how to live it?

Her accusations were doubly hard to accept because deep down, he sensed that she was right.

'And who exactly *do* you think I am?' he challenged her, far too incensed to acknowledge the truth now. 'What do you really know about me? My birthday, my past, my favourite ice cream flavour? Nothing. I'm just a guy who risked his life to save yours. And shit like this makes me wonder if I did the right thing.'

He could have sworn he saw a blush rising to her cheeks. 'I did not ask you to do that.'

'Would you rather I'd left your arse to freeze in that Russian jail?' he asked with brutal honesty. 'Because your life wasn't exactly party central before I got there.'

Anya said nothing. She had no answer for him. At least, not one that she was prepared to give. It gave him a small measure of satisfaction to know he'd backed *her* into a corner for once.

'Didn't think so,' he said, feeling that he'd made his point. 'But here's the thing, Anya. With all the fighting and the running and the killing, what have we actually accomplished? Cain's still out there, he's stronger than ever, and the list of people who want us dead is getting longer all the time. It's hard to keep playing the game when you do nothing but lose.'

'So what do you intend to do, Ryan? Run and hide? Hope that it all goes away?' She sighed and glanced away, reflecting on an old memory. 'We both know it doesn't work like that. It doesn't matter how far you run, or how well you hide. Sooner or later, our world always catches up.'

'Stop it,' he interrupted. 'Don't start comparing us, because we're not the same. Maybe I *have* learned to like it here. Maybe I've gotten more used to it than you'd prefer. Maybe I've had a taste of a normal life; a life without bullets flying over my head and fucking lunatics trying to kill me, and maybe I like it. And you know what? You're afraid of that.'

At this, he saw a blonde brow raised in silent question. No doubt it had been quite some time since anyone accused her of that. 'Afraid?'

'Yeah, afraid. Not of the mission or the danger or the bullets… You're afraid of what comes after. If we somehow take down Cain and put an end to this bollocks for good, then you'll have nothing left to fight for. You're afraid of what you'll do when all the dust settles, and what's left isn't fighting and killing, but living. All those long years stretching out in front of you, trying to fit in, trying to be something you're not. Trying to be… normal.

You want to talk about losing focus and perspective? Maybe you should take a look in the mirror.' He gestured around him, taking in their surroundings. 'So you can sit there and judge me all you want, but I need this. I need it because I don't want to end up more afraid of living than dying. I don't want to end up like you.'

He knew his words had been brutally harsh, knew it was unfair in some ways to lay into her like this. Part of him even regretted saying it, but it had come out all the same. It had come out because it had to, because three years of fighting and killing and watching good people sacrifice their lives in this increasingly desperate struggle had taken its toll on him. More than that, it had taken a toll on the people he cared most about in this world.

Sometimes he wondered if Anya even gave a shit about any of that.

But if he'd been in doubt, then her reaction to his stinging rebuke sank in told him otherwise. She was hardly an emotional person at the best of times, but he saw it all the same. He saw the hurt, the shock and the embarrassment flare.

Like his own reaction earlier, the words had cut all the deeper because on some level, she knew that he was right too.

'I took you for a lot of things, Ryan,' she said at last. 'But never a coward.'

'Then I'm happy to disappoint you.' Taking a breath, Drake downed the remainder of his beer and stood up from the table, laying down enough euros to cover the bill. 'Sorry you had a wasted trip.'

'Wait,' she said, gripping his arm. She too had risen to her feet, eager to make her point before he left, though for a moment she struggled to find the right words. 'Maybe… maybe you were right about me,' she finally acknowledged. 'But that doesn't mean I was wrong about you. Think about what I said, Ryan.'

'Likewise,' Drake advised, pulling free of her grasp.

Saying nothing further, he turned and strode off along the waterfront. He needed to think, he needed to work out the conflicting emotions her reappearance had stirred in him.

Most of all, he needed to be alone.

# Chapter 5

Gripping the edge of the chipped porcelain sink, Samantha braced herself as her stomach constricted into another painful knot, forcing up a surge of acrid tasting vomit. She felt like she'd already emptied the contents of her stomach, but apparently that wasn't good enough. All she could do was keep her breathing under control and let her body do what it had to.

Finally the most intense feeling of nausea began to abate. Turning on the faucet, she rinsed her mouth out and spat the last of the foul-tasting mucus into the bowl.

Raising her head to regard herself in the mirror, she wasn't pleased by what she saw. Her face was drawn and pale, her eyes red, her dark hair hanging limp. Fortunately she'd at least managed to keep it out of the way.

She was trembling. Not because of the sudden nausea and vomiting, but because of what it meant.

At first it had been easy enough to brush aside the less obvious symptoms, writing off the uncharacteristic fatigue and the stomach cramps as something women went through every month, or perhaps some minor ailment she'd contracted. But then she'd begun to notice her breasts growing swollen and tender to the touch, and realized suddenly that her period was late. Just a few days at first, then a week, then two.

She'd said and done nothing during this time, hoping she was wrong, hoping that her fears would be revealed as nothing more than foolish worry over nothing.

And then she'd felt the nausea hit her this very evening.

There could be little doubt now. She was no doctor, but even she could read the signs and symptoms, and draw a logical conclusion.

'Goddamn you,' she said, staring at her reflection as if she expected it to give her answers, to reassure her that everything would be all right, to tell her what the hell she was supposed to do with an unplanned pregnancy.

It was obvious enough how it had happened, yet of all the things that could have shattered their fragile existence here, she'd never contemplated something like this. Why now? She and Drake had slept together often, but they had always taken precautions. Neither had any interest in starting a family yet, least of all with their own lives still hanging in the balance. But it had happened all the same. Like millions of teenage girls the world over who thought they'd been careful, she'd somehow fallen victim to her own biology.

After everything else they'd been through, what a cruel joke.

Of course, she knew the sensible thing would be to deal with it quickly and discreetly, before it went any further. This was no happy families situation – they were a pair of rogue CIA operatives on the run from the authorities. They'd been able to keep a low profile thus far, but how the hell were they supposed to do that with a child in tow?

Pregnancies needed doctors, scans, tests, all kinds of red tape that would eventually unravel their false identities here. Not to mention the birth itself, or the sheer insanity of bringing a child into the world in which they still lived. No, it had to be taken care of now, before it became an even greater problem.

It wasn't just the right choice. It was the only choice.

But even as this very logical and pragmatic decision was being made, a voice of doubt and objection resounded in her mind. Where it came from, she couldn't rightly say. She'd never considered herself a maternal woman, had never felt a pang of longing or emptiness when she saw mothers or infants, and yet something had been stirred up by the realization that a life was growing within her at this very moment. A tiny, unaware, unplanned life to be sure, but a life all the same. A life started not just by her, but by the man she'd been living with for the past year.

Did he not have a right to know? Should she really just arbitrarily make such a decision without even consulting him? Would he even want to know, or would it simply drive a wedge between them?

And most of all, what would it mean for her true purpose here? How could she carry out her mission, knowing that Drake was the father of her child?

Splashing cold water on her face, she looked at her reflection again and mouthed a single word. 'Shit.'

Her conflicted musings were cut short then by the bang of the front door being thrown open, and the sound of footsteps in the hallway, fast and agitated. Drake had returned from his errand, and by the sounds of things, all was not well.

–

Breathing hard, Drake circled the heavy punch bag and laid into it with a flurry of lefts and rights. His T-shirt was soaked with sweat and his dark hair was plastered to his head. The impacts jarred his arms all the way up to his shoulders, the bruised joints of his already injured hand protesting the punishment they were taking, but still he kept on with grim determination.

After emptying out the decades of junk that the villa's previous owner had accumulated in the basement, he had taken the liberty of setting up some basic exercise equipment, chief among which was the heavy punch bag suspended from one of the more sturdy overhead beams.

It wasn't much, but it was a useful place to come when he needed time to think, to unwind, or just to let out some frustration. Tonight he needed all three, because Anya's stinging words from earlier echoed in his mind like the pealing of a bell.

*You're becoming soft, Ryan. Soft and complacent. Too much sun, too much drink… too much rest. You are losing your focus, forgetting the mission. Before you know it, this false life will swallow you up, and you'll forget who you really are.*

He gritted his teeth as his gloved fists slammed into the padded leather bag again and again. The heavy bag lurched and swayed with the impacts, but he paid it no heed. His mind was elsewhere, his thoughts turned to their parting words in Iraq three years ago.

*'I promised Hussam I'd protect you, Anya. Whether or not you think you need it, I'll be there for you, and I won't give up on you.'*

*He saw a change in her eyes then, a lowering of her defences. She looked as she had last night, when they had at last opened up to each other, bared their souls in the flickering light of the camp fire.*

*Hesitating a moment, she walked towards him and held out her hand, saying nothing, waiting for him to take it. He did so without reservation, without regrets or deception. He accepted her as she had accepted him.*

*Gripping his hand tight, Anya smiled. But it was a bittersweet smile, tinged with sadness and regret.*

*'You know your problem, Ryan? You're a good man.'*

His heart was pounding and his breath coming in gasps as he circled the bag, muscles burning and legs heavy. His knuckles ached from the punishment, blood seeping from the torn flesh to soak the tape and bandages around his hands, but he was indifferent to it.

Still the anger burned inside him, unquenched by his punishing workout, as he saw himself sitting on a grassy hillside back in the Welsh countryside last year. The day he'd parted company with the Agency and gone on the run. The day he'd been forced to say goodbye to the only family he had left.

*He reached out and gently touched Anya's hand. For once, she didn't move it away.*

*'Remember what I said to you once? I made a promise that I'd be there for you even if you didn't think you needed me, that I'd do everything I could to help you, and that I'd never give up on you. Because this is my fight now as much as yours. That hasn't changed. We started this thing together, Anya,' he said. 'You and me. That's how we're going to finish it. Together.'*

*The woman said nothing to this, but at that moment he felt it. He felt her squeeze his hand just a little.*

With an exhausted sigh, Drake landed one final blow before backing away and doubling over, struggling to draw breath.

'I think you've done enough for one day,' a voice remarked.

Swallowing, Drake straightened up and glanced over at Samantha, who had descended the basement stairs without him noticing. How long she'd been watching him, he didn't know, but it was obvious from the look of concern in her eyes that she'd seen enough.

'I was…' He trailed off, not sure what to say.

Fortunately, she was ready to jump in. 'Only one person I know of that can piss you off this much.' She nodded up the stairs. 'Come on. Let's talk.'

–

Drake winced as he wrapped a dish cloth filled with ice around his throbbing left hand, waiting while the cold slowly numbed the aching joints. He certainly hadn't done the old injury any favours tonight.

In the kitchen area nearby, McKnight had laid out a drinking glass. Pulling down a bottle of malt whisky from the cupboard, she poured a generous measure.

'I don't know what it is about you, Ryan,' she said, handing him the glass. 'Even when we're not in danger, you seem hell-bent on hurting yourself.'

Drake accepted the drink with a nod of thanks. 'Not joining me?'

She glanced down, avoiding his gaze. 'You need it right now. I don't.'

'Fair enough.' Drake tossed back a gulp of the potent drink, closing his eyes for a moment as it lit a blazing path down his throat, the glowing embers settling at last in his stomach.

'So tell me, what did she want?' McKnight asked suddenly. 'Come to demand another mission? Another errand to run with no explanation? That's how it usually works with her, right?'

He hadn't told her the real reason for his trip into Marseille earlier. Somehow he felt guilty for meeting with Anya, as if their encounter had been some kind of illicit tryst instead of a fraught, tense confrontation between two estranged allies.

McKnight had never met Anya face to face, but the animosity she felt towards the enigmatic woman was palpable. Not that he blamed her – from her point of view, Anya must have seemed like a tornado swirling through his life, leaving a trail of destruction in her wake before disappearing again. Sometimes he wondered if that wasn't closer to the truth than he'd like to admit.

'She came here to remind me of something. In her own way, at least.'

'Remind you of what?'

Opening his eyes, Drake reached out and gently touched her cheek with his bruised, bandaged hand, reflecting for a moment on how stupidly content they had both been that very morning, how far away their fears had seemed. How it was almost possible to forget everything that had happened.

'That nothing lasts for ever.'

'It's lasted this long,' she reminded him. 'What's changed?'

'Me.' He took another sip of whisky. 'When we came here, it was just supposed to be a place to lay low and plan our next move. It was never meant to last this long. But being here with you, just us and this place, it's been… like a dream, Sam. It was all I ever wanted. And I suppose, after a while, I started wishing it was real.'

'It *is* real, Ryan,' she said, taking his hand and staring hard into his troubled eyes. 'Don't you see? We're here, we're together, and none of the rest matters. It's a different world, and the one we left behind… it doesn't have to be part of our life any more. *We* can make that choice to leave it behind.'

'What about Anya?'

Her expression darkened at this. 'Fighting is all she knows. If she wants to fight this war, then let her. But enough good people have died in her name already. Don't add to it, Ryan. I know you want to help her, but… some people *can't* be helped.'

There it was; the same doubt that Drake had been privately harbouring for some time now. Hearing someone else say it only seemed to add more weight to his fears.

'I told her I wouldn't give up on her.' Drake looked down at his glass, torn between loyalty to the woman whose life he'd saved, and the woman he couldn't bear to lose. 'You're asking me to do exactly that.'

'I'm asking you to think this through,' she implored him. 'We're on the run from the Agency because we made a mistake in Libya last year. We rushed in without thinking. This isn't a time to make the same mistake again, especially not after what I saw downstairs.'

She was right. He didn't want to admit it even to himself, but she was right. Making decisions based on emotion had almost gotten them all killed in Libya. Tonight he was in real danger of doing the same thing again.

'At least sleep on it, Ryan,' Samantha went on, sensing her words were reaching him. 'If you still feel like this tomorrow, then… we can figure it out. Okay?'

Drake looked at her then. Samantha McKnight: always the pragmatist, somehow able to see through the conflicting loyalties and emotions clouding an issue. He knew her advice made sense, that it was the logical thing to do, and yet he couldn't shake the feeling that he was giving up something at the same moment.

Something he might regret later.

'All right, Sam,' he conceded, though the issue was far from resolved. 'All right.'

She brightened a little at this, offering a tentative smile as she reached out and pulled him close. The war might still be in doubt, but for tonight the battle was over.

# Chapter 6

*Munich, Germany*

'Another brew, dude!' Keira Frost said, slapping her empty beer bottle and a ten euro note down on the bar. She had to raise her voice to be heard over the thumping techno music that reverberated around the crowded bar, but she didn't really care. She'd never had a problem making her wishes known.

The bartender, a tall, skinny-looking guy in his early twenties, regarded the diminutive young woman standing before him with a mixture of irritation and uncertainty. This was her third beer in the past fifteen minutes.

Sensing his doubts, she looked up at him, her gaze sharp and challenging. 'Got a problem with that?'

He shrugged, apparently seeing the wisdom of not antagonizing her further, and quickly popped the lid from another bottle of Beck's.

'No problem,' he said, scooping up the money.

'Didn't think so,' she mumbled, tipping back the bottle and gulping down a mouthful. She could hold her drink about as well as anyone, but even she was starting to feel the effects of the previous three. And that was just fine by her. If she didn't walk out of here wasted, she was doing something wrong.

Like Drake, she had been forced to abandon her job with the Agency as a Shepherd team specialist and go on the run after their doomed attempt to take down Marcus Cain. They had gambled and lost, believing the evidence of arms smuggling and terrorist backing they'd uncovered could destroy Cain's career. Instead they had found themselves manipulated by the very man they sought to destroy, their failure placing them openly at war with both Cain and the shadowy group he represented.

After splitting with the others, Frost had ended up taking refuge in Germany's third largest city. With over 1.5 million inhabitants and a big migrant community, it seemed as good a place as any to disappear for the time being. With no work to occupy her, she'd found herself slowly drinking away the nights and sleeping away the days while she waited for orders from Drake.

Orders that never came.

She'd never expected to find herself wishing for the old days when Drake regularly presented her with daunting challenges and impossible deadlines, but there it was. Inactivity was eating away at her; lack of purpose causing her to dwell on the past and brood over what might have been.

She felt rather than saw someone sidle up next to her at the bar, interrupting her grim train of thought. 'Hey. *Wo warst du mein ganzes Leben lang, schön?*' a male voice spoke in her ear.

'*No sprechen sie Deutsch*, buddy,' Frost replied without turning around. She wasn't unreceptive to male company tonight if it helped work out some of her frustration, but she intended to put away a few more beers first.

'Ah, English then,' her new companion said, switching languages as smoothly as changing gears in a car. 'You're American, right?'

'Got it in one, Sherlock.'

He chuckled in amusement at her not entirely good-natured jibe. 'It's strange. I see this beautiful girl sitting all alone at the bar, and I ask myself, how can this be?'

'Maybe I'm waiting for someone,' she suggested.

'Not after four beers, I think.'

Intrigued, Frost spun around in her seat to regard this new arrival, and immediately reconsidered her options. Tall, blonde haired and well built judging by the sinewy muscles in his exposed arms, he was nothing like the lecherous, overweight older men that regularly tried their luck with her. The face that regarded her was good looking and youthful, his jaw coated with a couple of days' worth of growth, his dark eyes shining with attraction in the red lights glowing overhead.

Her thoughts must have shown in her facial expression, because she saw that handsome face brighten in a smile as he looked her up and down.

'You notice things, huh?' she said, not sure whether to feel flattered or irritated by the attention.

'I notice you. I'm surprised no one else did.' He shrugged. 'Their loss, I think.'

As far as opening gambits went, she had to admit his wasn't bad.

'So what should I call you?' she asked, deciding tonight might not be a bust after all. 'Sherlock doesn't quite fit.'

'Anton.'

She held up her bottle. 'Kate.'

She liked this guy, but no way was she giving her real name.

'I like that name. It suits you,' he decided. 'What brings you to Munich, Kate?'

'You mean business or pleasure?' she asked with a wry grin. 'Started out as the first…'

'Maybe it will end with the second.'

Ballsy, she thought. A little cheesy, but ballsy all the same. She liked that in a guy. 'Depends how good the company is.'

With that, they clinked their drinks together and drank. They only needed a mouthful to finish the toast, but a childish sense of competition meant neither was willing to stop first. As it was, they carried on until they'd drained their bottles dry, slamming them down almost in unison.

Anton beat her by a second or so, but she could live with that. He likely hadn't polished off three others in short order first.

'If I didn't know better, I'd say you were trying to get me drunk,' she said with a playful grin. 'Planning to take advantage?'

Good luck to him, if so. One handy bonus of being a former covert operative in one of the world's elite intelligence services was that she generally had little to fear from drunken assholes who didn't like the word 'no'.

'Hey, I'm a nice guy.'

'Really?' She leaned a little closer, lowering her voice as much as possible given their raucous surroundings. 'Well I'm not a nice girl.'

'Then you're just what I'm looking for.'

The booming techno music was still pounding inside her skull, and suddenly it seemed like an annoyance now that she'd found someone she actually wanted to talk to. Well, talk and other things.

'What do you think of this place?' she asked suddenly.

He glanced around for a moment or two before turning his attention back to her, guessing what she was hinting at. He was leaning a little closer to her now, his body language open and inviting. She wasn't complaining.

'I think it's a little loud. Maybe we go somewhere more... quieter?'

That was all right as far as she was concerned. One thing she appreciated about German men was that if they liked you, they let you know pretty quick. Better than fucking around with boring small talk all night. After all, it wasn't as if she was in the market for a long-term partner.

However, there was one thing she did need to take care of before she left this place, and her body was reminding her of that with increasing urgency. Four bottles of beer down, it had to go somewhere.

'I'm down with that,' she agreed. 'Do me a favour, order a couple of shots before we go. Something strong and clear. I'll be back soon.'

Anton's face was one of mock disappointment. 'You're leaving me all alone?'

Grinning, the young woman grabbed him by the T-shirt and pulled him close, her lips parting as she pressed her mouth against his, hard and insistent and leaving him in no doubt about her intentions tonight.

Releasing him at last, she took a step back, smiling at the reaction her kiss had provoked. 'Yeah, but I'm worth waiting for,' she assured him, then held up two fingers. 'Two shots. Make it happen.'

Fighting her way through the crowds of revellers who were waiting none too patiently to be served, Frost circled around the bar and headed for the restrooms at the back. Preoccupied with thoughts of the evening that lay ahead, she didn't notice two men following in her wake.

It was almost a relief as the door swung closed behind her, leaving her in the relatively quiet corridor beyond. She glanced up at the signs above the doors. Men's room, then ladies', then a third door at the far end that she guessed was a fire exit.

38

Alone for a moment, she paused, leaning against the wall and taking a breath as she ran her hands through her hair. At 31, she was probably a little old to be having one-night stands in foreign countries with complete strangers, but what the hell. There wasn't much in life that couldn't be sorted out with a good fight or a good fuck, and it had been a while since she'd had the latter.

She was just heading towards the restroom when she heard the door swing open behind her. It was a busy place after all, and likely the toilets saw frequent use, but instinct and habit prompted her to turn around anyway.

Had she gone easier on the drink, she might have seen what was coming half a second sooner, might have reacted half a second faster, might have avoided the blow aimed at the back of her head. But she hadn't, so she didn't.

*Crack!*

The explosion of white light and pain that reverberated through her head even worse than the music outside was almost enough to send her spiralling into unconsciousness. As it was, she pitched sideways and began to fall, clutching at the wall in a vain effort to support herself.

The first explosive impact was followed a moment later by a second vicious blow to the ribs that robbed her of whatever strength and resilience remained. She doubled over in agony, bile rising in her throat.

Through blurred vision, she was just about able to see a tall young man with short blonde hair rushing forward to grab her, then suddenly something heavy and was thrown across her head and body, and the world went dark.

'Grab her! Get her up!' Anton called out to his partner, a big shaven-headed Bavarian named Ruprecht.

'Are you sure it's her?' Ruprecht asked, securing the unconscious woman's wrists behind her back with plastic cable ties before heaving her up off the ground.

'I'm sure! Move! Go!'

Already Anton was sprinting towards the fire exit with Ruprecht close behind, breathing more heavily as he fought to manhandle his burden. Keira Frost's limp form was just visible beneath the cloth sack they'd thrown over her.

Kicking open the door, Anton found himself in a narrow alleyway at the rear of the club, used for deliveries and garbage disposal. And waiting for him there was a Volkswagen panel van driven by the third member of his crew, his brother Martel.

They had to move fast. Opening the fire door would trigger the alarm, prompting the bar's security team to investigate. He intended to be well out of here with his prize by then.

Giving Martel a nod as he passed, Anton made his way to the rear of the van and hauled open the doors. 'Get her in. Now!' he shouted, adrenaline and excitement causing him to speak louder than necessary.

Approaching the rear door, Ruprecht heaved his burden up and practically tossed her into the cargo compartment as if she were a piece of lumber. Her muffled cry on impact suggested she'd hit the steel deck with bruising force.

'Be careful, for Christ's sake!' Anton reprimanded the hired muscle. 'We kill her, we lose three million euros.'

Ruprecht fixed him with an angry glare. 'She'll live. Get in.'

The axles seemed to groan under his considerable weight as he clambered up, kicking the unconscious woman aside to make room, with Anton close behind. Pulling the doors shut, Anton hurried forward and slid into the passenger seat, leaning in close to speak to his brother.

'Where the fuck did you get this guy?' he asked, his voice low.

'Relax. He's cool,' Martel assured him with entirely too much confidence. The unfocused look in his eyes suggested he'd hit up a line or two while they'd been inside, despite his earlier promises to stay clean until it was over. 'Buckle up.'

With that, he threw the van into gear and accelerated away down the alley, turning right at the far end and onto the main road. In under a minute, they were clear.

Despite Anton's anger with his brother and his distrust of Ruprecht, he began to feel his anxiety abating. They had their prize, they were well away from the scene of the crime, and all of it had unfolded exactly as he'd planned. Considering the bounty on her head and the warnings about the danger she posed, he'd expected more trouble.

'Pull in up here,' Ruprecht said. 'The parking lot on the right.'

Anton frowned at the sudden change of plans. 'Why?'

The big Bavarian glowered at him. 'I want to make sure it's her. Now pull over.'

'Fuck that. Keep driving,' Anton instructed, wary of the man's intentions. The last thing they needed was to pull over and find a dozen of Ruprecht's friends waiting to relieve them of their prize. 'We're not stopping here.'

'Suit yourself,' Ruprecht grunted, switching on the internal light. 'But I want a proper look.'

Reaching into his pocket, he unfolded a printed photograph of the woman known as Keira Frost and laid it on the deck, then drew a Sig Sauer automatic from the back of his jeans and cocked the hammer.

Keeping the weapon in his left hand, he gripped the fabric hood they'd thrown over her and pulled it upwards, exposing her unconscious form.

It happened fast. Faster than Ruprecht could react. In a sudden blur of movement, the young woman sprang to life. Her right hand shot upwards, something metallic flashed in the harsh electric light, and suddenly the big

German grunted in pain. Staring at him in shock, Anton saw the haft of a flick knife protruding from his neck as the man lurched sideways, blood pumping from a severed artery.

His finger tightened convulsively on the trigger, the interior of the van resounding with the thunderous crack as the weapon discharged, sending a round into the deck.

'What the fuck!' Martel screamed, flinching at the deafening report and causing the van to swerve dangerously.

Belatedly Anton realized their target wasn't as helpless and subdued as they'd assumed, that she had used the knife to slice through her restraints, and he felt his stomach lurch at the realization she was still very much a threat. A threat that needed to be dealt with now.

But before he could clamber into the rear cabin to restrain her, he saw her make a grab for Ruprecht's weapon, saw her yank it from his faltering grasp as he tried to pull the blade free from his neck. He was screaming, a low and animalistic howl that was a mixture of pain, shock and growing fury.

There was another deafening crack, followed by a heavy thud as his body hit the floor, and the screaming abruptly stopped.

'Get her!' Ruprecht yelled. 'Before the stupid bitch—'

His sentence was abruptly cut off as a 9mm Parabellum slug tore a gaping exit wound in his throat, blowing out his windpipe and severing his spinal column in a single devastating blast.

No longer under conscious control, the van slewed sideways off the road. Anton turned, trying to grab for the wheel, and was just in time to see a concrete lane divider rushing forward to meet them.

The van impacted with all the force that several tonnes of steel moving at close to 50 miles an hour conveyed, crumpling the front chassis like paper and destroying the engine. Unrestrained by a seatbelt, Anton was flung forward like a rag doll by his own kinetic energy, his body tumbling through the shattered windshield and over the concrete divider with bone-breaking force, coming to rest in a bloody heap several yards beyond it.

For the next several seconds, silence descended on the scene of the crash, broken only by the dripping of oil from the ruptured sump and the steady ticking of the cooling engine block. Steam was rising from the shattered radiator, misting in the cool night air.

Then, suddenly, the van's rear doors shook with a resounding clang as something slammed into them from inside. The blow was repeated a second time with equal ferocity. Finally on the third attempt they flew open, allowing a battered, bloodied figure to tumble out onto the road.

Keira landed hard on the asphalt, letting out a groan of pain as fragments of glass from the shattered windshield embedded themselves in her arms and side. Her entire body radiated agony from both the beating she'd taken and the crushing impact that had crippled the van. Her vision swimming in and out of focus, she closed her eyes for a moment, tears trickling down her cheeks as she curled into a ball, trying her best to take the pain.

Get up, a voice warned her. Get up, you stupid bitch, before the cops arrive. Move!

Gritting her teeth and keeping a death grip on the gun she'd fought so hard to wrestle from her captor, Frost managed to get one bloodied hand beneath her and dragged herself to her feet.

The big guy and the driver were very much dead – she knew that because the contents of their skulls were splattered across the inside of the van – but a soft moaning from the other side of the road told her that her third captor was still alive. For now at least.

Wincing in pain, she limped around the remains of the van and approached the concrete lane divider, then somehow managing to heave herself over.

Anton was lying on the far side, moving sluggishly as if to get up. He wasn't going to be walking any time soon. Both legs were twisted and bent at an unnatural angle, and judging by his laboured breathing he'd broken several ribs, probably puncturing his lungs into the bargain.

Dragging herself forward, Frost knelt down beside him, gripping him by the T-shirt just as she'd done in the club earlier. But there was no kiss in store for him this time – just the barrel of the 9mm automatic.

'Who sent you?' she demanded.

Blood was seeping from the corner of his mouth. His eyes were on her, though she wondered if he was even still capable of speaking.

She held up the crumpled, bloody photograph of herself that had been lying in the back of the van, held it so close that he couldn't fail to see it.

'Who sent you to kidnap me?' she repeated, rage and anger overriding the agony of her own battered body. 'Answer me, you piece of shit!'

'Bounty…' he managed to choke out. 'For you… alive.'

Frost closed her eyes, letting out a sigh. He wasn't Agency; that much was clear. He and his two terrible chums were bounty hunters who made a living out of bringing in wanted fugitives. No doubt they'd seen her picture on Interpol, the FBI or some other website's Most Wanted list, and taken her for an easy payday.

It should have made her feel better instead of hurting more, but it didn't. Because it meant Anton probably wasn't such a bad guy; just another man trying to make a living. It was going to make it harder to do what she had to do.

A quick search of his pockets revealed no identification. No driver's licence, no credit cards – no wallet at all, in fact. Just some euros and loose change. He had a cell phone in his back pocket, but it was a cheap burner that had likely been purchased for this job. At least he'd been smart enough to go into it sterile.

'Go…' he whispered as she pocketed the cell phone. 'Leave… me here.'

Leave him to get picked up by the police, taken to hospital, nursed back to health and thoroughly questioned about what had happened. Leave him to tell them that a wanted criminal had murdered his two friends, and was still at large.

'Sorry, Anton.' Frost looked at him with a twinge of pity as she stood up and trained the weapon on his head. 'Guess those drinks will have to wait.'

She turned her head aside to avoid the resultant spray of blood and pulled the trigger. The weapon kicked back against her wrist with a sharp discharge, the ejected shell casing pinging off the tarmac a short distance away. It was done.

Only now that it was over did she begin to feel the warm wetness seeping down her right side. Closing her eyes, she pulled her jacket aside and reached in, almost surprised when her hand came away wet with blood.

She thought back to her brief, violent confrontation with the big man in the back of the van, and the sharp crack as he'd accidentally discharged a round into the steel deck. Only it hadn't just hit the deck – it had passed through her first.

'Fuck…' she said, her body seeming to weigh her down as if the gravity around her had suddenly doubled.

She had to leave this place. She was completely exposed here in the middle of the road, and likely the police were on their way already. The injuries she could sort out later, but for now she had to get out of here.

Steeling herself against the pain, she turned and made for the bushes on the far side of the road, quickly disappearing into the shadows.

# Chapter 7

*Milan, Italy*

'Yup, this'll do it,' Cole Mason remarked, leaning over the stripped-down scooter engine laid out on his workbench like a patient on an operating table. 'See, the problem with these old motors is the bearings. Damn things burn out quicker than a teenage romance. Why, you might ask? Because the assholes who run them never bother to check the goddamn oil levels.'

Prising the bearing ring free of its housing, he held it up to the work light for inspection. Sure enough, the inner shaft was scored and deformed by the little steel ball bearings that were supposed to ensure smooth operation.

Three more bikes were sitting in the improvised parking garage below, awaiting his attention. Scooters and mopeds were as popular as breathing in this part of the world, used by everyone from young waitresses zipping through traffic on their way to work, to old guys in their eighties making the morning milk run. Everyone used them, which meant sooner or later everyone needed them fixed.

'Still, keeps guys like us in business,' he concluded. 'Isn't that right, Rock?'

Spinning around in his chair, he regarded the big tabby cat that was sitting on the far side of the open space that served as his living quarters, kitchen, bedroom, workshop and just about anything else he needed it to be.

He had no idea where the feline had come from, except that he'd found it lurking in a corner of his improvised home about a week after he'd moved in. He hardly considered himself a cat person, but with no one else to talk to, he was happy to let it stay. It in turn seemed to tolerate him, which was probably the best you could expect as far as cats were concerned.

With no collar or owner that he knew of, Mason had taken to calling him Rocky on account of the fact he was Italian, and because he loved the boxing movies.

He supposed Italian heritage was something the two of them had in common. His original family name had been Martinelli, until his grandfather moved to the States at the turn of the century. He'd used that as his reason to reside here in Milan, as if he were somehow returning to his homeland.

'Knew you'd see things my way,' Mason said, regarding the cat's gaping yawn as a sign of agreement.

Pushing away from the workbench, he allowed his swivel chair to glide across the open space to his kitchen table, as if he were an astronaut making a daring leap from one spacecraft to another. He liked to challenge himself with these little exercises, trying to negotiate his trajectory through difficult obstacles and narrow gaps. Like a game of pool, it was all in the angles.

The haphazard layout of the room reflected its multipurpose nature, with a basic kitchen counter, fridge, cooker and table in one corner, a worn old couch and TV in another, and a simple metal-framed bed against the far wall. The remaining side was occupied by a long workbench cluttered with various tools and spare parts. The floors were bare wooden boards, the walls unpainted red brick, scant thought given to comfort or aesthetics.

That was how life had to be lived right now, both for himself and the small group of ex-Shepherd operatives he called his friends. Moving from one location to another, always ready to cut and run at a moment's notice. Though he had to admit, he'd be sad to leave Milan.

A coffee percolator was steaming away on the kitchen table. Bringing himself to a stop with a gentle nudge of his boot, Mason poured himself a cup. That was one aspect of life here that he really appreciated – the quality of the coffee.

'You know, I never quite saw myself moving from covert ops to engine repairs. Not a real logical career progression there,' he mused as he took a sip of the strong black liquid. 'Funny old world, huh?'

Rocky didn't seem too impressed by his philosophical thoughts, instead turning his attention to licking his paws.

That was the moment when Mason's world changed.

No sooner had he laid the cup back down than he was jerked out of his thoughts by the crunch of shattering glass as one of the nearby windows was blown apart. At the same moment, something flew through the jagged gap, slamming against the opposite wall before falling to the floor with an audible metallic thump.

Mason barely caught a glimpse of the explosive projectile before he realized what it was, and instinctively tried to turn away just as the grenade detonated. And for a few seconds, the world around him was obliterated by white light.

Opening his eyes, Mason shook his head, dust and fragments of glass falling to the floor around him as he tried in vain to clear the persistent ringing in his ears. His surroundings seemed to be moving in slow motion, once solid shapes rendered vague and dreamlike as his stunned brain tried to catch up with what was going on.

He'd managed to turn away from the flashbang grenade at the last moment, saving him from being blinded and rendered helpless by its intense burst of light. However, he could do nothing to protect his ears from the concussive boom that had deafened and unbalanced him, making it difficult just to move.

But move he would have to, and soon. He knew the effects of such grenades all too well, having used them in plenty of house assaults himself. Usually they were thrown by hand, just like conventional grenades, but there were rifle-launched variants that could be fired from further away. Either way, the intention was the same. They were designed to soften up and confuse an enemy, providing an opening for a strike team to move in and storm the building.

Dragging himself into a crouching position and swallowing back the lingering sense of nausea and vertigo, he chanced a look down into the workshop level below. Several bikes and mopeds were parked in the open space that had probably once served as a loading dock, all awaiting his attention. He doubted he'd be getting around to them now, especially since there were now several uninvited guests down there. The strike team, hurrying between the parked vehicles and converging on the stairwell leading up to his living quarters.

His brain was overcoming the effects of the grenade now, spinning up into survival mode like a chopper powering up, ready to take flight.

He counted at least four operatives, all geared up in body armour and armed with compact submachine guns. At first he thought his vision was still hazy from the effects of the grenade, but he soon realized that a layer of smoke was lingering in the workshop down below, probably caused by more flashbangs launched simultaneously for maximum effect. He hadn't heard their detonations because the first one had wiped out his hearing.

Despite the poor visibility, he could now see that the strike team were armed with Heckler & Koch MP5s; venerable old submachine guns that had been around for the best part of four decades, and still popular with everyone from special forces to police SWAT units. The long, bulky additions to the barrels told him they were using silencers, though Christ knew why after the racket made by the flashbangs. The red beams of the weapons' laser sights cut through the haze like crimson scythes, eagerly sweeping left and right as they sought a target.

It wouldn't take them long to find one if he didn't act now.

Ducking down so as not to be seen, he hurried over to the workbench where he'd been busily stripping down the damaged bike engine only minutes before. A shout from below told him the sound of his boots on the floorboards had been detected, and he winced as a burst of 9mm gunfire tore upwards through the floor just feet away, showering him with wood splinters.

Ignoring the sting as these slivers of shrapnel embedded themselves in exposed skin, he felt around beneath the workbench until his fingers brushed against what he was looking for. A single electronic switch, fixed to the wooden underside. Praying the mechanism hadn't been damaged by the grenade blast, Mason flicked back the plastic safety guard and pressed the switch.

There was a loud buzz as an electric motor went to work over near the stairwell, accompanied by a dull rasp as a steel bolt was withdrawn. Then suddenly it was gone, allowing the heavy iron gate it held in place to swing down, slamming into place across the stairwell with a resounding clang.

It was a primitive security measure reminiscent of the ancient portcullis used to protect medieval castles, but it would delay the strike team for at least 30 seconds, perhaps longer if they didn't have breaching charges. Hopefully enough time for him to escape.

Even as the grate resounded with the sharp impacts of a burst of MP5 fire, Mason sprinted over to the far corner of the room and yanked open the doors of a battered-looking wardrobe, slipping inside and pulling them shut behind him.

In reality it took just over 20 seconds for the strike team to break their way through the temporary barricade, blasting out the hinges using concentrated automatic fire. Kicking the heavy grate to one side, the first two members of the team advanced warily up the steps, their weapons sweeping left and right.

Senses were painfully alert and nerves fraught as they reached Mason's living space, eagerly searching for their target. They had been warned that this man was dangerous, highly trained and likely armed — a combination none of them relished. However, no target presented itself. The open area, still wreathed in smoke, was eerily quiet.

Their outside spotters had confirmed he hadn't escaped through the windows, and since the stairwell was the only way off this level, logically he had to be in here somewhere. He was hiding. Pointing left, the team leader directed one man to search the kitchen area, while he advanced further into the room.

Nothing beneath the work benches. None of the other furniture was large enough to conceal a grown man. No obvious hiding places, except…

He felt a tap on his shoulder, and followed the direction his teammate was silently indicating. A battered old wardrobe stood in one corner of the room, big enough for a man to hide inside.

The only hiding place left.

Tightening his grip on the weapon, he nodded affirmation and advanced towards it, broken glass crunching and old floorboards creaking beneath his boots. Ten feet to go.

Five feet.

Pressing the weapon tight against his shoulder, he put a single silenced round into the wardrobe, aiming low so as to injure rather than kill. The dry old wood splintered and fragmented as the 9mm round punched clean through.

But there was no cry of pain or fear from the occupant. No pleas for them to hold their fire, no offer to surrender. Nothing save the dull *whang* as the round ricocheted off something metallic.

Frowning, he began to sense something was wrong. Without waiting another moment, he reached out and yanked the doors open.

'Goddamn it,' he growled in Italian, staring at the metal laundry chute that the wardrobe had clearly been positioned to conceal.

'Target is on the move. I repeat, target is on the move! All units, be on the lookout!'

More Italian police units were already converging on the building, moving with the speed and efficiency that years of training imparted, quickly forming a tight cordon around the entire area. Unfortunately for them, the target had already slipped beyond their grasp.

The laundry chute had deposited Mason unceremoniously in the building's basement level, a couple of stacked-up old mattresses helping to absorb the impact of his fall from two floors up. His body had taken a beating on the way down, rattling around inside the metal chute like a brick in a washing machine, but he was still whole and relatively unharmed as he scrambled to his feet and dragged the mattresses out of the way.

Anyone who tried to follow him down was in for a hard landing, but given that they'd just stormed into his home and almost killed him, he felt no remorse.

This task done, he rushed over to the far side of the dimly lit room, where a couple of packing crates had been stacked against the wall. Pulling them aside, he exposed a low opening in the brick wall, barely large enough for a man to crawl through.

In truth, it wasn't just the cheap rent that had brought Mason to this place. He'd chosen it because of its proximity to one of the underground service tunnels that criss-crossed the area, used for everything from water to gas to electricity. Once he'd figured out which direction to go, it had been a simple matter of breaking through a section of the basement wall and digging for a short stretch.

Back-breaking and claustrophobic work it might have been, but the effort was paying off today. Crouching down low, Mason felt around for the flashlight he'd stashed at the entrance and flicked it on, illuminating about ten feet of bare earth walls and floor, braced in places with pieces of scavenged wood. It was hardly *Great Escape*-level engineering, but it did the job.

Within seconds he was crawling down this narrow subterranean passage, flashlight beam bouncing off the walls. He couldn't hear the rasp of his own breathing yet over the ringing in his ears, but he could feel the urgent pounding of his heart as it hammered away in his chest. He'd never had a great love of confined spaces, and that feeling had never been stronger than at this moment.

Just keep moving. Almost there.

A simple metal grate covered the far end of the tunnel, placed there as camouflage in case city engineers happened to be inspecting it. A single hard shove with his free hand was enough to dislodge it, allowing him to crawl through.

The service tunnel into which he emerged was barely three feet wide and no more than five feet high, much of its internal space crowded with a confusing network of cables, ducting and pipes of various shapes and sizes, many with different coloured stickers and hand-written notes affixed to them. It was a cramped, narrow, unlit space, but compared to what he'd just crawled through it felt as wide open as a football field.

Fifty yards further along, Mason knew that a short ladder topped with a manhole cover would allow him to ascend to street level and make his escape. From there, he would put his emergency fallback plan into action

'Sorry, Rock,' he said under his breath, thinking of the stray cat he'd befriended with a twinge of regret. One way or another, he doubted their paths would cross again. 'Looks like you'll have to find a new place.'

With that thought fresh in his mind, he turned and loped off down the tunnel, bent low to avoid cracking his head on the ceiling pipes. Time was against him. He needed to get out of Milan, fast.

# Chapter 8

*US embassy – Islamabad, Pakistan*

If Hayden Quinn had been a diplomat instead of a CIA station chief, he would have described the past couple of days as 'challenging'. As it was, he considered them to be about as shitty as they come.

After being effectively reprimanded by the deputy director of the Agency over the phone, he'd found himself trapped in limbo, with no clear idea of what the repercussions were going to be. Was he about to be recalled back to Langley to answer for his failures? Was he going to be fired altogether, his once promising career left in tatters?

He had no idea, and he'd been too frightened to call Marcus Cain back to clarify the situation. Thus he'd done what most employees do when their track record is called into question – thrown himself into his work, riding his subordinates as hard as he dared, pushing for reports and assessments as quickly as possible. In some self-deluded part of his mind, he still harboured the hope that a sudden burst of progress might assuage Cain's anger and restore his reputation.

It was a vain hope, and soon dashed one morning just after his first round of daily briefings, when his desk phone started ringing.

'Yeah?' he said, trying to skim-read an intelligence report.

Outside the bulletproof glass of his office window, the streets of down-town Islamabad were already packed with traffic of all shapes and sizes, from lorries to cars and pickup trucks, taxis and tiny motorized scooters that seemed barely large enough to accommodate their riders. Dust kicked up by the passage of countless tyres mingled with the acrid grey smoke of engine fumes to form a choking miasma that lingered over the city like a blanket. He had no idea how the locals tolerated it, but every time he looked out there he found himself missing home just a little more.

'Gate security here, sir. We've got a Mr Stryker here to see you. Says he's been sent from Langley, and that you're expecting him.'

Quinn felt his stomach tighten, realising Cain had made good on his threat.

Clearing his throat, he reached for the necktie already lying discarded on his desk. 'Okay. Send him on up.'

'Actually, sir, he's on his way already,' the guard reported. 'His security clearance is... well, he doesn't need our permission to enter, sir.'

Quinn hadn't thought it was possible to feel worse, but now knew how wrong he'd been. Before he could respond, the door to his office opened and the man he presumed to be Stryker entered without even bothering to knock.

Quinn's first impression of the man was that he was big. Not just tall and muscular, though he was certainly both of those. Rather, there was a presence about him; an aura of authority and quiet menace that seemed to enhance his already large frame. His walk was measured but purposeful, carrying a hint of the confident swagger that suggested he'd once been military, which wasn't surprising. Plenty of ex-military guys were snapped up by the Agency, their talents put to good use in field ops.

He was dressed in a dark grey business suit that looked like it had been tailor-made for him, and carrying an expensive leather briefcase. His short brown hair was neatly combed, his face clean shaven, his eyes betraying no hint of the fatigue that one might expect after a long-haul flight from the US to Pakistan. Indeed, in most respects he appeared to be a model Agency employee – clean-cut, fit and motivated.

In most respects, save for the scar that bisected his face. It was narrow and clean, suggesting a blade of some kind, running in a wicked curve from his chin, up across his left cheek, and ending just above his eyebrow. It had healed well, but the pink scar tissue suggested it was still fresh, probably within the last year or so. But whatever or whoever had caused it, the effect was to render his already intimidating visage almost frightening.

Killing the phone line, Quinn rose instinctively from behind his desk, his shirt collar still pulled up and the tie stupidly hanging loose around his neck. Talk about being caught with your pants down, he thought bleakly.

'You must be—'

'Stryker. Mark Stryker,' he began, cutting Quinn off. He moved forward and shook Quinn's hand, nearly crushing it in his grip. Glancing at Quinn's untied collar, he grinned in amusement. The scar tissue turned it into more of a wicked grimace than a true smile, though he suspected this had been the man's intention. 'Caught you at a bad moment?'

'I was—'

He'd barely begun to stammer a response when Stryker cut him off again. 'Hey, don't worry about it. I don't stand on ceremony, so why should you?' Glancing down at his own formal attire he shrugged, his strangely feral smile broadening. 'Tell you the truth, the suit was Marcus's idea. I'm more of a boots and jeans kind of guy, but he seems to think it sends the wrong message, know what I mean?'

He snorted with amusement and slapped Quinn jovially on the arm, nearly knocking him off balance with the force of it, before turning away and laying the briefcase down on his desk. Talking of messages, Quinn caught himself wondering just what kind this man had been sent to deliver.

'Now, Mr Quinn, as I'm sure Marcus explained, I've been sent here to help out on a few... sensitive matters.' He clicked open the clasps on his briefcase. 'First things first, I don't want you to see me as a threat or a problem. I'm not here to take your job or make you look bad, okay? It's not that kind of situation.'

'I understand.' Quinn might actually have felt reassured had such news been delivered by a different man. 'So why *are* you here?'

Stryker glanced up from his briefcase. 'Think of me as more of a... facilitator.' He smiled, the newly healed flesh tugging it into a brutal sneer. 'I know, it's one of those bullshitty corporate things people say, right? Normally I'd kick my own ass for it, but it's kind of true in this case. I'm here to... bridge the gap between you and our friends in Pakistani intelligence. I'm good like that, kind of a people person.'

Never had Quinn met a man to whom that moniker was less applicable, and who was more aware of that fact.

'Now, I've been reviewing your workups on potential ISI contacts, and I've...' He trailed off, noticing that Quinn was staring at him. More specifically, the damage to his face. Again he saw that unnerving, sneering smile. 'Checking out the paint job damage, huh?'

Quinn felt his cheeks turn crimson. 'I'm sorry, I didn't mean to—'

'Hey, it's cool. Don't worry about it. Kinda hard to miss, right?' Stryker remarked, clapping a hand on his shoulder and squeezing just a little. 'I don't want there to be any awkwardness between us. Anyway, I like it. It's a reminder for me.'

Quinn frowned. 'Reminder of what?'

'Not to piss off the wrong woman.' He chuckled in amusement at his own joke, though there was no trace of humour in his grey eyes. 'Anyway, that's all in the past, so let's get down to business, shall we?'

'O-of course,' Quinn agreed, eager to move the conversation on.

'Good. Now, as I was saying, I've been reviewing the list of ISI contacts you sent back to Langley,' he said, removing a series of personnel dossiers that Quinn's team had built up on key officers in Pakistan's Inter-Services Intelligence (ISI) agency. Leafing through them, he selected one in particular. 'What can you tell me about Majid Reza?'

Quinn frowned at his choice. 'Reza? He's an attaché for their Joint Intelligence North division, works in logistics mostly. He's small time, barely made the cut.'

'So he wouldn't have his own security detail?' Stryker prompted.

'No way.'

Stryker seemed to like that. 'What do we know about his personal life? He have a wife, children?'

Quinn closed his eyes, trying to remember the details. 'He's unmarried, both parents dead. Nearest next of kin are two sisters in Sindh province.'

He nodded thoughtfully. 'Anything else? Any vices? Women, drink… kids?'

Quinn was struggling now. Being a low-level player, the Agency hadn't devoted nearly as much time to researching a man like Reza as they had some of the bigger hitters in ISI. There was only one other thing that came to mind. 'We haven't confirmed it, but there was some suggestion that he's a heroin user.'

Again he saw that smile. 'Perfect.' Returning the dossiers to his briefcase, Stryker snapped the locks shut and turned back to the station chief. 'Okay, buddy, here's what I'm going to need from you…'

# Chapter 9

The first light of sunrise found Drake seated out on the patio at the back of the villa, staring out to sea without really seeing anything. The cup of coffee resting on the table beside him had long since grown cold, though he paid it no heed.

He'd slept little the night before, brooding on his encounter with Anya, the harsh words they'd exchanged, and most of all the grim proclamation she'd made.

*So what do you intend to do, Ryan? Run and hide? Hope that it all goes away? We both know it doesn't work like that. It doesn't matter how far you run, or how well you hide. Sooner or later, our world always catches up.*

Drake knew he needed to turn his mind elsewhere, to stop replaying her words. Seeking a distraction, he reached into his pocket and fished out the familiar object that he almost always kept on his person. An object that was as much a mystery to him now as the person who had given it to him.

It was a key, unusual in design and unknown in purpose, its length divided into four sets of teeth as an added security measure, making copying extremely difficult. Meanwhile its bow had been embossed with a set of precisely inscribed numbers, which again meant nothing to him. No discernable pattern came to mind.

It been left to him by his late mother, who had been brutally murdered just a few months ago. A parting gift for a son she'd dismissed as a child and barely known as an adult. The mysterious gift had been accompanied by a short missive expressing her regrets at how she'd treated him, and hinting at secrets she'd kept from him his whole life.

Presumably the key was central to uncovering those secrets, though her letter had neglected to mention its purpose or where it was to be used. Without it, Drake had been left frustratingly in the dark.

Attempts to glean some clues from the key itself had yielded little. Its metallic composition was unremarkable and failed to point to a specific place of manufacture, and there was nothing hidden within it. Its four-bladed shaft was unusual but not unknown, used in all kinds of high-security applications like weapons storage, safes, even banking. In short, it could be used for almost anything, anywhere.

And yet, his mother had chosen to impart it to him. If her letter was to be believed, it was vital to unravelling the truth about her own past, her involvement in the shadowy group known as the Circle and, most of all, the reason she had been murdered.

The dawn light glinted off the polished steel teeth, as if challenging him to decipher their purpose. He was missing something – he knew it. She wanted him to find the truth; she wouldn't have given him a problem that was impossible to solve. Presumably she wanted to be sure that only he could solve it using some unique scrap of knowledge that he alone possessed.

But what?

'I thought I'd find you out here,' McKnight said, taking a seat beside him. 'Couldn't sleep, huh?'

'A lot on my mind.'

Her eyes rested on the key. She knew what it meant to him, knew who had given it to him. But like him, she knew nothing of its purpose.

'You still think about her?' McKnight asked. 'Your mom?'

'Sometimes. But every time I do, I come away with more questions than answers.' He shook his head, still mystified that she could have kept an entire life hidden away from him for so long. 'Why didn't she tell me?'

'Maybe she was trying to protect you?' Samantha suggested.

Turning the key over in his hand one more time, Drake reluctantly slipped it back into his pocket. 'I don't need protection. I need answers.'

McKnight looked ready to say more, but didn't get a chance to respond; the buzz of Drake's cell phone alerting him to an incoming call. Since only a handful of people knew his number, any calls that came through were worth taking.

However, a quick check of the caller ID revealed a number that was unfamiliar to him. Frowning, Drake hit the receive call button and waited a moment while the line connected.

'Yeah?' he began, his tone guarded.

'Ryan, it's Cole.'

Drake's suspicion abated a little. It was his old friend and comrade Cole Mason. Judging by the loud rumble of a car engine and the rush of wind in the background, he was on the move.

'Cole, why did you ditch your phone? Something wrong?'

'All kinds of things,' the man responded with grim honesty. 'Ran into some trouble at the safe house, had to bail in a hurry.'

Drake's moment of cautious optimism vanished. 'What kind of trouble?'

'The Italian police kind. SWAT team, by the looks of it. They had grenades, automatic weapons, the whole deal. Barely made it out.'

'Shit,' Drake breathed. 'You all right?'

'Never better, but my cover's blown in Italy,' Mason said, his disappointment obvious. 'I ditched pretty much everything I owned and stole a ride out of Milan. And a new phone in case they were tracking the old one.'

Drake closed his eyes, still shocked by this sudden turn of events. Six months of inactivity had lulled him into a sense of complacency and security that was, it seemed, quite unwarranted.

'You want me to go to ground, wait it out?' Mason pressed him, though with no money or ID they both knew he'd have a tough time of it.

'No,' Drake decided, realising he couldn't just hang his friend out to dry. They had a contingency plan for just this sort of eventuality. 'Get yourself to the *Alamo*. You know what to do.'

The *Alamo* was their fallback plan in case one or more of them were compromised and forced to go on the run. It was a place to regroup, to arm themselves and prepare to counter whatever move their enemy had made. It had been intended as a last resort, to be used only in time of great need.

Now was such a time.

'Copy that. Mason out.'

Shutting down the phone, Drake let out a sigh and ran his hands through his hair, his mind racing with the implications of what he'd just heard.

'What's happened to him?' Samantha asked, having only caught one side of the conversation but drawn her own conclusions. 'Is he okay?'

Drake quickly relayed the gist of what Mason had told him, as well as his instructions for the man to head to the *Alamo*, watching as McKnight's face paled visibly at the news.

'Jesus Christ,' she gasped. 'If they can find Cole, we could all be compromised.'

But Drake didn't reply. Instead he paused, his keen senses alerting him to a noise on the winding road leading up to their villa. The rattle of an engine, the crunch of wheels on rough unpaved ground.

Someone was coming.

Right away Drake was moving, heading indoors and straight for a drawer in the kitchen. Inside he found a Browning 9mm automatic; a memento of their last job in Libya that had turned out to be a handy companion in the months since.

Pushing the magazine home, Drake pulled back the slide to chamber the first round, checked the safety was engaged, then shoved the weapon down the back of his trousers. It was purely a precaution, of course. Even in a rural backwater like this, passers-by weren't entirely unknown – usually lost tourists looking for directions, or the occasional delivery van gone astray.

Still, after his conversation with Mason, Drake was taking no chances.

'Hang back, okay?' he said to McKnight as he strode towards the front door. The engine noise outside was plainly audible now; whoever was coming must be moving at quite a speed. Then, abruptly, it stopped.

Approaching the door with one hand behind his back, gripping the weapon, Drake undid the big solid lock that held it shut, grasped the handle and, taking a breath to ready himself, yanked it open.

Straight away he felt the tension dissipate. It was no lost traveller or gun-toting terrorist that confronted him, but a short, petite young woman in dusty bike leathers. Her Suzuki bike was parked haphazardly on the gravel drive just a few yards away, the helmet still resting on the seat.

The young woman tried to flash one of her fierce, predatory grins, but it came off as a pained grimace instead. Drake noticed that her face was uncharacteristically pale and sallow, her eyes ringed by dark circles of fatigue, while the skin of her left cheek was grazed and cut. She was holding one hand against her side, leaning over as if favouring it.

'Keira, what the hell happened to you?' Drake gasped, startled by her appearance.

'Thought I'd drop in on an old friend,' she managed to say, taking an unsteady step forward. 'It's been a while, Ryan...'

Releasing his grip on the weapon, Drake rushed forward as her legs gave way beneath her, and she fell into his arms.

# Chapter 10

*Rawalpindi, Pakistan*

Majid Reza was sitting at the kitchen table in his small, cluttered apartment in central Rawalpindi, the twin city to nearby Islamabad. His shirt and jacket hung from the back of his chair as he bent forward, concentrating on his task. The drone of traffic and the occasional angry blast of a car horn filtering in through his open window, mingling with the thump of footsteps in the apartment above and the muffled shouts of an argument from his next-door neighbour. Petty irritations that regularly taxed his patience.

Like many in the ISI, he made a decent salary that should have afforded him a comfortable home in a respectable part of town, but it was not to be in his case. Circumstances had dictated that the bulk of his monthly pay check went to something less tangible than property.

Suspended over a flickering candle on the table, the soot-stained spoon in his hand had heated sufficiently to dissolve the crystalline material it contained, reducing it to a bubbling mass of dirty brown liquid. Soon the noise and the heat and the irritation of his dirty living space would be far behind him, he knew.

Laying the spoon carefully on the table lest he spill some of its precious contents, he unwrapped the hypodermic syringe from its protective packaging and screwed the needle into place. HIV and other blood-borne diseases were rife in this part of the world as users were forced to share needles, but that was one matter in which he took a kind of perverted pride. Every time, he made sure to use a fresh needle, straight out of its medical packaging.

It was his way of convincing himself he was better than the junkies living on the streets below. He still had a job, a career, a future. Certainly he enjoyed the occasional high, as did many in Pakistan, but that was all it was. A diversion, an entertainment little different from drinking or smoking. When it ceased to amuse or divert him, he would stop.

With the needle prepared, he held the tip of the needle in the brown sludge, slowly withdrawing the plunger and watching as the liquid transferred from the spoon to the syringe. One had to be precise and methodical about such things, he reflected, trying not to notice the slight tremor in his hands as he worked.

His task complete, he let out a sigh, savouring this moment before he shot up. He could feel the ache in his body, the desire for it, the anticipation at knowing his release was only moments away.

But before he could pick up the syringe, his thoughts were interrupted by a sudden banging at the front door.

'Go away!' he called out. 'I'm busy.'

The banging was repeated, louder and more urgent now.

'What do you want?'

'Majid Reza?' a voice echoed through the door.

'Yes.'

'We have a problem. I've been sent to collect you.' The voice that spoke was deep, resonant, but carrying a faint hint of an accent that he couldn't place. Nonetheless, the words they'd spoken were enough to send a chill through him.

Swearing under his breath, Reza laid the syringe down and blew out the candle. 'What kind of problem?' he asked as he hurriedly transferred the syringe and the associated paraphernalia into the old biscuit tin he kept it in.

'The kind I'd rather not shout about from the hallway,' the new arrival explained irritably. 'Now open the door so we can talk.'

Stowing the tin away in a drawer, Reza pulled his shirt over his thin, spare frame and hurried towards the door, though not before drawing his service pistol from its holster on the bed. Whoever this man was, Reza was taking no chances.

Making sure the security chain was in place on the door, and that the automatic was hidden from view behind his back, he gingerly undid the lock and pulled the door open to meet this new arrival.

He barely noticed the sudden blur of movement, or the glint of the electric lights on the strange plastic-looking gun that had suddenly appeared, but he certainly felt what happened next. There was a loud pop, and he flinched as something embedded itself in his right shoulder.

Then, an instant later, white-hot pain engulfed his entire body, short-circuiting every nerve ending and muscle under his control. No longer obeying his command, his body went limp as a rag doll and flopped to the floor, the gun simply falling from his grasp as his fingers ceased to work.

Lying prone and helpless in a foetal position, Reza barely heard the distinctive ping as a pair of bolt cutters severed the security chain and the door swung open to reveal a dark, blurry figure. A figure that had come for one thing only – him.

# Chapter 11

'Clear me some space on the table!' Drake called out, carrying the semi-conscious woman through to the villa's kitchen.

McKnight was way ahead of him, one sweep of her arm sending the few cups and plates on the table clattering to the floor. Approaching close behind, Drake hoisted Frost up and laid her down gently on the flat surface.

She was hurt – that much was obvious – but he wouldn't know how bad or what exactly was wrong until he had a chance to examine her. Unzipping her leather jacket, he pulled it aside to reveal what looked like the source of her pain.

The right side of her grey T-shirt was stained crimson with blood, some of it having dried and clotted already, but it was clear she'd lost a lot of it.

'Jesus, Keira, what the hell happened to you?' McKnight asked.

There was no time to ponder that right now. Answers could come later. For now, the priority was tending her wounds and stabilizing her.

'I've got to get a look at it. Pass the scissors,' Drake prompted, holding out his hand. Almost immediately he felt the requested implement thrust into his grip and went to work, cutting away the blood-soaked T-shirt so he could examine the wound properly.

'Anyone tries to cop a feel, I'll knock them out,' Frost warned, though her words were vague and mumbled as if she were intoxicated. Blood loss coupled with pain and fatigue had taken a heavy toll.

Even a cursory glance was enough to tell him she'd been in the wars. Several large, heavy bruises marked her body, the flesh already badly discoloured beneath her skin. There were also various small lacerations to her arms and hands, one or two of which seemed to contain fragments of glass. Those he could deal with later. It was the big injury that concerned him the most.

Some attempt had been made to dress the wound, Drake realized. There was a cloth pressed against it and secured in place with duct tape, of all things, but the makeshift bandage had only slowed the bleeding.

'Got some serious bleeding here. Doesn't look arterial, but it's a bad wound.'

'Why didn't she go to a hospital?' McKnight asked.

'People ask questions in hospitals.' Especially when the patient harboured the kind of injury he suspected Frost had sustained. Leaning in close, he looked the young woman in the eye, hoping she was still lucid enough to understand him. 'I'm going to take the dressing off, Keira. Might hurt a bit.'

He glanced at McKnight, who nodded and gripped the young woman by the shoulders, ready to hold her down if she struggled, which she was very likely to do.

'Like it matters – *Ow! Fuck!*' she cried out as he yanked the dressing off, duct tape and all. McKnight had to fight hard to keep her from falling right off the table as she bucked and thrashed.

'Easy, Keira. Easy,' the older woman whispered. 'You'll be okay.'

'Not with this guy tearing pieces off me,' Frost replied. 'Shit, Ryan. I hope I get to do this to you one day.' Her teeth were clenched tight, tears in her eyes.

Nonetheless, Drake was at last afforded a decent look at the injury. Sure enough, it was a gunshot wound; a snaking gash along her right side just below the rib cage. The positioning suggested she might have gotten lucky; any further to the left and it would likely have hit an internal organ. Then there would have been nothing he could do for her.

As it was, it was a messy but probably non-fatal flesh wound.

'Clean shot, through and through.' He looked into Frost's eyes, trying to sound jovial and relaxed. 'What are you complaining about, you wimp? This is a piece of piss.'

She tried for a defiant grin. 'Remind me to tell you that next time you get shot.'

'Don't count on it.' Looking at McKnight, Drake motioned to a cupboard at the far side of the kitchen. 'Grab the first aid tin. I need a clean dressing, and a suture kit.'

# Chapter 12

He couldn't move.

The moment Reza's mind at last drifted back into consciousness, he knew something was terribly wrong. His arms and legs were spread out wide, and he could feel his wrists and ankles restrained by something. But it wasn't until he looked up that he realized he'd been tied to the sturdy metal bars of his own bed.

The second thing he realized was that he couldn't speak. A rag had been forced into his mouth and a strip of duct tape used to secure it in place. He tried to cry out, but all that emerged was a feeble, muffled groan.

Panicking, heart pounding, he thrashed and bucked, pulling desperately on his wrists and ankles in a vain effort to break free. Muscles strained and burned with the effort, but nowhere did he even come close to freeing a limb. That knowledge only increased his fear.

'Wouldn't keep that up if I were you, Majid,' a voice warned. 'You'll hurt yourself.'

The realization that his attacker was in the same room sent Reza's heart into overdrive, and his struggles became frantic.

'Hey! Hey! I told you to stop it,' the voice called out. 'Calm down, or I'll have to shock you again.'

Reluctantly his struggles dissipated. Glancing over at the doorway, Reza was at last afforded a look at his captor. The man was big, both tall and broad, and dressed in civilian clothes – jeans, scuffed hiking boots, a casual shirt and a worn-looking leather jacket. He could have been anyone, if not for his face.

His face and head were covered with a black cloth balaclava, leaving only his eyes and mouth exposed. Clearly he didn't want Reza identifying him later, which kindled a tiny spark of hope in him that there might actually be a later.

He spoke flawless Urdu, but without the thick apartment door to muffle his words, the foreign lilt to his voice was unmistakable. American – it had to be. What on earth did an American want with him?

'That's better,' his captor went on, recognizing that he was calming down. 'Work with me here, Majid. No need for us to get off on the wrong foot.'

Leaving the doorway, he approached the bed, the slow measured tread of his boots thumping on the bare floorboards contrasting sharply with the wild, frantic beating of Reza's heart. But rather than attack him, he simply pulled up a chair and sat down next to the bed, as if Reza were a sick relative he'd come to visit.

'Right now, you're probably wondering why I'm here. We're both busy men, so I'll make it quick. All I want from you is information. That's not too hard, is it? Just give me a little honesty, and I'll be on my way.' He leaned forward, the chair creaking under his solid weight. 'I want to know who was responsible for the attack on Camp Chapman, and I want to know where al-Qaeda's senior leaders are hiding.'

Reza's heartbeat quickened once more. This man was asking for something he couldn't possibly give; not just because of the potential fallout from such an admission, but because he simply didn't know. He wasn't nearly important enough.

'Now, I know your first reaction will be to deny it,' the American went on. 'After all, we're playing for high stakes here. It's like a game of poker – everybody's bluffing, but everybody knows it. We know the ISI's been helping to shelter them for at least the past five years, and you know that we know. But you pretend you don't know, and for the sake of diplomacy, we pretend we believe you. Well, I'm here because it's about time everybody showed their hands. I've come to call your bluff.'

'We both know you're not a big player in this particular game, Majid. That's a shitty deal, but it's a fact, my friend. You don't hold any real cards, but *I'm* guessing you know a man who does. So what do you say? Will you point me in his direction?'

Reza shook his head, trying to shout through the gag that he knew nothing, that he was simply a low-level administrator with no knowledge of the ISI's higher echelons. But it was a wasted effort. The gag prevented more than a low groan to escape his lips.

'Thought you might say that,' the American conceded with disappointment. 'But don't worry. I've got something to help motivate you.'

Reaching into his leather jacket, he pulled something out. Something that glinted in the wan street light filtering through the grimy bedroom windows. Something that made Reza's guts twist in terror.

It was a knife, but a knife unlike any Reza had ever seen. The blade was curved almost at right angles, forming a strange L-shape that negated any potential as a weapon. It looked more like something used by a surgeon or a butcher.

'You know what this is?' he asked. 'It's a gelding knife. See, horse breeders often have problems with their herd stallions. All that testosterone pumping through their blood makes them wilful, aggressive, impossible to control. You can't break a stallion like that; no matter how much you whip or collar him, he just keeps fighting back. What you've got to do instead is take a

63

little something away, then he's as good as gold. And you know what? I've found it works just as well on men like yourself.'

Reaching into his pocket, he pulled on a pair of rubber surgical gloves, having to wriggle his fingers a few times to find the right holes. This done, he leaned over and yanked down Reza's underwear, exposing his genitals.

'The good news is that the bleeding's really not as bad as you'd expect,' he explained as he brought the knife closer. 'You won't die from it, at least. Infection could be a problem later, of course, but that's the least of your worries. The pain though… well, put it this way, I've never known a man who didn't talk afterwards.'

Restrained as he was, there was nothing Reza could do to cover or protect himself. Nothing except scream into his gag with absolute terror, buck and thrash around much like a horse trying to unseat its rider. But there could be no escape from this. Nothing he could do to prevent it except give the man what he wanted.

'Nod if you have something you want to tell me,' the American prompted, positioning the curved knife blade beneath Reza's testicles so that a single upward thrust would do the job.

Frantically he nodded, jerking his head with such force that it jarred his neck.

'I'm going to take off your gag now. If you're thinking about screaming, don't,' he warned. 'Believe me, this knife works just as well on tongues.'

Reza groaned in pain as the duct tape was ripped free, taking stray hairs and a layer of skin with it. Nonetheless, the feeling of relief as the rag was pulled from his mouth was tangible. Greedily he sucked in air through his mouth, filling his lungs.

'Who in the ISI knows?' his captor prompted. 'Give me a name. And don't even think about lying to me.'

'He'll kill me,' Reza protested weakly.

'Then you should probably think about leaving Pakistan once this is over.' He saw a dangerous glint in those eyes. 'You won't have a job, but at least you'll still have your balls. So… the name.'

Reza closed his eyes, knowing he could well be signing his own death warrant if he complied, knowing this man would certainly kill him if he didn't.

'Qalat,' he said at last. 'Vizur Qalat.'

'Who the hell is he?'

'A senior field agent with Covert Action Division.' CAD, as it was known, was the most secretive and elite branch of Pakistan's intelligence service, tasked with undertaking missions most rank and file officers never even learned about. 'I don't know the man, but I know he is well connected. If anyone can help you find them, it will be Qalat.'

The American eyed him suspiciously. 'Not holding out on me, are you, Majid?'

'It is the truth. I swear it.' Reza was staring right into his eyes, pleading with the man to show mercy. 'You must believe me.'

After several seconds of anguished silence, the American finally nodded. 'I do,' he confirmed. 'You've done well, Majid. Thanks for your help.'

Replacing the gag in Reza's mouth and securing it with tape, he laid the knife down and instead picked up the biscuit tin in which Reza had stored his syringe and other equipment.

'And because you've been so good, I've prepared a reward,' he explained, lifting out the syringe. 'I added a little something of my own, free of charge. Gives it an extra kick, if you know what I mean.'

Holding Reza's arm steady lest he struggle and break the delicate instrument, he carefully inserted the needle into a prominent vein and depressed the plunger.

'Happy trails, buddy,' he said, speaking in English this time.

Reza barely had time to question the meaning of his words before he began to feel the effects of the potent cocktail. For a few moments, he felt the characteristic rush and euphoria so familiar from the heroin he was used to, but then something else began to creep in. A darkness seemed to be enveloping the room, creeping in from the edge of his vision, slowly engulfing the world around him.

Reza cried out in fear, the gag rendering his final effort useless, as the darkness swallowed him up and his vision faded away.

In total, it took nearly three minutes for him to go into respiratory depression, and his vital signs to fade away completely. Longer than the typical administration, but Hawkins supposed the man's body had built up a tolerance to drugs like this.

Untying Reza's limbs from the bedposts, he carefully arranged the man in a foetal position on the bed, making sure to lay the empty syringe beside him. When he was eventually found, the cause of death would be obvious enough, and a toxicology report would confirm he'd died from a massive heroin overdose. Just another junkie who'd taken a little too much.

Packing away his remaining gear, Hawkins removed his rubber gloves, fished the cell phone out of his pocket and dialled a number back in the States. It was answered within moments.

'Cain.'

'I have a name,' Hawkins reported. 'Vizur Qalat. He's a field agent for their Covert Action Division.'

Silence greeted him for a couple of seconds. Tense, brooding silence, broken only by the drone of traffic outside and the occasional blare of a car horn.

'That name mean something to you?' Hawkins asked.

'Maybe,' Cain said without elaborating. 'How solid is this lead?'

Hawkins glanced at the dead man lying curled on the bed. 'Pretty solid.'

There was a momentary pause. He didn't expect thanks or congratulations, but he knew Cain would be mulling over the implications of this new development.

'Find out everything you can about him,' the deputy director instructed. 'And set up a meeting.'

Hawkins smiled, wondering if Qalat was the sort of man to deal rationally, or if he'd get a chance to put the gelding knife to use after all.

'Consider it done.'

# Chapter 13

Half an hour after her arrival, and Frost's condition had mercifully stabilized. The hastily applied sutures used to close the bullet wound seemed to be holding, and the bleeding had slowed enough that Drake was able to move her to the couch and apply a fresh dressing. Infection was still a danger, but that was a chance they'd have to take for now.

'Here,' McKnight said, handing the young woman a cup of sugary tea.

Frost took an experimental sip, wrinkling her nose as if it were poison. 'I'd settle for something stronger.'

'I bet you would. But you're dehydrated, in borderline shock, and you've lost God knows how much blood over the past twelve hours,' Drake said sharply. 'You need fluids, and lots of them. So stop bitching and drink.'

Frost knew when she was outmanoeuvred. Steeling herself as if she were about to down a shot of absinthe, she went to work on the mug of tea.

'How are you feeling?' McKnight asked.

'Well, aside from having a hole in me that wasn't there yesterday, pretty good.' The young woman glanced around at their surroundings and managed a grin. A real one this time. 'By the way, I like what you've done with the place.'

Her momentary smile soon faded, however. It was clear from her expression she had more she wanted to say.

'Listen, I'm sorry for showing up like this,' she finally managed. More than anything else in this world, she hated being indebted to people. 'I wouldn't have come here, but I didn't have anywhere else to go.'

Now they were getting down to it. Drake lowered himself into a chair opposite her. 'Tell us what happened.'

'Some fucking assholes jumped me in a club in Munich last night, tried to haul me off in a van.' Reaching down, Frost absently gripped one of the fragments of glass between her thumb and forefinger, yanked it from the flesh of her arm and laid it on the coffee table as if it were an empty chocolate wrapper. 'It was my fault. I let my guard down. They're dead now, but I got pretty messed up in the process. I knew I couldn't stay in Munich in case they'd been watching my apartment, and the police might be checking the local hospitals, so I patched myself up as best I could and got the fuck out of Dodge. Pretty much came straight here after that.'

'You mean you rode all the way from Munich to Marseille in one night?' McKnight asked, impressed by such a feat of endurance. 'With a wound like that?'

'It's okay, I had my little friends here to keep me company,' Frost said, reaching into her back pocket and holding up an almost-empty strip of painkillers. 'Goes down smooth with a can of Red Bull. The bleeding wasn't too bad at first, but it got worse the longer I rode. Have to admit, I was pretty glad to see this place when I pulled up. I'm just sorry for pussying out on you and fainting, though.'

Drake said nothing to that. As if she needed to apologize for almost dying. 'The men who jumped you. Were they field operatives?'

She shook her head. 'Too fucking stupid and sloppy for that. They were bounty hunters, probably hoping to make a big score.'

Unfolding a crumpled, bloodstained piece of paper, she held it up for Drake to see. It might have been taken a few years ago, but the printed image on the page was unmistakably that of Frost.

'Looks like I'm famous,' she remarked with grim humour.

Drake felt his heart sink, knowing the attacks on Frost and Mason had to be linked to this image. 'I thought you were monitoring all the Most Wanted sites.'

'I was.' She looked defensive at the implication that she'd dropped the ball. 'Doesn't mean there aren't others I don't know about. Shit, maybe there are bounty hunter-only message boards floating around out there.'

'Doesn't matter where it came from. Either way, someone tipped them off about you,' McKnight reasoned, giving Drake a meaningful look. 'Which means the rest of our faces have probably been circulated as well.'

'Cain,' Frost said, practically spitting the word.

She didn't need to say anything more. It was plain that the timings of the two attacks, coming within mere hours of each other, couldn't be a coincidence. And Cain was the only man with the influence and global reach to make that happen.

It was then that another thought occurred to Frost. Her face seemed to lose even more colour. 'Christ, what if he tracked me here?'

'Relax. Nobody tracked you here,' Drake said, rising from his seat to go outside and retrieve her bike, which he couldn't just leave sitting there in plain view.

'How can you be so sure?'

'Because we're still alive.'

Heading for the front door, he glanced over at Frost. 'You're staying here until you're back on your feet. No apologies, no arguments. What happened wasn't your fault, okay?'

She was avoiding eye contact, but he could tell his words had struck a chord. And for once she didn't have a smart-assed comeback for him.

'Whatever.' He was about to leave when Frost spoke up again. 'Ryan?'

'Yeah?'

She was holding out her hand. Drake knew what it meant, what she wanted to say but couldn't. Reaching out, he gripped her hand and clasped it tight. That one gesture meant more to him than any amount of thanks or flattery.

Letting go, he nodded gently. 'Stay here, get some rest. And for Christ's sake stay out of trouble.'

'No promises!' she called after him as he strode outside.

# Chapter 14

*CIA headquarters, Langley, Virginia – 30 April 1985*

*The young woman was being held in an interrogation cell, seated motionless at the metal table in the centre of the room, her hands resting on her lap, her head bowed as if in quiet contemplation. Locks of long blonde hair fell around her face, partially shielding it from view.*

*Watching her through the security cameras in the observation room nearby, Cain glanced at the technician manning the room.*

*'Has she said anything since she was brought in?'*

*'No, sir.' He looked like he'd been waiting too long for something to happen. 'Hasn't moved a muscle in the past hour. I actually sent a guy in just to make sure the camera wasn't malfunctioning.'*

*Frowning, Cain turned his attention back to her short personnel dossier, which he'd been skim-reading on the way here. There wasn't much to read. She claimed to have been born in a small village in one of the Baltic republics, and that her parents had died in an accident when she was still a child. Disillusioned with life in the Soviet Union and with no next of kin, she had eventually made the decision to defect to the West.*

*Thus she'd made the arduous trek northwards, crossing the border into Finland at night with the intention of reaching Norway and claiming asylum there. She'd been smart enough to know that Finland's official policy was to deport Soviet escapees back to their country of origin.*

*All had gone well until she'd become lost and disoriented in a snow storm, forced to wait several days in an improvised shelter before resuming her journey. Freezing, exhausted and close to death, she'd been picked up by a Norwegian border patrol. The medical report confirmed that she was physically fit and apparently in good health despite her ordeal.*

*Aside from these snippets of information, however, she appeared to be a blank slate. The only way to learn more was by speaking with her.*

*'All right. I'm going in,' Cain decided, tucking her dossier under his arm.*

*Making his way into the short hallway leading to the adjacent room, he flashed his ID to the security agent on duty there. There was a loud buzz as the electronic lock disengaged, and the door swung open.*

*Only then, as he approached the table, did the young woman at last look up, affording Cain his first proper look at her.*

With a strong jawline, high cheekbones and straight forehead, her facial structure was faintly Nordic in appearance, characteristic of peoples living in the Baltic states, as opposed to the oval shape that was more common amongst ethnic Russians. Her blonde, slightly wavy hair was worn long, reaching well past her shoulders, with loose strands falling on either side of her face. Her full lips were closed, her chin raised slightly as if in quiet defiance of the authority he represented.

She was seated, and wearing a plain white T-shirt and slacks, so her height and build were hard to judge, but in her exposed arms he saw the lean, wiry muscles that spoke of an active, physical life. He had little reason to believe the rest of her body was any different. He also spotted a number of small scars on both hands, which he'd come to recognize easily enough in those who had fought up close and personal.

But most of all, it was her eyes that caught his attention and held it. Stark blue and cold as glacial ice, they were fixed on him with an unwavering intensity that was almost disconcerting, as if she were somehow seeing right through him. The look in those eyes spoke of a soul that had witnessed a great many things in its short life.

Taken as the sum of her parts, this woman seated before him was both strikingly attractive and oddly beguiling, her appearance somehow combining youthful prettiness with the harder edge and confidence that came with experience and age. She was a strange but compelling contradiction – young and impetuous yet cunning and resourceful, beautiful yet tough, calm and composed yet apparently no stranger to violence and fighting.

Who was she? What did she want? And what had brought her here?

'Good morning, Anya,' he began, settling himself into the chair opposite. 'My name's Mike Cunningham.'

'No,' she said simply.

'Excuse me?'

She was looking at him curiously, as if he were a puzzle that would require a little work to solve. 'That is not your real name. I think you were not telling the truth.'

She spoke English quite well for one so young, though with an obvious accent. Some words clearly took some effort to pronounce.

'What makes you say that?' he asked, keeping his expression carefully neutral.

'When you say the name, you hesitate, it does not come naturally to you. I think this name was not true. And I saw your identification for a moment as you entered the room.' Her lips parted slightly in the beginnings of a smile, the pieces of the puzzle coming together in her mind. 'It was a test, yes? You were testing me.'

Cain's brows rose for a moment in surprise at how easily she'd seen through the ruse. Sharp and observant. He made a mental note to add those to the list of attributes he was compiling about her.

'Very good, Anya,' he allowed, setting the dossier down on the metal surface. 'My real name is Cain. Marcus Cain.'

That seemed to satisfy her. At least, she didn't try to correct him.

'You are in charge here?'

Cain chuckled at this notion. 'Not exactly. But I'm about as far up the chain as you're going to get. You can speak with me, or we can put you on a flight back to the Soviet Union. Fair enough?'

She shrugged, conceding to his terms. 'Fair enough.'

'Good. So...' He leaned forward, resting his arms on the table. 'Let's talk about you, Anya. You went to a lot of trouble to get here. What exactly do you want from us?'

'I want to work for you.'

'Why?'

She swallowed, glancing down for a moment before carrying on. 'Because I want my country to be rid of the Soviets for ever. I want my people to have freedom and decide their own future. America was born from the same ideas, yes? Well, I want the same thing. And I am willing to give everything I have to make it happen.'

Cain hesitated before replying. Coming from another person, such words might have seemed overblown and idealistic, nothing more than youthful fire and passion. But in this woman, he saw something more. He saw purpose and iron determination behind the rhetoric.

'That's quite a goal,' he said, hoping it didn't sound like mockery. 'What makes you think you could work for us? Do you have any skills? Technical expertise? Connections in the Soviet regime?'

She shook her head.

Cain let out a faint sigh of disappointment and flipped her dossier closed. 'Then I'm sorry, Anya.'

'Wait,' she said, reaching across the table with surprising speed to clasp his hand. Glancing up, Cain found himself staring into those hard, intense blue eyes. 'You do not understand. I have no family, no friends, no one who depends on me. No one who can be used against me. The State saw to that,' he added with a bitter look. 'I have nothing, so I have nothing to lose.'

'Just your life,' he pointed out. 'You really so eager to give that up?'

She thought about that for a moment. 'What did your General Patton say? It is better to die for something, than live for nothing.'

'I think it was fight rather than die,' he mused. Still, he had to commend her on her enthusiasm if nothing else. 'You understand that even if I was to consider this for a moment, it could take months just to vet you, not to mention the training that comes after. Being a field operative isn't like working at a 7-Eleven.'

At this, her blonde brows drew together in a frown. 'A seven-what?'

'Doesn't matter. The point is, we get a lot of people like you. People who want to play spies. Most don't even come close to making it.'

'Yet you are talking to me now,' she observed. 'And I did not come here to play games.' She sighed, looking him right in the eye, her former defiance and confidence gone now. 'Please, Marcus Cain. I do not want pity, just a chance to prove myself. So far my life has meant nothing to anyone. Let me do something with what I have left.'

*The intensity, the determination, the sheer force of will behind this final plea was startling. Cain could practically feel it emanating from her, and wondered once more about what had driven this young woman to make such a dangerous gamble, to come all this way and risk everything.*

*And much to his own surprise, he found himself wanting to agree with her. There was something compelling, almost magnetic about her. The simple but heartfelt ideals she held, the drive that lay behind them, the determination and confidence of youth seemed to resonate with him. It was a stark contrast to the cynical and pragmatic old men he was so used to dealing with.*

*Perhaps she did deserve what she was asking for. Didn't everyone at least deserve a chance?*

*'Leave it with me. I'll be in touch,' he promised, retrieving the dossier and standing up to leave.*

–

*CIA headquarters, Langley, Virginia – March 2010*

Cain was in his office, engrossed in the classified intelligence dossier that the Agency had compiled on Vizur Qalat, the Pakistani intelligence operative Hawkins had singled out for further attention. It was fragmented and incomplete, but even the list of career postings began to paint a picture that Cain could make sense of.

An interesting man who had lived an even more interesting life, much of it intriguingly entwined with the Agency itself. Forty-seven years old, he'd started his career in the Pakistani army, quickly rising through the ranks before being promoted to their military intelligence division. He'd played an active part in aiding US operations against the Soviets in Afghanistan back in the 1980s, helping funnel intelligence on Russian troop deployments and even to smuggle arms across the border.

That was why the name had struck a chord with him the first time Hawkins mentioned it. Cain remembered Qalat from personal experience, especially now he'd seen a recent photograph. He might have aged somewhat since their last encounter, but it was unmistakably him. What a strange sense of humour life seemed to have, Cain reflected, throwing this man back into the mix after two decades.

Intrigued, he carried on reading. In 1999, Qalat had helped orchestrate the military coup that had seen the overthrow of Pakistan's democratically elected Prime Minister Nawaz Sharif. By the time of the September 11 attacks, Qalat had already moved into ISI – Pakistan's premier intelligence agency. From there he had overseen a number of joint operations against Taliban cells hiding in the mountainous tribal regions near the Pakistan border, most of which had been successful.

Little was known about his personal life, save that he was unmarried and had no close next of kin. A grey man, then, often to be found at the periphery of major events but never at the epicentre. A man who had somehow remained under the Agency's radar for most of his life, but who might now hold the key to destroying their greatest enemy.

If they could get him to cooperate.

Cain blinked, brought back to reality by the buzz of his cell phone. Laying the folder down on his expensive mahogany desk, he fished the phone out of his jacket and hit the accept call button. As he'd hoped, it was coming from one of his field ops teams in Italy.

'The police took the bait, sir,' the man reported, his voice surprisingly soft and quiet considering his profession. 'They moved in on Mason's safe house just like we predicted.'

'Did they get him?' Cain asked with mild interest.

'Negative. Seems he was prepared for an assault. They're expanding their perimeter, but it looks like he gave them the slip. We no longer have eyes-on ourselves.'

Mason, like his comrade Frost, was a wily one, employing every trick in the book to stay under the Agency's radar and rarely letting his guard down. In fact, if it hadn't been for the clues provided by Cain's mole, he suspected both operatives might have remained at large for some time. As it was, Cain's agents had finally tracked him down about a month ago, and had been discreetly watching him ever since.

'Doesn't matter. We know where he's heading.'

A few discreet tip-offs, first to local thugs in Munich and then to the police in Milan, had yielded exactly the kind of results he needed. Now both of Drake's comrades were on the run, and he knew exactly where they would run to.

'Get yourselves out of Italy,' Cain ordered. 'And get ready for Phase Two. I want you ready to launch within the hour. Clear?'

'Crystal, sir.'

Satisfied, Cain closed down the phone and pocketed it, before turning his attention back to Qalat's dossier. The pieces of this puzzle were moving into position almost of their own accord, needing little more than the odd nudge now and again to keep them on course. Soon enough, they would be exactly where he wanted them.

All he needed was the final piece. The one vital element that still eluded him.

Anya.

# Chapter 15

It was early evening in southern France, the sun slanting towards the western horizon and setting the sky alight in a blaze of colour, as Drake prepared a simple dinner in the villa's kitchen. He had too much on his mind to be hungry, and in truth he wasn't a great cook at the best of times, but they all needed to eat regardless. Anyway, even he could reheat a can of beans, some potatoes and a bit of tinned meat without killing someone.

They would be leaving soon to rendezvous with Mason at the *Alamo*, staying only to give Frost a little time to regain her strength for the journey. After that, they would have to decide their next collective move. Drake already had a plan in mind, based on the very real threat they now faced, but whether the others would agree to it was another matter.

His preparations were interrupted by the sound of footsteps, and he looked up as Frost emerged from the bathroom, her hair still damp from the shower.

Her bloodstained jeans and bike leathers were gone now, replaced by a pair of jogging pants and a plain white vest that could be pulled up easily to inspect the dressing on her abdomen. She had a towel draped around her shoulders, and was clearly in pain, but she at least looked more like her normal self.

'Don't say it,' she warned. 'I know I've never looked more beautiful than this moment, but try to keep it under control. I'm not up for partying right now.'

'I'll do my best,' he promised. At least her sense of humour was back up and running, though whether that was a good thing or not was questionable.

'The shower sucks, by the way. Can't decide if it wants to be hot or cold,' she remarked as she eased herself down at the small dining table, wincing in pain as her battered and bruised body reminded her once again of the punishment it had taken over the past 24 hours.

'It's on my to-do list,' Drake said with the weary resignation born from long experience. 'Anyway, how are you feeling?'

'Tip top. Haven't had this much fun since my last exorcism.' She ran her hands through her short, dishevelled black hair. 'And I'm starving.'

Drake wasn't surprised. Frost might have been half his size, but she ate and drank like a professional rugby player. He had no idea how her metabolism worked, but it must have functioned very differently from most humans because she somehow remained lean and trim regardless of what she ate.

Spooning some of the mixture he'd been preparing onto a plate, he laid it down in front of her. 'Here, dig in.'

The young woman eyed the meal suspiciously. 'What the hell is this?'

'You Americans call it hash.'

'Yeah? What do you call it?'

'Fuck knows, but it got me through army basic training, so it can't be all bad.' He handed her a fork. 'Eat.'

She didn't thank him, because she knew it wasn't expected. Instead she set about tackling the food. Though tentative at first, she soon began devouring it like what she was – someone who hadn't eaten a proper meal in close to 24 hours.

'You know, this would go down better with a little—'

'Forget it, Keira,' Drake cut her off, feeling like an exasperated parent having to deal with a demanding child. 'Not happening. Deal with it.'

'Fucking typical,' she mumbled. 'Worse than living with my mom.'

It was then that she paused for a moment. To Drake's surprise, there was a sad, mournful look in her eyes, as if dark thoughts had intruded on her mind. 'Something wrong?'

She looked around, taking in their modest surroundings. The simple rustic furniture, the old doors with peeling paint, the worktops cluttered with utensils and personal items, the sunlight slanting in through shuttered windows. The silent evidence of two lives entwined beneath one roof.

'It's this place,' she said quietly. 'It's all so... normal.'

Drake gave her a wry smile. 'Is that a bad thing?'

'No, I mean...' She shook her head, looking almost angry at herself. 'Shit, Ryan, I don't really know what I mean.'

'Give it a try,' he prompted. 'You're not usually lost for words.'

'It's just... you really look like you're making a go of things here. You and Sam, you've got... a home.' She said that word as if it were unfamiliar to her. 'I mean, it's not exactly white picket fences and two-and-a-half kids, but it's a real place, a real life. I just never expected it, that's all.'

'Things change for all of us eventually.' He spread his arms out to encompass his surroundings. 'Maybe this place has given me some perspective.'

'That how you want to live?'

She wasn't asking that question with her typical sarcasm or disdain, but genuine interest, as if trying to understand the man sharing the room with her.

'Isn't that what we all want?' Drake asked, not even sure if he knew the answer himself. 'A home. A life.'

She smiled at him then, a hint of her former bravado returning. 'You know me. I never plan that far ahead.'

Outside, not far from the villa, McKnight was standing near the cliff edge, looking westward across the bay at the small fishing boats bobbing on the gentle swell. The breeze had risen a little with the onset of evening, stirring up the sea so that it was studded with whitecaps, but air still retained the sultry warmth of the afternoon.

She swallowed hard, trying to fight back the rising tide of nausea that had been growing all afternoon. She tried to tell herself that it was just a result of the tumultuous events of the day, but deep down she knew it was a silent reminder of the secret she was keeping from her companions.

But that would have to wait for now. Too much was at stake for them to be distracted by something like that. Right now, she had other matters to deal with. Glancing over her shoulder to make sure Drake couldn't see her, she dug her cell phone from her pocket and quickly dialled a number. A number she was careful to delete from her phone records every time she used it. A number she was required to call every three days without fail.

It didn't ring for long before he answered.

'Yes, Samantha?'

Marcus Cain always called her by her full name. She didn't know why, but she always sensed an edge of mockery and condescension in it. Because he held all the cards against her. He always had.

'What the hell do you think you're doing?' she demanded right away.

'Excuse me?'

'You know goddamn well what I'm talking about. Frost and Mason. You tried to have them killed last night!' It took no small measure of self-control to hold her anger and hatred in check. Anger towards him, hatred towards herself.

'Samantha, I think you need to calm down. For both our sakes.'

He was playing the voice of reason, his tone carefully neutral, almost compassionate. But beneath this veneer lay a harder undertone, warning her such insubordination wouldn't be tolerated for long.

'Don't tell me to calm down. They almost died,' she said, her voice low.

If she was hoping for any kind of concession from him, she was to be disappointed. 'And what if they had?'

'This wasn't our deal, Marcus,' she said, though her resolve was wavering now. 'I didn't sign up for this.'

'And what exactly *did* you sign up for, Samantha? To keep Drake out of trouble? To tell me his favourite movies?' He paused for a moment, and she sensed something devastating was about to come. 'What about fucking him? Was that part of our agreement?'

At this, she felt the colour drain from her face, her heart beating wildly in her chest. He knew. He knew everything. How could he not? Marcus Cain had made a career out of finding out what people didn't want him to know.

'You asked me to gain his trust. I did what I had to do,' she said once she'd recovered her composure sufficiently to speak.

'I bet you did.' His disdain was obvious, and she felt hatred swell up inside her at the notion of him watching them together. 'But maybe you're confused about the nature of our agreement, Samantha. If you think this is some kind of partnership where you get to pick and choose which directives to follow, you're very wrong. You were nothing when I pulled you out of that military prison – just another dumb jarhead who got caught with her hand in the cookie jar. I gave you a second chance; a chance at a fresh start. But I can't emphasize enough how easily I could take that away again.'

McKnight tried to swallow, but her throat was like sandpaper, tight and dry and constricted. He was right, of course. Every word he said was the truth. He had given her a second chance, pulled her out of a 15-year prison sentence with an offer she simply couldn't refuse.

But many times since then, she wished she had. She'd made a deal with the devil when she accepted Cain's offer. When this was over, she doubted he would lose any sleep over what happened to her. She was simply a tool to be used until it had served its purpose.

And what a terrible purpose it was.

'Are we clear on that?'

She had to force the words out. 'Yes. We're clear.'

'Good. Now talk about me about Drake. What does he intend to do now?'

She and Drake had planned for many contingencies during their time here, and she could guess well enough what was on his mind now. Once he reunited with Mason, he would want to hit back, to take the fight to his enemy. And if she tipped Cain off about it now, she was effectively signing their death warrants.

Until now she'd always told herself there was no alternative but to play Cain's game, that Drake and the others were doomed to failure no matter what they did. They were up against an enemy that was far beyond any of them. That was why she had actively tried to stop them taking action against Cain, believing that if she could maintain the uneasy ceasefire between them, then she could protect Drake's life.

No longer.

At that crucial moment, Samantha did something even she hadn't expected – she hesitated. Reaching down, she laid a hand gently on her stomach, still hard and flat, giving no outward sign of the tiny life growing within. But it was there.

Her child. Drake's child.

'Nothing.' The word had escaped her lips almost before she knew it.

Silence greeted that statement. She could practically sense his doubt, his suspicion. Cain wasn't stupid, nor was he gullible. He was a shrewd enough judge of character to know that running and hiding wasn't Drake's style, especially not when his friend's lives had been put at risk.

'Nothing?'

Samantha stared out to sea, watching the distant shape of a helicopter skimming a few hundred feet above the choppy waters. A sightseeing flight perhaps, or one of the wealthier yacht owners looking to arrive in Marseille in style. Angling in towards the coast, soon disappeared beyond the rocky headland on the other side of the bay.

'He doesn't have a plan. I don't think he ever did,' she said. 'And now he's all out of options.'

She could barely believe she'd said it. Just like that, she'd crossed a line, making an enemy not just of the friends she had betrayed all this time, but also of the man who held a noose around her neck. And yet, for the first time in a long time, she didn't hate herself. For the first time in a long time, she had done the right thing.

'Not holding out on me, are you, Samantha?'

She knew she was going to have to sell this one, to flesh out the details and keep the lie alive. Simply asking him to believe her wouldn't be enough now.

'You don't understand Drake; not like I do. He's been different ever since what happened in Libya.' After all, the best lies were the ones closest to the truth. 'He's not looking for ways to fight back any more, he's not trying to win this thing. He's already lost so much, I think… all that's on his mind now is survival, for him and the others.'

She could still hear the distinctive thump of the helicopter as it lurked somewhere beyond the hillside that blocked her view, though the noise was barely noticeable over the hammering of her own heartbeat.

'I see.' His tone of voice made it impossible to gauge whether he did or not. 'So you don't think he's a threat any longer?'

He was pressing her, and she knew that her next answer would be crucial. To be too emphatic in her denials would alert him that she was lying, whereas sticking too closely to the truth might prompt Cain to act anyway.

'I don't know yet,' she replied, though she had to hold the phone closer to her ear to shield it from the growing noise of the chopper. 'But I know he cares more about his friends than he does about fighting you. As long as they're safe, he won't risk getting involved.'

'Interesting,' Cain mused, intrigued by the possibility.

Samantha let out a breath, for a moment daring to hope that perhaps she'd managed to avert further bloodshed. Perhaps she had done enough to convince Cain that Drake and the others were no longer worth his attention.

'Maybe you're right,' Cain went on. 'Maybe everything you've told me is true. But then, maybe it isn't. I'm afraid I can't afford to take that chance.'

Suddenly a dark shape rose up from behind the rocky hillside on the other side of the bay, silhouetted against the setting sun, wide rotor blades

79

swiping the air as it descended towards her. Only then did she realise this was no sightseeing flight, no rich playboy looking to impress his peers.

Oh Christ, her mind screamed. Oh God, no!

'Marcus, please,' she said, her voice trembling. 'You don't have to—'

'You knew it would come down to this in the end. Did you really think I could leave Drake and the others alive, after everything they've done? The man will always be a threat, no matter how much you try to rein him in. I'm sorry, but that's one threat I have to deal with.'

It was all a ploy, to draw them together, get them to close ranks so that Cain could kill Drake and his team in one strike. How stupid she'd been to think otherwise.

'If I were you, I'd put some distance between myself and that villa, fast,' Cain advised. 'The chopper crew are under orders not to fire on anyone outside their zone of engagement, but I can't protect you if you don't help yourself. Walk away, come home and consider your mission completed. I'll take care of the rest.'

She couldn't believe what she was hearing. Cain was offering her a way out; a final chance to come home and have her slate wiped clean. Put all this behind her, start a new life. At the cost of her friends'.

She knew right away that was a deal she could never live with.

'Fireworks are about to start, Samantha. You can't do anything for Drake now, but you can save your own life. Isn't that worth anything to you?' he asked. 'Your call, but for what it's worth I hope you make the right choice.'

With those parting words, Cain closed down the call. McKnight no longer cared. Abandoning the phone, she turned and sprinted towards the house even as the chopper swept across the bay, downwash from the rotors whipping up the sea below.

'Ryan! Chopper coming in!' she screamed, pounding towards the building, fear and adrenaline lending greater urgency to her frantic burst of speed.

Inside the villa, Drake started at the sound of her voice, and turned instinctively towards the windows. Peering through the blinds, he caught a glimpse of the aircraft as it swung round towards them, nose flaring upward to slow its forward motion out over the water.

He could make out the blue and white fuselage that marked it as a civilian aircraft, probably a variant of the Bell Huey. Sunlight glinted across the curved dome of the cockpit, while the side door rolled back to reveal two men in the crew area, both of whom were armed.

Instinct took over in that moment. Turning away from the window, he rushed towards Frost who was just now rising from the table, caught her around the waist and forced her to the ground. At the same moment, the villa's back door flew open and McKnight practically threw herself inside.

'Get down!' Drake called out.

A second later, the shuttered windows disintegrated beneath a storm of automatic fire as the chopper's two passengers opened up with a pair of light machine guns. Heavy calibre rounds slammed into the far wall, shattering bricks and plaster that then rained down on the kitchen's three occupants. The roar of both weapons firing on full automatic seemed to blend together into a constant deafening cacophony that echoed and reverberated off every surface.

'Who the fuck is shooting at us?' Frost screamed. 'How did they find us?'

Those were questions to ponder later, assuming they survived that long. In any case, Drake wasn't listening. Reaching out, he clutched at McKnight's outstretched hand and pulled her towards him, her body having to force a path through the shattered glass, wood and stonework that littered the floor.

'You okay?' he asked, yelling right in her face. She didn't appear injured, but he needed to be sure.

She nodded, eyes wide with shock. 'He found us. He's going to kill us all. What do we do, Ryan?'

That was the question. To stay here or attempt to fight back would be futile, he knew immediately. Likely the two gunners in that chopper were using belt fed machine guns, likely M60's or some derivative, based on the familiar noise, which was bad news for him. Those guns were accurate and powerful, and unlikely to fail a competent operator.

Judging by the amount of fire they were laying down, they had enough ammunition to sit there taking pot shots for quite some time. Anyone who exposed themselves to such murderous fire would be cut down before they could get off a single shot. Then again, to simply cower here hoping to survive might be playing right into their hands, buying time for a ground assault team to storm the house.

Run or fight. Live or die.

In that moment, he made his decision.

'Stay low and follow me. Move!' he hissed, crawling through the debris that now littered the devastated kitchen area, heading towards the main hallway.

A hundred feet above them in the Bell 206 helicopter, the pilot adjusted his pitch slightly to give the two gunners an optimal line of fire on the villa below.

Reaching up, he keyed his radio mic to connect him with the two operatives in the crew compartment. 'Light them up.'

'Copy that,' came the curt reply. Laying his M60 light machine gun aside, the first gunner hoisted the long slender frame of an RPG-7 grenade launcher up onto his shoulder. These powerful anti-armour weapons had been around since the Soviets developed them in the early 1960's, and were still the bane of tank commanders the world over. Easy to maintain and use, they could be loaded with everything from fragmentation to armour piercing to gas or smoke rounds, but this one was something special.

Inserted in its launch tube was a single TBG-7 thermobaric warhead, designed to suck in all the surrounding oxygen when it detonated, creating an intense high temperature explosion and an accompanying blast wave far more powerful than conventional explosives. And they were particularly effective when used in confined spaces like tunnels, bunkers, or civilian houses like the one below.

There was an audible *whoosh* as the initial charge forced the projectile from the launcher, followed a second later by a more powerful roar as the rocket's own propellant ignited. The pilot watched as the single warhead streaked down towards the villa, disappearing through the gaping hole that had once been a window.

A dull red flash from within the building told him the payload had just detonated. Craning his neck to survey the destruction, he watched as the remaining windows exploded outwards in a hail of fire and glass, the door was torn from its hinges and the tiled roof seemed to bulge upwards, like an overfilled balloon about to pop. Weaker sections gave way under the strain, allowing jets of smoke and flame to erupt into the evening air.

'Good hit,' the gunner called out, lowering the now empty launch tube. 'I see no movement below.'

The pilot was inclined to agree. Anyone caught within that building would have certainly been killed, either by the concussive blast wave or the resulting hail of shrapnel.

'Roger that. They're toast.' Keying his radio to a different frequency, he hit his mic again to send out an encrypted burst transmission. 'Karma One, we have good impact. Target building is neutralised. No survivors on site.'

'Understood, Karma One,' came the crackly voice over the radio. A man's voice. Marcus Cain's voice. 'Good work. Withdraw.'

'Copy that. Karma One is out of here.'

Wasting no more time here, he swung them away to starboard in a wide arc, heading out to sea to dump the weapons overboard, along with any other evidence of the clandestine raid. Their meeting rally point was a tiny air strip fifty miles to the east, where they would land and quickly change the aircraft's registration numbers and colour scheme, returning it to its original red and black trim. Within the hour, nobody would even know this chopper had existed.

As the French coast receded behind him, the pilot glanced one last time at the smoking, ruined building they had left in their wake. Like the rest of his crew, he didn't know who'd been unlucky enough to be living there or what they'd done to earn such a violent demise.

As the chopper receded into the distance, silence descended on the ruined villa, broken only by the crackle of smouldering wood and the groan of the partially collapsed roof threatening to give way entirely.

The freshening sea breeze whipped across the devastated structure, whistling through empty window frames and stirring up smoke and embers.

Then, suddenly, the charred and blackened door leading up from the villa's basement rattled and shuddered, struck by a blow from the other side. The blow was repeated a second time with greater force, and the door juddered open an inch or so in its damaged frame. Then, with a final effort born of pure anger and frustration, the third blow succeeded in forcing the cracked and warped barricade open.

Emerging into the ruins of what had once been the villa's main hall with his Browning automatic in hand, Drake's eyes swept his immediate surroundings. Right behind him was McKnight, also armed, with Frost bringing up the rear.

'Jesus Christ,' the young woman whispered, stunned by the destruction that had been wrought on the once peaceful and secluded dwelling.

Drake said nothing to this, keeping his thoughts to himself.

'I don't hear anything,' McKnight said after a moment or two, head cocked to one side. 'The chopper's gone.'

'Must have figured us for dead,' Frost reasoned. 'They weren't too far off. If you hadn't gotten us into the basement, that fucking thing would have vaporised us.'

It had been a close-run thing, Drake barely managing to heave the door shut and take cover before the thermobaric warhead detonated on the upper level. Even underground in the relative safety of the basement, they had been thrown against the ground and stunned by the force of the blast, the sudden change in air pressure leaving their ears ringing and their heads aching.

But it was more than just material damage. Drake knew all too well what this attack meant. The life he and Samantha had made for themselves here over the past six months had abruptly vanished.

'Christ, I'm so sorry, Ryan,' Frost said, her voice close to breaking as the realisation dawned on her that this attack had coincided with her arrival. 'They must have found me, followed me here, used me to get to—'

'Save it, Keira. We need to get out of here,' Drake decided, lowering his weapon. 'Everyone within ten miles will have heard that blast. The police are probably on their way already.'

'But where are we supposed to go?' the young woman asked.

Drake turned to look at her. 'I hope you're up for a climb.'

–

Though the villa sat on a hillside overlooking a sheltered little bay below, the natural harbour was too shallow to be of much use to yachts or fishing boats, and what little beach existed there was too narrow and rocky to be of interest to tourists. However, it was just fine for what Drake had in mind.

Hurriedly descending a steep, uneven path that wound its way down the hillside, the three survivors found themselves on a wide spur of rock that jutted out into the bay, forming a natural jetty. Moored close to this was an inflatable boat, big enough to hold three or four passengers, an outboard motor fixed to its backboard.

'Not exactly the QE2, Ryan', Frost said, eyeing the modest vessel dubiously.

'It's enough to get us where we need to go. Anyway, the roads are probably being watched. Here, climb aboard,' Drake said, holding out his hand.

The young woman was breathing hard after the difficult and painful descent from the villa, and was for once prepared to accept his help. McKnight, having become well acquainted with the craft, leapt aboard without difficulty as Drake dropped the engine into the water and gave the starter cord a sharp pull.

As the engine coughed into life, Drake stole one last look up at the villa they had abandoned. Smoke was still drifting up through the shattered roof and empty windows, and he imagined the fires started by the blast would consume what remained of the building before fire crews could get out here to tackle it. Good news for them at least; it would buy them some time before the French police realised the owners of the house hadn't been killed in the blast.

However, that thought did little to assuage the aching sadness he felt to be leaving this place, knowing he would likely never return.

He felt a hand on his shoulder, and glanced around at Samantha who was standing beside him. 'We can find another place,' she said quietly.

Drake said nothing as he settled himself in front of the outboard motor and twisted the throttle, accelerating away from the scene.

# Chapter 16

The sun was low on the horizon by the time Drake eased off the throttle, allowing the little speedboat to drift to a halt about a mile out from the harbour at Marseille. None of them had said much during the fraught journey away from the villa, though they were relieved to have encountered no pursuit.

At least, none that they could see. For all they knew, there could be a Predator drone shadowing them, or a satellite looking down on their progress.

'You know, sometimes I can't help thinking we got the shitty deal in life,' Frost remarked, staring longingly at the big luxury yachts moored near the harbour mouth, the sound of music and revelry already drifting across the water.

'You just realising that now?' Drake asked, as he fished out his cell phone and started dialling.

She shrugged. 'Be nice to see how the other half live.'

Drake didn't respond as he waited for his call to connect. To his relief, it was answered within seconds. 'We're in position. Give us a signal.'

Sure enough, a second or two later, he caught the flash of a signal lamp a mile or so to the west. The low sun made it difficult to pick out the source, but Drake had the bearing fixed in his mind.

'Good man. Stand by, we're on our way.'

Gunning the throttle once more, he powered the small craft at top speed across the choppy waves, salty spray stinging his eyes and the small cuts on his arms from the earlier attack. He cared little for such minor discomfort, focussing on the task at hand as their destination at last came into view.

An old, worn out, wooden-hulled fishing trawler that looked like it hadn't seen a lick of paint in her lifetime, the *Alamo* seemed painfully outclassed by the ultra-modern pleasure craft that populated the big harbour at Marseille. But then, that was the point. Nobody took much notice of her, least of all the thieves who made a profitable living by slipping aboard untended vessels at night and helping themselves to the valuable equipment on board.

Drake brought them alongside the bigger vessel and throttled back on the engine, keeping pace with it. A moment or two later, a figure appeared at the guard rail above.

Drake let out a sigh of relief as Cole Mason grinned down at him, looking tired and dishevelled but heartily glad to see them. The feeling was mutual.

'Ahoy there,' he said, his grin broadening in amusement. 'Always wanted to use that in context. Hang tight and I'll throw you a rope.'

In short order a line was tossed down to him, which Drake used to secure the inflatable against the side of the *Alamo*. Holding the line tight to keep them in place, Drake watched as Samantha clambered up the steel rungs fixed to the hull of the vessel, followed a little more tentatively by Frost. He went up last, relieved as much to be on a more substantial vessel as he was to see his friend.

Mason had greeted McKnight as soon as she was aboard, grabbing the woman in a bear hug that practically lifted her off the deck. 'Damn good to see you again, Sam.'

Despite herself, she couldn't help but return the gesture in equal measure. She hadn't known him as long as Drake or Frost, but the two had enjoyed an easy, relaxed camaraderie that had only grown stronger over the years.

'And you. I'm glad you got out of Milan in one piece.'

'Hey, dickhead,' Frost said with a dash of her typical brashness. 'You'll forgive me if I don't pick *you* up.'

Mason threw her a glance, ready to reply in kind, though his smile soon faded as he took in her pale and dishevelled appearance. 'What the hell have you been doing to yourself, Keira?'

'Long story. Don't get all Florence Nightingale on me, though.' She gave Drake a meaningful look. 'Ryan's already got that covered.'

Turning his attention to Drake, Mason caught the man's expression and realised he had his own story to tell. 'What's been going on, Ryan?'

'A lot.' Drake let out a breath. 'Better if we talk it over below. Have you secured the main cabin?'

The older man shook his head. 'Nah, just the engine room and wheel-house. Only what I needed to put this tub to sea.'

Nodding, Drake approached the rusty steel-covered hatch leading below decks and knelt down beside it. It was secured with a heavy-duty padlock, which he disengaged and removed. Pulling the hatch open an inch or so, he felt around for the length of fishing line he'd secured there. A single deft motion was enough to unhook it, preventing it from triggering the homemade scuttling device that McKnight installed as a precaution against unwanted boarding.

He certainly didn't want the contents of the vessel to fall into the wrong hands.

'Let's go,' he said, helping the injured young woman down the hatchway into the belly of the ship. It was no easy task given the steep angle of the stairs, but with some coaxing and support he was able to get her below. The others followed behind.

Flicking on the light switch by the entrance, Drake watched as the darkened cabin flickered into life.

'I'll say one thing for you, Ryan,' Frost said, taking it all in. 'You certainly plan ahead.'

To casual observers the *Alamo* appeared to be a neglected, dilapidated old fishing smack, likely one storm away from sinking. But as Drake had learned all too well, appearances could be deceptive.

The main cabin, measuring about 30 feet long and 15 across, was, in contrast to the exterior, clean, orderly and well maintained. The floor was sanded and polished smooth, the walls recently repainted, the fixtures and fittings brand new.

A communications terminal and work area had been set up on the port side, with a pair of laptop computers linked to a larger flat-screen monitor fixed to the bulkhead above. Alongside them was an encrypted radio unit, a radar console and a satellite phone plugged into a charging port.

On the other side of the cabin was a simple but efficient galley, with a couple of storage units stocked with fresh water and tinned foods. The *Alamo* was, at Drake's insistence, stocked with enough food, fuel and provisions to sustain a crew of four for up to a month. In his view the only thing better than a safe house was a safe house that could relocate virtually anywhere with a port.

Toilet and washing facilities were located further aft, but it was the berthing area in the bow that Drake was most concerned about. Easing Frost onto the leather chair by the communications terminal, he moved forward, producing a second key from the chain he carried with him.

Unlocking the padlock that kept the area secured, he swung the hatch open to inspect the small V-shaped room beyond.

Food and provisions were one thing, but a group such as his might well have need of weapons to defend themselves. For this reason, the *Alamo*'s berthing room was stocked with an array of assault rifles, submachine guns, shotguns, pistols, cases of ammunition and spare clips. Beside these weapons were several sets of body armour, tactical radios, medical kits, survival gear and just about anything else a small group of field operatives might need.

Satisfied that the armoury hadn't been tampered with, Drake returned to the main cabin. 'We're good,' he said simply. 'How are you feeling?'

'I fucking hate boats. How's that?'

Drake gave her a disapproving look. 'There any form of transport you *do* like?'

'Yeah. Bikes. That's why I own one.'

'Very funny. You weren't laughing when you showed up this morning, though,' Drake reminded her, before turning his attention back to Mason. 'Cole, tell us everything that happened. Two of my friends have been attacked within hours of each other, and I need to know how and why. Then we have more.'

It took about ten minutes for Mason to recount his experience of the raid in Milan, for Frost to explain the attack and attempted abduction in Munich, and finally for Drake to relate the assault on their villa.

'Cain came after us first, but not in force,' Mason said, summing up his thoughts. 'If he'd wanted us dead, there were easier and more certain ways of making it happen.'

'He was baiting you, trying to hurt you so you'd come to me,' Drake reasoned. 'He wanted us all here, so he could kill us together.'

'In short, we be fucked, mateys,' Frost concluded.

'In short, Cain's not worried about keeping this behind closed doors any more,' Drake corrected her with a sharp look. 'This was a declaration of war.'

For once, Frost seemed to be at a loss. 'But we were careful, covered our tracks, used false IDs, the works.'

For Drake, the answer was chillingly obvious. 'When you've got every police and intelligence service in the western world at your disposal, that has a way of levelling the playing field. Everyone you pass in the street, every traffic camera, every man and woman in a uniform... All of it could be working against us now.'

'But why? Why now, after all this time?' Frost asked.

'To force our hand,' Mason surmised. 'He takes a jab at us, backs us into a corner. He knows we'll have no choice but to react.'

'So how *do* we react? Do we relocate, create new identities?'

Drake shook his head, his expression grim. 'That's only delaying the inevitable. Cain wants us dead, and we all know that's a battle we'll never win. We can't fight the Agency, and we can't run from it – not for long.'

'So what do you suggest?' Mason asked.

Saying nothing, Drake stood up and backed away from the impromptu meeting. He needed to clear his head and think this through, because what he was contemplating could be the biggest gamble they had ever taken.

Emerging up onto the deck, Drake stared out across the sea with his arms folded. Normally this kind of view had a calming effect on him, but not today. Today every muscle in his body felt like it was tensed, ready to spring into action, his instincts compelling him to make that ancient primal choice – fight or flight.

But the enemy facing him wasn't one that could be fought with tooth and claw. He knew all too well what the Agency was to those unwise enough to make it an enemy. It was a monster whose insidious tendrils stretched into every aspect of the world around them, able to creep through the darkness and hide in plain sight. The threats it presented were as complex and multifaceted as a diamond, able to wield both overt strength and hidden menace, to turn good people against them, to call on virtually any resource it needed to achieve its aim.

They were fighting a monster whose body could never be defeated. Only its head remained irrevocably human, and therefore vulnerable.

'I know that look all too well,' McKnight said, having followed him outside. 'You're planning something.'

'Yeah.' No point in lying to her.

'You want to lash out, hit back after what happened today.'

Drake said nothing to that. She knew the answer well enough.

He heard McKnight sigh in frustration. 'Don't you see, that's exactly what Cain wants? If you try to strike back now when we're off balance and outnumbered, you're playing right into his hands.'

'Maybe,' he agreed. 'But I'd rather make a play while we still can.'

Like the fighter he'd once been, he'd rather go down punching than throw in the towel and meekly submit to an enemy who would show them no mercy. He'd take a fighting chance over no chance at all.

'But for all Cain knows, we're dead. Why not leave it that way?'

'Because it'll never be over,' Drake said, turning to face her. 'Sooner or later he'll figure out there were no bodies in the rubble, then he'll come after us again. And again, and again until he succeeds. No matter how far we run or how well we hide, he'll find us.' He sighed and shook his head. 'It'll never be over. Not as long as Cain's alive.'

She caught the dangerous glimmer in his eyes, saw the cold determination that was growing in him, and knew then what he was contemplating.

'You're talking about—'

'I'm talking about Downfall,' he finished for her.

He saw her exhale, saw the muscles in her throat tighten as his words sank in. She knew he would never make such a suggestion lightly, would never even mention it unless he was dead serious.

And now he was.

In truth, Ryan hadn't been as idle here as Anya had imagined. The lull in action had given him the time and space he needed. He had tackled the challenge with the same single-minded focus and determination that had marked him out as one of the Agency's best Shepherd team leaders, ruthlessly tearing through possibilities, theories and conjectures to arrive at a cold, calculated solution.

Their previous opportunistic and badly coordinated attempts to find incriminating evidence, to blackmail, disrupt or otherwise unravel Cain's plans had all failed. It had since become clear to him that they'd likely been doomed to fail right from the start, because they were trying to beat Cain at his own game, playing by his rules. He'd been playing those games long before any of them, and his deadly cunning combined with years of experience had allowed him to pre-empt their every move.

The only option left was to take a far more direct approach. Thus, over the past several months he had composed, discarded and refined more operational plans than he could remember, each focussed on a single, specific objective. And at last he had arrived at one that might just work.

Downfall was the codename for the plan to assassinate Marcus Cain.

# Chapter 17

Special Activities divisional leader Dan Franklin eyed up the stretch of carpeted floor that stood between himself and his office desk. Six, maybe seven feet separated him from the simple wooden-topped unit, the short distance stretching out like a yawning gulf before him.

'One small step for man...'

Taking a breath, he lifted his left foot and planted it firmly on the carpet, working carefully to keep his balance. It was a small step, but an unaided one, and he felt his heart beating faster in excitement. Focussing his mind on the task at hand, he raised his right foot and swung it forward, then straight away used the shift in momentum to bring his left foot back into play.

He must have looked like a toddler wobbling unsteadily forward, trying to coordinate limbs he was unfamiliar with using, but he didn't care at that moment. All that mattered was reaching his desk. That was the sole focus of his world.

Another step, and another. Almost there. He could do it. He *would* do it.

A minor wrinkle in the carpet, scarcely enough to impede a vacuum cleaner's progress, was enough to silence those thoughts. The tip of his left foot catching on the minor obstacle, he suddenly lost his tentative sense of balance and pitched forward, throwing out his arm to catch the edge of his desk and save himself from a painful and humiliating fall.

He succeeded, just, but his hand clipped a mug of coffee that was resting there, sending it rolling across the table to clatter on the floor.

'Shit,' he growled, using the solid support of the desk to pull himself upright.

No sooner had he spoken than the door to his private office flew open and his secretary Barbara approached, quickly surveying the room. The look in her eyes was one of concern and, as she began to understand what had caused the commotion, pity. The one thing Franklin couldn't abide.

'Mr Franklin, is everything okay?'

'Yeah,' Franklin replied, straightening his tie. 'Everything's fine.'

The woman nodded, then suddenly spotted the coffee mug lying on the floor. The thick carpet had stopped it from breaking on impact, but the dregs of coffee that had lurked in its depths had spilled out in a wide arc, staining the floor.

'Oh no. Let me get that for you,' she said, instinctively moving to pick it up.

'No!' He'd said it with more heat than he'd intended, and quickly softened his tone. 'It's fine. My own stupid fault. I'll clean it up in a minute.'

His secretary hesitated, wanting to help but wary of embarrassing him. More than most, she knew how much this meant to him.

Seeking to ease the uncomfortable situation, Franklin pushed himself away from the desk, standing tall and straight as he could. 'Since you're here, though, would you do me a favour and push out my meeting with Breckenridge by half an hour? I need more time to get through the field reports from Baghdad.'

At this, Barbara nodded, looking grateful to have a reason to leave. Franklin waited until she'd shut the door before slumping forward with an exhausted sigh, resting both hands on the desk for support.

Threading his way around it like a child clutching at the edge of a swimming pool, he eased himself back down into his padded leather chair and let out a breath of relief. It was a good 30 seconds before he felt ready to bend down and retrieve the fallen coffee cup, and as he straightened up, he found himself staring at something propped against the wall in the corner of the office.

A walking stick.

He'd been given it when he'd finally been discharged from hospital after undergoing successful spinal fusion surgery last year. Successful, in that he was no longer plagued by the chronic back pain that had become increasingly debilitating in recent years; the result of a roadside bomb that had ended his military career. However, the long-term merits of the operation were questionable. For a terrifying few days, he'd even lain in bed without any feeling whatsoever in his lower body, facing the prospect of life confined to a wheelchair.

That had eventually changed of course, and the months since then had seen him push through a gruelling rehabilitation and physical therapy programme, determined to return to work as soon as possible. He'd made great progress since that first day when he'd managed to wiggle his toes, but the doctors had warned him that he might never walk again without a stick.

'Fuck that. I'll never walk *with* one.'

That had been his reply at the time. Brave words, driven as much by fear as bravado, and since proven all too wrong. Nonetheless, Franklin was determined to get himself back in shape, to reclaim the life that had been limited by injury for so long.

One step at a time. That was the best he could manage right now.

His train of thought was interrupted by the buzz of a cell phone in his desk drawer. Not one of the secure encrypted phones he used as part of his day job, but a cheap burner he'd bought a few months back. The kind of phone whose number was known only to a precious few.

Glancing at his office door to make sure it was closed, he leaned over and used his personal key to unlock the drawer, then felt around the underside until his fingers brushed against the plastic casing taped in place.

Removing the burner and keeping it out of sight, he brought up the messaging service and quickly scanned the list. Only one new message was waiting for him, and he knew who it had come from.

A single word confronted him when he opened the message.

DOWNFALL

'Shit,' he breathed, realizing that Drake had at last decided to put his desperate plan into action. Months of inactivity had almost convinced him that his old friend had given up on the scheme, opting instead to vanish and live out the rest of his life in relative peace.

Such had been his hope.

Something must have happened to change his mind. Something big. Franklin had no idea what was going on, but he knew Drake wouldn't put this plan into action if there was any other choice. All he could do was play his own part.

Leaning in a little closer, he typed out a brief acknowledgement.

*I'll be in touch.*

With that, he returned the phone to its resting place inside the drawer, pushed it closed and locked it. As he did so, his eyes rested once more on the walking stick.

'I hope you know what you're doing, Ryan,' he whispered.

# Chapter 18

*US embassy – Islamabad, Pakistan*

Quinn was just leaving his office when he ran into Bill Barratt, one of the senior analysts with the Agency's Pakistan mission. Tall, silver haired and sporting the kind of moustache that would have made Clarke Gable proud, Quinn had always thought the man had missed his calling as a matinee idol, perhaps having the ill luck of being born a couple of decades too late. Still, he'd been with the Agency for ever and was probably one of the most knowledgeable men on the payroll when it came to making sense of the complex political, tribal, ethnic and military landscape in this part of the world.

Normally laconic and easy-going in his manner, he looked uncharacteristically on edge today. 'Quinn, you got a minute?' he asked, speaking in a hushed tone.

Quinn frowned, wondering what he was about to hear. As if the situation here couldn't get any more difficult, he thought bleakly.

'Yeah, sure,' he said, beckoning Barratt into his office. 'What's on your mind, Bill?'

The old man made sure to close the door behind him before talking. 'NSA just intercepted a report over the local police network. You know that ISI agent you asked me to check up on?'

'Majid Reza? What about him?'

'He's dead. Found in his apartment this morning. Died of an overdose, apparently.' Barratt's expression made it clear he didn't believe that for a second. 'Just thought you ought to know.'

Quinn could feel himself paling at the realization. It didn't take a genius to see that Stryker – if that was even his name – had had a hand in Reza's demise. He'd had a bad feeling about that man from the moment he'd met him, waltzing into his office with an access-all-areas endorsement from Marcus Cain.

But this was taking it to the next level. What the hell did Stryker think he was doing – trying to provoke an international incident with an already tenuous ally? If he'd been seen entering or leaving Reza's apartment building…

'Has there been a reaction from the Pakistanis?' he asked instead, hoping his concern didn't show.

Barratt shook his head. 'It's too soon to say. I'd guess they'll want to know all the facts before making their next move, but they tend to circle the wagons when they lose one of their own.' He regarded Quinn in thoughtful silence for a moment or two. 'You want to take any precautions? Tighten security here?'

No doubt he was wary of a reprisal attack on the US embassy. It had happened right here in Islamabad 30 years ago when protestors, believing the US had been involved in the bombing of a mosque, had stormed the walls and burned the place to the ground.

'No,' he decided at last. 'We don't want to tip them off that we know something.' Taking a breath, he turned to face the old analyst once more, pasting on a fake smile. 'Thanks for the heads-up, Bill. And... let's keep this between us for now, okay?'

Barratt hesitated for a moment, torn between loyalty to his station chief and concern over a potentially brewing conflict with Pakistan. Still, he'd played this game long enough to know that the one person you didn't want to piss off was the head of operations at your own posting, and wisely left without another word.

Quinn, however, was not so confident in his position. Ever since his posting here, he'd sensed the ominous weight of Cain's expectations hovering over everything he did, even from seven thousand miles away at Langley. The deputy director was pushing hard for results, and when conventional means failed, he'd turned to more unorthodox channels.

And he was knee-deep in it. It was obvious enough that if this whole thing turned into a clusterfuck, then as station chief it would be his head on the chopping block. Was Cain setting him up for a fall? Was he witnessing the beginning of the end of his career?

He glanced out of his window at the sprawling city that lay beyond the heavily fortified embassy compound. 200 million people in this country, most of whom already distrusted America. For a moment, he felt a cloying sense of claustrophobia as he imagined those same streets filled with thousands of angry protesters, armed and fired up and baying for blood.

It took him about thirty seconds of fraught, anxious contemplation to reach his decision. Snatching up his encrypted cell phone, he strode out of his office, making sure to lock the door behind him. With the phone secure in his pocket, Quinn made his way through the network of corridors, office space and conference suites that represented the beating heart of the Agency's operations in Pakistan. He paid the other employees little notice as he made for the stairwell leading up to the roof.

Like most big US embassies, the Islamabad compound had its own heliport for bringing in high value personnel at short notice, and more importantly in case an emergency evacuation was ordered. It was empty at the moment of course, and mercifully the big open rooftop area seemed to be deserted.

Fishing out his phone, Quinn enabled the encryption mode, preventing anyone from eavesdropping on the conversation, and hurriedly dialled a number back in the US. A number he'd hoped he would never have to use.

'Franklin,' came the answer after a few rings.

Quinn swallowed hard, knowing he was about to cross a line, knowing his career might be over either way. But if he had to go down, he'd rather do it for the right reasons.

'Dan, it's Hayden. We need to talk.'

# Chapter 19

The coffee house was bustling at such an early hour, as patrons queued to collect their takeaway cups en route to work, while others with more time on their hands sat at tables along both walls talking, eating, smoking and drinking together. The air was filled with the buzz of conversation and the heady aroma of tobacco smoke and steaming beverages, the atmosphere relaxed and genial.

For Vizur Qalat, however, the outlook was less agreeable.

'Your problems don't concern me, Rashid. What concerns me is losing control of our northern provinces because we don't know what the hell is going on. So I'll make this very simple – either get me the information I asked for today, or I'll find someone who can. Do I make myself clear?' he demanded, forced to lower his voice as he spoke into his cell phone so that his words were lost amidst the general hubbub.

'You do, sir,' his subordinate agreed, his voice charged with determination and something else – fear. Fear was what motivated men above all else, because losing what you had was far worse than failing to gain something new. 'It will be done.'

'See that it is,' Qalat said, snapping his phone closed just as his takeaway cup was presented to him. It was an uncouth state of affairs to have to gulp down coffee on the move, but his demanding schedule no longer permitted a leisurely morning visit here. The best he could manage was to drop in briefly on the way to ISI headquarters, as always accompanied by his two personal bodyguards.

Both men were veterans of the Pakistani army, chosen specifically by him because he was more inclined to trust men from a military background, and had already fought in more campaigns than most men would see in a lifetime. He trusted them about as much as he trusted anyone in this world. Giving the barista a nod of acknowledgement, he turned away with the coffee in hand and headed for the exit.

It was already shaping up to be a warm and sunny spring day outside, but in truth he had little appreciation for the fine weather. His thoughts were turned inward, brooding on the problems that now beset him. Namely, the CIA and their never-ending meddling in affairs that didn't concern them.

Their drones flew over Pakistani airspace on a daily basis, often striking at targets deep within the republic's sovereign territory, while their special operations teams roamed with impunity through the mountains and remote passes along the Afghan border. Their embassy in the heart of Islamabad was nothing but a front for their spies and systems of surveillance. And all of it was tolerated by the Pakistani government. Where was it going to end?

The suicide bombing at Camp Chapman had dealt them a blow and curtailed their ambitions to be sure, but it was only a matter of time before they regrouped. And there was no telling whether he'd be able to stop them again.

His contemplations were rudely interrupted when someone tried to enter the coffee shop just as Qalat was leaving, bumping right into him. The ISI officer winced as a splash of scalding hot coffee landed on his hand, and turned angrily towards the oaf who had walked into him.

Whoever he was, he was big. Far taller than Qalat's five feet ten inches, and heavily built beneath an expensive tailored suit. His shirt and belt strained against his ample stomach, while his fleshy neck and jowls were largely hidden beneath a greying beard. His hair was blonde, or had been once, and was now turning that dusty brown colour that blonde hair often does in middle age. A Westerner.

'I'm terribly sorry,' he stammered, looking down at Qalat through a pair of thick lenses that magnified his eyes to almost ludicrous proportions. 'I didn't—'

His sentence was cut short when one of Qalat's bodyguards thrust himself between them, shoving the big man backwards onto the street with the brute force that only two hundred and ten pounds of solid muscle allowed. The man was zealous if nothing else, alarmed that someone had gotten so close to his principal unchecked.

'Hey! Steady on, old boy. It was an accident,' the fat businessman protested in a pronounced English accent, his expression bordering on panic at the violent reaction.

Qalat's second operative, obeying the unspoken agreement made between the two men, hovered protectively close to his boss.

'Are you all right, sir?' the bodyguard asked, speaking low and fast, eyes darting in every direction. His hand was on the concealed weapon inside his suit jacket, ready to draw down in case the seemingly accidental encounter had been intended merely as a diversion for something more sinister.

'I'm fine, damn it,' Qalat replied irritably, flicking the coffee off his hand. His bodyguard handed him a handkerchief without saying a word, and he accepted it in similar fashion.

Outside, the first operative was briskly frisking the fat businessman, who had already turned red with embarrassment. Qalat could hear his protests as he made his way out onto the busy street.

'Now look here, I've had just about enough of this Gestapo routine,' he said indignantly, though it was clear these words were just empty bluster.

'It was an accident. If it's about the coffee, I'll happily buy your man a new one.'

As Qalat approached, his bodyguard tossed him the man's wallet. Qalat flipped it open, glancing at his identification. Colin Davies, a stockbroker for Millennium Brokerage, operating at the Islamabad Exchange.

'Colin Davies,' he said, eyeing the man for a moment or two.

'That's right,' Davies replied, flashing the kind of crooked-toothed smile that could only belong to an Englishman, as he glanced nervously at the two bodyguards. 'Look, I think there's been—'

Qalat tossed the wallet back to him, and Davies caught it with the awkwardness of a man who hadn't done anything more physical than climb a set of stairs since he was a child. He didn't need the hassle of dealing with buffoons like this. People were already staring at the potential confrontation brewing; Qalat saw no sense in giving them a show.

'Perhaps you should take more care in future, Mr Davies,' Qalat replied acidly before strolling past him, heading for his parked Mercedes SUV. His two bodyguards took up flanking positions beside him, hovering a little closer than usual after the tense encounter, and leaving the stunned foreigner in their wake.

'Let's go. We've wasted enough time here,' Qalat said as he settled himself into the plush, air-conditioned rear seating area.

As the SUV sped away from the sidewalk and merged with the busy traffic, Colin Davies turned away and walked purposefully over to his own car, parked just a short distance away. Starting up the engine, he pulled away from the scene as if he were consumed with embarrassment over the awkward scene he'd created.

Only when he was a block or so away, and quite certain he wasn't being followed, did he reach up and peel off the fake beard he'd been wearing. The theatrical wig went next, and the glasses that made his eyes hurt, then the false teeth. The fat suit was too awkward to remove now, so he'd have to settle for turning the air conditioning up to maximum.

Christ only knows how fat people survived in this country, Hawkins thought as he wiped a sheen of sweat from his brow and loosened his tie. Just pretending to be overweight had left his shirt damp with perspiration.

Still, it had been worth it to accomplish his task. Qalat was a careful man, but he was also predictable and therefore vulnerable. A couple of days spent observing him and learning his habits had been enough to discover the location of his favourite coffee house, visited with almost regimental punctuality every morning. What else could one expect of a military man, after all?

Enabling the car's Bluetooth system, he punched in a phone number.

Half a mile away, Qalat frowned at the unexpected sensation of something vibrating in his jacket. He always kept his phone in his left trouser pocket.

Reaching inside, he found a cell phone that hadn't been there before. A cheap burner of the kind sold everywhere in Islamabad. The kind that was perfect for surreptitiously making contact with someone.

Instantly his mind flicked back to his encounter outside the coffee shop, the chance collision with the fat Englishman which hadn't been chance at all.

Not many operatives could pull off such a piece of legerdemain in the half second they'd been close enough to make it work, and certainly not without his knowledge. This man, whoever he was, was good at his tradecraft. That made Qalat nervous.

Hesitating a moment or two, he hit the accept call button and held the phone to his ear. 'I presume your name is not Davies,' he began.

'Bingo, Mr Qalat.' The voice that responded was American; brash and confident as only those people could be.

If he was trying to rattle him by mentioning his name, it wasn't going to work. 'You have me at a disadvantage, my friend,' he said, keeping his voice smooth and relaxed. 'You know my name, but I don't know yours.'

'We'll get to that,' the American assured him. 'Let's talk about you first. I already know a few things about you.'

'I'm sure you do.' He wouldn't have gone to such trouble if he didn't.

'I know that last year you chartered a private jet from Pakistan to Turkey, and that subsequently you ordered all copies of the flight plan destroyed. Of course, you didn't take into account the AWACS jets that were tracking the movements of all suspected ISI flights, but who can blame you? Nobody really knows if someone's watching.'

'Quite impressive.' Qalat had to work hard not to show how much the man had rattled him with this revelation. 'But I'm sure my travel history is not why you made contact today.'

'Very true. I'm not interested in where you went, but what does interest me is *why* you went there. I want to talk to you about the Black List, Mr Qalat.'

At this, Qalat felt a chill run through him that had nothing to do with the cool air blasting him from the car's air vents. How could this man know about that?

The failure of his errand in Turkey still lingered with him, like a wound that wouldn't heal. The Black List was an encrypted directory of the CIA's blackest of black operations. Only the highest echelons of their command structure even knew of its existence, and even fewer had access to it. Qalat had paid a great deal to find out the truth of its origins and purpose, and had risked even more for a chance to steal it. To have access to their darkest secrets would have given him almost unlimited leverage over them, allowed him to bend them to his will, and paved the way for his rise to true power.

But it was not to be. His chosen agent, a British self-styled computer hacker by the name of Arran Sinclair, had failed to secure the Black List, coming back instead with an empty computer drive he'd been duped into accepting. Sinclair had paid for that failure with his life, but such petty revenge was cold comfort for a man of Qalat's ambitions.

'All right,' he conceded at last. 'You have my attention. What are you proposing?'

'We each have something the other wants. Maybe we can find a solution that benefits us both.'

Alarmed he might have been, but Qalat couldn't suppress his curiosity either. Clearly this man was both knowledgeable and well connected – two attributes it was unwise to ignore in this line of work.

'I'm listening.'

# Chapter 20

*CIA training facility, Camp Peary, Virginia – 2 August 1985*

Taking a breath, Anya cautiously circled her opponent, hands up and ready to defend herself, waiting for him to make his move. She knew it was coming. He wasn't a big man, but he was fast, strong and aggressive, and happy to employ all three attributes to their fullest effect, his short and stocky frame commanding a brute strength she couldn't hope to match. Her body already bore the bruises of several failed attempts to counter this deceptively effective strategy.

He was playing to his strengths. She had no choice but to play to hers.

There! She saw the muscles across his broad shoulders tense up, rippling with energy as he prepared to move. Instinctively she readied herself to counter it.

Sure enough, he came at her a moment later, feinting to the left before switching direction and throwing a sharp jab aimed at her throat. Such a blow to the windpipe could drop even the most hardened operative, and even with the padded gloves they both wore, it would certainly add to her growing collection of bruises.

But the blow never connected. She had already twisted sideways, neatly avoiding it, before landing a couple of sharp strikes to his unprotected side as he moved past her. Not enough to disable him, but a stinging reminder that she was no pushover either.

Irritated by the near miss, he lashed out with an elbow, hoping to catch her off guard. But his efforts were hopelessly wasted. Anya had already ducked beneath it, and watched his arm sail harmlessly over her head.

She was enjoying herself now. She had the measure of this man, knew his favoured tactics and how to counter them, and was already certain she would beat him. Having spent her formative years literally fighting for her life in a young offenders institute in the Soviet Union, these restrained sparring sessions with fellow CIA candidates were positively relaxing by comparison. And at least here she didn't have to worry about someone trying to shove a knife into her back.

But even now, she never let her guard down, and that natural wariness served her well. She heard the sound of footsteps approaching fast from behind, and whirled around just as a second opponent launched himself at her.

Two against one. She'd fought this kind of fight before, and knew the only way to win in a situation like this was to end it quickly, before weight of numbers overwhelmed her.

Dropping to the ground to avoid the kick he'd aimed at her midriff, she lashed out with her left leg, catching him from behind and buckling his knee. He went down hard, landing on his back. She had leapt on him before he had a chance to recover, driving her fist into the base of his chest with as much force as she could muster. She heard a grunt as the air was forced from his lungs, and knew he'd be out of action for the next ten seconds or so while he tried to get his breath back.

Enough time to deal with his comrade.

The first combatant had rounded on her now and threw himself at her in a rough tackle, knocking her to the ground. He was on top of her in a heartbeat, pinning her down with his considerable weight so that he could pummel her into submission. Ground and pound – standard tactic when you had an advantage in both size and strength.

She saw his clenched first coming down towards her. She couldn't twist aside or dodge it, so had to settle for turning and allowing her shoulder to absorb most of the impact. She winced as bone and sinew slammed into the flesh of her upper arm with bruising force, but knew her move had nonetheless saved her from being knocked out.

She knew she could yield at this point. A simple tap of the mat would end the sparring session before any real injuries were inflicted. But doing so would be an admission of defeat; a sign that she couldn't handle herself. She'd never submitted in a fight in her entire life, and she didn't plan to start now.

Watching as the second crushing blow rained down, Anya suddenly jerked her head to the side, causing him to miss by mere inches. Had his hands not been protected and the floor cushioned with crash mats, the impact of fist against floor would likely have shattered bones. As it was, he let out a growl of pain.

Anya wasn't about to let him swing at her a third time. The injury to his hand had distracted him for a moment, causing his grip on her to slacken, but his sheer weight was still enough to prevent her escaping. The only way to get him off was to fight dirty.

Reaching between his legs, she felt the bulge of his genitalia through the fabric of his sweatpants and gripped hard, twisting at the same time with savage force. The reaction was immediate. Groaning in pain, he pitched forward and fell against the floor, trying to roll away from her. Springing up, she threw herself on top of him and grasped one of his arms, managing to twist it behind his back and lock it, preventing his escape.

That was when she heard it. The slap of his other hand against the mat. The signal of his surrender.

'Time!' the fight instructor called out from the edge of the training area.

It was still something of a novelty for her to have fights ended so suddenly, to simply turn off the aggression and the natural survival instinct that came in the heat of the moment. But she knew she had to. Showing restraint and discipline was just as important as the proverbial killer instinct, even though the latter had served her far better in her short life.

'I said break it up!'

Releasing her hold, Anya rose to her feet and let out a frustrated breath, wiping her arm across her brow. Judging by the way he was clutching at his groin, she suspected it would be a while before her opponent got up.

'Take five,' the instructor ordered her.

She shook her head. 'I am ready to fight now.'

He glanced at her two opponents, both of them candidates in the same training programme as herself. 'They ain't.'

'Then find someone who is,' Anya said, an edge of impatience in her voice. Rather than feeling elated at her victory against two larger and stronger opponents, she was keyed up and irritable, filled with nervous energy she couldn't seem to expel.

'I said take five,' the instructor repeated, staring her hard in the eye as he spoke each word. A simple but potent reminder that she wasn't the one in charge here.

Shrugging in reluctant acquiescence, she turned and strode off to the edge of the training area to get a drink of water. But it was obvious from the tension in her posture and her fast, purposeful strides that she wasn't happy.

'Too much for you guys to handle?' Marcus Cain asked, mesmerized by what he'd just witnessed from the observation room overlooking the training hall. It wasn't often one saw an unarmed woman take on a pair of male trainees and come out on top, but this was something else entirely.

The senior instructor on site glanced at him. 'You kidding? Those were the only two guys in her selection group willing to take her on.' He shook his head. 'Never seen anything quite like this one. She seems to know what her opponents are going to do before they do. And as you can see, she's no stranger to fighting dirty. Where did you dig her up?'

'Long story,' Cain said, reluctant to take his eyes off the young woman. Much like that first day they'd met in the interrogation room, there was something compelling, magnetic about her. 'How's she handling the rest of the programme?'

'Marksmanship is right on the money. Physical fitness, aptitude, problem solving, situational awareness, all top notch.' He snorted in amusement. 'If you don't find a job for her, let me know. I think she could teach some of our instructors a thing or two.'

Cain smiled as he watched Anya taking a drink of water, preparing herself for the next fight. 'Don't worry about that.'

Making his way downstairs into the training hall, he found her stretching on the crash mats, the exercise helping to stop her muscles from cramping up between fights.

'Not working you too hard, are they?'

Glancing up at him, Anya sprang to her feet, self-consciously reaching up to move a stray lock of blonde hair away from her face. 'Marcus. What are you doing here?'

He smiled, finding her embarrassment amusing and perhaps a little endearing. 'Thought I'd drop by and check in on you, see how the training's going. You sure taught those two a lesson.'

Her face, already flushed, seemed to colour a little deeper at that. 'I was just—'

'I know what you were doing,' Cain assured her. 'I saw it when you were talking to the instructor. You've been here three months, and you're going stir crazy, right?'

She frowned in confusion at this, then seemed to take his meaning. She silently mouthed the words as if committing them to memory. 'I have passed every test the CIA set for me, but still I am kept here. Why?'

'Well, that's what I'm here to talk to you about,' he admitted. 'The truth is, the Agency doesn't exactly trust you, and they didn't expect you to make the grade anyway. Now that you have, they don't know what to do with you.'

His revelation went down about as well as he'd expected. Turning away, she hurled her water bottle to the floor, prompting a concerned look from the two students on the far side of the hall. 'Then I am wasting my time. What more must I give them before they believe in me? My life?'

Cain couldn't blame her for being pissed off. She had risked everything to come here, had thrown herself into training with the dedication of a professional athlete for the past few months, and until now had nothing to show for it but some painful-looking bruises. But perhaps now he could offer her something more.

'Like I said, I came here to talk about your future. You ready to listen, or would you like to smash this place up some more?'

Her blush deepened, and she glanced down at the floor, for once unable to meet his gaze. 'I apologize. I should not have lost control.'

He decided not to push that one, instead getting down to business. 'The Agency's putting together a joint operation with the US military, sending... foreign operatives like yourself behind enemy lines. I can't promise it'll be easy, or safe, but if you're determined to get into the field, it's probably your best shot. Interested?'

Now she was able to look at him, and when she did, he could see the growing excitement in her eyes, her face already lighting up with a smile. Christ, she truly was beautiful when she smiled.

'I am interested.'

–

*Washington, DC – March 2010*

That had been the start of it, Cain knew. The beginning of the path that had led them to where they were now. Even today, a quarter of a century later, he still debated his decision to put the untested young operative forward for such a dangerous mission. Perhaps he'd known even then that she was up to the challenge, that her iron will and utter determination would allow her to survive just about anything the world threw at her. Or perhaps he'd sensed an opportunity to put her unique skills to good use, giving the entire hazardous venture at least a fighting chance. Perhaps he'd even cynically seen an opportunity to use her to enhance his own prestige, claiming the heroic field operative as his own discovery.

Perhaps, but they weren't the real reasons. The truth was, he'd known even then that much of what the Agency did wouldn't appeal to someone like Anya. Subterfuge, deception, misinformation, slow and methodical intelligence gathering... those were not the things she was seeking. She wanted revenge; direct and violent and destructive. She'd wanted to hurt the men who had taken everything from her, to make them feel a measure of the pain and loss she'd endured.

Anya wasn't a spy – she would never truly be a spy – but a warrior. It was in every fibre of her being, every thought, every action she took. And that innate potential had only grown and been nurtured by a life spent fighting for survival, battling and clawing through each day. She might have had the misfortune of being born a few centuries too late, and into the body of a woman no less, but that didn't change who and what she was. She was a warrior, and a warrior needed a war.

Fortunately for her, he'd found one. Though he never could have imagined the terrible toll it would take on both of them.

Reaching for the crystal decanter on his sideboard, Cain poured himself a glass of malt whisky. He was in his home now, away from the pressures and the constant demands of Langley, and no doubt this was when most people found time to relax and reflect on the day that lay behind them. Yet for Cain, being here in this big house all alone with nothing but his own thoughts for company posed its own kind of challenge.

He was 58 years old now. An age when most men should long since have settled down to raise a family, perhaps even prepare for the next generation. He'd started one a long time ago, but his career had finished it for him. He supposed he should have seen it coming, should have listened to the old veterans who warned him the job didn't tolerate distractions like that, but it hadn't made it any easier.

Perhaps that was for the best, he reflected as he knocked back a gulp of whisky. He'd played at being a husband for a brief time, but it was clear he wasn't cut out for that kind of life. Some essential aspect of his character, the part that allowed men to put their family before all other considerations, was missing in him.

Men like himself weren't supposed to settle down, weren't supposed to find peace and contentment in the mundane details of life, weren't supposed to be happy. They had a different purpose, a higher calling, a final goal that made all the sacrifices worth it. That was what he told himself.

His private cell phone was ringing, and he could guess who was calling. Laying down the whisky, he picked up the phone and hit the button to take the call.

'Talk to me, Hawkins.'

'Qalat took the bait,' his operative reported. 'I was right about him – he was in Turkey a few months ago looking for the Black List.'

Cain might have smiled if this revelation had been less alarming. Anya herself had come dangerously close to getting her hands on the Black List in a daring cyber attack several months ago. Naturally Cain had dealt with the situation as he always did, using the list as bait to lure her out and almost managing to capture her in the process. But in the end, Anya had escaped with a fake copy of the file that had led her nowhere, and both sides had withdrawn to lick their wounds.

The Black List had been deleted now, having become more of a liability than the security measure it was intended to be, but the fact that a man like Qalat even knew about it was cause for concern. What was he up to? And how much did he really know?

'Then he's a threat to us,' Cain concluded, knowing Hawkins would quite happily eliminate the man if ordered to.

'Maybe, but he could still be useful. He's prepared to meet with us in Pakistan to discuss a trade. The man's ballsy and ambitious, but he's not stupid. If we play him right, he might just give us what we want.'

And what do we have to give him in return, Cain wondered? Becoming indebted to men with less than noble intentions had caused him enough trouble already in life. Nonetheless, such an opportunity was unlikely to come up again.

'Set up the meeting,' he ordered. 'Make sure it's in one of our safe houses in Islamabad – high security. Report back when everything's in place.'

'Your call,' Hawkins conceded. He was after all, a killer, not a protector. Cain doubted he'd lose any sleep if something were to happen to him, and that was fine. At least Hawkins had never pretended to be other than what he was.

Ending the call, Cain put the phone down and picked up his glass of whisky, taking another mouthful and relishing the fire it lit within him. One way or another, this meeting in Islamabad was going to change everything.

# Chapter 21

The *Alamo* was cruising westward at a steady eight knots, its bluff bow churning through the light swell beneath a vast night sky studded with stars. Drake was up on deck, surveying the distant coast with his binoculars when he felt his phone vibrating in his pocket. It was someone whose call he had been awaiting ever since he first sent out the Downfall codeword.

'Yeah, Dan?' he said, putting down the binoculars.

'Ryan, I think we've got some magic happening,' Franklin began without preamble, sounding out of breath. 'My contact in Islamabad says Cain is heading out there in the next couple of days.'

Drake's heartbeat shifted up a gear. In all the time he'd contemplated Downfall, Drake had never known Cain to venture far from the protective cordon around Langley. The man was more paranoid than Stalin when it came to his safety, and almost as well guarded.

'How solid is this?' he asked, wary of staking everything on a false lead.

'As a rock,' his friend confirmed. 'He might be a secretive son of a bitch, but even he can't fly halfway around the world without people in the Agency knowing about it. He's going, all right. He's already chartered a private jet from Andrews, scheduled to leave in 48 hours.'

'Shit,' Drake breathed, hardly believing their luck. Forty eight hours wasn't a lot of time to put Downfall into effect, but they were unlikely to get a better chance. 'What does Cain want in Islamabad?'

'Hard to say, exactly, but he's been making a lot of moves towards the Pakistanis over the past couple of weeks. Even sent one of his own operatives out there to make contact with their intelligence service.'

'The ISI?'

'Yeah. My guess is he's putting together some kind of closed-door deal with them, on their home turf no less. Must be something pretty big to risk exposing himself like this.'

Drake's mind was racing, quickly churning through everything he'd heard as he tried to make sense of the deputy director's actions. 'So he wouldn't want to meet with them at the embassy, and there's no way he'd risk going to their own headquarters. He must have a neutral location in mind. Can you pull up a list of Agency safe houses in Islamabad, see if any of them have been cordoned off?'

'Way ahead of you, buddy. He's already staked his claim on one of our most secure locations in central Islamabad. No reason given, according to the station chief.'

Nor would there be, Drake knew. Cain didn't want anyone seeing or hearing what was discussed in that safe house. Pre-prepared locations like that were deceptively hard to penetrate, and protected against all forms of surveillance, from visual to electronic. In short, they were a nightmare to bug and virtually impossible to break into.

But not for him, because he had an advantage that no foreign intelligence service could call upon. With Franklin's help, he would know exactly how that safe house was designed, what its security measures were, and what their weaknesses might be. And given time, he would figure out how to defeat them.

'Can you send whatever you've got on that safe house to me?' he asked, fervently hoping he wasn't asking for something his friend couldn't give.

'I had a feeling you'd ask that,' Franklin acknowledged. 'That kind of information is held on a secure network; anyone trying to access it is logged automatically – even me. I don't have the expertise to get around that kind of security.'

Fortunately, Drake knew someone who did. 'Keira can do it. All she needs is a valid access code to get through the Agency's firewall.'

'Mine, you mean.' Franklin hesitated. 'You sure she can do it?'

'She's the best hacker I know.' She was also the only hacker he knew, but that was beside the point. 'If anyone can get in, it's her. But she can't do it without you.'

His old friend sighed. 'One of these days I'm going to regret helping you.'

'Wouldn't blame you, but we can make this work. I know it.'

'And you're set on going through with this?' Franklin asked. 'No backing out?'

Drake glanced out to sea for a moment, his thoughts lingering on his three teammates, on Anya, on the sister he'd left back in the UK. All of their lives might rest on Downfall.

'I've come too far to back out now,' he said honestly. 'Downfall is my last option.'

Silence descended between them, broken only by the faintly audible crackle on the long-distance line. Drake could sense how conflicted Franklin was, how much he was asking the man to risk. Normally he'd never consider putting someone else at risk, but they both knew Franklin was living on borrowed time just as much as Drake. Cain might not have openly declared him an enemy, but sooner or later he would outlive his usefulness.

The only question was whether he was prepared to risk the time he had left on one last gamble.

'All right, Ryan,' he said at last. 'I'll make it happen.'

Drake closed his eyes for a moment and let out a breath. 'Good man.'

'Just make sure you don't fuck this up,' Franklin said, trying to adopt a tone of faint mockery to lighten the mood. 'Cats might get nine lives, but you're coming up short.'

Drake grinned. 'I'll keep that in mind.' However, his smiled faded as he reflected for a moment on everything Franklin had risked to help him. 'Oh, and Dan?'

'Yeah?'

'Thanks… for all of it. I mean that. I won't let you down.'

The good humour was gone now as the reality of what Drake was about to undertake sank in. For all they knew, this could be the last time they spoke.

'Take that son of a bitch out, for both of us. Good luck to you, Ryan.'

Pocketing the phone, Drake strode back along the deck, making his way below. If Franklin was right, then time was already against them.

As he'd hoped, Frost was sitting at the communications console, her feet up on the desk as usual. Both laptops were up and running, one of them set to a music download site while she tapped away on the other. Tinny dance music was faintly audible through the headphones she was wearing.

Sensing his presence, she pulled off the earphones and spun around in her chair to regard him. 'What's the good word, captain?' she asked, noting his purposeful stride.

'I've got some good news for you.'

She cocked an eyebrow. 'Don't tell me. They're remaking *Final Fantasy VII*?'

'No idea what that means,' he said, brushing off the facetious remark. 'But how do you feel about doing a spot of computer hacking for me?'

That got her attention. 'Against who, exactly?'

'The CIA.'

She seemed to deflate then. 'In that case, no fucking way. I'm good, but even the best hacker on the planet can't get past their firewall.'

'You don't have to,' he assured her. 'Dan's going to send you his access codes. What I need *you* to do is find something for me without being detected, otherwise they'll track it back to him. Can you do that?'

'Hell, yes.' A slow smile began to spread across her face. 'What do you need?'

'Better if I explain it to all of you.'

Summoning Mason and McKnight to their makeshift conference room, Drake hurriedly explained what Franklin had revealed to him during their call. All three operatives listened in rapt attention as he laid out what he knew so far, and more importantly what it could mean for their plans.

'In the past three years, Cain has never ventured this far from Langley. He'll obviously have security with him, but only those he trusts to keep secrets. He'll be outside the Agency's umbrella, and that makes him vulnerable.' Drake looked at each of them in turn. 'If we're going to make Downfall work, we won't get a better chance than this.'

The look on Mason's face suggested he wasn't inclined to argue. However, that didn't mean he was entirely pleased with the proposal either. 'So we've got to put together a plan to take down one of the most paranoid men on the planet, including all the equipment, weapons and resources we'll need, then get our asses to Islamabad and implement all of it within 48 hours.'

Drake glanced at his watch. 'Actually it's more like 47 now.'

His friend snorted in grim amusement. 'You're spoiling us, Ryan.'

'We've done this sort of thing at short notice before,' Frost reminded him. 'In Libya.'

McKnight raised an eyebrow. 'Hardly a great example. We almost died in Libya.'

'Nobody's pretending this will be easy, or pretty,' Drake said, stepping in before an argument flared up. 'But we only have to make it work once. Downfall is our endgame, our last play. We do it right, and all of this goes away for ever.'

As always, they had to be unanimous. Drake would never consider ordering his friends to risk their lives on something like this, because none of them owed him anything. All he could do was give them the choice and let them make it.

'Shit, I'm in,' Mason said right away. 'Not like I've got anything to go back to in Milan.'

Frost too seemed to be of like mind, and her usual dark sense of humour was never far away. 'I'd rather die than live here without cable TV. I'm on board.'

Drake's eyes turned to McKnight, who had remained largely silent for now. He had come to recognize her as a voice of reason and restraint amongst the group, her cautious and pragmatic outlook in stark contrast to Frost's gung-ho impetuousness and Mason's stubborn refusal to back down. He didn't always agree with her, but he did respect her opinions and value her advice.

'Sam? What's it going to be?'

To his surprise, there were no words of caution or pleas for rationality this time. This time her thoughts seemed to mirror those of her comrades.

'If this is our last play, then I say we make it together. We go all the way this time,' she said, her tone one of deeply buried anger and hatred that was at last bubbling to the surface. 'Find that asshole and kill him.'

Such was Drake's surprise at her change in attitude that it actually took him a moment or two to find the words. Still, perhaps she had finally come to accept what he'd tried to tell her the other day: that as long as he drew breath, Cain was a deadly threat.

'All right, we go for it,' he decided. 'Keira, get online. Dan should have sent through his access codes by now. As soon as you're inside the Agency's network, find everything you can on that safe house: Cain's travel plans, security measures on site… Everything. Understand?'

'On it,' Frost replied, spinning back around to face her workstation. 'Better get some coffee on the go. We'll need it.'

Drake nodded. 'Cole, I need a list of weapons and equipment for this job. Sam, vehicles and a staging area to operate from.'

'What about you?' McKnight asked.

Drake raised an eyebrow. 'I'm going to figure out a way to get us into and out of Pakistan without being caught or killed.'

'That would be preferable,' Frost remarked without looking up from her work.

Indeed, but it didn't mean he had the answers yet.

'All right, the clock's ticking. Let's get to work.'

# Chapter 22

'Yo! I've got it!' Frost called out.

Drake and the others were by her side within moments, watching as she brought up a series of construction blueprints on the flat-screen monitor fixed to the wall overhead.

'Can anyone tell you're accessing this?' Drake asked.

'Only if they're smarter than me, which is unlikely,' she said with no trace of humour. 'We're under the radar.'

Drake leaned in closer, his eyes rapidly scanning the screen, taking in as much information as possible as if it might suddenly be whisked away from him without warning.

Safe houses by their nature could come in all shapes and sizes depending on what the Agency needed them for, from tiny one-bedroom apartments in the middle of a crowded city up to luxurious country houses set within acres of carefully maintained grounds. The things they had in common, however, were that they were secure and closely monitored, offering their occupants a high degree of both privacy and safety. In short, they were ideal places for carrying out clandestine meetings with foreign intelligence agents.

In this case, the structure appeared to be an actual house; a modern two-storey villa set within a walled compound of some sort. The kind of place that was particularly hard to bug because there were no other buildings physically connected to it. Cain had chosen his location well. Even a cursory glance at the blueprints was enough to tell Drake that this was going to be a tough nut to crack.

'Jesus, this place is a fortress,' Mason said, echoing his thoughts as he surveyed the plans. 'Double-layered walls reinforced with steel rebar, structural I-beam frame, solid concrete base… Looks like it was built to survive a siege.'

Drake rubbed a hand along his stubble-coated jaw. 'Or an earthquake.'

Mason glanced at him. 'Huh?'

'Islamabad's near the edge of two tectonic plates. They get earthquakes all the time there, so any new buildings have to be designed to survive major ground tremors.' He pointed to several unusual looking structures laid out at regular intervals in the building's foundations. 'See these? Seismic dampers, designed to absorb shockwaves and isolate the building's core from ground movement. Like a shock absorber on a car.'

'How do you know so much about this shit?' Frost asked.

'Because I studied structural engineering at university for two years,' he replied without looking away from the screen. 'I was planning to go into architectural design.'

'Jesus.' For once she actually looked impressed. 'Why'd you quit?'

'This is all very interesting, but maybe we could get back to the matter at hand?' Mason suggested impatiently. 'Ryan, you said this is all down to earthquake proofing. What does that mean for us?'

'Well, it means we're not going to be tunnelling in,' Drake concluded. 'Even if we could dig through the subsoil in time, the villa's basement is structurally isolated. We'd have to break through two feet of solid concrete without anyone hearing us.'

'So we can't make entry from below. What about from above?'

'We ain't going to be parachuting into this one, that's for sure,' Frost remarked with no small measure of relief. 'There's a small terrace up top, but the roof's nothing but angled tiles, and they'd spot us in a heartbeat if we landed in the courtyard.'

Drake turned his attention back to the blueprints, looking for something within the perimeter that might help. Internally there was little to give him cause for optimism.

'That looks like a panic room right there,' Mason said, pointing to a small rectangular space near the core of the house. 'Cain gets inside, and the whole thing's a bust.'

They had encountered a similar feature during a house raid in Libya several months earlier, and it very nearly derailing their entire plan.

'So if we're going to get to him, it has to be done quickly and quietly. We can't afford room-to-room fighting,' Drake concluded.

'Main gate?' McKnight suggested.

Frost shook her head. 'If I'm reading this right, it's locked electronically. Numerical keypad, and the approach is covered by cameras.'

'We could use signal jammers on the cameras,' Mason said. A signal jammer emitted a powerful electronic surge across all wavelengths, effectively nullifying anything that tried to transmit a signal, including radios and security cameras. Again, it was a tactic they had used before with considerable success.

'But they'd know something was wrong if all of them suddenly went down,' Frost pointed out.

Mason grunted in disapproval. 'And Cain heads straight for the panic room.'

Drake said nothing to this. His mind was racing ahead of them, already deep within the bowels of that target building, devising and discarding possible alternatives far quicker than the group could discuss them. The entire safe house had been designed to resist both overt attacks and infiltration. Its electronic and physical security measures were both sophisticated in their design and deceptively simple in their implementation. A potent combination.

As he'd surmised, it was going to be a tough nut to crack.

No attack force could overcome its formidable security measures quickly enough to catch their target; that much was plain. But there was one element which the designers of this safe house, for all its clever design and safeguards, couldn't anticipate any opponent ever getting their hands on.

'The Judas code,' he said suddenly.

All eyes turned to him.

'Huh? Sounds like a shitty adventure novel,' Frost snorted. 'What is it?'

'Every high-level safe house has an override code built into their security system. We called it the Judas code,' he explained. 'It's a safeguard against hostage taking. In the event the building gets compromised, the Agency can remotely take control of the security system. Cameras, alarms, electronic door locks… they can override anything that's linked into the system, so they'll know exactly where their enemies are when they try to retake the place.'

Frost was incredulous, clearly having never heard of such a code. 'How the fuck do you know about all this?'

'Shepherd team leaders were all briefed on it, in case we ever needed it for mission planning.' He looked at her, unable to hide a wry smile. 'Sorry, but you weren't important enough.'

At this, she gave him the finger.

'So that code is our ticket in,' Mason said, bringing them back on track. 'We take control of the security system, which is all well and good, but we still have to get our asses inside without being seen by Cain or his men. We can't come in from the air, we can't approach on the surface, and we can't tunnel in from below. What does that leave us with?'

In that respect, he was right. They may have overcome one problem, but there were plenty of others to contend with.

'Can you pull up a view of the surrounding area?'

Frost went to work, calling up an online satellite map of the area around the safe house. Like most major cities, Islamabad had been photographed extensively from the air, allowing her to project a pseudo three-dimensional image of the surrounding landscape onto the screen.

As Drake had supposed based on its size and quality of construction, the safe house sat in the midst of what looked like a new high-end residential development. Most of the properties seemed to be of similar size, if not design, and laid out to give the impression of space while packing in as many units as the housing company could get away with.

'Come on. Somewhere high, somewhere high,' Drake said under his breath as he surveyed the isometric view of the city, looking for a suitable target. Then, suddenly, he spotted a candidate. 'There! That building right there. Can you give us a better look at it?'

Zooming in as much as the program's limited resolution would allow, Frost called up an image of a low-rise residential apartment block near the edge of the development, perhaps intended for those who couldn't afford their own villa but still wanted to be part of the prestigious neighbourhood. It looked to be about five storeys high, with a flat roof accessed via a central stairwell.

Perfect, assuming it was within range.

'How far would you say that building is from the safe house?' he asked, hoping his hasty calculations weren't proven wrong.

Zooming out once more, Frost used the site's scaling tool to estimate a rough distance. 'About…70 metres, give or take.'

Drake let out a breath. 'That'll do.'

'What are you thinking, Ryan?' McKnight asked.

Tearing his eyes away from the screen, Drake briefly outlined his plan to them. It was unorthodox to say the least, and not something he expected to be met with great enthusiasm.

He wasn't wrong.

'Are you fucking kidding me?' Frost protested. 'That's some James Bond bullshit you're talking about there. This is reality, Ryan. Even if we don't fall to our deaths, they'd see us coming a mile away. We might as well paint a target on our heads.'

'It can work,' he insisted, careful not to say that it *would* work, because given all the variables at play, that would be a bold claim indeed. 'I've seen it done before, and the safe house is well within range. If you can think of a better way in, I'm all ears.'

Frost threw her hands in the air. 'Just because I've got nothing better doesn't make your idea good.'

Drake shrugged. 'It's a proven concept that works. That's good enough.'

'So let me get this straight. We break into this apartment building nearby, get up on the roof without anyone seeing us, take control of the safe house security system, then make like Tarzan across the rooftops, get inside, taking out any guards who stand in our way, all without Cain or his buddies noticing us. Then we fight our way past an unknown number of ISI and CIA agents to reach a man that's been one step ahead of us every time we've gone up against him. Then, assuming we somehow manage to take him out, we somehow get our asses out of a hostile country before the wrath of two whole intelligence agencies descends on us.' Mason exhaled slowly. 'That's pretty fucking thin, Ryan.'

When he put it like that, it didn't exactly sound like a winning scheme.

'Thin is all we've got right now,' he conceded. 'But we've done this before, and there's nobody I trust more than you three.'

'Isn't that the point, though? Four of us, one of whom is still hurt,' McKnight added with a glance at Frost. 'That's not enough. If we were planning this as a legitimate op, we'd need a team twice as big to even consider it.'

'Sam's right; we're way short on manpower,' Frost added. 'I don't want to sound like a pussy, but I don't want this to be our last stand either. We need more guns on our side, Ryan.'

Drake looked at her, contemplating what she was asking. She was right, of course. They were woefully undermanned for taking on an enemy like Cain on foreign soil. Fortunately for them, they weren't entirely without allies in this fight.

Whether or not that ally was still prepared to help, and whether his team would accept that help was another matter.

'I might know someone.'

# Chapter 23

*Both Cain and his ward Anya were seated in uncomfortable silence, Cain keeping himself occupied by watching the constant ebb and flow of military personnel as they traversed the long corridor.*

*The seat of American military power since the Second World War, its sheer dimensions were almost mind boggling. Six million square feet of floor space, seventeen miles of corridors and over 25,000 employees resided within its high imposing walls. It was enough to make Langley look like a hobby farm.*

*The five concentric rings of office blocks that made up the entire facility were designated A through to E, with the E ring office blocks being the only ones whose windows actually offered views of the outside world.*

*The corridor in which they were seated was part of the A ring; the innermost ring of the building. This was where the most secretive and sensitive of operations were conceived. The uniformed men and women who trod these corridors reflected the clandestine nature of the work being done. Nobody made eye contact, because they knew better than that.*

*He supposed that was one thing the place had in common with Langley.*

*Beside him, the young woman remained resolutely silent. Her expression was hard to read, but he'd come to know the subtle changes that came over her when she was nervous or agitated. A lot rested on the outcome of this meeting, and they both knew it.*

*His thoughts were interrupted when the door opposite him was opened and a young female secretary emerged into the corridor. 'Mr Cain, the colonel will see you now.'*

*'Let's go,' he said, rising to his feet.*

*Colonel Richard Carpenter was seated behind his desk, staring down at the stack of paperwork before him with the look of casual disdain that field officers often reserved for admin tasks. A big, tall man in his mid-forties, he still had the square build and broad shoulders of one used to hard physical exercise. Only a light smattering of grey at his temples suggested a wavering battle with age.*

*He looked up from his work as Cain approached, flashing a smile that seemed at least somewhat genuine. 'Marcus, damn good to see you.'*

*He rose from his chair to shake hands, drawing himself up to his full height. The US Army uniform sat on his intimidating frame like he'd been born to wear it, and indeed, from what Cain knew of the man, he'd spent most of his adult life doing just that. Military through and through, he'd come from a long line of Carpenters that had served in the forces, and didn't seem likely to quit any time soon.*

*'You too, Rich.'* Cain exchanged a handshake, then gestured to his female companion. *'This is Anya. I wanted you to meet her face to face.'*

*Carpenter's smile faded a little as he regarded the young woman. Already she'd become a source of tension in the ambitious project he was trying to get off the ground, and meeting her in the flesh had clearly done little to change his opinion.*

*'So you're Marcus's pet project, huh?'* Without waiting for a reply, he gestured to a couple of spare chairs facing his desk. *'Okay. Take a seat.'*

*Without saying a word, Anya lowered herself into a chair. Cain was grateful for the restraint she'd shown thus far. She knew when to speak, and more importantly when to stay quiet.*

*As he'd come to expect when she was in a new environment, her eyes were everywhere, taking in the details of the small but comfortably appointed office. Carpenter wasn't top brass, wasn't a starred general, but he certainly had a sense of style, Cain mused. And a keen interest in military history.*

*Anya had noticed it too. Her attention had rested on the framed painting hanging on the wall behind Carpenter's desk. Unsurprisingly it depicted a historical battle scene, though oddly it wasn't some rendering of American heroism. Rather, this one showed Napoleon Bonaparte in his distinctive bicorne hat and grey overcoat addressing his assembled troops from horseback, the mud and gunpowder smoke suggesting a battle was still being fought.*

*'You like it?'* Carpenter prompted, noting her interest. *'Napoleon at Waterloo, right before the Imperial Guard went into battle.'*

*Cain knew enough history to understand the significance. At the very climax of the battle, Napoleon had unleashed his hitherto undefeated Imperial Guard to break through the Allied lines. But instead of completing his victory, the Guard had walked into a trap and been driven back, the shock of their retreat quickly causing the entire French army to collapse.*

*'I like to keep it here as a reminder. Every soldier can be broken, no matter their reputation,'* Carpenter explained, smiling at her without warmth. *'Kind of makes you wonder, doesn't it? What was going through his mind when he saw the Old Guard break and run. I wonder if he knew right then that he'd just lost his empire.'*

*The young woman said nothing to this, and Cain began to wonder if the colonel's philosophical musings were falling on deaf ears. He didn't imagine military history was a great passion of hers.*

*'Middle Guard,'* she said abruptly.

*Carpenter frowned. 'Excuse me?'*

*'The final attack at Waterloo was mounted by the Imperial Middle Guard. The Old Guard stayed with their emperor, fighting to the last man while the rest of the army retreated.'* She turned her head to look at him, flashing a tentative half smile that he'd come to recognize when she felt she'd scored a point. *'A true soldier never breaks, colonel.'*

For the briefest of moments, Cain saw a scowl forming on Carpenter's face. A scowl of anger that she'd made him look bad, that she knew more than him, that she had dared correct him.

'You know your history. Very good,' he allowed reluctantly. 'But I'm more interested in the present. Marcus here tells me you want to get involved in the unit I'm putting together.' He shook his head. 'That's very noble of you, but I'm afraid it's the policy of the US military not to allow women to serve in frontline combat units, never mind special forces teams behind enemy lines.'

As before, she didn't respond right away. She was weighing up how much to say, how firm a line to take. It was obvious he didn't like or respect her, but to appear submissive would only solidify his view. On the other hand, to be defiant and obstinate would mark her out as a troublemaker, someone who couldn't be counted on. That would be all the excuse he needed to ditch her.

'Is that not the point of having… What is the term you use? Plausible deniability?' she asked. 'You want to be able to wash your hands of this unit if they are captured. Who would believe America would send women into combat?'

'She has a point,' Cain remarked.

Carpenter wasn't so easily swayed, however. 'There's a reason we don't send them in, and it's got nothing to do with deniability. What makes you think you're up to something like this?'

'You have read my dossier, I assume.'

'Paperwork,' he said, gesturing to the stack of forms spread across his desk. 'Never did care for it. Anyway, all the test results in the world don't mean shit out there in the firing line, where lives are at stake.' He sighed and leaned back in his chair, surveying her critically. 'So I ask you again, why should I let you in?'

'I do not want special favours. All I ask is a chance.' Anya glanced up at the picture hanging above his desk. 'Let me train with your team, on equal terms. If I break, then it is over.'

That was when Cain saw it. The smile forming on a face so unaccustomed to it. The smile of a soldier seeing a fatal weakness in his enemy.

'All right,' he conceded. 'You'll get your chance. No favours, no special treatment. You break, you walk. Fair enough?'

'Fair enough,' the young woman agreed.

–

*Marseille, France*

Twenty-four, twenty-five, twenty-six…

Anya could feel beads of sweat forming at her brow as she gripped the metal pipe running along near the ceiling, using it to pull herself up so that the top of her head was almost touching the roof. The muscles in her arms and shoulders, long since accustomed to physical exertion, burned with the strain of raising and lowering her full body weight over and over.

It was one of the many tests that Carpenter had set for her – 30 pull-ups unaided. The US Marine Corps required its male candidates to do ten, but he had been as inflexible as the pipe from which she now hung. As far as he was concerned, his unit was to be a cut above everything else, with only the mentally and physically strongest candidates making it. He certainly wasn't going to lower his standards for a woman.

And he never did.

Twenty-eight, twenty-nine…

Letting out a strained breath each time she lowered herself down, and drawing fresh air into her lungs as she pulled herself back up, Anya pressed on with the simple but effective exercise routine that had become so familiar to her over the years it was almost as if she didn't have to think about it. Her body knew what to do.

Thirty, thirty-one.

She always did one more than Carpenter's old benchmark, just to prove that she could. Satisfied by this petty victory, Anya dropped to the floor and turned away from the improvised exercise equipment, heading into her hotel room's cramped bathroom.

Outside she could hear the drone of traffic on the busy roads, the occasional blast of a car or ship's horn, even music from countless restaurants and apartments. All of it pressed down against her like a suffocating cloak.

She'd never cared much for big cities, even as a child. The teeming mass of humanity all crowded together, all vying for position and advantage and superiority, the noise and the chaos and the tall buildings seemed foreign to her somehow, as if it were a different world she could observe but never really be part of.

She dimly recalled one childhood memory of being taken on a school visit to Moscow, far from her own home. The teachers and official guides had been so enthusiastic to be showing them the great metropolis at the heart of the Soviet Union, but almost as soon as Anya arrived there, she'd hated it. To her young eyes it had been a grey, cheerless world of concrete, grotesquely large buildings and exaggerated statues of fallen Soviet heroes.

The longer she spent in such places, the more she craved silence and isolation.

After splashing water on her face and cupping her hands to drink a few mouthfuls, she raised her head up to regard her reflection in the mirror. Her cheeks were flushed from the exercise, her blonde hair in disarray, lips slightly parted as her breathing settled down and her heartbeat quietened. The lean, hard muscles in her arms and shoulders stood out sharply beneath tanned skin.

A lot of years had passed since the day Cain first led her into that office in the Pentagon. A lot of things had changed for both of them. Carpenter was dead now of course, killed by her own hand, and she was an outcast from the Agency. A fugitive to be hunted. Only Cain remained, though he wasn't the same man she'd known back them.

She wasn't the same either, she acknowledged. Physically she supposed she wore the extra years about as well as anyone, and training and discipline meant she still possessed much of her hard-won strength and fitness. But more and more, she felt the passage of time deep inside.

There was a weariness about her that she hadn't known in those days. It was the weariness of one who had run for too long, witnessed too many bad people do bad things and get away with it, seen too much of their own efforts come to nothing.

Then, unbidden, she recalled what Drake had said to her during their brief meeting a few days ago.

*You're afraid of what you'll do when all the dust settles, and what's left isn't fighting and killing, but living. All those long years stretching out in front of you, trying to fit in, trying to be something you're not. Trying to be… normal. You want to talk about losing focus and perspective? Maybe you should take a look in the mirror.*

Anya wasn't normally given to deep introspection, considering it self-indulgent and sentimental. But there was a part of her that avoided it for another reason, because she was worried what she would find if she looked too deep, if she exposed the things that lurked in the dark corners of her soul.

If she did look in the mirror, what would she really see? Not the young and passionate woman she'd once been, that was for sure. Anya feared she would see someone her former self never would have recognized. Someone so filled with bitterness and anger and vengeance that it had become not just a part of her, but the very core of her being.

Was that to be her true legacy? After everything she'd done, everything she'd risked and sacrificed, was she truly nothing but a ghost for ever condemned to brood over what might have been?

Her hands gripped the edge of the sink tighter as she lowered her head, closing her eyes and exhaling slowly. She wasn't even sure why she was still lingering in Marseille when Drake had made it clear he wanted nothing to do with her.

Not that she could blame him, after the way she'd dealt with him.

*So you can sit there and judge me all you want, but I need this. I need it because I don't want to end up more afraid of living than dying. I don't want to end up like you.*

Her head rose up, glaring at the woman she saw before her. Drawing back her fist, she slammed it into the mirror as if it were her most hated enemy, shattering her reflection in an instant. The musical tinkle of broken glass clattering into the sink and the tiled floor beneath was lost on her. Looking down at her hand, she frowned at the bright red tracks of blood oozing from her torn knuckles. There was no pain.

Drake's words had cut far deeper than the broken glass, and she knew why. Of all the people she'd encountered in this world, good and bad, Ryan Drake was one of few who understood her. Or at least he had accepted her, and that had meant more than she'd ever been able to express. She cared about him, and against her better judgement, she trusted him.

And she'd pushed him away. Like everyone else in her life.

She would be leaving Marseille tonight, she knew then. Where she would go next, she hadn't yet decided, but she knew it was time to move on. She had come here to make contact with Drake, to decide whether his commitment to their mission was still intact. Well, she had her answer.

So she would leave. She would go her own way, as she had for most of her life. Perhaps it was better for everyone, Drake included. He had made a life for himself here, and as much as it was fragile and vulnerable, it was real. A life away from the Agency, away from Cain. Away from her.

She was heading back into the bedroom, a towel wrapped around her injured hand, when her phone on the dresser started vibrating. Reaching for it, she felt her heartbeat quicken at the caller's number.

It was him. Why was he calling? Normally their communications were done via text message or emails. Something must have changed.

'I'm here.'

'We need to talk. Can you meet today?'

Curt and to the point, all business now, just as she had been with him.

'I'm surprised you want to meet at all,' she replied, allowing a little of her simmering frustration to creep into her voice.

'This is important. Can you get here today?'

She knew he wouldn't give any details over an unsecure line, but it was clear from his tone that this wasn't a meeting for personal reasons.

'I can,' she said at length. 'Same place as before?'

'No. Meet us at a town called Collioure, down by the old port. We'll find you.'

Anya frowned, both at the change in location and his choice of pronoun. 'We?'

During all of her meetings with Drake, it had always just been the two of them. She had been very specific about that point. She didn't trust anyone else to be there.

'It's simpler if you just come. I'll explain when you get here.'

'I had plans with Anatoly today,' she said. Anatoly was their challenge codeword, to find out if Drake was under duress. If he didn't respond with the name Natasha, she would avoid the meeting and ditch the phone.

'Tell him to meet with Natasha instead,' Drake countered. 'This is more important.'

Anya let out the breath she hadn't realized she had been holding. 'Fair enough. I'll call you when I get there.'

'We'll be waiting.'

The *Alamo's* main cabin was beginning to look more like a military command centre with every passing hour, albeit a ramshackle, improvised one. Frost was busy working at the computer terminal, tapping away at one of the laptops while using the overhead monitor to project important images or plans onto a larger viewing area.

Mason meanwhile had taken over one entire wall in order to plan the house assault. Already it was covered with printed images of the building, design plans, maps of the local streets, and even handwritten Post-it notes scrawled with hastily thought of ideas, equipment requirements and countless other reminders that would be needed later.

McKnight had been tasked with finding a base from which to operate once they were in Pakistan, which was easier said than done. Entry to the country required a visa signed off by the Pakistani foreign ministry, which they had nowhere near enough time to organize. The alternative was to enlist a local sponsor with a letter of recommendation from the Pakistani government. Again, not an option.

Flying to neighbouring Tajikistan seemed like the best – if only – viable prospect, as they had the option to apply for a temporary tourist visa within three days of arrival. With luck, they would have slipped over the border to Pakistan, completed their mission and been on their way home before then.

There were, however, two problems with this plan. The first was that commercial flights from France to Tajikistan weren't exactly easy to come by. The second, far more concerning problem was that to get to Islamabad, they would have to travel across country through the mountainous border region shared by Tajikistan, Afghanistan and Pakistan. That was shaping up to be a nightmare.

With virtually no government or law-enforcement presence, the entire area was effectively ruled by bandits, tribal warlords and countless terrorist groups displaced by the fighting in Afghanistan. In fact, it was widely regarded as one of the most dangerous places on the face of the earth. And they would have little choice but to drive right through the middle of it.

Her thoughts were interrupted by the sound of the deck hatch swinging open, and steps descending the stairs. Instinctively she reached for the weapon she kept with her at all times, though she felt herself relax a little as Drake descended into the cabin.

The man himself looked tense and nervous, his jaw set and his shoulders tight as if he were expecting a battle to erupt at any moment. Only the battle he was expecting wouldn't involve guns or bloodshed. Not yet, at least.

'Heads-up, everyone,' he announced. 'We've got a… visitor.'

She could feel her heartbeat quicken in anticipation as he stepped away from the stairs, allowing the new arrival to descend. Samantha knew then who Drake had taken the *Alamo*'s small inflatable speedboat ashore to retrieve. It was someone she had waited a long time to encounter.

Everything she'd heard of this woman's exploits over the past couple of years, all the incredible tales of survival and endurance, the accounts of her deadly skill and martial prowess had coalesced in Samantha's mind, imbuing her with an almost superhuman aura.

Instinctively she rose to her feet, wanting to face Anya on equal terms.

This was the woman who had defected from the Soviet Union when she was just 20 years old, who had survived some of the most gruelling training programmes ever devised, fought and nearly died alongside the Mujahedeen in Afghanistan, and endured months of torture and interrogation at the hands of the KGB. A woman whose two decades of service with the Agency had brought her to the highest echelons of power, and whose destructive downfall had shattered countless lives and careers.

This was the woman people had fought and died for, who inspired devoted loyalty and abiding hatred in equal measure, whose bitter quest for vengeance had pulled in Drake and everyone around him, and on whom all of their fates now hung. The woman Cain had recruited her to help destroy.

She was standing not more than 15 feet away.

Almost without thinking about it, Samantha's hand crept towards the pistol hidden at her back. Anya was unarmed so far as she could tell, not expecting danger amongst a group of supposed allies. She could do it, a voice whispered in her ear. A single shot was all she needed. One smooth motion would see her draw the weapon, take aim and fire.

Two seconds at the very most.

None of them would expect it, and they certainly wouldn't be able to stop her in time. Anya would be dead before they could do a thing, and her mission would be complete. She would have done everything Cain had demanded of her and more. It would be over.

They would hate her of course, and Drake most of all. She was under no illusion that he would ever forgive such a betrayal, or that he wouldn't kill her in retaliation. He would be angry, bitter and stricken with grief, but he would be alive. By killing Anya, she might well be saving all of their lives. Wasn't that a worthy sacrifice? Wasn't that worth one person's life?

She could feel her heart pounding, adrenaline surging through her veins as she was seized by an agony of indecision, conflicting thoughts and loyalties locked in deadly battle. Her hand was trembling even as it hovered inches from the weapon.

It was at this moment that Anya, perhaps sensing something was wrong, turned to Samantha. Those eyes, as cold as a glacier and as piercing as a needle, were locked with hers. And for a heartbeat, Samantha was permitted a glimpse of the mind and the will that lurked behind them, the fierce predatory soul that had survived the very worst this world could throw at it. That mind and that will was focussed on her, questioning, evaluating, searching for a possible threat.

She could feel her throat constricting, and fought a sudden urge to swallow. The colour seemed to have drained from her face, as if her very heart had paused in its beat, frozen in place like everything else around them.

'Oh fuck, no!' Frost exclaimed on seeing the woman. 'No way, Ryan. If this is your solution, forget it.'

Anya's eyes instinctively flicked towards the source of the noise, breaking contact momentarily. The moment had passed, like a spell had been lifted. It was all Samantha could do not to let out an audible sigh of relief as she lowered her head, her heart still pounding so hard she could hear the rhythmic thud in her ears.

'Good to see you as well, Frost,' Anya said, eyeing the young specialist with distaste.

Frost however had no interest in conversing, instead focussing her attention on Drake. Rising from her station with difficulty, she moved over to him, speaking in a dangerously calm voice. 'Ryan, I know we're up shit creek without a paddle here. But I'm telling you now, this is not the answer.'

'You said we needed more manpower,' Drake reminded her. 'Here it is.'

Frost raised her chin defiantly – always a bad sign – and glared at him. 'That's not what I had in mind, and you know it. I'd rather have fucking Hannibal Lecter watching my back.' Only then did she spare Anya a disparaging look. 'No offense, of course.'

'None taken,' Anya replied coldly, before turning her eyes on Drake. 'You asked to see me, so here I am. Now I would like to know why.'

Drake exhaled and nodded agreement. 'Introductions first. Keira you already have a long and fruitful relationship with,' he said, giving the young woman a look that warned against further outbursts. Seeing that she was wise enough to hold her tongue, he gestured to Mason, who had hung back a little during this argument. 'This is Cole Mason. Second in command of my Shepherd team.'

Anya studied him for a long moment with a look of mild recognition. 'I know you,' she said at last. 'You were at Khatyrgan prison.'

'That's right,' Mason said, his tone guarded. He had met Anya, albeit briefly, during the mission to break her out of a maximum security Siberian prison. Unlike Frost, however, he'd had no further involvement with her after that night.

'You were wounded.'

Mason cocked an eyebrow at this. A stray round had hit him in the shoulder during their escape. Several reconstructive surgeries and a year of gruelling rehab had at last seen him return to active duty, albeit unofficially. No wonder he wasn't exactly effusive in his welcome, McKnight thought. Anya had almost ended his career.

'That was then, this is now,' he said, no doubt eager to move past the unhappy memory. 'Let's concentrate on the now, shall we?'

She gave a shrug, unconcerned. 'As you say.'

Drake cleared his throat, hoping to interrupt the uncomfortable encounter, and nodded towards McKnight. 'This is Samantha McKnight. She joined our team in Afghanistan; been with us ever since.'

McKnight's heart, which had only just started to calm down, suddenly leapt into overdrive again as she approached the older woman. She could practically feel the tension radiating from Drake. Two of his team had already been cold or openly hostile towards Anya. If the third member of his group was equally unwelcoming, it might prompt her to leave altogether.

Never had she felt the weight of expectation so keenly. She was unsure what to say, how to act. Somehow she doubted *I've heard a lot about you* was going to cut much ice.

But to her surprise, it was the other woman who made the first move. 'Good to meet you, McKnight,' she said, holding out her hand.

Knowing she couldn't refuse it, McKnight shook hands with her. 'And you.'

Anya's grip was strong; stronger than it needed to be, and lingering just a moment too long. McKnight looked into her eyes, caught off guard, and that was when she knew Anya had played her.

'I assume there is at least one person here who isn't against me?' she asked.

It was a test, McKnight realized. Drake had warned her about Anya's ability to detect deception in others, to read the subtle nuances of body language that most people were oblivious to. Like a poker player who can find their opponent's tell, she'd sensed Samantha's unease when she arrived, and she was suspicious.

'Wouldn't let Keira get to you,' she replied, feigning a smile. 'She's like this with pretty much everybody.'

Anya said nothing more to that, but Samantha sensed a slight easing of the tension between them, a fractional acceptance of this new acquaintance. She might not have passed the test, but she hadn't failed it yet either.

Her grip relaxed then, and she let go of Samantha's hand, turning her attention fully on Drake once more. 'You called me here for a reason, and it was not to meet your team. What do you want?'

Drake was of like mind, it seemed. 'You might want to take a seat for this one,' he said, gesturing to a bench next to the small dinner table.

Anya folded her arms and stood her ground, saying nothing. It was plain she was perfectly comfortable standing.

'Suit yourself,' Drake conceded.

For the next ten minutes, Anya listened while Drake related the events of the past few days: the attacks on Mason and McKnight, the raid on the villa, their retreat to the group's fallback position, and the conclusion that the only course of action left was to go on the offensive.

'No more games. If he wants a war, we give him one,' he said, speaking with the iron resolve of a man set on his course, no matter what Anya might say or do. 'Cain's going to be meeting with an ISI agent at a safe house in Pakistan two days from now. Don't ask me how I know this, but I do. We've got a chance to take him out; maybe the last chance we'll get. So we go there, we find him, and we end this thing.'

To McKnight's surprise, Anya didn't react to this right away. There was no hint of vengeful enthusiasm in her expression, no glee at the thought of taking down her nemesis, not even the kind of grim determination she might have expected from one of such stoic demeanour. If anything, she looked almost taken aback by his suggestion, as if a direct confrontation was something that hadn't occurred to her.

'Getting to Marcus Cain is no easy task,' she said at last, speaking from long experience. 'I assume you have a plan of some sort?'

Indeed he did. Despite the occasional argument, his collaboration with Mason had produced the beginnings of an operational plan. Conscious of their tight timescales, Drake immediately launched into a step-by-step description of the assault on Cain's safe house, with Frost projecting images of the house plans and maps of the local area onto the overhead monitor for clarity. Anya made no attempt to interrupt or question him, content to simply listen.

'It's not pretty, but it's what we've got,' he concluded, bringing the impromptu presentation to a close. 'And with the right people involved, it can work.'

Anya was staring at the screen, on which was projected a street-level view of the target house. As always, it was difficult to gauge her thoughts from her guarded expression, but clearly her mind was deep in contemplation.

'So what do you need from me?'

'For a start, we need another pair of boots on the ground,' he began. 'There's not a lot of people I'd trust to work with us on something like this, and even fewer who have experience at this kind of op, but you're one of them.'

She glanced at him then, her lips parted in an ironic smile. 'Flattery is wasted on me, Ryan. You need something more. What is it?'

Drake held her gaze for a moment or two, then reached into his pocket and unfolded a sheet of paper, on which he'd written a shopping list of equipment. The *Alamo* was well stocked with weapons and gear, but this plan called for a few items that were decidedly harder to come by.

'We need everything on this list,' he said, seeing no point in sugar-coating it for her. 'Plus covert transport into Pakistan at short notice.'

Anya's eyes travelled down the hastily scrawled items, her brows rising when she caught sight of something unusual or problematic.

'Arranging all this at short notice will not be easy, or cheap,' she warned.

'Put it on our tab. We're good for it,' Frost countered with a wry smirk.

Anya gave her a sharp look. 'Money does not concern me. But there are only a few men in Pakistan with access to this kind of equipment, and even fewer are trustworthy.'

'But you know someone,' Mason pressed her, guessing from her evasive demeanour that such a request wasn't impossible.

'Perhaps,' she said, thrusting the list back into Drake's hand. 'The more relevant question is what you plan to do when you get your hands on Cain.'

'Isn't it obvious? This all started with him. It'll end the same way.'

To Samantha's dismay, Anya shook her head. 'You will not kill him, Ryan.'

Time seemed to stand still for Samantha in that moment as the full implications of her statement sank in. Anya wanted Cain alive? Why? What possible reason could she have?

'Bullshit we won't,' Frost snapped, fists clenched in anger. 'Good people died because of that son of a bitch. One way or another, he's going down.'

'Yeah, watch us,' Mason added coldly, though no less angrily.

But Anya was oblivious to both of them, as if they were nothing more than buzzing insects to be ignored and tolerated. Her gaze was on Drake, because she knew he was the real decision maker here.

'You will not kill him,' she repeated.

'Give me a reason.'

Anya nodded to the list he was still clutching. 'Without me, this operation is over before it begins. I will not help unless you promise not to kill Cain.'

Drake sighed and shook his head, mystified as to her change of heart. He wasn't angry, because he understood that anger would achieve nothing against someone like her. 'After everything he's put you through, why would you spare his life?'

McKnight felt like she were living inside a bad dream. She watched as the muscles tightened in Anya's throat, and the seemingly impenetrable armour she'd surrounded herself with appeared to weaken for a moment.

'Because I want answers,' she said, her voice carrying an underlying hint of something Samantha had never expected. Pain. 'I want to know why he did the things he did, why he became this man, why he betrayed me. Only he can answer those questions.'

'Fuck answers,' Frost retorted, growing more incensed by the moment. 'He's an asshole – isn't that answer enough? If you think we're risking our lives just so you can have a Q and A session, you're deluded. The only answer that piece of shit deserves is a bullet between the eyes.'

Again, Anya paid her no heed.

'Hey, I'm talking to you,' Frost said, taking a step towards her.

At the same moment, Anya began to turn, hands already raised to defend herself.

It was then that Samantha intervened, placing herself firmly between the fiery young specialist and a woman who could likely kill her with ease if provoked.

'Take it easy,' she said quietly, gripping Frost's arm with enough force to show she wasn't going to take no for an answer. 'This isn't worth it. Not when you're hurt.'

It wasn't much of an excuse, but the recent gunshot wound to her side at least provided a credible reason for Frost to back down without losing face. And even she began to see the sense in her companion's words. She had clashed with Anya before, and it had left her with a dislocated shoulder and a mild concussion. Anya was unlikely to be so merciful again.

Letting out a breath, she yanked her arm out of McKnight's grip and turned away, running a hand through her short dark hair. 'Fucking waste of time,' she hissed, shaking her head in disgust.

This minor irritation dealt with, Anya gave Samantha the barest nod of acknowledgement before turning her eyes on Drake again.

'If this is to happen, then it will happen my way. We go in, we abduct Cain and take him to a safe location, and I get the answers I need from him,' she said, speaking with the slow, patient self-control of a teacher addressing a particularly defiant student.

'As long as he's alive, he's a danger to all of us,' Drake replied, folding his arms. 'You know that as well as I do.'

Anya nodded, reluctantly conceding his point. 'Maybe so. But if he is to be killed, *I* will be the one to do it.'

She straightened up a little as she said that, raising her chin as if killing her most powerful enemy was some unpleasant task she was only taking on out of necessity.

'Those are my terms. If you give your word to honour them, I'll help you. If not…' She shrugged. 'Then I wish you luck.'

Drake was caught between a rock and a hard place. To accept Anya's offer would mean jeopardizing the very objective they were risking everything to achieve, not to mention introducing an unpredictable new element into the team. On the other hand, to refuse her help would mean cutting off a vital ally, crippling the operation before it had even begun.

For Samantha, the situation was even worse. If Cain was kept alive long enough for them to question him, then he would almost certainly reveal that she had been his mole for the past year. There would be no reason for him to hold back. He would destroy her, dragging her down with him.

Drake glanced upwards for a moment and let out a breath – a gesture she had come to recognize when he'd made an unpleasant decision – before finally nodding acquiescence.

'Fine,' he conceded unhappily. 'You'll get your chance to question him.'

Anya held out her hand to cement their deal. Drake reached out and gripped it, pulling her a little closer and staring her hard in the eye.

'But I'm warning you now, if he puts my team at risk, or it looks like we can't get him out, we're not leaving him alive. Understand?'

'Perfectly.' The woman released her hold, turning her attention to the blueprints laid out on the table before her. 'Let me see your deployment plan again.'

As Drake sat down to walk her through the plan once more, McKnight turned away, needing to get out of the room. She ascended the stairs and strode towards the ship's bow, taking a deep breath and trying to calm her wildly beating heart.

The deal struck between Drake and Anya might be enough to get them into that safe house, but it would mean the end for her if Cain started talking. She couldn't allow that to happen. The only choice was to make sure he didn't get the chance.

One way or another, he was going to die.

# Chapter 24

*Andrews Air Force Base – 21 October 1985*

*So this was it. They had come down to it at last. The months of training, planning and preparation were over. The unit that he and Carpenter had put together was about to deploy to Afghanistan, to go into battle together for the first time.*

*There was no telling what might happen to them, whether any of the soldiers hauling weapons and other gear towards the C-130 cargo plane nearby were going to make it back alive. But Cain could at least take comfort from the fact that they were probably as ready and prepared as any group could be for what lay ahead.*

*Carpenter was nothing if not a man of his word. He'd promised to whip the disparate collection of mercenaries, foreign defectors and exiles into shape, to form them into a true unit, and he'd done exactly that. Three months of brutally effective training and careful selection had gradually whittled away those who lacked the mental and physical strength to make it, those who panicked under pressure, who hesitated under fire, who thought of themselves first and the unit second.*

*Those who had emerged from this fiery crucible were as hard as iron, as strong as any soldiers that had ever taken to the field, as intensely trained and conditioned as any human could be. They were a spear, honed to a razor edge, ready to be used.*

*And Anya was one of them.*

*Even now, he didn't truly understand how she'd done it. Somehow she'd survived Carpenter's tortuous selection process when others who were bigger, stronger and fitter had fallen away. Somehow she had found the strength to keep going, to persevere against everything he threw at her, every attempt to make her break. Somehow she had even earned a modicum of respect, both from him and the rest of her unit.*

*And now she was about to venture out into the field with them for the first time, to go deep behind enemy lines, far from any help he or the Agency could offer. The thought of what the young woman might face out there stirred an odd mixture of pride, protectiveness and trepidation in him.*

*'Anya!' he called out, striding across the tarmac towards her.*

*Laying down the heavy rucksack she'd been about to hoist onto her shoulders, Anya flashed a welcoming smile. The kind of smile that seemed to linger with him long after he'd parted company with her, that he found himself longing to see again.*

*'Marcus. I didn't know you were coming,' she said, looking almost flustered.*

*Her English was more fluent now, he noticed. She'd been working hard on it during her time in the States, and could even approximate a pretty good American accent when called upon.*

And that wasn't the only change that the last few months had wrought in the young woman. Her body, already fit and athletic, had hardened and filled out, adapting to the relentless and intense demands that her training had placed on it. Her blonde hair, once falling in loose waves well past her shoulders, was cut short and tied back now so as not to interfere with her vision at a crucial moment.

There was something else, too. Something a little less tangible, but real all the same. A certain confidence that hadn't been there before; the kind that many tried to emulate but only soldiers truly possessed. Had she been a man, Cain might have called it swagger. But whatever it was called, it was hers now. And she'd earned it.

'Hey, I couldn't let you go without wishing my protégé luck. If you're Luke Skywalker then I'm Obi Wan Kenobi, just better looking,' he said with a playful grin.

Her baffled expression told him his reference had fallen on deaf ears.

'Still haven't watched Star Wars, huh?'

She shrugged and gestured to the operatives nearby. 'I have been a little busy lately. What is the thing you say here? It's on my doing list?'

Cain couldn't help but laugh at this. 'To-do list.'

'To-do list,' she repeated, committing it to memory. One thing about Anya; she never made the same mistake twice.

Cain's laughter subsided a little as he looked her up and down. 'Seriously, though, I just... wanted you to know how proud I am of you. I know these last few months haven't been easy, but... Well, I'm sorry for what you've had to go through, but it had to be difficult. I had to know you were ready for this.'

Anya took a step closer, staring up into his eyes. 'All I asked for was a chance. You gave me that, when no one else would. You have nothing to be sorry for, Marcus.'

Christ, if he had a hundred of Anya, he could change the world, Cain thought in that moment. But maybe he didn't need a hundred, he realized as he looked at her. Maybe, in the end, one would be enough.

Reaching out, he held his hand out to her, and she took it without hesitation. The touch of her skin was like electricity, the warmth of her hand lighting a fire inside him that he'd sensed growing these past few months.

Cain had never been a superstitious man, had never believed in premonitions or fate or any of that other nonsense, and yet he sensed somehow the weight of significance that lay in this moment. This was a turning point, for both of them. He felt himself seized by the sudden notion that this young woman who had arrived so unexpectedly in his life, who could so easily have passed him by without the slightest ripple, was going to have a profound impact not just on himself, but on many others.

She was going to help him change the world.

'Look after yourself out there,' he said, wishing he could think of something more profound or moving at such a moment. But then, perhaps she didn't need noble words or stirring sentiments. Perhaps it was enough to know that he meant what he said.

She smiled. One of those achingly beautiful smiles he always longed to witness, made all the more bittersweet because he didn't know when or if he would see it again.

'Anya, we're almost loaded. Get your skinny ass over here!' Carpenter called out from the big aircraft's rear cargo ramp. 'We ain't waiting for you!'

A blush rose to the young woman's cheeks then and she glanced away, breaking the spell. 'I have to go now,' she said, reaching down to heft the bulky rucksack onto her shoulder. 'I'll see you again, Marcus Cain.'

With that, she turned and hurried towards the waiting aircraft, leaving Cain standing alone on the tarmac.

'I know,' he said quietly as he watched her go.

–

Cain sighed as he stared out across those same tarmac runways a quarter of a century later. Only this time, he was viewing them from the comfort of the Andrews AFB executive departure area – the kind of place reserved for serious players in the military and intelligence communities. The kind of place his younger self could scarcely have imagined having access to.

And yet here he was, preparing to travel halfway around the world for a meeting that could lead to the death of the most wanted man on the face of the earth and the decapitation of the terrorist network he commanded. Preparing to change history, just as he'd once envisioned with almost childish *naiveté*.

But this time he was doing it alone.

His Gulfstream C-37A executive jet was being fuelled at this very moment, getting ready to make the transatlantic flight to Ramstein AFB in Germany, where it would once again stop for refuelling. From there, it would be another eight or nine hours to Pakistan depending on local weather conditions. A long journey, but a worthwhile one.

He'd left Hawkins to handle the security arrangements for the meeting. He was certainly aware of how much depended on this. And yet, Cain couldn't help but wonder if all his preparations would be enough, whether Anya might actually make a play despite everything.

Whether she might succeed.

Moved by a sudden impulse, Cain reached for his cell phone and selected a number from his list of contacts. It was a number he hadn't dialled in some time. A number he often found convenient excuses not to call, because it was easier for both of them.

He hesitated, his thumb hovering over the call button. It would be so easy to avoid it, to make yet another excuse so he didn't have to face another strained conversation, didn't have to face one of his many past mistakes. But what if this turned out to be his last chance? What if he never got to speak to her again?

Almost without realizing it, he'd pressed the call button. Taking a breath, he held the phone to his ear, staring at the sombre grey clouds overhead as he waited for it to connect.

It was ringing. Cain held his breath, waiting for her to pick up, but the ringing just carried on for what felt like minutes. Maybe he'd caught her at the wrong time, he thought, almost hoping for the reprieve. Maybe she was busy.

Or maybe she just didn't want to talk to him.

'Yeah?' a young, impatient female voice demanded suddenly.

Cain let out the breath he'd been holding. 'Lauren.'

It had been so long since he'd said that name out loud, the very sound of it was almost foreign to him.

'What is it?' she asked. No greeting, no attempt at small talk, not even a veneer of warmth. But then, what had he been expecting?

'I just...' He hesitated, feeling awkward and tongue-tied. 'It's been a while since we talked. I wanted to check in... see how you're doing.'

Did he really just say 'check in', as if she were a side project he'd kept on the back burner for the past few months?

He heard a sigh down the line. The vexed sigh of a young woman called upon to go through the motions of a conversation she had no enthusiasm for. With a man she had no desire to speak to.

'Fine, I guess,' she conceded at last. 'No different from usual.'

He was getting nothing. 'How's school going? Your dissertation coming together?'

She snorted in amusement at this. 'And what's my dissertation about?'

Cain swallowed and looked down. He had no answer for her, and she knew it. 'I'm trying here, Lauren.'

'Why?' she countered. 'Why the sudden interest? You worried I'm spending my allowance too fast or something?'

He might have laughed himself if the situation had been less strained between them. If money was the biggest issue he had to worry about in life, Cain would have considered himself a happy man indeed. Normal concerns for a normal life.

But not his.

'No, of course not. It's just that... Well, I haven't seen you for a while—'

'And whose decision was that?' she interrupted heatedly. She took a breath, calming herself before going on. 'Listen, I don't know what's brought this on. If you're going through guilt issues or you're just feeling lonely, whatever, but that's something *you* need to deal with. Calling me out of the blue and expecting me to act like nothing's happened... I don't know what you want from me. We haven't known each other for a long time.'

'*That's* what I want to change, for Christ's sake,' he said, allowing some measure of the frustration he felt to show in his voice. Frustration that was directed solely at himself.

'A little late for that, don't you think?' There was no anger in her voice now. It was cold and clinical, like a physician pronouncing a patient's death. Maybe that wasn't so far from the truth.

Spotting movement to his left, Cain glanced over at an air force flight sergeant, who was holding up her hand with all five fingers extended. Five minutes until his flight was ready to board. Cain gave her a nod.

'Look, Lauren, I don't have a lot of time right now—'

'Surprise me,' she said with unveiled sarcasm.

'But that's going to change soon,' he pressed on. 'I'm about to finish something that's been hanging over me for a long time. And when I'm done, a lot of things are going to change. I don't blame you for doubting me, but I mean it. I don't expect anything from you, I don't want anything and I don't deserve anything. But I'll be there. And if you think we could at least talk to each other... I'll be waiting for you.'

For once, she didn't immediately hit back with a scathing remark or a sarcastic put-down. Silence echoed down the line. Cain waited, saying nothing, knowing he had to give her the time and the space she needed.

'Look, I... I have to go,' she said, but this time she sounded a little less sure of herself. 'My friends are waiting for me.'

Cain let out a sigh. 'I understand.'

Another pause. Strained, awkward, hesitant. 'Look after yourself, Dad.'

The line went dead then, but Cain didn't care. It had been a long time since she'd called him 'Dad'. Maybe that was as good a start as he could hope for.

In that moment as he made his way towards the waiting aircraft, it was enough.

# Chapter 25

*St Luke's Medical Center, Denver*

Pete McKnight let out a weary sigh as he lowered himself into his chair. He was tired and out of breath after walking back up two flights of stairs from the hospital news-stand, but nonetheless he had returned with a couple of magazines tucked under his arm. Enough to keep him occupied for a while.

He was a busy, energetic man by nature; the kind who always had a project on the go. Idling away his days reading books and flicking listlessly through TV channels was as foreign to him as the hospital he now found himself in.

He could have taken the elevator back up to his private room, but he'd insisted on struggling up the stairs, determined to push his ailing body to its limits because he needed those limits to become a damn sight bigger than they were.

Still, at least he was feeling better than a few weeks ago, when he'd been so floored by the combination of chemo drugs and radiation therapy that he could barely make it to the bathroom to throw up. That had been a low point, but as the doctors had assured him, it would all be worth it when he came out the other side. He couldn't be cured – the pancreatic cancer had advanced too far for that – but assuming his immune system recovered from the treatment, his chances of seeing another five years were considered 'reasonable'.

Reasonable – a strange word by which to measure one's life span. It was even stranger that he considered himself lucky at the prospect of having a few more years left in him. But he did – he very much did. A year ago, armed with substandard medical insurance that would pay only for the most basic palliative care, his lifespan had been measured in months rather than years.

He'd been all set to make a one-way trip to his hunting cabin up in the Rocky Mountains with enough supplies to see him through a few weeks, and a bottle of sleeping pills for when they ran out. Pete McKnight certainly didn't consider himself one of those macho death-before-dishonour idiots, but he'd been around long enough to recognize the difference between being alive and actually living. No way was he going to end his days in some sterile hospital room, clinging desperately to each miserable moment.

But his situation had changed suddenly and dramatically last year. Somehow his daughter had found a loophole in her military health insurance, allowing for his life-saving treatment. She'd tried to explain it to him once, but the complex legal technicalities had been lost on his drug- and pain-dulled mind. He'd cautioned her, wary of her good-hearted but dangerous manipulation of the system, but she had brushed away his objections, telling him everything would be fine, that she knew someone who was an expert in these things.

So he'd accepted her offer. Even if he didn't fully understand it, even if he harboured a lingering suspicion that the scheme wasn't entirely above board, Pete McKnight had accepted the chance of life against the certainty of death. Because first and foremost he wanted to live, not just for himself but for Samantha. He was all she had left as far as family went, and he knew his death would hit her hard. Harder than she deserved.

Why shouldn't a man fight for his life, both for his sake and those he loved?

He was halfway through an article on deep-sea tuna fishing when the cell phone in his pocket started to go off. Samantha had given it to him when he started his treatment, made him promise to keep it with him at all times no matter how sick he got.

He could feel his excitement growing at the prospect of speaking with his daughter again. It had been too long since he'd heard from her, though she'd explained that she was overseas on deployment and might not be able to call him as often as she'd like. He understood from his own experiences in the Marines decades earlier. It was the nature of a life in the military.

'Sam. Damn good to hear from you, girl,' he said, grinning despite the fatigue. 'How you doing?'

'Good… Dad.' Her tone made it plain she wasn't doing good at all. 'What about you? How's the treatment going?'

'Getting better every day,' he said, hoping he sounded strong and confident. Unconsciously he reached up to touch the smooth, hairless dome of his head. 'Plus I've saved a fortune on shampoo lately, so it's all good here.'

He heard her chuckle down the line, though he sensed it was more for his benefit.

'Listen, kiddo. What's going on?' he asked, his voice growing quieter and softer now. The way he used to talk to her when she was a little girl and upset about something. 'Something you want to talk about?'

'It's complicated.'

'I'm not going anywhere.'

Samantha sighed then. A weary sigh, such as he hadn't heard from her in a long time. But he knew it meant she was going to tell him.

'Remember when you started your treatment, and I said there might come a time when I'd need you to do something for me?'

'Of course.'

'That time's now, Dad,' she admitted, her tone grave.

Pete swallowed, feeling his stomach tighten up. A familiar sensation over the past few months, but in this case it wasn't caused by the cocktail of drugs he was taking, or the radiation he'd been blasted with.

'Okay. What do you need?'

'I'm going to send someone to your hospital today. An old army buddy of mine. His name's Taylor. When he comes for you, I need you to go with him, no questions asked.'

Pete frowned at these bizarre instructions, his mind racing. 'What do you mean? Where's this guy supposed to take me?'

'Somewhere safe. Somewhere they can't find you, at least until things calm down.'

His concern and surprise was giving way to real fear for his daughter's safety now. All of a sudden, he began to see his miraculous treatment in an entirely different light, and cursed himself for ever agreeing to it. 'Sam, what have you done?'

'It's going to be okay, Dad.'

Going to be okay? Those were the kind of reassuring words a father was supposed to say to his daughter, not the other way around. 'Sam, listen to me—'

'I don't have time to argue, Dad,' she cut in, a harder edge creeping into her voice for the first time. 'I need you to do this for me, okay? You made a promise that you'd help me when I asked for it. Well, I'm asking now.'

'I won't help you get in more trouble.'

If it came to it, he would accept full responsibility for what had happened, perhaps claiming he'd bullied or blackmailed his daughter into helping him. If it meant spending what time he had left in a prison cell, then so be it. He'd lived his life already. Perhaps not as long or as well as he would have liked, but well enough. She still had hers ahead of her.

He heard an exhalation of breath as she searched for the right words. 'Bad people are after me, Dad. They might use you to get to me. I can't let that happen, and I can't do the things I have to do unless I know you're safe.'

'What are you going to do?'

'That's all I can say right now,' she evaded. 'I'm asking you, please, do this for me. I'll explain everything when it's over, but for now please trust me.'

Pete glanced up at the ceiling, torn by indecision. Would he make things worse by cutting and running, or would it give her the breathing room she needed to make this right? How was a man supposed to make a choice like this?

'I trust you,' he said at last.

It was a moment or two before she responded. 'Thanks,' she said, her voice close to breaking. 'Get your things together, get ready to move. He'll be there soon.'

That wouldn't take long, he thought as he surveyed the sparse room. His worldly possessions here could comfortably fit into a small gym bag.

'Change of scenery couldn't hurt, huh?' he quipped, hoping to lighten the mood.

It wasn't going to work. Not now.

'I'll speak to you soon, Dad,' she managed to say before hanging up.

–

Closing down the phone, Samantha let out a sigh and wiped the tears from her eyes, doing her best to regain her composure. After all, she had to keep up appearances amongst the group. Keep the act going just a little longer.

'McKnight?'

The sound of a voice from behind startled her, and she whirled around to find Anya standing close by. How had the woman approached without making a sound?

'What is it?' she asked, irritated and a little unnerved by her sudden appearance.

The older woman glanced away for a moment, looking a little uncomfortable herself, as if she had a difficult topic to broach.

'I came to thank you,' she said at last.

'Thank me?' If Anya had a clue who and what she really was, she imagined thanks would be the last thing on her mind.

'For calming Frost down earlier. I...appreciate the gesture.'

McKnight could feel colour rising to her face. Already strained after the difficult conversation with her father, the thought of having earned Anya's gratitude, of all things, only served to raise her ire. This woman who was at the centre of the maelstrom that had consumed so many lives already now wanted to thank her?

'Let's get one thing straight, Anya,' she said, taking a step closer. 'I don't like you any more than Cole or Keira do, and I sure as hell don't trust you. As far as I can see, you bring nothing but pain and death wherever you go.'

Anya regarded her without emotion. 'So why help me?'

'Because I like Cain even less. I want that son of a bitch to pay for what he's done, and right now you're our best... our *only* chance at making that happen. I stopped a fight – that's all. I did it because I didn't want Keira to get hurt, and I didn't want our only ally to walk out the door. So don't fool yourself that we're going to be friends after this is over. We won't. I'd sooner you went on your way after we take Cain down.'

Outwardly Anya gave little sign that McKnight's outburst had affected her. She didn't recoil, didn't clench her fists in anger, didn't show shock or indignation. But McKnight could sense that some hidden switch had flicked inside Anya's mind. She had changed for good in Anya's estimation, going from a possibly ally to something quite different.

'That's your choice,' she conceded, dismissing the matter from her thoughts. 'In that case, I'll take up no more of your time.'

She was just turning to leave when she paused, another thought occurring to her. 'Oh, and McKnight?'

'What?'

She nodded to the phone McKnight still clutched in her hand. 'It was a wise move, getting your father to a safe place. I hope for his sake you were not too late.'

Leaving that thought to linger in McKnight's mind, she turned away and walked off, heading back below deck.

# Chapter 26

Working alongside Mason, Drake was putting the finishing touches to their plan of attack. Anya had agreed to handle transport into Pakistan, and to supply the equipment they'd requested. He had little understanding of the financial resources she could call upon, but based on past experience he doubted she was short of cash.

In any case, planning the complex and difficult assault on the safe house was going to require most of his attention. Logistical difficulties were one burden he was happy to be relieved of.

He was disturbed from his contemplation as a shadow fell across the design blueprints he'd been studying. Looking up, he saw Frost standing close by. The look on her face made it plain this was no time for light-hearted banter.

'A word,' the young woman said quietly. 'In private.'

'I'm busy,' he said, all too aware of their limited time.

He felt her hand on his arm, the grip strong and urgent. 'Make time, Ryan.'

On the opposite side of the table, Mason glanced at the pair of them, giving Frost a meaningful look. He wondered suddenly if the two specialists had been conspiring together.

Chewing his lip in frustration, Drake nodded towards the armoury room at the bow. 'Fine. Let's go.'

Leading the young woman through, he closed the heavy hatch behind her. The bulkheads in this old vessel were thick and airtight, as were the internal hatches, making eavesdropping difficult at best. Whatever she wanted to say, she could say in relative privacy here.

'We're short on time,' he warned without preamble. 'Spit it out.'

Frost, direct as always, was happy to oblige. 'It's about Cain. More to the point, it's about what we plan to do with him.'

'You were in the room, same as me. Would you like the Cliff's Notes?'

'Don't bullshit me, Ryan,' she hit back. 'You know what I'm talking about. The whole point of Downfall is to kill that son of a bitch, not to abduct and interrogate him. Christ, we'll be lucky even to get within kill range as it is. But if we're not going to finish the job, what the fuck are we risking our lives for?'

'Nobody's talking about keeping him alive. Anya wants him dead, just like us.'

'Does she?' Frost asked. 'Because from where I was sitting, it sounded an awful lot like she was trying to save his ass.'

As much as he knew that was a ridiculous assumption, there was a part of him that struggled to dismiss it. He could understand Anya's desire for answers, considering Cain was the last man left alive who could explain why exactly she'd spent four years in a Russian prison, but he was unnerved by her reluctance to kill him.

'Why would she do that? You know what she's been through because of him, you know what she's lost. She wants revenge.'

'I don't know what the fuck she wants, and frankly I don't care. You want to bring her to Pakistan with us? Go ahead – I can't stop you. But Anya's screwed us over too many times for me or any of us to trust her. She might be part of this operation for now, but only as long as she's useful.'

'What are you saying, Keira?'

There was a dangerously mutinous look about her now. 'I'm saying that if Anya doesn't have the guts to complete Downfall, someone needs to do it for her.'

'And I suppose that's you?' he challenged her.

'If I have to. One way or another, that bastard's going down. And he is *not* getting up again.'

'That's not your call to make.'

'You're right, it's not,' she countered. 'This decision belongs to all of us. We're each risking just as much on this job, so we each have a say in how this goes down. If not, you'd better cut us loose now.'

'And does this "we" include anyone else?'

Frost sighed. 'Cole's with me on this one, Ryan. You know he is. And Sam wouldn't take much convincing either.'

Drake exhaled slowly, taking a moment to compose himself. Now was not a time to lose his temper, because he knew it would accomplish nothing. Worse, he knew he had no right to do it. She and the rest of the team were not soldiers under his command any longer. They followed him because they chose to, because he'd earned their respect and their loyalty. If he lost either, he lost the team as well.

'And what exactly should I tell Anya if this goes down?'

At this, Frost moved a step closer and lowered her voice. 'Extractions are messy affairs, Ryan. We both know things can go wrong real fast. Wouldn't take much for Cain to get hit by a stray round – nobody's fault, just bad luck.'

Bad luck. They'd seen enough of that already without inviting more.

Glancing down at the floor, Frost sighed. 'I never wanted to have this conversation. I feel like shit that it's come to this. You know we'd move heaven and earth for you if we could, but what Anya's asking...' She shook her head. 'We need more. We can't...*I* can't leave something like this in her hands. Please tell me you understand that.'

What could he say? He couldn't tell her she was wrong, that she was out of line, because in truth he knew exactly how she felt. Cain was always their endgame, their final objective. Maybe they wouldn't get all the answers they wanted, maybe they'd never know what he'd truly been trying to accomplish, but he would still be dead and they'd be alive.

Drake could live with that.

'I do understand,' he said at last, and he saw the tension leave her body in that instant. But no sooner had she let out a sigh of relief than he moved forward and gripped her arm. 'But you need to understand that nobody is going to kill him without my permission, Keira. *Nobody*. If it comes down to it, if Anya can't or won't kill pull the trigger, I'll take care of it myself. And I'll take responsibility for it myself. You can pass that on to the rest of the team with my regards. Do I make myself clear?'

If it meant as much to Anya as he suspected it did, then she would likely show no mercy to anyone who broke their agreement. Except perhaps himself, though that was questionable. Whether or not he was in a position to give orders, he was still the leader of this group. If the burden had to fall to anyone, it would be him. That was the responsibility he had assumed.

Frost's eyes were wide as she stared back at him. She had seen many sides to Drake over the years, had witnessed most aspects of his personality manifest themselves, but this was something new. There was a colder, darker, more ruthless element lurking in the depths of his soul. And it was coming out now.

'You do,' she said quietly, visibly shaken.

Drake relaxed his grip then, allowing her to back off. She looked as if she were about to reach up and rub her arm, but thought better of it, unwilling to show weakness. 'Then you'd better get back to work.'

For once, she looked happy to escape this confrontation. Pulling the hatch open, she turned to leave, pausing in the doorway as if to say more. Then, shaking her head faintly, she walked off in silence, leaving him alone.

Letting out a breath, Drake turned away from the hatchway. This situation was growing more difficult with every passing hour. He'd expected Anya's arrival to ruffle a few feathers, but her presence was driving a wedge between himself and the rest of his team. And yet, he needed the help of both if Downfall was to succeed.

The choice then was clear – betray Anya's trust, or betray his friends.

'Fuck,' he said under his breath, heading for the hatch. He needed to get back to work; he couldn't afford to waste any more time.

Returning to the main cabin, he briefly caught Mason's eye. The man was quick enough to glance away, suggesting Frost had already given him the gist of their conversation. It was as well for him.

'Heads-up. Just had word from Franklin back at Langley,' Frost called over from her computer, having returned to her station. 'Cain's flight lifted off from Andrews about ten minutes ago, en route to Pakistan.'

Silence descended on the cabin then. Their target was already on his way to the meeting. True, he had a good deal further to travel than them, but he was airborne already and they quite clearly weren't.

'Then it's going to happen tomorrow night,' Drake decided.

'How do you figure?'

'It's a 7,000-mile flight from DC to Islamabad. Factor in at least one refuelling stop, and you're talking 16, 17 hours' flight time at a minimum.' Drake did some rough mental arithmetic, trying to take into account the various time zone changes that Cain's flight would pass through. 'That puts his ETA at about 5 a.m. local time. No way is he going straight into a meeting like this after flying halfway around the world.'

'Ryan is right,' Anya said, descending the stairs with a cell phone in hand. 'Marcus always believed in preparation, especially for crucial meetings like this. He would not go into it tired and jet-lagged.'

Drake looked at Frost. 'Can you pull up a copy of his flight plan?'

'Not unless I made a copy of Franklin's secure access key, which I did,' the young woman replied, going straight to work. 'There's no passenger manifest, but there's a flight number and a destination. Looks like they scheduled an eight-hour layover at Ramstein before going on to Islamabad.'

'So we're talking a midday arrival,' Drake concluded. 'If he has any sense, he'll wait until after dark, which is...'

'About 19 hundred hours local time,' McKnight said.

'About 19 hundred hours,' he repeated, giving her a nod of gratitude. 'Multiple vehicles and new arrivals at a suburban house will attract attention during the day. At night it'll be easier to hide.' He pointed to the printed map of central Islamabad pinned to the wall, where the safe house had been encircled by red pen. 'So, tomorrow evening. If we're not there at least 12 hours in advance, we can forget about being ready in time. That means we need to be out of here and on our way to Islamabad today.'

'We will be,' Anya said, holding up her cell phone. 'The arrangements have been made. Our transport should be waiting by the time we get there.'

McKnight glanced at her, frowning. 'What transport?'

Anya pocketed her phone, offering a rare smile. 'You'll see.'

# Chapter 27

About an hour later, Drake found himself in the passenger seat of Anya's rental car, with Frost, McKnight and Mason squeezed into the back and most of the contents of the *Alamo*'s armoury secured in the trunk. Anya herself had been noticeably diligent about following the rules of the road during their drive from Collioure, lest some overzealous traffic cop pull them over and find a whole lot more than an expired tax disc.

Nonetheless, they'd made it here without incident, though he wasn't sure exactly where here was. Driving in the dark through twisting mountain roads hadn't done his sense of direction any favours.

'We are here,' Anya announced, nodding towards a cluster of single-storey brick buildings up ahead, possibly offices or reception areas. Looking ahead, Drake spotted a small sign for Aérodrome Mont Louis La Quillane.

Whatever kind of airfield this was, it didn't seem like it saw heavy use. The runway lights were still switched on, but there was no control tower that he could see, no perimeter fence, no security. Likely it was nothing more than a small private facility used by local flying clubs, which made it an ideal place for a clandestine meeting of the sort Anya had in mind.

'Party central here,' Frost remarked from the back seat. 'What exactly are we looking for?'

'Patience,' Anya advised, glancing at her in the rear-view mirror. 'He'll be here.'

Swinging the rental car off the main road, they passed what looked like a pilots' rest area, all dark and shut down at such an early hour. Beyond it lay a pair of corrugated steel hangars; the only substantial structures Drake had seen in the modest facility.

Anya made straight for the closest of two hangar buildings. Sure enough, the big sliding doors were open, allowing them a clear view of the cavernous space within. That was when they at last caught sight of the transport Anya had arranged.

'Holy shit,' Mason breathed, staring at the gleaming contours of the Gulfstream G280 executive jet sitting in the centre of the hangar, its graceful sweeping wings barely fitting within the structure.

'You own a goddamn private jet?' Frost asked, incredulous and more than a little envious of their new benefactor.

'No. I *rented* a private jet,' Anya explained. 'And it was not an easy matter to arrange at short notice. Luckily the pilot owed me a favour.'

Drake glanced at her. 'I presume this one's off the books?'

'Very,' she confirmed. 'The pilot is no stranger to jobs like this, and I trust him not to speak of it to anyone. He is also the only man I know who can get us to Islamabad ahead of Cain. That being said, he is a little... different.'

Frost was quick to pick up on this. 'Different how, exactly? *Rain Man* different? Jeffrey Dahmer different?'

'You can judge when we meet him. But let me do the talking,' Anya cautioned. 'He doesn't like Americans very much.'

Bringing the vehicle to a halt outside the hangar so as not to impede the jet's departure, Anya killed the engine and stepped out, with Drake close behind. The cold unyielding metal frame of his Browning pistol pressed uncomfortably against his back as he straightened up, but it was one discomfort he was happy to endure. He trusted Anya to a degree, but he knew nothing about the pilot of this plane. There was no way he was walking into a situation like this unarmed.

The jet's access hatch was already open and the collapsible stairs extended. Drake watched as what he presumed to be the pilot slid down using just the hand rails, landing with casual ease on the hangar's concrete floor.

A tall, thin man in his late forties with close-cropped dark hair, he had the strong-featured, swarthy complexion that Drake recognized as typically Slavic. He was wearing the short-sleeved white shirt and trouser combination common to private pilots, but there was no name tag or corporate logo anywhere on his outfit.

Ignoring Drake and the rest of the group, he walked straight towards Anya. However, one look at his expression was enough to confirm that greetings were the last thing on his mind.

'Anya, what the fuck?' he demanded in a pronounced accent, his sweeping gesture encompassing the modest airfield around them. 'You tell me this is perfect place to meet. You say, 'Don't worry, Yevgeny, everything will be taken care of. No problems there.' And what do I find when I get here? A runway shorter than my brother's cock.'

Anya for her part looked distinctly unimpressed with his colourful assessment of the situation. 'You are unharmed. And so is your plane, I assume.'

'Only because I am best pilot in Russia,' he admitted without a hint of irony.

Anya seemed content not to dispute that assertion. 'The airfield staff have been taken care of?'

Yevgeny held up a broad shovel-like hand, rubbing his thumb and forefinger together. 'I pay a little extra for them to open early. They will close up when we leave, and keep their mouths shut.' This point made, he at last turned his gaze on Drake and the others, acknowledging them for the first time. 'So these are your crew, yes?'

'Correct,' Anya confirmed.

Tapping out a cigarette from the packet he kept in his breast pocket, Yevgeny lit up and took a long, thoughtful drag as he surveyed the four operatives. No doubt it was obvious even to him that they weren't planning a sightseeing trip.

Sensing that Drake was the leader of this group, he approached slowly, staring him in the eye as if sizing him up. Drake stood his ground, waiting to see what would happen.

'Where are you from, my friend?' the Russian pilot asked.

'Doesn't matter,' Drake replied. 'What matters is where I'm going.'

A smile crept onto his face as he stared Drake down. Exhaling, he allowed his lungful of smoke to drift into Drake's face. 'A brave man, huh? You give me trouble, cowboy?'

He was pushing, testing Drake to see what kind of man he was, perhaps whether he could be intimidated into handing over more cash. Drake didn't bother looking to Anya for assistance, knowing he would find none there. Anyway, to do so would mark him out as weak in Yevgeny's eyes, and only encourage further provocation.

'Only if you give me reason to,' he said, meeting the man's stare without fear.

The smile broadened, and in an instant the tension between them seemed to vanish. Yevgeny clapped a friendly hand on Drake's shoulder. 'Ha! Very cool. I like this guy,' he decided, taking a final deep drag on his cigarette before dropping it on the ground at his feet. 'Okay, cowboy. Get your shit on board so we can go.'

'That's it?' Drake asked, surprised the man was willing to let them on board without knowing a thing about them.

'Who cares about the rest? Anya pays, so we go.' Striding towards the waiting jet, he called back over his shoulder, 'Hurry up! I must be back in Moscow tomorrow or Petyr will cut my balls off.'

'Who's Petyr?' Drake asked as he followed in the pilot's wake.

'This is his jet,' Yevgeny announced, unconcerned. He practically flew up the stairs, taking them two at a time. 'I borrow. It is cool, but wipe your feet! If you get dog shit on carpet, I kill you myself.'

This time Drake did glance at Anya, his expression making it plain what he thought of her improvised transportation. For her part, the woman merely shrugged.

'All right. Grab the gear, let's go,' Drake decided.

Popping the rental car's trunk, they retrieved the canvas bags filled with the weapons and equipment they were taking with them, and hurried towards the jet. Ascending the stairs and manoeuvring his unwieldy burden through the narrow hatch, Drake suddenly found himself in a different world. A world very different from the sleek, clinical corporate interior he'd been expecting.

The reclining leather chairs and expensive wooden finishes were all present and correct, but the decor reminded him more of a night club than an executive jet. The walls and carpets were coloured deep blue and purple, illuminated to maximum effect by the glow of neon strip lighting positioned behind every console and fixture. Almost the entire forward bulkhead was given over to a massive flat-screen TV, into which several different games consoles and what looked like a karaoke machine had been hooked up. There was even a miniature disco ball mounted in the ceiling, positioned so low that a man would have to duck aside to get past it.

The only thing that seemed to be missing was a dance pole, though he wouldn't have been surprised if there was one hidden away somewhere.

'What the actual fuck am I seeing?' Mason said, echoing Drake's thoughts.

Frost too was overawed by the scene that confronted her. 'I genuinely have no words,' she proclaimed. That was a first.

'Yevgeny, what exactly does Petyr do?' Drake felt compelled to ask. His life was complicated enough without incurring the wrath of a Russian oligarch, especially one rich and crazy enough to install a disco ball in a private yet.

Pausing at the cockpit door, Yevgeny grinned at him like a lunatic. 'Whatever the fuck he wants, man.'

That sounded about right, Drake thought.

'Have to hand it to the guy, he travels in style,' Frost conceded, admiring the bottles of luxury vodka and champagne in the plane's decidedly well-stocked on-board bar. 'I could get used to flying like this.'

'Don't even think about it,' Drake warned her. The next 24 hours were going to be difficult enough without adding a hangover into the mix.

'Sure thing, Dad,' the young woman replied with a sulking look, returning a bottle of Grey Goose to the drinks rack.

'Close the hatch, cowboy,' Yevgeny called from the cockpit, already strapping himself in.

Drake duly obliged, hauling up the stairs and pulling them flush against the fuselage until the door locked in place with a pneumatic hiss. 'All right, pick a seat, I suppose,' he advised as the engines powered up.

As the rest of the team sat down and fumbled with their restraining seatbelts, Drake caught Anya's arm and leaned in close, keeping his voice low so as not to be overheard.

'How the hell do you know this guy?'

'I killed his brother,' she replied with mild indifference.

Drake frowned. 'Why?'

'He asked me to.' She shrugged, dismissing it. 'It is a long story. But since then, he has owed me a favour. Today I collected.'

Drake released his hold and sat back in his chair without another word. Sometimes it was better simply not to know, he reflected, as Yevgeny

149

throttled up and the aircraft began to bump and roll towards the grassy runway nearby.

Pausing only a moment or two to line the nose up, the Russian called back to them over his shoulder. 'Hold on! May get bumpy.'

That was the understatement of the century, Drake thought as the engines roared with sudden power and the jet lurched forward, gaining speed and momentum with every passing second. The undercarriage rumbled and jolted as they hit small lumps and potholes on their violent journey, the hydraulic shock absorbers practically groaning under the impacts.

Drake and his team could do nothing but clutch their seats and try not to think about how much runway still lay before them as the nose slowly, reluctantly rose up into the sky. Drake could have sworn he heard a muffled curse from the cockpit over the whine of the straining jet turbines, but tried to dismiss it as his mind playing tricks on him.

With a final shuddering lurch, the rear wheels at last parted company with the ground and the jet rumbled skywards, engines roaring on full power. Not wishing to betray his own apprehension, Drake resisted the urge to let out a sigh of relief as the darkened countryside below rapidly receded from view.

For better or worse, they were on their way.

# Part II

# Incursion

According to former members of the US National Security Council, the Pakistani intelligence service has for years been recruiting and radicalizing young Pakistani men, before sending them to al-Qaeda training camps in Afghanistan.

*Chapter 28*

A little over six hours after departing southern France, Drake was in the Gulfstream's compact if opulent galley, waiting as the coffee machine slowly dispensed its steaming black liquid into his cup. He suspected the drinks bar saw a lot more use than this machine.

Despite the bumpy take-off, the flight since then had been a largely uneventful one, with good weather conditions and favourable winds hastening their journey. The respite had also afforded the team some much needed time to gather their thoughts and prepare themselves for what lay ahead.

Drake had used the time to learn as much as possible about their area of operations. Having served in Afghanistan during his military career, he was somewhat familiar with the complex and often dramatic history of its southern neighbour Pakistan, and had been doing his best to deepen that knowledge.

Like many countries in South Asia, Pakistan's early history had been characterized by the successive invasions of foreign powers, from the ancient Persians to Alexander the Great to the Sikh Empire. But it was the British who had truly shaped modern-day Pakistan, ruling it as part of their Indian Empire for more than a century, and profoundly influencing its culture and traditions. Two world wars, declining British influence and civil unrest had prompted a growing desire for independence, and in 1947 India had been split up, with Pakistan becoming a new sovereign country.

Its postcolonial history had been a chequered one, marked by political instability, conflicts with its larger neighbour India, civil wars and periods of military rule. These days it was viewed as a country at something of a cross-roads, with a comparatively moderate democratically elected government, good industrial infrastructure and strong, well-equipped armed forces, but also marred by tribal conflicts, terrorism, ongoing border disputes, government corruption, religious radicalization and widespread poverty. In short, its 200 million inhabitants were being pulled in many different directions.

Ostensibly Pakistan was an ally in the War on Terror, but a deep Islamic influence at all levels of society, growing distrust towards America, and strong ethnic ties to neighbouring Afghanistan meant the alliance was tenuous at best. With Pakistan possessing the eighth largest military in the world, not to mention nuclear weapons, it was no wonder Washington was keen to keep them onside.

The coffee machine pinged, disturbing his contemplations. Taking his cup, Drake turned back into the main cabin and surveyed the scene before him.

Mason, true to the military creed of grabbing food and rest when you could get it, had destroyed several packets of nuts and potato chips, then promptly fallen asleep. Frost meanwhile was glued to her laptop as she pored over details of the safe house's security system, a pair of earphones blasting tinny dance music making it obvious she didn't wish to be disturbed.

McKnight seemed to be dozing in one of the rear seats. She had spoken little since the group had disembarked the *Alamo*, seemingly lost in her own thoughts. Drake could guess what was on her mind, and had tried to broach the subject with her a few hours ago, only for her to dismiss his concerns out of hand. Not wanting to risk a confrontation in front of the group, he had opted not to push her.

The only person in the cabin who seemed awake and receptive to his presence was Anya. She was sitting apart from the others, staring out the little window towards the western horizon, the glow from the setting sun reflecting off the clouds beneath them bathing her face in crimson light.

Drake approached and sat down opposite, placing his coffee on the table that lay between them. For a moment or two he just sat there watching her, struck by the way the light played across her features. She knew he was looking at her, but she made no move to question or protest, perhaps sensing the meaning of this moment. It occurred him then that this was the first opportunity he'd had to speak with her alone since she'd joined the group.

'Been a while since shared a flight together,' he said quietly.

He saw a wry smile then. Her vivid blue eyes turned away from the sunset, regarding him. 'I think this one is a little more comfortable.'

'Well, this time around you haven't tried to kill one of my teammates, so that's a good start,' he said, reflecting on the moment where a paranoid and traumatized Anya had taken Frost hostage mere minutes after being freed from a Russian prison.

Anya leaned forward, lowering her voice conspiratorially. 'There is still time,' she assured him, her gaze flicking to Frost.

Drake smiled in response to this, though it wasn't quite as relaxed as before. With Anya, one learned not to take anything for granted.

'Relax, Ryan. It was a joke,' she said, leaning back in her seat. 'Even I know how to make them from time to time.'

'Never thought otherwise.' He took a sip of coffee to hide his discomfort.

Anya regarded him for a moment longer. 'I presume you didn't come here to reminisce about old times.'

'Not exactly. I came to find out where your head's at.'

'Where it normally is, I would hope.'

Twice in one year. Truly she was on a roll with this whole humour thing, he thought. 'You know what I mean. I want to know about Cain.'

She tilted her head quizzically. 'What would you like to know?'

She wasn't going to make this easy – that much was obvious. But neither was he. He wanted answers from her, just as much as she wanted them from Cain. And perhaps now that it was just the two of them together, she might open up.

'If this plan comes together... If we get to him, and he gives you the answers you need, what then? Will you kill him, or let him go?'

Anya was silent for a few seconds, weighing up the implications of that question. 'I don't know,' she judged at last.

Drake still couldn't get his head around her attitude. Anya was many things, but forgiving was not one of them. Why was Cain worthy of her mercy, when he had caused more damage to her than almost any other man in this world?

'Do you think he'd hesitate if the situation were reversed?' Drake asked bluntly.

She exhaled, as if this were something she hadn't wished to contemplate. 'Cain was not always a bad man. When I met him, he was... very different. I can't believe that person is gone completely.'

Drake certainly didn't share that opinion. Cain's actions over the past couple of years, his avaricious quest for power, his willingness to sacrifice innocent lives and his callous disregard for the consequences of his actions gave little evidence of a once good man upholding noble ideals.

'So what changed?'

In that moment a change seemed to come over Anya; she looked suddenly weary, as if a great weight had settled on her. Even if Drake had known nothing of her life, it would have been obvious how much Cain had once meant to her, and what an impact his betrayal had had.

It was but a momentary lapse, and soon overcome. Drake watched as her jaw clenched, her shoulders straightened, and the look of hurt and lingering sadness vanished like shadows at the coming of dawn. When she looked up at him again, Drake saw only the cold, hard resolve and iron will that had driven her from the first moment they'd met.

'That is what I'm going to find out,' she promised.

Such was Drake's focus on the woman seated opposite, he didn't notice McKnight watching them in silence from her seat further aft. He didn't see the pain, the worry or the anger in her look.

'Hey! Wake up, cowboy,' Yevgeny called out from the cockpit, interrupting their conversation. 'We are near the drop point. Fifteen minutes.'

Anya blinked, turning her thoughts to more practical matters. 'Drink up,' she advised, rising from her seat.

Nearby, Mason opened his eyes and looked around, roused from his sleep by the call from their pilot. He'd always possessed the innate ability to come back into full consciousness within seconds, no matter how deep his slumber.

Downing his coffee, Drake stood up to address the others. 'All right, guys. Gear up. We don't have much time.'

'Much time for what?' Frost asked, yanking out her headphones. Yevgeny's shout had been loud enough to overcome the music blasting in her ears.

Making her way aft to where the group's equipment bags were stowed, Anya knelt down, unzipped one and pulled out a pair of compact black nylon rucksacks.

'To prepare for our jump,' she replied, tossing one of the parachute packs to the young specialist.

'Wait, what the fuck is this?' Frost demanded, looking to Drake for answers. 'Nobody told me we'd be parachuting into Pakistan.'

Anya tilted her head quizzically. 'How else did you expect to get on the ground?'

'Erm, I don't know. Maybe by landing at a fucking airfield?' Frost suggested. 'That's why we're in a private jet, isn't it?'

'The jet was to get us over the target area, not to touch down. Their military will have us on radar already,' Anya explained, handing a second parachute to Drake. Already the deck was tilting beneath them, the engines throttling back as the plane began to bleed off altitude and airspeed. 'If we try to land outside a major airport, they will scramble fighters to intercept us.'

Drake for his part had known about this part of the plan, as had most of the others, though he'd opted to let Anya break the good news to Frost, reasoning it was someone else's turn to incur her wrath for once.

The technical specialist was virtually without fear in most situations, but she was what seasoned veterans referred to as a 'five-jump chump' when it came to parachuting – someone who had done the bare minimum to earn their certification, but hated every minute of it. It had taken all his powers of persuasion to get her to take part in a risky high-altitude jump into Russia two years ago, and she'd vowed never to do it again.

'Screw that. I am *not* jumping out of another goddamn plane,' Frost decided.

Anya shrugged, unconcerned with her reservations. 'Suit yourself. Pakistani security forces will be waiting for you in Islamabad. I hope you have a good excuse ready.'

If it came down to a battle of wills, Frost was never going to win against such an opponent. Anyway, she could see the logic in Anya's argument, even if she didn't want to admit it.

She was full of accusation as she turned on Drake. 'You knew about this, didn't you?'

'Don't know what you mean,' he lied, concentrating instead on fixing his harness in place and making sure the rip cord was within easy reach.

'Relax, Frost,' Anya said, no hint of sympathy in her voice. 'Just open the door and step out. Gravity does the rest.'

Frost shot her a furious look but said nothing further, concentrating instead on preparing her gear. The rest of the team did likewise, quickly changing out of their civilian clothes and donning the black assault gear and body armour that they would be wearing when they attacked the safe house. Since there was no other way to transport it in, all of their weapons and equipment would have to go with them when they jumped.

Still, as far as Drake was concerned, this jump was a piece of cake compared to the HAHO (High Altitude, High Opening) insertion they'd made three years ago. They would be bailing out at relatively low altitude, so wouldn't need any of the bulky respirators, oxygen tanks and thermally insulted suits they'd worn last time. And despite Frost's protests, all of them were trained in airborne insertions as part of their former roles as Shepherd operatives. As long as they all made it to the ground in one piece, that would be good enough for him.

With his harness in place and his other gear secured, Drake lifted out the last item from his equipment bag – a simple steel-bladed knife. Though it could be used as a weapon at a pinch, it was really intended as an emergency measure in case his parachute fouled on deployment, forcing him to cut away the tangled lines so he could deploy his emergency chute. Fortunately he'd never had to do it.

As he sheathed the blade, Anya approached him. She was already harnessed up and armed, a similar knife secured across her chest. 'Ready?'

He shrugged. 'Getting there. Listen, don't take this the wrong way, but when was the last time you did something like this?'

She'd enjoyed a varied and lengthy career as a paramilitary operative, which no doubt included covert parachute drops, but she'd been out of the loop for a long time. Too long, perhaps.

'Feels like yesterday,' she evaded, her expression warning against further enquiries. 'And since we are asking honest questions, who packed these parachutes?'

Sensing just a hint of unease in the normally composed veteran, Drake flashed a conspiratorial grin. 'I did. Feel better now?'

'Ask me once we are on the ground.'

'Five minutes!' Yevgeny called out.

Crossing the cabin, Drake approached McKnight. 'Let's have a look.'

Part of the procedure before any jump was for each member of the team to have their rig checked by one of their comrades, so that nobody was left solely in charge of their own safety. It didn't guarantee a flawless jump, but it shortened the odds. And it was good for morale.

'How are you feeling?' he asked as he tugged on her shoulder straps, making sure they were securely fastened.

'Peachy,' the woman replied, though Drake noticed she was avoiding his gaze, and her complexion seemed to have taken on a noticeably sickly pallor.

'Sure you're okay?' Lifting up the deployment flap, he took a quick look at her chute to confirm it was properly packed.

'I'm fine.'

'Listen, there's nothing to worry about here,' he promised her. 'You step out, give it a couple of seconds and pull your rip cord. That's all there is to it.'

'I know how to jump, Ryan,' she said with a flash of irritation.

Drake nodded, saying nothing further. Whatever was eating her, now was not the time to address it. But he made a mental note to speak to her in private once circumstances permitted.

With final checks complete, Drake raised his voice to address the team. 'All right, listen up. We're cruising over the mountains about 20 miles north of Islamabad. The terrain we'll be dropping into is mountainous and pretty heavily forested, so keep your eyes open, watch for boulders and sudden drop-offs. And for Christ's sake, try not to get hung up in a tree when you touch down. Once it's safe, get on the radio net and sound off so we know you're in one piece. Everyone clear?'

He was met with a round of affirmatives, though Frost's hostile glare was enough to remind him she was likely to hold a grudge over this.

'Good. Then I'll see you on the ground.'

Having engaged the aircraft's automatic pilot, Yevgeny ducked through into the cabin, surveying the small group with amusement. If he was unnerved by the black combat gear, body armour and automatic weapons, he gave little sign of it.

'We are almost at drop point,' he reported. 'I go as slow as I can without stalling, but it will be rough when you jump.' He flashed a grin at Drake. 'Try not to die, huh cowboy?'

'Yeah. Thanks, mate,' he replied. Fucking prick, he decided not to add. He could practically feel Frost's eyes boring into him after the Russian's remark.

'Get ready,' Anya said, reaching for the door-release handle. She would be out first, followed by Mason, then Frost and McKnight.

Drake would bring up the rear, since he was one of the most experienced of the group. If one of the others got into trouble, he could in theory go into accelerated freefall, get to them and assist before they impacted. If he was already below them, they were on their own.

Glancing at his watch, Yevgeny gave her a nod. Anya slipped on her protective goggles and pulled hard on the release lever. The sudden inrush of air coupled with the roar of the slipstream and the whine of jet engines outside was almost enough to make them recoil in shock. Drake was vaguely aware of alarms blaring in the cockpit, probably triggered by the change in cabin pressure, though they were at a low enough altitude that oxygen deprivation was unlikely to be a problem.

Standing by the hatch, Anya halted and looked back over her shoulder. Her face was partially covered by the protective goggles, but Drake was able to make eye contact with her for a brief moment before she turned, gripped the edge of the hatch and launched herself out into the darkness. Mason was next, not even bothering to pause at the door. He just went for it without fear or hesitation, calmly stepping out with his arms crossed in front of him.

Frost was another matter, freezing by the doorway. Drake saw her turn towards McKnight and lean in to say something, but the roar of the wind made it impossible to hear her words. In any case, McKnight shook her head and jerked her finger towards the door, frantically motioning for Frost to go. Every second that passed would leave the group more widely dispersed when they landed, wasting precious time regrouping.

Drake was about to move forward and speak with the young woman when she suddenly turned away, rushed forward and threw herself out the hatch. Either she'd found the courage to overcome her fear or she was more afraid of what Drake would do. Whatever the reason, she was out.

McKnight glanced at him only for a moment. Reaching out, he touched her hand, hoping the simple gesture was enough to express what he hadn't been able to say to her earlier. He saw a faint nod, then she too turned away and stepped out over the edge.

It was time to go. Yevgeny was watching him, one arm up to shield his eyes from the howling wind. He grinned at Drake and opened his mouth to say something, but the noise made it impossible to hear. Drake didn't care much anyway, though despite himself, he hoped Yevgeny's boss didn't learn of this little clandestine venture and punish him in the manner he'd so colourfully described. Maybe the world could use a few more mad bastards like him to keep things interesting.

Giving the Russian pilot a nod of grudging thanks, Drake gripped the edge of the hatch, rocked back once on his heels to build up some momentum, and leapt out into the night.

## Chapter 29

Drake was falling, plunging through the night sky like an ungainly bird, arms and legs outstretched to increase his drag and even out his downward acceleration until he reached terminal velocity. Howling winds tore at the fabric of his clothes, while chilling high-altitude air clawed at his exposed skin and roared past his ears as the aircraft receded into the darkness somewhere above.

The sun had set not long before, and although night had fallen there was enough ambient light for him to make out the residual glow on the western horizon. Far to the south lay a different kind of light. It was the harsh orange glare generated by tens of thousands of electric lights in the sprawling twin cities of Islamabad and Rawalpindi, rendered vague and indistinct by the blanket of smog that lingered over the metropolis.

Bringing his left hand up in front of his face, he consulted the digital altimeter unit strapped to his wrist. At roughly 10,000 feet deployment altitude, they could afford to freefall for nearly 60 seconds before they needed to pop their chutes. Likely they would open earlier than that for safety's sake, but it gave them a decent margin in which to get their bearings and orient themselves.

Below him lay a world of rocky mountain peaks, winding river valleys and ancient weathered highlands; the eroded stumps of far older and taller mountain ranges. There were no lights that he could discern in the vicinity, either from vehicles or settlements, which could only be good news.

The low ambient light made it difficult to see his comrades. They had all exited the plane in short order, but even a delay of mere seconds could mean a gap of hundreds of yards during freefall. All he could do was hope each had their shit together.

He glanced at his altimeter. Eight thousand feet.

There! Below, off to his right, he spotted the first blur of movement as a chute blossomed into life. He'd deliberately chosen dark fabric for their parachutes, reasoning that if they ever used them, it was likely to be for a night insertion, and therefore concealment was a priority.

As if everyone had been waiting for one team member to make the first move, other parachutes soon began to open up. Drake spotted the second one closer at hand, followed almost immediately by a third off to his right. One to go.

Come on, come on, he thought, willing it to open. He'd been last out. It was his duty to wait until the others had deployed their chutes properly.

Thirty seconds of freefall left.

That was when he spotted movement almost directly below, perhaps 400 feet away; the sudden rush of an uplifted parachute as air began to fill it. But this chute didn't blossom into a neat, engorged circle like the others. Rather, it remained stalled in a straggling line of fabric and tangled cabling, flapping and straining ineffectually against the wind. It was caught on something, preventing it from opening.

'Shit!' he hissed, though the howling wind stole his exclamation away.

He reacted instinctively, tucking his arms flat against his body and drawing his feet together, doing his best to make his body as streamlined as an arrow as he dove towards the struggling jumper. The sense of acceleration was immediate and profound, and Drake gritted his teeth as the wind tore at his clothes and skin, focussing his eyes on the straggling folds of canopy below as it crept closer and closer.

Three hundred feet.

Drake chanced a look at his altimeter. Six thousand feet to go.

Every second that passed brought him closer to his stricken comrade, but also to a crushing, fatal impact with the ground. This was going to be a narrow margin.

Two hundred feet from the chute.

He tried to picture his comrade struggling with the tangle of lines above their head, trying to fight back the rising sense of panic that always came with a chute malfunction, trying not to think that every second that passed brought them closer to death. He just prayed they were smart enough not to try to pop their reserve chute before the main chute was cleared, otherwise it would simply become fouled in the mess overhead.

One hundred feet. Five thousand feet of freefall remaining.

Come on, come on.

Suddenly, after approaching with agonizing slowness since he'd started his maximum speed descent, the chute rushed up to meet him, forcing him to twist sideways to avoid becoming ensnared in it as well.

As it drifted past him on his left side, Drake began to spread his arms and legs, slowing his descent so that he could meet with the jumper and avoid overshooting. If that happened, he might never be able to get back up to them, and his one chance to help would be gone.

Almost there now. He could see the darkened figure just below him, fighting with the tangled cables trailing from their pack. He couldn't tell if they were aware of his approach, but that didn't matter. He was coming in fast, and needed to catch them.

As they swept by, Drake reached out with both hands, grasping for whatever he could get a firm grip of. His right hand met only fabric, and he felt a moment of taut resistance followed by a sudden release as it ripped under the strain. However, his left managed to close around a strap of some kind, and he tightened his grip as he was jerked to a muscle-straining halt.

The stricken jumper was pulled forward by the sudden change in weight, bringing them face to face with him. In that instant, Drake found himself staring into a pair of vivid blue eyes. Normally cool and reserved, he saw something else in them now. Fear.

Of all the people he'd expected to encounter a problem like this, Anya hadn't been one of them.

'Anya, you're hung up!' he screamed, hoping their physical closeness would help her hear what was being said. 'Can you cut away?'

No such luck. She shook her head, pointing up at the fouled canopy above. Though they couldn't communicate verbally, it was obvious enough what she wanted. She couldn't reach far enough back to detach the main chute by herself.

Only one option left.

Reaching down, Drake closed his free hand around the haft of the knife she'd given him, and yanked it free of its sheath. Sensing what he was doing, Anya wrapped her arms around his waist, steadying him enough so that he could use both hands to work.

A tangle of different lines trailed from her pack, leading up to what should have been a full canopy above. But down by the base, they were clumped together into an almost solid mass. That was where he'd aim.

Closing his left hand around the cables to bunch them together, Drake attacked them with the knife, sawing at the bundle with savage, powerful thrusts. Straight away the first few lines began to fray and pop, giving way under the strain.

As he worked, Drake couldn't help but glance at his altimeter, and immediately wished he hadn't. Four thousand feet to go.

'Come on, you bastard!' he snarled, working the razor-edged blade back and forth with increasing urgency. More lines were snapping and whipping aside now as the knife sliced its way through the nylon fibres, but still the canopy above remained firmly attached.

Three thousand feet.

Almost there. More lines were coming away with every thrust, and the remainder had been stretched to their limits by the increasing load.

Two thousand.

It was at this moment that Anya's grip suddenly released, forcing Drake to clutch at the bundle of lines itself just to stay in position. For an instant he wondered what the hell she was doing, but this confusion quickly gave way to stark realization. Anya, pragmatic to the end, was letting him go, forcing him to pop his own chute and save his life rather than die with her.

Maybe she was right. He was out of time, out of options, and if both of them were killed in the drop, the mission was over before it had begun. There would be nobody left to stop Cain.

'No,' he said through gritted teeth, working the blade one more time with savage, desperate fury, as if he were locked in mortal combat against a hated enemy. He had no idea what his altimeter said now, and nor did he care.

He wasn't leaving her now.

Then, with an audible snap and a sudden rush of movement, the canopy above finally tore itself free, vanishing into the night as the howling wind gusted through it. Robbed of his only handhold, Drake found himself tumbling head over heels in an uncontrolled spin, the world now frightening close whirling around him. He paid it no heed as he reached up for his ripcord, knowing there was no time left to try to stabilize his flight.

Closing his fingers around the steel ring that marked the end of the cord, Drake closed his eyes and braced himself for what was coming. A single hard pull was enough to trigger the spring-loaded deployment mechanism for his main chute, ejecting it from the top of his pack.

His last thought was to hope that he'd done a better job of packing his own parachute than Anya's. Then he felt himself jerked to a sudden, violent halt, the straps of his harness biting into his flesh as the canopy above unfolded and air resistance worked desperately to slow his descent. Drake opened his eyes and looked down just as a rocky, undulating hilltop rushed up to meet him like a giant fist.

One of the first things he'd learned in jump school was how to absorb the sometimes violent impact of a hard landing and avoid the broken bones that were all too easy to earn in situations like this. The instant he felt his boots make contact, he allowed his leg muscles to relax, falling forward and twisting slightly so that his right shoulder absorbed most of the shock. He was aiming to drop and roll, just as he'd done countless times before.

The unyielding ground had other ideas, and he felt a stab of pain as sharp stones tore at his clothes and skin, and the rocky wind-scoured hilltop beneath slammed into him like a sledgehammer. Nonetheless, he managed to tuck his head in and transfer his momentum into a forward roll, which served to bleed away the last of his kinetic energy.

For a moment or two Drake just lay there staring up at the darkened sky above, gasping for breath, his heart pounding. The sheer adrenaline surge of the last 30 seconds was making it hard to think clearly, but gradually this was easing off as he came to terms with the fact he was no longer in mortal danger. And as the adrenaline thinned out, so his body began to react to the punishment it had just taken. He was bruised and bleeding, and altogether felt like he'd just gone ten rounds against an opponent with bricks for fists.

But he was alive. That meant he could still move and act; both of which he needed to do now. Taking a deep breath, he clenched his fists and tensed up for a moment or two, focussing his mind on what was happening around him.

Get up. Get up now.

The canopy was settling around him as it descended the last few feet towards ground. Grimacing in pain, Drake heaved himself up from the ground and reached out to grasp at the material, bundling it into a ball so that it couldn't unfurl again. It wasn't unknown for a sudden gust of wind to catch fallen parachutes and drag their unfortunate owners along the ground like rag dolls. After surviving that landing he had no desire to die by being swept off the edge of a cliff.

This done, he unclipped his harness and shrugged out of it, allowing the pack to fall away. He was alive and he was on solid ground – two things for which he was equally grateful at that moment. Now that the most immediate concern of landing was out of the way, it was time to focus on the next problem – reuniting with his team.

Reaching behind him, he drew the Browning automatic free of its holster and pulled back the slide just far enough to make out the gleam of a brass shell casing in the chamber. With his weapon at the ready, Drake crouched down and took a couple of deep breaths to settle his heart and calm his body, allowing his senses to tune into his new environment.

A light breeze sighed past him, carrying with it the lingering warmth of evening and the smell of juniper, spruce and cedar trees, while the air seemed to be alive with the clicks and chirps of cicadas and other night insects, their calls blending together into a background hum that served to mask small movements.

With his eyes now adjusted to the low light, Drake scanned his surroundings. He had landed near the edge of a broad rock escarpment overlooking a wide, heavily forested valley below. There was more cover in the form of brush and small trees not far away where the escarpment met the slope of the valley wall, and instinctively Drake crept towards it, moving slowly and carefully, senses on constant alert as his booted feet picked a path through loose rocks and tree roots.

Crouching down in the shade of a gnarled spruce tree, Drake powered up his tactical radio unit. Like the others, he'd left it powered down during the jump since the noise of the wind would render such communication devices thoroughly useless, but now was the time to put it to the test.

'This is Unit One. All elements, sound off. Over,' he said, keeping his voice low.

Whispering was counterproductive at times like this as the high-pitched noise carried over great distance at night. In any case, the radio microphone strapped to his throat was designed to pick up the vibrations of his vocal chords rather than the sounds coming from his mouth, so he had no worries about being heard. The question was whether anyone would answer.

'Two is on the ground. Over.' That was Mason. There were no fancy code words at this stage – each member of the team had simply been assigned a number as their call sign, making it easy to sound off in sequence.

'Three is all good. Over,' McKnight reported.

'Four is very fucking glad that's over,' came Frost's angry sound-off. 'Over.'

Drake might have smiled at that remark, were it not for the fact that one member of their group hadn't checked in.

'Unit Five, sound off,' he spoke into his radio.

Nothing, save for the pop and hiss of static over the airwaves. Drake felt a wave of foreboding descend on him like a pall as he replayed those last few moments before he'd released his parachute. Was it enough, or had he been too late?

'Unit Five. What's your sitrep? Over.'

Still no reply. Had Anya been able to deploy her reserve chute, or had her body slammed into the ground with bone-shattering force before it could open? Was she lying out there at this very moment, broken and dying in agony?

'Unit Five, come—'

'Will you stop that?' an irritated voice demanded from somewhere behind him.

Drake whirled around and raised his automatic, instinctively thumbing off the safety catch as he brought the weapon to bear.

Even as he did so, a figure emerged from the undergrowth not more than 20 yards away, dressed in black assault gear like himself and armed with a compact submachine gun that she kept up at her shoulder even as she approached.

'Anya. Jesus Christ, why aren't you answering your comms?' Drake hissed, lowering his own weapon. Such had been his preoccupation with raising her over the radio, he hadn't detected her approach over the sounds of nocturnal wildlife and the rustle of foliage in the night breeze. At least, that was what he told himself.

Reaching down, Anya held up her radio unit. Even in the low ambient light he could make out the shattered casing and the exposed wires and circuit boards within.

'Took a hard landing. Not that I needed a radio to find you,' she added with a disapproving look. 'A blind man could have found his way here.'

'You know, some people actually show a little gratitude when someone saves their life,' he pointed out none too gently.

'I didn't need saving, Ryan. And I have never had a chute fail before. Never,' she contended, though her voice was lacking its usual air of authority. If anything, she actually seemed a little embarrassed.

That was when the puzzle seemed to come together in his mind. She'd come perilously close to dying up there, and though the experience had left her shaken up, she didn't crave comfort or reassurance in the way a normal person might. Those feelings were as alien to her as the surface of the moon. Instead her instinct was to lash out, to go on the offensive just as she always had.

'Really? Tell that to your radio,' Drake hit back. 'I'm fine too, by the way. Thanks for asking.'

Anya opened her mouth to retort, but seemed to think better of it. Perhaps for once she recognized when not to argue her case.

His radio earpiece crackled with an incoming transmission. 'One, this is Two. What's your sitrep? Any sign of Five?'

Giving Anya a meaningful look, Drake keyed his transmit button. 'Roger that. Five is with me now.'

'Good to hear, One.'

Now it was time to bring the rest of the team together. 'All units, rally on my position. Stand by for visual reference. Over.'

Reaching into a pouch in his combat webbing, he pulled out a metal object roughly the size and shape of a ballpoint pen, though considerably heavier. Pointing it skyward, Drake pressed the single button moulded into its side, and watched as a thin beam of green light shot up into the night sky.

High-intensity laser emitters weren't exactly popular with aircraft pilots these days on account of the assholes who shone them at cockpit windows, but there were few better ways of marking a position from the ground. Drake kept the beam pointed skyward for a good five seconds or so, allowing his teammates to get a solid fix on his position.

'All units, converge on my reference now,' he instructed. 'Over.'

'Copy that, One. En route,' McKnight replied, quickly followed by her two comrades.

'Unit One, acknowledged. Out.'

Clicking off the radio, Drake reached up and felt the torn fabric of his tunic, damp and sticky with congealing blood. He'd taken a beating during the landing, and although the lacerations were unlikely to slow him down, they would likely need tending before they went much further. Rolling his shoulder experimentally, he was rewarded with a stab of pain that caused him to tense up involuntarily. Hopefully it was nothing but bruised muscle, and not something more serious.

'You're hurt,' Anya said, moving towards him.

'I'm fine.'

'You're not. Let me look at it.'

'I said, I'm fine.' Drake gave her a look that warned he would debate the matter no further. Instead he unstrapped his radio unit and tossed it to her, which she caught out of instinct rather than desire. 'Just get on stag, and keep the comms open in case they need another signal. Can you handle that?'

She didn't reply, which was probably for the best. Leaving her to keep watch, he moved off a short distance to tend his wounds and await the arrival of his friends.

# Chapter 30

Despite his fears of the team being dispersed over miles of mountainous terrain, Drake was relieved that his teammates were able to answer his summons without difficulty. Frost and McKnight arrived at the rendezvous point together, having exited the plane within seconds of each other and likely reunited shortly after landing.

Unsurprisingly, Anya spotted their movement amongst the boulders and wind-sculpted trees that littered the hillside. Instinctively she crouched down and trained her weapon on the approaching figures.

'Red,' she called out in challenge, awaiting the countersign that would confirm the two arrivals were friendly.

'Dwarf,' McKnight replied, emerging from cover with Frost by her side. Anya lowered her weapon in response, though she didn't seem any less wary.

Frost shook her head as she approached. 'You must be a closet geek, Ryan.'

'You're just as bad for knowing what it means,' he reasoned. He'd decided on the sign-countersign combination himself, reasoning that if anyone in this remote part of the world knew of the old British sitcom that had spawned it, they deserved to get the better of his team.

McKnight, however, was in no mood for jokes, particularly when she saw Drake's shoulder. 'Ryan, you okay?'

'Never better,' he lied, brushing aside her concerns. He'd applied a basic dressing to the lacerations to stop the bleeding, and was busy clipping his webbing back into place.

'Does it hurt?' Frost asked, looking uncharacteristically concerned.

'A little.'

She flashed a satisfied grin. 'Good.'

'Keira, quit it,' McKnight warned her. 'What happened, Ryan?'

Drake glanced over at Anya who studiously avoided his gaze, concentrating instead on keeping watch. 'Had to open my chute a bit later than planned. It was a hard landing.'

'Why? Something go wrong?'

'My parachute failed,' Anya said without turning around. 'Ryan stayed behind to cut it away so I could open my reserve.' She paused for a moment or two before continuing. 'Without him I would be dead.'

Well, shit, Drake thought. Finally an acknowledgement, albeit a grudging one.

'Sounds like a lovely fuck-up to kick things off,' Frost remarked unhappily. She seemed to have inherited a superstitious outlook when it came to operations like this, viewing early difficulties as a bad omen. 'Who packed your chute?'

'Ryan did, just as he packed all of yours.' Anya glanced around then, fixing her eyes on McKnight. 'And *she* checked it for me.'

For a couple of seconds, not a word was exchanged amongst the group as the weight of her words, and their implications, settled on each of them.

Typically, it was Frost who reacted first. 'What's that supposed to mean?'

'How did it look, McKnight?' Anya asked. 'You seemed to take your time over it.'

McKnight for her part had remained silent throughout, watching Anya as if she expected the woman to pounce on her at any moment.

'You'd better think real careful about what you're implying,' Frost warned.

'It is a question.' Anya's deceptively calm tone was in stark contrast to the baleful look in her eyes. 'One that McKnight has not answered.'

Drake had heard enough of this. 'Stop it, both of you. Shit like this can and does happen, so stop bitching at each other and deal with it. Just be grateful nobody got killed.'

Anya said nothing, merely turning away to resume her watch.

'You,' Drake said, pointing a finger at Frost. 'Check your gear. I need you thinking with a clear head.'

She shrugged unhappily. 'Whatever.'

'Say it,' he ordered her.

'I got it!' Frost snapped. Throwing him an irritable look, she removed the equipment pack she'd been carrying slung across one shoulder, and crouched down to check the contents.

Satisfied that this would keep her occupied for a while, Drake turned away to deal with the next problem. As he did so, McKnight approached him. 'Thank you, Ryan,' she said quietly. 'For what you said.'

'The minute we stop being a team, Cain's already won.' Drake exhaled, offering a tentative smile. 'How's that for a cheesy motivational quote?'

She shrugged, but he saw his smile reciprocated. 'Not bad.'

'Contact,' Anya called out from her vantage point. Once more she had her weapon up and ready. 'One man, approaching from the north.'

Sure enough, about a minute later the last member of their team responded to Anya's challenge in similar fashion to McKnight, and appeared at the crest of the slope, weapon in hand. He was a little out of breath after what had likely been a strenuous run, but otherwise appeared to have survived the jump and the journey here without so much as a scratch.

'You all right, dude?' he asked, noting Drake's injuries.

'Caught a rough landing, that's all.'

Mason frowned, sensing the simmering hostility in the group. 'Why does this place feel like an awkward Thanksgiving dinner?'

'You're here now, so get ready to move out,' Drake said, eager to focus on the mission. 'Anya, the clock's ticking. We need to find your contact and get out of here.'

'That won't be a problem,' the woman replied, staring past him into the darkness.

'Why?'

She rose slowly to her feet, keeping a tight grip of her weapon. 'Because he has already found us.'

# Chapter 31

The reaction of the Shepherd operatives was immediate and instinctive. Whirling around to face this new and unexpected arrival, Drake immediately went for his weapon, as did his three companions.

A trio of shadowy figures had appeared not 20 yards away, seemingly having emerged from the darkened forest like ghosts. They were dressed in dark cloaks that masked outlines and covered even their faces, leaving only their eyes exposed, and had likely allowed them to approach so close unseen. But even in the general darkness in which they lurked, Drake was able to recognize the distinctive frames of AK family assault rifles pointed his way.

There were many variants – and reproductions – of these legendary old Soviet rifles, but it didn't matter too much at that moment which ones were pointed at him. They all went boom on command and they were all capable of punching a sizeable hole in pretty much anything they hit. All three firing on full automatic were more than enough to reduce his team to bloodied corpses in seconds.

'Don't,' Anya warned, likely harbouring similar thoughts. 'Make no move.'

'They've got the drop on us,' Frost hissed.

Ignoring her, Anya holstered her weapon and slowly approached the new arrivals, keeping her hands in plain sight. Her face betrayed no hint of fear or hostility, but Drake could see the tension in her body, like a coiled spring straining to be released.

'Malak,' she began, before continuing in Pashto, one of the many languages used amongst tribesmen in this part of the world.

Drake himself had a working knowledge of Arabic, but Pashto was too far removed for him to make any sense of her conversation. He could only hope the three masked gunmen were more receptive.

Having said her piece, Anya fell silent. In the uneasy stand-off that followed, Drake could have sworn he'd have heard a pin drop. Even the ubiquitous cicadas seemed to have ceased their song.

Then, just as suddenly as they had appeared, one of the figures lowered his weapon and pulled back his hood, exposing a craggy, thickly bearded face that looked like it had lived a life neither short nor easy. One dark, hawkish eye was fixed on the woman. The other was a gaping, empty socket partially covered by old scar tissue.

But to Drake's surprise, the man he presumed was called Malak let out a peal of hearty laughter, the jovial sound of genuine amusement quite at odds with his grim visage.

'Your Pashto is as ugly as my face, Anya,' he remarked in English, striding towards her with one gloved hand outstretched.

The tension seemed to leave Anya's body then as she met him halfway, grasping his hand as if he were an old friend. The other two gunmen had lowered their weapons, and Drake silently nodded to his own teammates to do likewise.

'It is good to see you again, Malak,' Anya replied, releasing her grip. 'Your tracking skills are getting better.'

'Better than yours, I think. But then, we were waiting for you.'

She said nothing to that, instead turning her attention to matters closer at hand. 'Did you bring everything I requested?'

'Straight to business, as always,' Malak observed. 'Of course I got everything. Have I ever let you down?'

'Would you like me to be honest?'

The man grinned, exposing a set of white, perfectly aligned teeth that would have been the envy of any Hollywood movie star. Strange that he should have invested so much money in his dental care when a simple eye patch might have served him better, Drake couldn't help thinking. But then, perhaps his friends were simply too frightened to tell him so.

'Ha! Still got some fire in you, just like the old days,' he said, slapping her on the arm. 'Speaking of which, why are you back in Pakistan? Surely you are not working for the CIA again?'

Anya's expression made it plain this was one conversation that wasn't going anywhere. 'I would like to see the gear, Malak.'

Malak regarded her a moment longer, then shrugged. 'As you wish. Come, our truck is not far from here.'

Without saying a word to Drake and the rest of the team, he turned away and began to stride off down the forested slope, making remarkably little noise considering the rough terrain they were traversing. Drake was beginning to realize it hadn't just been a lapse in vigilance that had allowed these men to approach so close; likely they had spent most of their lives in these mountains, and could move through them as silently as shadows.

With little choice, Anya, Drake and the others followed behind. Instinctively they formed a standard patrol column, keeping about five yards between each member to avoid bunching up and making themselves an easy target.

Drake, however, slowed his pace, allowing Anya to catch up with him so they could converse without being overheard by their new guides.

'Doesn't seem too interested in us,' he observed.

It wasn't as if he was eager to swap names and addresses with a Pakistani arms dealer, but he was surprised Malak didn't want to know anything about them. In his experience, such men were notoriously paranoid, as well they should be. The Agency had run plenty of sting operations against his kind.

'Malak knows the situation. No names, no details. Nothing that could compromise us if he is caught.' The woman shrugged. 'And he trusts me.'

Drake was curiously reminded of the Russian pilot who had brought them here. 'I take it this is another one of those long stories, right?'

Anya said nothing.

He shook his head, dismissing it. There was something more important he needed to address anyway. 'Listen, about what happened with the others—'

'Save your breath,' she interrupted. 'I don't care if your team likes me. All I'm interested in is Cain. Once we have him, they will not see me again.'

There wasn't much he could say to that. She had made her views perfectly clear. Drake quickened his pace a little, giving her some space. But as he did so, she called out after him. 'Ryan.'

He glanced over his shoulder.

'What you did for me... up there,' she said, looking suddenly unsure of herself. The way she always did when she had to let down her guard. 'I won't forget it.'

It wasn't much, but it was about as close to a 'thank you' as he was likely to get. And he supposed, given what they were about to face together, it was enough for now.

# Chapter 32

*St Luke's Medical Center Denver*

Jack Taylor made his way along the corridor at a slow, casual pace, doing his best not to look uncomfortable at the smell of antiseptic, the whitewashed walls and the doctors in medical scrubs doing the rounds of the wards.

Hospitals had never sat well with him, even as a kid, and that feeling had only intensified during his career in the military. Too many of his buddies had ended up in places like this – proud and dedicated soldiers reduced to broken, burned, mutilated shells of men.

Most of the time it had been nothing more than bad luck. Maybe they'd tried to walk across the wrong field, driven down the wrong road, made a wrong turn. He'd visited each of them after it happened, offered reassurance and even shared a few jokes with one or two, but he'd always hated it. Hated the feeling of desperation, the despair, the loneliness that seemed to linger around such places.

Pushing past these thoughts, he followed the corridor as it took a right turn, keeping his eye on the door numbers. He'd been sent here by an old friend, to find her father and escort him to safety. He'd promised Samantha that if the need ever arose, he would be there for her, and he had no intention of breaking that promise.

He knew all too well what she'd sacrificed, what she'd given up to protect the other members of her group, including him, after their foolish adventure in Iraq. A plan that should have made them all rich, but instead landed her a 15-year prison term.

Finding Room 6C at last, Taylor paused for a moment outside the door to straighten his jacket and check his shirt for creases. He was wearing casual clothes, but old habits die hard, and he wanted to make a good impression on Pete McKnight.

There was no reply to his polite knock. Perhaps the old man was dozing. She'd warned Taylor that he was sick and likely weak from his treatment. He knocked again, a little harder this time to give the man fair warning, then pushed it open.

But there was no sign of Pete McKnight, either in the bed or on the seats over by the window. Not only was he missing, but there was no trace of his presence. No clothes, no personal effects on the bedside table, no books or magazines.

'Shit,' he said under his breath.

Leaving the room, he hurried back around to the nurse's station and approached the duty nurse, a middle-aged black woman who looked like she was at the tail end of a long shift. A stack of folders were piled up on the desk in front of her.

'Excuse me. I'm looking for the patient in Room 6C. Has he been moved to another ward?'

She glanced up from her work, regarding him dubiously. 'You his next of kin?'

'Family friend,' Taylor explained, seeing no point in lying to her. 'His daughter's on active duty overseas. She asked me to swing by, check in on him.'

At this, her expression softened a little, as people's often did when families were separated by military service. 'Too late, I'm afraid. He checked himself out this morning.'

'Checked out?' Taylor's brows drew together in a frown. 'Isn't he going through chemo right now?'

'You know we can't discuss a patient's treatment, sir. But for what it's worth, the doctor did everything to make him stay, short of locking him in his room. Legally we can't stop a patient of sound mind from discharging himself.'

Taylor held up a hand, uninterested in the legal details. 'Did he at least say where he was going?'

She tilted her head. 'You tried his house?'

Taylor was already moving, heading for the elevator that would take him down to the hospital's underground parking lot. Naturally Samantha had given him her father's home address in case the man needed to pick up some supplies or personal effects, so at least he knew where he was going next.

He just hoped Pete McKnight was there waiting for him.

–

*Margalla Hills, Pakistan*

The truck which according to Malak was 'not far from here' proved to be over two miles away. An easy 20-minute march under normal circumstances, but made substantially more difficult by the rough terrain and poor visibility.

The arms dealer and his companions were as sure footed as mountain goats and almost as nimble, easily leaping across narrow gullies or descending unstable scree slopes like they were paved highways. Even Anya, no stranger to terrain like this, was hard pressed to keep up.

Sure enough, they at last dropped onto a rocky, unpaved track that somewhat resembled a road. It was hardly pristine blacktop, but compared to the difficult ground they'd just covered, it felt like they were walking on air.

A few hundred yards further down this trail they found a pair of vehicles parked nose to tail. The one at the back was a panel van of some kind, most likely of Russian origin, while the vehicle in front was an old model Isuzu Trooper 4 x 4. One was certainly more suited to this kind of terrain than the other, and Drake had a feeling he knew which one Malak and his mates would be driving away in.

A fourth member of Malak's crew was guarding the two vehicles, similarly armed with an AK assault rifle. He tensed a little as the group approached out of the darkness, but a bird-like whistle from Malak was enough to allay his fears.

'Everything you asked for is in the van,' the arms dealer explained. 'You want to check it?'

Anya nodded. 'Of course.'

Moving forward, he unlatched the van's rear doors and pulled them open. Sure enough, several large packing boxes had been laid out in the cargo area, fixed against the walls with bungee cords to keep them from spilling out during the rough drive up here.

Drake and Anya moved towards the van at the same time, each eager to verify that the gear they needed was present and correct. Anya gave him a sidelong look, perhaps not expecting him to get involved, though she voiced no objection as he went to work on the first box.

The *Alamo* had been well provisioned in terms of weapons and gear, some of which they'd brought along with them, but there was only so much they could transport into the country by parachute drop. Staging a complex house assault of the kind Drake had in mind, not to mention gathering the supporting elements needed to sustain the team during their time here, required more than they could be reasonably expected to carry. That was where Malak came in.

Five minutes of careful examination was enough to satisfy Drake that everything was as it should be. He certainly couldn't find any obvious flaws or defects that would warn him this deal had gone sour. Of course, some of the equipment was impossible to test properly without actually using it, but as far as he could tell Malak had been true to his word. Whoever this man was, he must have had quite a network of contacts within the military to make this happen. No wonder the guy could afford to fork out for his winning smile.

'This will do,' Anya decided, closing the box she'd been examining.

'Such praise.' Malak grinned at her, then gestured to the Russian van. 'The van is yours as well. The tank is almost full, and the engine is in good order.'

'It's not stolen, I assume?' she prompted. The last thing they needed was to be pulled over by Pakistani police for car theft.

The weapons and equipment were of course another matter. Drake was under no illusions that they'd been obtained anything close to legally, but that didn't matter. Once they were done here, everything here would be left behind.

'What do you take me for?' Malak asked, though his playful words elicited no response from her. 'So, we are done here?'

'We are,' she confirmed. Reaching into her webbing, she handed over a thick wad of US dollars. Given that the Pakistani rupee was currently worth somewhere between very little and fuck all, the choice of currency made sense to Drake. Malak certainly wasn't complaining as he thumbed through the greenback, checking it hadn't been padded out with one-dollar bills.

'I will not insult you by counting it,' he said as he pocketed the bills, despite the fact he'd pretty much done just that.

A quiet order in Pashto prompted his comrades to return to the 4 x 4 up front, and a moment later the engine shuddered into life. With their business concluded, they were no doubt eager to get out of here.

Lingering a moment longer, Malak took a step towards Anya. 'I don't know what you have in mind here in Pakistan, but I wish you luck.' He glanced at Drake and the others, acknowledging their existence for the first time. 'All of you.'

The woman nodded curtly. 'And you, Malak.'

Drake doubted Anya would lose much sleep over Malak's welfare, but he sensed a certain grudging respect for the man all the same. It was more than most people earned from her, at least.

Leaving them to it, Malak returned to the 4 x 4 and clambered up into the passenger seat. With only one eye, Drake imagined his night-driving skills weren't exactly top notch. The main beams flicked on then, and with a throaty growl the vehicle took off down the road, the glow of its headlights soon lost as it disappeared around a bend in the valley.

Once more the group were alone, albeit far better armed and equipped than they had been before, and with a vehicle to get them where they needed to be. It was time to make use of it.

'We'd better be on our way,' Drake said, pointing towards the van's rear doors. 'Cole, up front with me. Everyone else in the back. Let's move.'

'I'll drive,' Anya said.

Drake looked at her. 'You're a woman.'

Her expression made it plain she didn't like where this was going. 'Your point?'

'We're in an Islamic country.'

'So? Women can drive in Pakistan.'

'Yes, but it's the middle of the night. And this is a van, not a family saloon. And you're clearly a Western woman. You'd draw attention to us. Isn't that something you said we should avoid?'

Drake and Mason both had naturally dark complexions aided by much time spent outdoors in hot countries, and though they wouldn't fool anyone on close inspection, at night and from a distance they might just pass for locals. The same couldn't be said for their blonde haired companion.

Anya crossed her arms, saying nothing. The way she often did when she didn't want to concede a point. No doubt she was also aware that the whole group was watching to see how this little contest of wills played out.

Moving forward, Drake took her arm and gently steered her away from the others, lowering his voice so that only she could hear.

'I know this isn't how you're used to doing things, but I need you to work with me now, yeah?' he urged her. 'This isn't a competition. Believe me, you'll get your chance.'

Anya met his gaze, and for a moment he could have sworn he saw a flicker of amusement. It was hard to tell if she was mocking him, but it was preferable to outright hostility. 'Are you this diplomatic with your own team?'

Drake nodded to Frost, who was idly poking around in one of the boxes in the van's cargo area. 'I've learned to be.'

Christ knows, I've had plenty of practice over the years, he thought.

This time he definitely saw the beginnings of a smile. 'Fine. We do it your way,' she conceded. 'For now.'

With the matter reluctantly agreed on, she turned away, marched towards the van and clambered up into the rear compartment. Another obstacle overcome, Drake thought. He wondered how many more stood in their path.

'All right, the night's not getting any younger,' he said, pointing towards the vehicle. 'Get changed into your civvy clothes and get aboard.'

As the others removed the combat gear that would only draw attention in populated areas, Drake headed for the cab with Mason in tow.

'Played that one pretty cool, buddy,' the older man observed with a wry grin. 'Ever think about going into bomb disposal?'

Drake shot him a sidelong look. 'Probably safer than this.'

A closer inspection of the van confirmed his earlier suspicions about it being of Russian origin. It was a product of the Ulyanovsk Automobile Plant, a formerly state-owned enterprise dating back to the Soviet era. Externally it looked like a rounded, featureless rectangle resembling a loaf of bread on wheels. Indeed, its appearance had earned it the nickname *Bukhanka*, literally meaning 'loaf', amongst Soviet drivers.

Drake was familiar with them because the Russian military still used them as field ambulances, with only minor modifications. They weren't fast or elegant, but they used the same power plants as 4 x 4 military jeeps and were generally considered rugged and reliable vehicles. He hoped so, because the drive that lay ahead was not going to be easy.

The *Bukhanka*'s interior was as plain, functional and thoroughly aged as the outside, with cigarette burns on the upholstery and all manner of stains on the centre console that he preferred not to think about. Nonetheless, the engine fired up first time.

As the rear doors slammed closed, Drake engaged first gear and eased off the brake, beginning their unsteady, jolting journey towards Islamabad.

# Chapter 33

## Goodland, Kansas

It was about 200 miles from Denver to the small town of Goodland in Kansas – a three-hour drive according to Taylor's satellite navigation unit – but with only one brief refuelling stop and the judicious application of speed on the open highway, he made it there in a little over two.

It was just as well, because after traversing endless miles of flat open farmland that stretched all the way to the horizon, he was ready for a change of pace.

Arriving at the address given to him by Samantha, he brought his car to a stop outside the modest single-storey house and sat there, just observing the building and its surroundings. It seemed like a decent neighbourhood that was more or less representative of small town America: lots of big open lawns, painted fences and people carriers parked in wide driveways. A few stars and stripes wafting in the gentle breeze suggested some households had people serving in the forces.

The McKnight house was typical of others in the street. Low and compact, wood panelled – why people in one of the country's most tornado-prone states still made their houses from wood was beyond him – and in need of a fresh coat of paint. The lawn was overdue a cut as well.

There was no car in the driveway, but the garage door was closed. It was too early in the evening for the lights to be on, and blinds over the windows shielded the interior from view. If Pete McKnight was home, he was keeping a low profile.

Opening his door to get out, Taylor paused for a moment. Popping open his glove box, he pulled out the Beretta 9mm he always kept there, checked that there was a round in the chamber and the safety was engaged, then pushed the weapon down the back of his jeans. He was hoping to avoid trouble, but if it found him then he intended to be ready.

Stepping out onto the sidewalk, he locked the car and headed towards the house, his eyes scanning the porch area and the front door itself for any sign of forced entry. There were a few potted flowers laid out on the wooden decking, all shrivelled and dried up, but no signs of anything untoward.

Pausing by the door, he leaned in close to the window and peered inside, using his hand to shield his eyes. No sign of movement in the living room.

The TV was turned off, and there was nothing to indicate anyone had been there recently.

There was no doorbell, so he settled for knocking firmly on the front door.

No reply.

'Mr McKnight, it's Jack,' he called out. 'Sam sent me. Are you there, sir?'

Still no reply.

Glancing over his shoulder to check nobody was watching, he left the porch and circled around to the rear of the building. The back yard was in much the same shape as the front, with all signs pointing to a property that hadn't been lived in or maintained for several weeks at least.

A quick examination of the windows and back door suggested the building wasn't alarmed. The door was secured with a simple pin-tumbler style lock that a man with his training would have little trouble overcoming, given time and the right tools.

As it turned out, however, he didn't need to bother, finding a spare key hidden beneath a cracked plant pot. Hailing as he did from inner-city Pittsburgh, it never ceased to amaze him how trusting and naive people in these small towns could be.

Gaining entry, Taylor found himself in a small, cluttered kitchen. Lots of magazines, tools and unwashed dishes scattered around, none of which looked like they'd been used recently. A quick inspection of the refrigerator told the same story.

'Mr McKnight?' he called out one more time, just in case the man suddenly awoke to an intruder in his kitchen. Unsurprisingly there was no response.

Not wanting to leave any avenue unexplored, Taylor made a quick recon of the rest of the house, clearing each room one after the other until he was satisfied Pete McKnight wasn't here, and hadn't been for some time.

'Goddamn it,' he said under his breath, returning outside and locking the door.

Circling back around to the front of the house, he spotted a boy of perhaps ten years wheeling a bike along the opposite side of the street.

'Hey, kid,' he called out. 'You know the guy who lives here?'

The boy looked over. 'Mr McKnight? Yeah, I know him.'

'Seen him around lately?' Taylor asked without much hope.

'Don't think so. Why?'

Taylor was no longer listening. Fishing the phone out of his jacket, he hurriedly punched in Samantha's number and hit the dial button.

The connection seemed to take longer than usual, and he paced back and forth beside his car in agitation as a series of clicks and buzzes sounded in his ear. The call went straight to voicemail.

What a hell of a time to be ignoring calls, Taylor thought angrily.

'Sam, it's me. Your dad checked himself out of hospital before I could get there. I tried his place, but he's not home.' He sighed. 'I'm all out of options here. Give me a call back as soon as you get this.'

Hanging up, he glanced around one more time and shook his head. 'Where the hell are you, old man?'

# Chapter 34

Sitting on the hard, uncomfortable floor of the *Bukhanka* van as it chugged along a roughly paved road, Samantha McKnight let out a breath, trying hard to keep from worrying about her father. She assumed Taylor had picked him up by now, and was eager for confirmation that he was safe and well, but knew she couldn't risk powering up her phone with the rest of the team around.

So for now, she had little choice but to wait it out.

Just concentrate on the mission, she told herself over and over again. The mission was all that mattered now. It was the end, not the means. Once Cain was dead and Anya taken care of, then perhaps she could begin to contemplate a life afterwards. Perhaps, in some scarcely hoped-for reality, she could even salvage something from this.

Almost without being aware of it, she found her hand straying down to her abdomen, as if to protect the life that was growing within. She knew it was wrong to think of it that way when she might well have to end the pregnancy, but some scarcely understood part of her psyche already saw it as something precious, to be defended at any cost.

Those were dangerous thoughts to entertain, she knew. Yet try as she might, she couldn't quite silence them.

Having survived the almost impassable mountain track before the suspension or the unfortunate passengers buckled under the strain, they had mercifully found something resembling a real road, which had eventually brought them to the small town of Khanpur. There they had joined one of the main highways heading south.

Islamabad might have been the capital of Pakistan, but in reality it was little more than a district within a larger conurbation formed from the much older city of Rawalpindi. Two cities occupying the same space, radically different but inexorably intertwined.

This curious state of affairs had existed since the 1960s, when Islamabad had been constructed from scratch as a purpose-built capital for the newly independent country. With a simple grid street layout, wide tree-lined avenues and grand government buildings every other block, it had reminded Samantha a great deal of Washington D.C..

Its neighbour Rawalpindi was another matter, having grown organically over long centuries of expansion, conquest, ruin and reconstruction. Its roads were narrow, potholed and meandering, choked with vehicles of every make and model known to man, criss-crossed by haphazardly laid phone and power lines, and crowded in by market stalls, cafés, restaurants and shops. Dilapidated residential blocks, their balconies festooned with ancient satellite dishes and garish banners, seemed to lean in overhead as if caught in the process of falling.

And everywhere she looked there were people. Pedestrians darting in amongst the slow moving traffic, cyclists and moped riders squeezing through gaps they had no business attempting, beggars approaching unlucky motorists with hands outstretched, vendors hawking their wares to anyone in range, and uncountable numbers of citizens simply making their way around town. The overall impression thus conveyed was of a chaotic, intimidating, thronging mass of humanity.

'For fuck's sake,' Drake swore, leaning on his horn as an overloaded cattle truck lurched into their path, cutting him off. Normally he would shy away from doing anything that might attract attention at a time like this, but in such a chaotic environment it seemed that *not* blasting his horn every 30 seconds would mark them out as unusual.

'Can't say I envy you,' McKnight said as she crouched behind him to survey the scene beyond, for once relieved not to be driving.

He gave her a sidelong glance. 'I'm starting to wish we'd parachuted straight into the safe house after all.'

Reaching up, she gave his shoulder a gentle squeeze. 'How far out are we?'

Drake glanced up at a nearby street sign. One advantage of Pakistan's colonial history was that English was widely spoken here, to the extent that it was still officially taught in schools. More importantly, most road signs were perfectly legible, making the navigation, if not the actual driving, a little easier.

'Shouldn't be more than five or ten minutes, if we can get a clear run at it,' he replied, stamping on the accelerator and forcing his way between a pair of mopeds and a decrepit-looking taxi. 'For the record, I'm not responsible for any fatalities along the way.'

'Duly noted.' Despite herself, she couldn't help but smile as she eased herself back into a seated position in the cargo area.

Straight away she could feel a pair of eyes on her, and knew well enough to whom they belonged. Anya had said almost nothing throughout the journey, and that had suited her just fine. After her confrontation with the woman before their flight, and again after their landing, she was in no mood to exchange words with their dubious ally.

Nonetheless, the sensation of being watched continued unabated. Samantha shifted position, her discomfort growing as the minutes crawled by. No doubt Anya knew exactly what she was doing. Was she enjoying making her feel like this?

Irritated, she looked up at her adversary. Sure enough, Anya was watching her from the other side of the cargo hold. A monster lurking in the darkness; silent, unpredictable deadly.

'There a problem?' she asked.

Anya didn't answer right away. She rarely did, McKnight noticed, as if intent on drawing out the tension and discomfort.

'You seem nervous, McKnight.' She leaned forward a little, emerging into the light filtering through the windshield like a ghost suddenly turning corporeal. 'Maybe I should ask *you* if there is a problem.'

'How about you don't talk to me for the rest of this trip?' McKnight retorted. 'That's one problem solved.'

She saw a flicker of a smile then. 'People get nervous for all kinds of reasons at times like this. Worries about the mission, fear of capture, fear of letting the team down… Especially when they keep secrets from their friends.'

Don't lie to her, a voice in McKnight's head warned her. She'll know.

'You're not my friend,' she said, an edge of defiance in her voice. 'What business is it of yours?'

'It is my business, because there may come a time when I have to put my trust in you. I would hate to think that trust was misplaced.'

'Hey,' Frost interjected from the rear of the cargo area. 'Sam already told you she's done listening to you, and so am I. What part of "shut the fuck up" don't you understand?'

Anya's penetrating gaze shifted towards the young specialist. Her posture seemed to change somehow without moving, tensing up like a predator preparing to launch itself at its prey, and for a moment McKnight genuinely feared she might retaliate against Frost with more than words.

Then, just like that, she saw the muscles relax, the spring uncoiling as she eased herself back against the wall of the van. The monster disappearing back into the shadows.

'Heads-up!' Mason called from up front. 'Got a security gate coming up. Everyone stay down until we're clear.'

McKnight pressed herself against the wall of the vehicle, doing her best to disappear into the shadows like Anya as Drake brought the van to a halt and cranked down his window.

'Morning,' he said, forcing a cheerful air into his voice. 'Robert Douglas from Apex Deliveries. My company should have a unit set aside here.'

Their plan naturally required a base from which to operate. Hotels and apartments were out of the question, partly because they attracted too much attention but mostly because the team needed to be able to move weapons and equipment to and from the van. What they required instead was a big, secure internal space that could accommodate vehicles.

The best solution they'd come up with was to take out a short-term rental agreement on a small warehouse, situated in one of the many industrial estates in Rawalpindi. It had been easy enough to organize at short notice using a fake company name, claiming they were moving to new offices and so needed a place to store their supplies and remaining stock during the transition. Paying a month in advance had helped grease the wheels somewhat as well.

McKnight listened to some muffled conversation coming from somewhere outside, likely from the facility's night watchman. She hoped they didn't require an inspection of vehicles coming in, otherwise they were in trouble.

'Identification? No problem,' Drake said, handing over his fake passport along with a business card for Apex Deliveries. 'Our Islamabad branch is closed, obviously, but feel free to call head office for confirmation. The number's at the bottom there.'

More muffled voices, followed by silence. What was going on? Was the night watchman logging their details on his computer? Was he calling a supervisor, or even the police? The seconds crawled by, seemingly stretching out into minutes while the three passengers sat in the darkness of the van's cargo hold, not moving, barely breathing.

'Look, I don't want to be a pain, but we've got a long day ahead tomorrow,' Drake said, sounding bored and tired. 'Could we move this along a bit?'

He might be feigning the bored labourer, but McKnight could practically feel the tension radiating out from Drake. He was playing a dangerous game now, risking the wrath of the one man who had the power to admit or refuse them access to the warehouse.

Finally she saw Drake reach out the window, then hand his documents and a set of keys over to Mason in the passenger seat.

'Unit Five? Take the first left, then all the way to the back? Sounds good, I'm sure we'll find it,' he said, all smiles now. 'Thanks for your help.'

McKnight couldn't help but let out a breath as they pulled away from the security gate, relief flooding through her. Another obstacle overcome.

It didn't take long to find the building in question and for Mason to leap out, unlock the door and guide them into the warehouse. As soon as they were inside, he hauled the big doors closed on their rollers, shielding the interior from outside view.

No sooner had Drake brought the van to a stop and killed the engine than Frost stood up and unlatched the doors, allowing harsh electric light to flood the van's interior.

'Home sweet home,' the young specialist said, leaping down from the van's cargo bed and glancing around. Her voice seemed to echo in the cavernous space.

'For the next 24 hours, anyway,' Mason replied, having finished securing the warehouse doors.

McKnight felt like a cave dweller emerging into the sun for the first time, squinting in the bright light as she too jumped down, her boots making contact with solid concrete.

This had been the smallest unit available that could accommodate their needs, but even this modest warehouse easily dwarfed the single van parked within its vast interior. Illuminated by arc lights mounted high up in the roof frames, one or two of which were flickering as they struggled to stay lit, she was afforded a decent all-round view of their new base of operations.

It was easy to see why the rental had been cheap. The walls and ceiling were corrugated metal built around a steel framework; pretty much standard construction for a building of this type. The floor was poured concrete, roughly finished, and studded with pieces of paper, packaging and cigarette butts that had been pressed into its surface by the passage of countless vehicle tyres.

A well-used storage space, then, and judging by the visible rust marks that streaked the walls and, more worryingly, many of the support beams, one that had seen better days. The air smelled of damp and mould, undercut with old engine oil and other less savoury odours that she preferred not to contemplate.

Towards the far end of the cavernous space, an area had been partitioned off with dented plasterboard walls in which light switches had been crudely wired, presumably to serve as offices or work areas. In their case, however, it would likely be used for sleeping, eating and washing.

It was hardly the best field ops station she'd worked in, but it would serve.

The sound of boots hitting the ground behind told her that Anya had just exited the vehicle. She resisted the urge to turn around or move aside, thinking somehow it would be perceived as a sign of weakness. Ignoring her, the older woman simply brushed past, bumping her shoulder without uttering a word.

'All right, we've got a lot to do and not much time,' Drake announced. 'Let's get this equipment unloaded and prep the van. I want to recon the target while it's still dark.'

'I'm on it,' Mason replied, unlatching the straps holding the first box in place.

'Keira, you're with me. I want to test the Judas code.'

'Why not? Sounds like fun.'

'That's what I want to hear,' Drake said. 'The rest of you, focus on getting this place up and running. We need a functioning ops room by the time I get back, but weapon and equipment checks have priority.'

'Would you like a hot tub and cocktail bar while we're at it?' Mason asked.

'Only if it does pina coladas,' he called over his shoulder.

Anya, however, was not interested in their banter, and caught Drake's arm as he strode past. 'I'm coming with you.'

He shook his head. 'Bad idea. You're needed here.'

Her grip tightened a little. 'I didn't come halfway around the world to unload equipment, Ryan.'

Drake eyed her sceptically. 'This is just a recon trip. The fewer of us there, the better.'

Anya shrugged, as if his concerns meant nothing. 'I am going all the same. I want to see the safe house for myself.'

For a moment Drake seemed poised to argue the point further. But, perhaps sensing that they'd been in conflict with each other enough already, he reluctantly nodded acquiescence.

'Fair enough,' he conceded, removing his arm from her grasp. 'We leave in five, so if there's anything you need to do, I'd do it now.'

'The only thing I need to do is get there. Anything else can wait.'

Feeling no need to respond to that, Drake consulted his watch. 'All right, we've only got a few hours of darkness left. Let's make them count.'

As the others went to work, McKnight waited until Anya was out of earshot before approaching him. 'Ryan, listen... be careful out there.'

'Always am.'

'That's not what I meant.' She nodded towards Anya, who was cautiously exploring the office area at the back of the warehouse. 'I mean, be careful around *her*.'

Drake eyed her curiously for a moment, wondering what had prompted this unease. But sensing how much it meant to her, he nodded.

'All right, Sam.' Turning away, he hesitated, glancing over his shoulder with a wry grin. 'Hold the fort. If we're not back in an hour, call the president.'

Even she couldn't help but smile at that.

# Chapter 35

*Islamabad, Pakistan*

It was always a strange experience seeing a target for the first time with your own eyes, after poring over blueprints and satellite images for hours or in some cases days, committing every possible detail to memory. Whatever one's mental image, nothing compared to actually being there.

Ryan and Anya were crouched on the rooftop of the apartment block they had identified on the map, situated about 70 yards west of the safe house. The rooftop access door had been locked and alarmed when they arrived, but a little lock-picking and electrical bypassing on Drake's part had taken care of both minor impediments, allowing them to creep out onto the flat roof unseen.

By now it was well after midnight, and even the bustling city of Islamabad had begun to settle down. Traffic on the streets had all but vanished, and though some houses and apartments were still illuminated from inside, it seemed most citizens had turned in for the night.

'How does it look?' Anya asked, crouched down beside him at the low parapet that encircled the rooftop. For the past minute or so, she had been busy fitting a metal restraining piton used by professional climbers into the wall opposite, knowing they would need it tomorrow night. But with her work done, she was eager to learn more about their target.

Adjusting the focus slightly on his camera's telescopic lens, Drake shifted his gaze along the building's perimeter.

'Cameras are right where they're supposed to be,' he said, taking a quick photograph of each security camera as he found it.

He angled the camera upwards, focussing on a big satellite dish fixed to the roof. Ostensibly it was nothing more than a commercial TV receiver, little different from the countless others in this neighbourhood, but Drake was willing to bet it was a satcom array for sending and receiving secure communications.

'There's some kind of antenna cluster mounted on the roof. It's not much of a target but it should make a good grapple point, and there's a rooftop terrace beneath it.' Sure enough, a closed doorway at one end of the terrace led deeper into the house. 'That's our way in.'

'Is it strong enough to take our weight?' she asked.

'We'll find out tomorrow night.' Drake smiled as he spotted another little detail that no construction blueprint could have warned him about. 'Looks like they stuck broken glass on top of the perimeter wall. It's the personal touches that really add character to a place.'

Fortunately for them, they wouldn't have to scale that wall to get inside. Drake had a far more audacious entry plan in mind.

Reaching for the radio unit hidden inside his jacket, Drake hit the transmit button. 'Unit Two, what's your sitrep? Over.'

'Still working on it, One,' Frost's voice crackled through the little radio earpiece he was wearing. 'Stand by.'

'How much time do you need?'

'I'm sorry, would you like to take a shot at this?' she hit back irritably. 'You'd be surprised to know this isn't like turning on the kitchen light. So stand by and let me do my job.'

'Very professional, Two.'

Frost was currently positioned a few hundred yards away, trying to tap into a local telephone junction box. It wasn't an easy task, but it was necessary if she was to wrest control of the safe house's formidable security system. As she had explained, a hardline connection was the only way to make it work.

'Any movement inside?' Anya asked, concentrating on matters closer at hand.

Drake shifted his focus to the upper storey windows, which were big full-length affairs designed to provide optimal views over the city. A couple of external lights were burning, but otherwise the house was shrouded in darkness. 'Looks quiet. No sign of activity.'

'Cain's security team will likely arrive a few hours before the meeting to sweep the place for bugs,' Anya agreed. 'Then we will know it's going ahead.'

'Sounds about right. Then we just have the small matter of fighting our way through them.'

'That won't be easy. He will likely be well protected.'

He nodded. 'Standard protective detail for a bigwig like him is half a dozen agents, suited and booted. Low key but packing plenty of firepower.'

Having served with the Agency for several years, he was well versed in their protocols. All of his operatives would be wearing Kevlar vests, and armed with a mixture of semi and fully automatic weapons, probably MP5-Ks for easy carrying and concealment, plus fragmentation and stun grenades if they were feeling creative.

'I would expect more,' she countered. 'Not to mention that his Pakistani contact is likely to bring his own detail.'

Drake had feared as much. That was a lot of guns for a small assault team to go up against. The potential for a massacre was frighteningly high.

He glanced sidelong at her. 'Listen, you've been around a while.' Seeing her look, he added, 'And I mean that as a compliment. You've seen and done all there is to do in this game. Be honest – did you ever go up against something like this?'

Anya pursed her lips, considering it. 'No,' she decided. 'Not like this.'

He'd asked for honesty, and sure enough she'd given it to him. Even if he didn't like the answer.

'And there I was, starting to worry,' Drake remarked with dry humour, turning his attention back to surveying the house. 'But look on the bright side – this is another feather in your cap. Assuming we live through it.'

'Are you actually enjoying this?' she asked, surprised by his flippant remark.

He shrugged, his first instinct being to dismiss her question as a simple misunderstanding of his intent. And yet, when he paused to consider it, he had to admit that things had been different for him lately. He felt, if not exactly enthused, then certainly more focussed, more driven, more *connected* than he had in a long time.

He had a purpose now; a mission, an objective to strive towards. The danger and challenges that stood in his way were problems that he would overcome. The enemy he faced, though cunning and ruthless, was something real and tangible to pit himself against.

'I'd rather fight than hide,' he said without looking around. 'We tried that already. Didn't work out too well.'

'Since we are being honest with each other, there was something I wanted to ask you.' Anya hesitated then, searching for the right words. 'You questioned what I would do once this was all over, and maybe you were right to do it, but did you ever ask that of yourself?'

Drake should have been able to reel off a dozen answers for her. A few days ago he might well have been able to, but now...

Now he found it hard to picture anything beyond their objective tomorrow night, as if Downfall were an end rather than a means. Was that the truth of it, he wondered? All that talk about not wanting to end up like Anya, about trying to protect the life he'd created for himself in Marseille, about having something to go back to once this was all over... How real had it actually been?

Or was there another reason he found it so hard to focus on the future, he wondered? A reason much closer at hand?

Mercifully, his earpiece crackled into life then, breaking the awkward silence. 'Unit Two. Ready to turn out the lights.'

Drake let out a breath, relieved both at her success and the welcome interruption. 'Copy that, Two. Do it.'

For the next few seconds, nothing at all happened. Cars cruised along on the nearby roads, dogs barked off in the distance, muffled music resounded from inside houses and apartments, and air conditioning outlets hummed away. The world around them continued on as normal, unaware of the clandestine work being done right in their midst.

Drake was oblivious to all of this, however. All of his attention was focussed on the surveillance camera mounted on the wall of the distant safe house, willing the indicator light to switch off as the seconds crawled by with agonizing slowness.

'Come on, come on,' he whispered.

Every moment that passed decreased their chances of success.

He couldn't rightly say how much time had passed. Then, just like that, the little red indicator light mounted in the side of the unit blinked off.

'That's it,' he called out, hardly believing it had worked. 'Two, what's your sitrep?'

'I'm in, One. It's a little clumsy to operate, but I've got it all – phones, door locks, cameras. The code works.'

Drake let out a breath, hardly believing it. It wasn't going to be easy, and there were at least a dozen things that could still go wrong and spell doom for their mission, but it was at least possible. That was enough for now.

'Then we have what we need here,' he concluded. 'Pack it up, Two. We'll meet at the rally point in five. Over.'

'Understood, One. I'm on it. Out.'

Turning to face Anya, Drake gave her a nod. 'No rest for the wicked. Let's go.'

She wasn't inclined to argue as he packed up his gear and retreated back into the stairwell, closing the door behind but leaving the alarm disabled. It would save time when they returned tomorrow night.

Exiting the apartment block, Drake turned right and hurried back along the street with Anya following close behind, a drab coloured *shemagh* pulled up over her head to cover her face and distinctive blonde hair. In this part of the world, a Western woman walking the streets at night would attract all kinds of attention they didn't need.

'You know, you're surprisingly resourceful when it comes down to it. Is this how you ran all your Shepherd missions?' Anya asked, curious.

'Fuck, no,' Drake snorted, keeping a wary eye on their surroundings. 'I'm winging it here. Normally we'd have satellite recon, drones, thermal imaging and about a week of planning time. Why, how did you do things?'

'We worked for a living. We didn't rely on computers for everything.'

Drake rolled his eyes. 'Jesus, you're starting to sound like my dad.'

He couldn't see her expression from where he was, but he could practically feel those steely blue eyes boring into the back of his head.

The *Bukhanka* was sitting parked in an alleyway off the main road about 50 yards further down, and he was relieved to find it untouched as they approached. He'd been loath to leave the vehicle unguarded, but there hadn't been much choice. Anyway, it was hardly a top-end Ferrari. In an affluent neighbourhood like this, there wasn't much chance of someone stealing such a dilapidated vehicle.

'Unit Two is en route,' Frost's voice crackled in his ear. 'Be there in 60 seconds.'

'Copy that, Two,' Drake replied. 'We're standing by at—'

'Don't move!' a hard, commanding voice called out from his left.

Drake's head snapped around just in time to see a man emerge from the shadows on one side of the alley. A moment later, a second man appeared from behind the van.

It seemed that both had been lying in wait for them.

Immediately Drake's body tensed up, muscles readying themselves for the sudden, explosive bursts of movement and aggression that might soon be required of them. At that same instant, his mind went into threat assessment mode, eyes sweeping between the two potential enemies, taking in as much detail about them as possible.

Both men were wearing matching uniforms of some kind, but they didn't look like military or even the blue and khaki of the local police force. Intelligence operatives would likely have been dressed in plain clothes, so that ruled them out. Likewise, a potential carjacking was also unlikely for the same reason.

If he had to guess, he'd say these men were private security, hired to patrol the neighbourhood and keep it clear of undesirables. An old, shitty-looking panel van of Russian manufacture lying abandoned in an alleyway had likely caught their attention.

'You've got to be shitting me,' Drake said under his breath, hardly believing their misfortune at being caught off guard by a pair of rent-a-cops.

'Hands up!' the first man demanded. 'Both of you.'

The arrival of these men might have been a cruel joke, but there was nothing funny about the pair of square framed automatics they had trained on him. Doing his best to examine them in the dim light, he reckoned them to be Glock 17s; a favourite of police forces worldwide.

One of the first handguns to be made of synthetic polymer rather than standard gunmetal, the Glock had quickly become well regarded because of its lightweight design, resistance to rust and dirt, and its accuracy. They came in lots of different calibres, and in the poor light it was impossible to tell what kind of rounds these weapons were chambered for, but it made little difference. At such close range even a 9mm weapon was more than enough to take down himself and Anya, neither of whom were wearing body armour.

Drake's first instinct on seeing them had been to go for his own concealed weapon, but one look at the security guards was enough to persuade him otherwise. Their fingers were on the triggers. It wouldn't take more than one sudden move to start them shooting. And even if he and Anya survived the encounter, an armed confrontation on the streets just hours before the house assault would likely see the entire meeting abandoned.

The fact that nobody had started dying yet suggested Anya was of like mind. How long she stayed that way, however, would likely depend on how things played out in the next few seconds.

'Woah! It's okay, guys. It's okay,' Drake said, raising his hands and doing his best to look as unthreatening as possible. Just a scared tourist caught off guard by two armed cops. 'Take it easy. We're not armed.'

'Is this your van?' the man on his left demanded, his English surprisingly good for low-rent private security. He looked a little older than his companion, and was likely the decision maker of the two. In that case, he was the one Drake needed to win over.

Drake nodded emphatically. 'Yeah, that's right.'

'What are you doing here?'

'We're from Vancouver,' he began, feigning his best Canadian accent.

The golden rule at moments like this was never claim to be American or British. Between them, they'd bombed and invaded half the Muslim countries in the world, and pissed off a lot of people in the process. Drake always chose countries like Canada, Australia or New Zealand – neutral, inoffensive English-speaking nations that nobody really gave a shit about.

'We're on vacation in Islamabad, and we have friends who live near here. We just stopped by for dinner.'

Why a couple on vacation would be driving a beat-up old utility vehicle instead of a rental car was another matter, but he was gambling that these men were unlikely to detain foreign nationals without good reason.

'I see,' he said, lowering his Glock a little. The look of suspicion in his eyes made it clear he wasn't buying it. 'Then you will not mind if I check with your friend. I am sure he can confirm your story. What is his name and address?'

Drake chewed his lip, knowing this was going to be tough to explain away. Just their luck to run into the one rent-a-cop in the world who actually cared about his job.

'It's late,' he said, stating the obvious. 'He's probably in bed already, and I'm sure he wouldn't appreciate security knocking on his door in the middle of the night. I'd rather not trouble him with this.'

That gave him pause for thought. Detaining potential burglars was one thing, but disturbing and harassing the very residents who paid his wages was another.

'Then you can at least give me his name and address,' he decided, opting for a compromise. 'I can check with our controllers.'

The guy had him, and they both knew it. But before he could say anything further, Anya weighed into this discussion.

'Look, it's late, we're tired and we'd like to get back to our hotel,' she said, adopting an accent much like his. 'You've got no right to detain us. So are you going to step aside and quit harassing us, or are we going to have to take this up with your boss?'

Drake glanced at her, giving her a sharp look that warned against further provocation. She was playing a risky game right now, and there was no telling how they might react to such a blatant challenge to their authority, especially from a woman.

'We are here to protect the safety of our residents, miss,' he replied, hiding behind official policy. 'I must see some identification. I will not ask again.'

Anya shook her head. 'I haven't got time for this. Get lost, go bother someone else.'

With that, she strode forward with her head high, making straight for the van before Drake could stop her. He knew that such blatant defiance was likely to lead a confrontation, and suspected that was her intention.

Sure enough, it was the younger of the two guards who took the initiative. Moving forward to block her path, he raised his weapon, pointing it right in her face. A young man, full of bravado and pride, who wasn't about to let a woman disrespect him.

It was likely to be the last mistake he ever made.

'Get back,' he snapped, brandishing the Glock as if he were a gang member defending his territory. 'Now!'

Drake knew then that there was only going to be one way out of this. Reluctantly he gave Anya the faintest nod of acknowledgement as the guard closed in one her. There was no need to speak. Each knew what the other was thinking, what had to be done. It was just a question of timing.

She waited until he was almost on her, a set of handcuffs clutched in his free hand, before springing her trap. Her right hand shot out, grasping the frame of the Glock and jerking it backwards, wrenching it free of his grip before his finger could tighten on the trigger.

Even as she did this, she struck upwards with the flat palm of her left hand, catching him on the point of his chin. The concussive effect of having one's jaw slammed upwards into their skull was not to be underestimated. Drake had seen everyone from boxers to seasoned operatives go down with a single hit like that, and this young security guard was no different. As his head snapped back with the force of the blow, he let out a low groan and began to topple.

Drake didn't wait around to see what happened next. Already the first man was swinging his weapon towards Anya, instinctively acting to protect his injured comrade.

Taking a couple of steps forward to bring him in range, Drake kicked out with his boot, catching the man's right knee with a powerful lateral strike. The knee joint simply isn't designed to bend in that manner, and Drake could practically hear the cartilage and tendons popping as they gave way under the blow. Unable to support his own weight, the man began to topple sideways, looking almost confused by what was happening.

The weapon, however, was still a threat that needed to be removed. Sweeping his right arm upwards, Drake managed to catch the automatic from below, knocking it clean out of the man's grasp before he could fire.

He almost felt bad about what happened next. Grasping his olive green shirt to prevent him falling to the ground, Drake turned the guard's head towards him so that it presented the optimal target. There was no need for a dramatic haymaker punch that would take time to draw back and might actually give his opponent a chance to dodge or block. That was pure fantasy. The reality was that a short, sharp jab straight to the chin, delivered with the force and precision that years of training had endowed him with, was enough to put his adversary down.

He released his grip of the man's shirt then, allowing his limp body to slump forward in a heap. His heart was thumping hard and urgently in his chest, his body now thoroughly pumped up by the violent if one-sided confrontation. Letting out a breath to calm himself, he turned towards Anya. Her own opponent was similarly incapacitated, and even as he watched, she was stooping down to retrieve the same handcuffs he'd intended to use on her.

'What the hell was that?' he snapped, irritated that she'd pre-empted him, that they'd been forced to defend themselves like this.

Anya looked at him in genuine bewilderment. 'What do you mean?'

'I could have talked our way out. Instead you had to leap in and fuck it up.'

'He attacked me. I defended myself.'

'Bollocks. You provoked him. You know you did.'

The woman let out a short, exasperated breath. 'There was no talking our way out of this one, Ryan. We both knew this had to happen the moment they found us.'

Drake opened his mouth to respond, but before he could say anything, he was interrupted by the sound of approaching footsteps. Drawing his weapon, he was just in time to see Frost appear at the entrance to the alley.

Surveying the scene, her response was typically sarcastic. 'All good here?'

Drake snatched the Colt Cobra up from the ground. 'We ran into some trouble.'

'No shit.'

He ignored her. 'Give us a hand, Keira. We need to get them off the street.'

Clearly they couldn't leave them here. They might have been neutralized for now, but sooner or later they would wake up, and they were sure to be mightily pissed off when that happened.

'Great, but where are you planning on taking them?' the technical specialist asked, moving forward to help. 'I don't think the others are ready for guests back at the warehouse.'

Anya avoided Drake's gaze as she hooked her arms beneath the young man, dragging him towards the rear of the van. Whatever she was thinking, she seemed content to keep it to herself for now.

In any case, he had his mind on other matters. Frost was right that they couldn't afford to hold these men captive. They were dangerously short-handed already, and the possibility that two prisoners could escape or raise the alarm was a risk they simply couldn't afford to take.

'I've got an idea,' Drake said, rifling through the older guard's pockets until he found what he was looking for – a wallet filled with some crumpled rupees, a couple of bank cards and a driver's licence.

# Chapter 36

This was as good a place as any.

Drake brought the *Bukhanka* to a halt on a patch of rough, scrub-covered dead ground just off the narrow country road they'd been following. They'd been driving for about 30 minutes, and were by now a good 15 miles outside Islamabad. The last settlement of any sort they'd seen had been a little village several miles back, which was far enough off the grid that their house lights had been powered by diesel generators.

In short, they were in about as remote a spot as one could feasibly be.

For a moment or two he just sat there staring ahead into the darkness, silently debating the wisdom of what he was about to do. It wasn't an ideal solution, but then, nothing about this mission was.

Just get it done.

Having reached a decision, he swung his door open and stepped outside, circling around to the rear of the van. Anya followed him.

Both security guards had awoken by now, and both were handcuffed and gagged. Gone was the bravado and pride that had prompted them to act so hastily before. As Drake hauled open the rear doors, their dark eyes swung around to face him, filled with fear and trepidation.

'Out,' he ordered. 'Let's go.'

Struggling up with difficulty, both men jumped down from the van on shaky legs, the older one nursing a noticeable limp after Drake's takedown. Frost followed close behind. She still had them covered, though it was clear neither man posed a threat now.

The younger one was mumbling something, his eyes shining with tears, but the gag made it impossible to make out his words. Drake had little doubt, however, that he was begging for his life. The older man, to his credit, remained stoically silent. Either he was too proud to beg, or he was wise enough to realize it would make no difference.

Drake stepped forward to address the two captives. 'Listen up, both of you. I'm going to ask you some questions, and I want honest answers. Nod if you understand.'

Both men exchanged a look that was part confusion, part cautious hope. They'd stepped down from the van expecting to be executed, and now they were apparently being offered something else. Realizing the opportunity that might just have presented itself, both men nodded agreement.

'Were there other security patrols on duty in that area tonight?' Drake asked.

After a moment or two, they shook their heads.

'Did either of you radio in to report the van you found?'

Again, it was a negative.

He knew he had to ask the next question, had to give them a chance to prove themselves.

'Take a moment to reflect on the fact that we know who you are and where you live.' Drake held up the two wallets they'd confiscated for emphasis, and saw the naked fear in their eyes. 'If we let you go, are you going to tell anyone about what happened tonight?'

There was no hesitation this time. Both men couldn't have been more emphatic.

Drake glanced at Anya, who seemed unmoved by what she'd heard. Gifted as she was with the ability to detect deception, he imagined she would have been quick to let him know if she thought they were lying.

Making his decision, Drake pointed off into the darkness, where the landscape seemed to have formed a depression running generally north-east, likely an ancient river channel that had long since dried up. It was the kind of topographical highway that men could follow with ease even in pitch darkness.

'I want you both to start walking in that direction. Don't look back and don't turn aside. Keep going until sunrise, then you're free to go home. If you do as I say and keep your mouths shut, I give you my word you'll never see us again. But if you tell a soul about what really happened tonight, we *will* find you, and we *will* make you wish we'd killed you. Now, think very carefully about this, because once you make that choice there's no going back. Do you really want to be dead heroes for the shitty minimum wage they're paying you?'

Both men exchanged a look. The kind of look only condemned men offered a last-minute reprieve could share. Their simultaneous head shakes came a moment later, and he didn't blame them one bit. In their position, he would likely do the same.

Drake drew his weapon and gestured towards the river bed. 'Then get moving.'

They needed no further prompting. Turning aside, they hurried away from their captors as fast as their legs would carry them, stumbling and limping across the uneven ground.

'Gutsy move, man,' Frost said, watching them go. Nonetheless, it was clear she approved of his decision. 'You know there's no guarantee they—'

Her voice was drowned out by the heavy thump of a silenced pistol discharging, and she let out a gasp as the older of the two guards jerked violently, then fell to the ground in a heap, like a puppet with its strings cut. Half a second later, a second shot rang out, and a cloud of red mist sprayed from the top of the younger guard's head. Without making a sound, he stumbled forward and collapsed in similar fashion next to his comrade.

Neither man got up, and they never would.

'Jesus Christ!' Frost cried out, shocked by the cold-blooded murder she had just witnessed. 'What the fuck was that?'

Wisps of smoke still trailing from the barrel, Anya lowered her weapon, her face devoid of emotion. It was as if she'd done nothing more than turn out a light.

Tearing his gaze off the two dead men, Drake rounded on her, his eyes blazing with fury. 'What the hell do you think you're doing?'

'What had to be done,' she replied coldly. 'They were dead the moment they tried to arrest us. We both know that.'

'They were just a pair of scared civilians. They took our deal, for Christ's sake.'

'*Your* deal,' she corrected him. 'It was not yours to offer. There was always a chance they would have talked, and I don't deal in chances. Not with so much at stake.'

'You fucking—' Frost took a step towards her with her fists clenched, but stopped abruptly when the silenced automatic rose up to face her.

'Do not test me, Frost,' the older woman warned, finger resting lightly on the trigger. For a moment, Drake genuinely didn't know what she intended to do, and that scared him more than anything else.

Frost's eyes flicked from the weapon to Anya's face, and back again. The flare of anger had abated now with the threat to her own life, but it had been replaced by something colder and more dangerous.

Hatred, deep seated and abiding.

'Or what?' she spat. 'You'll kill me too?'

'I have done worse. Much worse, all for the sake of the mission,' Anya promised. 'That's the way it has to be now, for all of us. The second you let fear or remorse or compassion cloud your judgement, Cain has already won.'

The look Frost gave her was caught somewhere between contempt and, to Drake's surprise, grim amusement. 'You're fucking beautiful, you know that? For all your cunning and your experience and all that other bullshit, you still don't see what's in the mirror staring back at you.' She shook her head as if this were a joke whose punchline only she understood. 'You and Cain are just different sides of the same coin. No wonder you can't kill the son of a bitch – you've already become him.'

Drake saw the muscles in Anya's throat tighten, saw her mask of stern composure waver as Frost's scathing words, delivered not with malice but with pity, slowly sank in. And it was then that he saw her finger tighten just a little on the trigger.

'Anya,' he said, speaking quietly and gently. 'Keira isn't your enemy, and neither am I. You're better than this. Lower the gun before you do something we'll all regret.'

But Anya didn't respond. She remained frozen like that as the seconds crawled by, her body held tense and ready, her gun trained on the young woman standing not more than ten feet away. Standing this close, Drake could tell her breathing had quickened, her heart beating faster as adrenaline raced through her bloodstream.

'Don't do this.'

Finally his words seemed to penetrate through to her. He watched as the silenced automatic slowly dipped towards the ground, her taut muscles relaxing. In response his grip on his own weapon eased off. Whether Anya knew it or not, he had a round chambered and the safety disengaged, ready to be used.

Thank Christ she hadn't forced him to make that choice.

The uneasy stand-off was over. Giving Anya a look of simmering disgust, Frost turned away and started walking towards the fallen men.

'Where are you going?' Anya called after her.

'To give them a decent burial,' she spat. 'They deserve that much, at least.'

Anya sighed and looked at Drake. 'We don't have time for this.'

If she was expecting backup from him then she was to be sorely disappointed. Part of him knew she was right about the burial, just as part of him knew that letting those men go had been a risk they couldn't afford to take. But Drake didn't want to listen to those voices in his mind, didn't even want to acknowledge them at that moment. Or her.

'Here,' he said, thrusting the two dead men's wallets into her hand as he brushed past her. 'Keep these. You earned them.'

He didn't look back as he strode over to assist Frost in her grim task.

# Chapter 37

*White River National Forest, Colorado*

Pete McKnight took a breath, inhaling the chill mountain air as he stared out across the small lake, the sun's late afternoon rays sparkling across the still water. Beyond the tree-lined banks of the lake, the stark snow-covered peak of Mount Thomas rose up into the almost cloudless sky.

Wrapped up in several layers to keep the chill away from his ravaged body, he eased himself into the chair he'd built himself many years ago. Back when he'd still been young and strong. Back when he could still do such things.

He was sitting on the porch of the simple log cabin he'd purchased nearly two decades earlier, intending to use it as a summer hunting lodge. In reality he'd begun to see the simple two-room dwelling as more of a home than the place in Kansas ever had been. Here, he had nothing but good memories. Memories of long summer days spent with Samantha as a child, walking for miles together, talking of everything and nothing, sleeping out under the stars, doing the kind of things parents were supposed to do with their kids. Not a care in the world between the two of them.

One of his biggest regrets about the cancer treatment was that he'd rarely had the time or the energy to come here. It would have been nice to spend one more summer here with Samantha, just the two of them like it used to be, but he knew that was never going to happen. She was a grown woman now with her own path to follow, and little time to indulge a sentimental old man.

He took a sip of coffee, brewed on the old-fashioned iron stove that was about as sophisticated a cooking implement as he possessed here. It tasted good for all that, especially with the healthy splash of bourbon he'd added.

Screw it, he'd thought. Not like he had to worry about his liver.

He could feel the phone ringing in his pocket, the vibrations somehow making it through all the layers of clothing. He'd been tempted to throw it away when he came here, to disappear altogether. Going off the grid, as they were fond of saying these days. But he knew she would only worry if she couldn't contact him, so he'd kept it, knowing this conversation would come sooner or later.

Better to get it over with, he supposed.

Laying his coffee aside, he fished the phone out of his jacket. 'Yeah, Sam.'

'Dad, where the hell are you?' Her voice was hushed, urgent, edged with tension. 'Jack left a message, said you checked yourself out of hospital without him.'

'Yup,' he concurred.

'Why, for Christ's sake? I sent him to keep you safe.'

'I don't need some young man playing hero, putting himself at risk for me. I can look after myself just fine,' he promised her, glancing at the bolt-action hunting rifle resting against the cabin wall beside him. Good for killing reindeer; perhaps not so useful against men who could shoot back.

Pete McKnight smiled then. A bittersweet smile. 'I'm looking at the most beautiful view, Sam. The one we used to sit out and look at together. I wish you were here to see it.'

He wasn't going to say where he was over an open line, but she'd spent enough time there to know what he was referring to.

'You're sick, Dad,' she replied, her voice strained and brittle. 'You can't be alone out there. If something happens to you—'

'Sam, listen to me,' he cut in, a harder and authoritative edge in his voice now. 'I'm an old man. I know you don't want to believe it – shit, I don't even like to admit it – but it's true. I've had my time. You've given me a little more than I expected, and I'll always be grateful for that, but the rest is up to me now. Don't send your friend to come looking for me. Let me do this my way, and you concentrate on what you have to do. I'll be waiting for you here... when it's over.'

He heard a noise over the line then. He couldn't be sure because the signal wasn't great, but he thought it might have been his daughter choking back a sob. A sound that had always made his heart ache.

'I'm scared, Dad,' she finally said. 'I've tried to do the right thing, but... I don't know how this is going to play out. I don't know what's going to happen.'

It was heartbreaking to hear her like this, to know that she was afraid and probably in danger, and that there was absolutely nothing he could do to help her. A man was supposed to protect his daughter, but instead she'd ended up protecting him. That wasn't how it was supposed to be.

'Not everything's up to us. Only the man upstairs really knows how things are going to play out,' he said gently. 'But if you've done right by the people around you, they'll do right by you. Okay?'

She sniffed, doing her best to pull herself out of it. 'I hear you.'

'Damn right you do. And listen, don't go counting your old man out just yet,' he said, forcing optimism into his voice. 'I've made it this far. Maybe I've got a few more miles left in me.'

A sudden mechanical noise in the background told him something was happening on her end. 'I have go, Dad. I'm out of time here.'

'I love you, Sam,' he said quickly, wanting her to hear it one last time, but the line had already disconnected.

Letting out a sigh, Pete McKnight replaced the phone in his pocket. Whatever dangers or enemies his daughter now faced, he couldn't be there to help her. All he could hope was that other people were.

–

*Rawalpindi, Pakistan*

Wiping her eyes, Samantha pocketed her phone and drew a deep breath, trying to put aside thoughts of her father and compose herself. She had retreated to a quiet corner of the warehouse to make the call, despite the danger of discovery, because she'd needed to know where he was, whether he was safe. Well, now at least she had her answer.

He'd always been stubborn, always insisting on doing things his own way. Always seeing her as his little girl to be protected. She supposed she'd been naive to think he would change now.

A metallic grinding and clanking nearby told her that the warehouse doors were being opened to admit a vehicle. Drake, Frost and Anya were back from their recon mission.

Running her hands through her hair, she sniffed, took a couple of deep breaths and strode out of the empty office she'd been using for the call.

The van had just pulled to a halt in the centre of the warehouse. Shutting down the engine, Drake stepped down from the driver's cab while Frost and Anya exited through the rear doors. Judging by their tense expressions and the chilly atmosphere between all three operatives, it was safe to say all was not well.

'You're late,' McKnight observed as Drake approached. 'Something happen?'

'Ran into some trouble,' he said, avoiding eye contact. Never a good sign.

'What kind of trouble?'

That was when she saw it; saw his gaze flick towards Anya, who was already heading towards the makeshift ops centre that had been set up on the other side of the warehouse. As far away from Drake and the others as possible.

He shook his head, forestalling further questions on the subject. One thing she'd come to know all too well about Ryan Drake was that he didn't talk about something until he was good and ready. Clearly now was not the time.

At least his preoccupation meant he didn't notice the redness in her eyes, the tension in her body or the grief and worry that hung over her like a pall. She supposed she was thankful for that reprieve, short-lived though it might be. Drake trusted her implicitly, would never suspect her of wrongdoing, but even he must have sensed something was on her mind lately. How long would it be before he forced the issue?

'Keira's going to be uploading the images we took of the target area,' he said instead. 'Do me a favour and go see if she needs a hand.'

McKnight frowned, knowing full well Frost needed no assistance when it came to computers. 'But she hasn't—'

'Just do it, Sam,' he snapped, turning away and heading towards the weapons station that had been set up in his absence.

McKnight swallowed and nodded. Just a little while longer, she told herself. She only had to keep this up a little longer, and Cain would be dead. And all of this would be behind them.

–

Nearby, Cole Mason was busy checking the batteries on the team's encrypted tactical radios when he spotted Anya approaching. It was plain she'd come to speak with him, though he had no idea why.

'What do you need?' he asked, realizing she wasn't one for small talk.

As he'd expected, she wasted no time on greetings. 'Has there been any activity outside while we were gone?'

'Nothing. Quiet as a grave out there.'

He couldn't have known how poor his choice of words had been. 'All the same, we must set up a watch overnight. Why don't you go out there and walk the perimeter.'

Just like that, he thought. As if he were some lackey to be ordered around.

'Two reasons. First, there's no need for roving patrols.' He nodded to the laptop that had been set up on the table beside him, its screen split into four different video images showing the exterior of their warehouse from multiple angles. 'Wireless cameras transmitting on a secure Wi-Fi network – a little gift from Keira's bag of tricks. Set them up while you and Ryan were out sightseeing. Anybody tries to get near us out there, we'll see them coming a mile off.'

Anya leaned over, examining the laptop dubiously as if she expected it to spring up from the table and attack her. From what Drake had told him, she'd never been entirely comfortable with advanced technology and wasn't inclined to put her faith in it. People like Anya belonged to a different generation of operatives, but that didn't mean they were right.

'Chill,' he advised, wishing she would go away and let him get back to work. 'We've got enough to do as it is. Let technology do some of the work.'

'Technology can be fooled and overcome all too easily. This operation should be proof enough of that,' she said, fixing him with a disapproving look, as if she'd expected more from a former soldier like him. 'And it is only as reliable as the person behind it.'

Mason said nothing to that. In truth, he was growing increasingly uncomfortable under her scrutiny, as if she were a teacher and he a misbehaving student trying to cover up some illicit deed. The veteran operative had a way of making them all feel that way, and it wasn't something any of them appreciated.

'What was the second reason?' she asked, suddenly changing the subject.

'Huh?'

She gave him a look of strained patience. 'You said there were two reasons for not going outside. What is the second?'

Laying down the radio, Mason rose from his chair and looked her square in the eye. 'I take my orders from Ryan. Nobody else,' he said, speaking calmly and quietly. No need to provoke a confrontation. He just needed her to understand that he wasn't someone to idly fuck with or disrespect. 'We clear on that?'

Drawn up to his full height, he was a good five or six inches taller than her, and a great deal larger and stronger. None of those facts were lost on either of them in that moment. And yet, they seemed not to make the slightest impression on Anya. He detected no sign that she was intimidated by him.

She stared right back at him, holding his gaze as if he were a curiosity to be examined, a minor puzzle to be solved before she moved on to more important matters. And much to his chagrin, he began to feel oddly self-conscious and perhaps even a little foolish standing before her.

'You don't like me, do you, Mason?' she asked then, speaking candidly. 'You resent me. You resent what I am, what I've put you all through. You think I'm responsible for all this, and you blame me for getting you injured three years ago.'

Mason clenched his fists, finding it a little harder to keep his voice calm like before. 'You said it, not me.'

'You don't have to. I know it's true, and… I can't say I blame you.' She spread her hands in what might have been seen as a conciliatory gesture. 'So, what do we do about it?'

'Do about it?'

'I am short on friends in this team, it seems. Frost will never trust me, and as for McKnight… she has her own reasons for not accepting me. But you and I are soldiers, we both recognize the need for mutual respect. And since we might soon be going into battle, I would rather do it as your ally than your enemy. So I'll ask you again, Mason, what are we to do about this?'

He honestly couldn't tell if this was a genuine attempt at reconciliation, or simply another means of taking control of the situation. Mason wasn't by nature a vindictive man, didn't relish the thought of holding grudges, but considering everything Anya had put them through, everything they had risked for this woman without the slightest thanks or reward, he couldn't bring himself to make that leap of faith.

'The only thing we need to do is keep our distance,' he said at last, his gaze hardening. 'You do your job. Let me do mine. That'll work just fine for me.'

He saw what might have been a fleeting look of disappointment.

'It is your choice.' She took a step back, defusing the momentary tension, though he wasn't under any illusions that she was backing down or retreating. 'Don't let me waste any more of your time.'

Watching as she walked away, Mason let out a frustrated breath and sat back down. Whether he'd made his point or not, he didn't feel any better about it.

–

Drake meanwhile was busy in the makeshift armoury that had been set up in one corner of the warehouse. McKnight and Mason had clearly not been idle while he'd been out scouting the target area, and he was relieved to find that all of the gear and weapons they would be using on the house assault had already been unpacked, stripped down, checked and reassembled before being laid out on a pair of collapsible wooden tables for inspection.

At Drake's insistence, the assault group was going to be heavy on firepower when they went in, since they were almost certain to be outnumbered. But as Drake had learned many times both as a soldier and as a field operative, numbers alone counted for little. Surprise, aggression and a carefully coordinated plan could allow even a small force to overcome an enemy many times their size. Drake would be counting on all three factors when they breached that safe house.

This was going to be no stealthy recon mission, where shots were to be fired only as a last resort, but rather a short, brutal, bloody assault. Casualties would be high, so every shot had to count.

Their enemies were likely to be wearing body armour, which would deflect the fire from most pistols and other small arms. The obvious solution was to use heavier weapons with greater stopping power, but the problem was that their method of entry, as well as the tight confines of the building, wouldn't allow for the cumbersome assault rifles they needed.

Thus, Drake had been forced to go for the best compromise between size and firepower that he could find in the *Alamo*'s armoury – the Heckler & Koch MP7. Resembling a compact machine pistol with a collapsible stock and fore grip, the MP7 was one of the most cutting-edge firearms available anywhere in the world, able to be fired ambidextrously, aimed with one or two hands, and holding up to 40 rounds. The 30mm hardened steel ammunition it fired was capable of defeating most body armour at close range, while its largely polymer construction rendered the weapon lighter than many contemporary pistols. Combined with the silencers he'd brought along, they were capable of spitting out a hail of armour-piercing projectiles while making very little noise.

It wasn't just the assault team that were to be well armed. Resting on its collapsible bipod beside the smaller MP7s, like a lioness presiding over its brood of cubs, was the long menacing form of a Knight's Armament Company SR-25 semi-automatic sniper rifle. Their plan called for at least one member to cover the assault team as they made entry, and perhaps lay down cover fire as they pulled out.

For this task, he'd wanted a weapon with long range, heavy stopping power, and a high rate of fire, and in that regard he could think of nothing better than the SR-25. These rugged and reliable weapons had proven themselves on numerous battlefields over the past 20 years, most notably in the desperate street fighting in Mogadishu in 1993 where fewer than a hundred US Rangers and Delta Force operatives had held their own against several thousand Somali militia.

These primary weapons were supplemented with both stun and smoke grenades, USP 45 pistols – another heavy hitter – as backups, and breaching charges that could be rigged and blown within a matter of seconds. If they made it that far without the alarm being raised, Drake had the option of using them to blast into the room where Cain was meeting. Failing that, if Cain made it to the panic room then they could always try blowing it open, or even collapsing the building around him and burying the son of a bitch under hundreds of tonnes of rubble. If the man somehow survived all of that, it wouldn't be through lack of effort on Drake's part.

Picking up one of the MP7s, Drake pulled back the charging handle to check the chamber was empty, then raised it up to his shoulder and stared down the sight before squeezing the trigger. As expected, there was a sharp, crisp click as the firing mechanism engaged.

He knew such checks were unnecessary, knew that he'd already checked their weapons before leaving Marseille, but he went through it anyway. Focussing on something practical like this, something he understood and could control, served to take his mind off the disturbing events of this evening.

'I'll say one thing for you, Ryan,' a voice remarked, interrupting his thoughts. 'You certainly have a flair for the dramatic.'

Glancing around, Drake found Anya holding what looked like a long, bulky rifle with a metal grappling hook fixed into the end of the barrel, and an attached cable snaking into a plastic drum suspended beneath. It might have vaguely resembled a weapon, but in reality the Plumett AL-52 she was holding was more of a tool than a gun. A vital tool as it happened, which was why Drake had requested two of them from her contact Malak.

However, the dubious expression on Anya's face as she hefted the unwieldy device made it clear she was far from convinced by his plan. Not that he could blame her. It had all seemed quite rational on paper several thousand miles away, but being confronted with the reality of what they were about to attempt was disconcerting to say the least.

The idea of a grappling gun seemed like something out of a bad spy movie, and in truth the bizarre devices depicted by Hollywood as capable of lifting grown men up the sides of buildings were pure fantasy. But the principle of using compressed air to launch a hook with an attached line that could be climbed, or in this case zip-lined down, was perfectly valid. Devices like this had actually been in use for decades, dating back to the Second World War when soldiers used them to scale cliff-top defences at Normandy.

'Haven't you got somewhere else to be?' he asked, in no mood to converse.

She regarded him with a raised eyebrow, as if deciding on her plan of attack. 'We should talk. About what happened earlier.'

'I don't have time for this,' he said, turning away to resume his work.

'Then make time,' she said, grabbing his arm and turning him around to face her. 'Because if we have a problem, it needs to be fixed before—'

'The only problem here is you,' Drake accused, yanking his arm free. 'Don't you get it? You're pulling this team apart, turning them against each other, against *you*. And I don't know how to stop it.'

'You're angry with me—'

'Angry? Angry is what I'd be if you'd used the last of the toilet paper or deleted my favourite TV show.' He pulled her closer, lowering his voice. 'I watched you murder two men in cold blood tonight. What do you expect me to think of *that*?'

'I expect you to see the truth,' she said. 'You know it had to be done, Ryan. Lie to me if you must, but don't lie to yourself. Those two men would have gotten us all killed. *All of us.* So I killed them, because I knew you couldn't. Maybe that's the real reason I am here, to do the things the rest of you can't.'

'No,' he said, shaking his head. 'You went too far tonight.'

'What are you saying?'

'Killing those men wasn't for you to do, Anya. It was a decision we should have made together. But you still don't get that, and that's what worries me. You're here, you said you'd help, but the fact is don't trust any of us. Your fucking paranoia is going to get us all killed.'

'Paranoia has kept me alive this far.'

'And those people over there have kept *me* alive more times than I can remember,' Drake countered, pointing towards his team. 'I've been with them through more shit than even you can imagine. I'd trust any one of them with my life, any time.'

This time he saw a flicker of something behind those eyes. Pain. Old pain, long buried, but no less raw. 'I was like that once,' she admitted with some reluctance. 'But I learned that trust is a dangerous thing to give. And even more dangerous to receive.'

'Do you trust *me*?'

She didn't answer right away. Not because she was trying to put him off guard or avoid the question, but because she didn't know how.

'I trust your intentions, Ryan.'

That was about as good as he was going to get.

'Then stop treating my team like the enemy, otherwise that's exactly what you'll make them.' He let out a breath, holding his mounting temper and natural protectiveness towards his friends in check. 'You don't like them? Fine, I'm sure the feeling's mutual. But you've *got* to find a way to work with them, because like it or not, you need them. This is one thing you can't do alone.'

Leaving that thought to weigh on her mind, Drake brushed past, heading to confer with the others. Anya made no move to stop him. Instead she watched him go in sullen, brooding silence.

# Chapter 38

Marcus Cain shivered as another chilly blast of wind whipped into his face, carrying stinging pellets of rain and sleet that stung his exposed skin. The weather was lousy, as he'd been warned to expect at this time of year, and made all the worse by their remote location high in the Hindu Kush mountains.

Then again, that was the idea. No Soviet patrols would be foolhardy enough to venture this far into the mountainous border region, where tanks and artillery couldn't support them, and where aircraft were vulnerable to ground fire. Places like this were by now far outside their control.

Even for Cain, who had no such concerns, getting here had been an ordeal, requiring a tortuous four-hour drive by jeep from Islamabad, then another hour of slogging on foot when the ill-defined jeep trail finally became impassable.

Not for the first time, he was glad of the regular daily exercise he took, otherwise he doubted he would have made it here. He was the first non-field operative to venture this far out, to come within a few scant miles of the Afghan border. A few of his colleagues had tried to dissuade him, but he'd ignored their warnings, knowing he had to come.

Knowing who he had to come here for.

Pulling the collar of his heavy winter jacket a little tighter, he pressed forward, his boots squelching in the mud with each step. Looking around the meagre encampment, he saw little that was heartening. The term 'Forward Operating Base' conjured up images of a fully equipped military establishment, of choppers thundering overhead, trucks and armoured vehicles roaring past, troops marching back and forth.

That was the fantasy. This was the reality of the CIA's clandestine war in Afghanistan. A squalid collection of rain-soaked tents, mud and freezing rain, populated by hunched figures with rifles cradled to their chests like newborn infants.

'Where is she?' he asked the soldier who had accompanied him in.

'Over there. Third tent in,' the man grunted, pointing with a gloved hand. 'She just got back a few hours ago.'

Cain nodded. 'Thanks.'

Leaving his handler behind, he plodded towards the tent. For the first time in months, he felt a sense of anticipation, even excitement at the prospect of seeing the young woman again. A woman he hadn't seen since her departure from Andrews AFB.

209

The tent was a decent size, and tall enough for a man to stand upright in. The door was pegged shut, and lacking any means of announcing his arrival, he settled for just pulling it open and stepping inside, grateful to be out of the wind and rain.

In the dim orange glow cast by a couple of kerosene lamps, Cain was able to take in the interior of the shelter. Ammunition and supply crates stacked haphazardly together, weapons dismantled for servicing and repair, a big regional map covered in handwritten annotations pinned to a cork board, along with kit bags, dirty boots, uniforms and countless other pieces of military paraphernalia.

One of the only concessions to comfort were a couple of collapsible beds and a steel water basin heated by a gas burner below. It was over this makeshift sink that Anya was standing, bent over as she splashed warm water on her face and down her neck.

'If Luka wants my report, tell him I'll be there soon,' she said without looking up. 'I haven't eaten hot food in a week.'

Cain smiled in spite of himself. 'I don't think many restaurants deliver out here.'

Caught off guard by the unexpected voice, Anya whirled around, her face still dripping water. It was then that Cain was afforded his first look at the woman he'd last seen boarding that plane six months ago.

His first impression was that she had aged a great deal in that short time. Not her face as such, but rather that a profound change had been wrought in the person behind it. It was clear she had seen things most people could scarcely imagine.

He'd heard stories of her exploits here, read the mission reports filtering through from their assets in the field. If they were even half true then it was little wonder she'd been changed by her experiences.

His second impression was that however grim and forlorn this encampment might have appeared to him, it likely seemed like the Hilton compared to what she'd been through. Her face was smeared with dirt and grime despite the dousing she'd given it, her hair greasy and tangled, her skin grazed and cut in places. She was still wearing the torn, frayed, mud-splattered battledress uniform that she'd marched over the border in. He didn't care to imagine when she'd last bathed.

And yet, in that moment none of those things mattered to him. If anything, they only increased the respect and admiration he felt towards her. She'd endured everything her male comrades had endured, had put up with the same hardships they had, and from what he understood, she'd done it without a word of complaint.

'Marcus,' she stammered, staring at him as if he were a ghost. 'I... No one told me you were coming. What are you doing here?'

He grinned. 'Had to come visit my protégé, find out if you've seen Star Wars.'

Her expression of shock at his unexpected arrival quickly gave way to relief, and her face lit up with a smile of such unabashed joy that he couldn't help but respond. Without thinking she strode forward and threw her arms around him, pulling him close in a tight embrace.

That was something he appreciated so much about Anya. There was no guile, no attempt at deception or flattery when it came to the two of them. She was as open and trusting towards him as one could be, and somehow he felt honoured by it.

She looked up at him then, and her pale blue eyes no longer seemed cold and intense. There was something else in them now; something he'd sensed when they parted company at Andrews all those months ago, but which burned far stronger and more urgently now. He suddenly became aware of their closeness, of her breath on his neck, the warmth of her body pressed against his, even through her damp clothing.

He couldn't explain it, but standing there with her in that rain-soaked tent in the midst of those desolate mountains, he felt more intimate, more personal, more connected than he had lying naked with most women in the throes of passion. It was as if they were two magnets inexorably drawn to one another, each pulling the other in no matter the time or distance that separated them.

Then, just as suddenly as she had approached, Anya pulled away from him, a blush rising to her face as she glanced down at the floor.

'I'm sorry,' she mumbled, and he saw that she was shaking. 'My clothes are filthy and soaking, I haven't even washed.'

Cain too felt his composure and common sense reasserting itself. What the hell was he thinking, letting her get to him like that? She was an asset and he was her case officer, and there was a reason such relationships had to remain detached and professional. Anything else was dangerous to them both.

'Don't worry about it,' he said, taking a step backward. 'Take all the time you need. I'll be outside when you're done.'

In truth, he had another reason for being here than simply catching up. Something he hoped would benefit both of them. But it could wait until she was properly ready for it.

For Anya, he would wait as long as it took.

–

*Polish airspace – March 2010*

Cain took a sip of his scotch, staring out into the darkness beyond the window of his Gulfstream jet. Thousands of feet below lay the rivers and forests of southern Poland, illuminated in places by the scattered lights of towns and small villages. And far to the east, at the end of another eight-hour flight, lay his final destination of Pakistan.

Just like during that first tentative venture into the field to meet with Anya, there was still a war being fought in neighbouring Afghanistan. A war whose seeds had been sown two decades earlier by men just like him, and which now threatened to consume the entire region in chaos and death.

If only he could have foreseen the damage they would do with their rash, short-sighted efforts, he reflected sadly. If only they could have recognized the monster they had created in the fragmented and unpredictable Mujahedeen. If only they could have anticipated the civil war that would engulf the country after the Soviets pulled out, the legacy of bitterness and betrayal and radicalization they would leave behind.

If only…

'Excuse me, sir?' a female voice asked.

Cain looked up from the window, his mind dragged from its grim musings as he regarded the young air force corporal standing over him.

'What is it, corporal?'

'The pilot says we could be in for some turbulence. I'd suggest you fasten your seatbelt.' She paused for a moment, perhaps not wishing to offend a man of Cain's rank. 'It's just a precaution, sir.'

Cain nodded, draining the remainder of the scotch in one gulp. It wasn't on a par with the stuff in his own private collection, but it did the job. It would hopefully be enough to quiet his restless thoughts tonight and allow him to grab a few hours' sleep.

'Get me another, would you?' he said, handing her the empty glass.

'Of course, sir.'

'What's your name, by the way? Your first name, I mean.'

The tag on her uniform said Peters, but he wasn't interested in a bland, impersonal surname. You couldn't really know much about a person until you knew their first name.

The young woman looked briefly taken aback by his question. This had changed the dynamics of the situation, crossed a small but significant line, taken their interaction from professional to personal. He couldn't blame her for being uneasy.

'Alyssa, sir.' Then, growing a little bolder, willing to give just a little more than politeness demanded, she flashed a wry smile. 'But… most people call me Allie. Seems to have a better ring to it.'

He nodded, reflecting sadly on a time when he'd been as young as the woman standing before him. 'You like the air force, Allie?'

'I get to serve my country, sir.' She seemed a little less sure of herself now. She was giving him a standard answer to an awkward question.

'That's not what I meant.'

Only then did she properly make eye contact with him, engaging with him for the first time as one human being to another. 'It's what I wanted to do since I was a kid,' she said, confidence and conviction in her voice now. 'I might not be flying fighter jets but I wouldn't change it for the world.'

Christ, when was the last time I thought like that, he wondered?

'That's good,' he acknowledged. 'Keep that. Hang on to it. It's more precious than you think. And a lot more fragile.'

'Will do, sir,' she said, turning away and leaving him alone, though she glanced at him once over her shoulder as she retreated to the galley. Perhaps she was wondering at the hidden burdens he carried that had prompted such an odd line of questioning.

Cain was oblivious, his gaze already returned to the darkened world outside.

# Chapter 39

Drake took a gulp from the garishly coloured can of energy drink. He didn't recognize the logo boldly emblazoned across the side, not that it mattered much – it contained more sugar and caffeine than he was probably meant to consume in a week. And it was doing its job of keeping him awake.

He was seated in the midst of their makeshift ops planning area, the laptop connected to their wireless security cameras humming away in front of him. Aside from a small work light, the ghostly pale glow of its screen was about the only source of illumination in the big darkened warehouse, the internal lights turned off to avoid attracting attention.

In the past two hours, the most exciting thing he'd seen outside had been a mangy-looking stray cat prowling around in search of food. And every so often, the screen would flicker into darkness as the laptop tried to go to power-saving mode, forcing him to lean forward and hit a key to prove he was still alive.

He could have disabled the feature, but it served its purpose of forcing him to move regularly, whereas inactivity might have lulled him off into sleep.

He'd volunteered to take first watch of the night, allowing the rest of his team to grab some much-needed rest before sunrise. The accommodation here wasn't exactly luxurious, consisting of nothing more than a couple of sleeping bags laid out on the floors of the empty offices at the rear of the warehouse, but he imagined they would find a way to make it work. Hell, Anya seemed to prefer a hard floor over a warm bed anyway, so he doubted she would have any problems.

It was fair to say he had a number of headaches at that moment, the biggest of which seemed to be Anya herself. He hadn't been naive enough to expect smooth sailing where she was concerned, but the strife she was causing amongst the others was bordering on intolerable.

He had ventured into dangerous situations before as a Shepherd operative, but always with a unified team behind him. The prospect of trying to lead the house assault tomorrow night with a group who didn't trust each other and couldn't work together was a recipe for disaster.

And yet, trying to make her do anything against her will was an exercise in futility. He reflected that despite all their encounters – the information they'd shared, the plans they'd made, the enemies they'd taken on – he had never once had to integrate her into a larger whole. He had never seen her deal with others as equals, cooperate with them, listen to their opinions, put her trust in them and ask them to do the same.

Had she simply been out in the cold too long? Was she too far gone to work with his team, or any team for that matter? He didn't doubt Anya's commitment or even her bravery in the fight that lay ahead, but it was becoming obvious that she would do her fighting alone.

'Shit,' he mumbled, taking another gulp of the sickly-sweet drink as he returned to his lonely vigil, feeling like he was no closer to a solution. So much for sorting through his problems.

Hearing the sound of footsteps on the concrete floor, Drake spun around in the office chair he'd been reclining on as McKnight approached him, emerging from the shadows at the rear of the warehouse.

'Doesn't quite measure up to the view back at the villa, does it?' she remarked, nodding to the nondescript black and white images displayed on the monitor.

'I don't know. Somehow I doubt it looks quite as good as it used to,' Drake mused sadly, then glanced at his watch. 'Next shift doesn't start for an hour. You should try to get some sleep.'

Samantha made a face. 'Tried it, failed. I figured you could use some company instead.' She shrugged, looking a little self-conscious. 'Or if you'd rather be alone—'

'Nope,' Drake was quick to jump in. 'Pull up a chair. But I can't offer you much apart from whatever this shit is.'

He held out an unopened can to her, which she declined with a weak smile. 'Not exactly what I had in mind.'

'You and me both,' he admitted. 'But don't worry, once this is over we'll make up for it. And then some.'

She smiled at this notion, but he could tell her heart wasn't really in it. In fact, if anything his mention of what they were going to do after this seemed to have stirred some unpleasant emotion, as if he had reminded her of something she'd tried to forget. She was putting on an act, trying to make him feel better. Trying to hide something.

Despite his earlier rebuke of Anya for indulging in paranoia and mind games, even he couldn't deny the change that had come over Samantha of late. If something was worrying her, he wanted to help. As irrational and foolish as it sounded given their occupation, not to mention what they were about to venture into, he wanted to protect her.

He always had.

'Mind if I ask you something?' he began, reasoning now was as good a time as any.

'Sounds ominous.'

Drake took another gulp, grimacing as the sugary liquid settled in his stomach.

'What's going on?'

Her dark brows drew together, a frown creasing her forehead. She wouldn't look at him, which told him a lot. 'What do you mean?'

He didn't want to push too hard, but this could be their last chance to talk privately. 'Well, you seem a little...'

'Tired? Edgy? Short-tempered?' She flashed a rueful grin, but he couldn't tell if it was forced. 'All of the above, I'm afraid. It's been a long night, you know?'

He did. But that didn't mean fatigue and stress were the root of the problem.

'I know, but... we've both had our share of long nights. This is different. I've seen you beat down, hurt, exhausted and very, very pissed off,' he added with a knowing smile, hoping to lower her guard. 'But this is the first time I've seen you... scared.'

She didn't say anything; didn't agree with him or contradict him. That alone was enough to convince him to keep going.

'I'm not in the business of judging people. Least of all you,' he ventured. 'If you want to keep stuff to yourself, that's your choice. I won't hold it against you. But it's just the two of us here, and I'm not going anywhere for at least...' He checked his watch. 'Fifty-eight minutes. If you want to talk, I'll listen.'

He could see she was struggling, torn between loyalty to him, and... what? Fear? Fear of him, or something else?

'Do you trust me, Ryan?' she finally asked, staring off into the shadows.

'More than anyone in this building,' he answered truthfully. And that was saying something, considering some of the people under this roof.

'And you trust that I'm a good person.'

'Of course.'

She sighed and nodded, though it was a while before she felt ready to speak. 'I told you once about my family, that my dad was all I had. It wasn't always like that.'

Drake said nothing. She needed to get this out, but she needed to do it in her own time, without prompting.

'I had a brother. Liam, three years older than me.' She smiled as her mind replayed old, bittersweet memories. 'There's no other way of saying it – Liam was a real pain in the ass. Always teasing me, playing pranks, making fun of me in front of his friends. The way big brothers do, I guess. We used to argue and fight like cat and dog... drove Mom and Dad crazy.

'But you know the funny thing? Once a year we'd go on vacation – we'd head to Colorado for the summer, camp out in the Rockies. I used to love it there, and so did he. That was when he was different with me. Because no one knew us there, didn't expect anything, we didn't have to be brother and sister. For a week or two, I guess we could just be... friends.'

He saw her swallow, saw her blink back tears and guessed what was coming. 'I was eight when he died. My mom was driving through an intersection with Liam in the back seat, some guy ran a red light… usual story. She didn't even see it coming, and neither did Liam. He took the full force of the hit, died pretty much instantly. Just like that, done.'

'I'm so sorry, Sam,' Drake said, well aware of how inadequate such words were. She had never told him any of this before.

She managed a faint smile, acknowledging his intent. 'My mom… I think that crash broke her. I don't mean physically. She walked away with barely a scratch, but she was never the same. I heard her arguing with Dad later, heard her say she wished she'd been killed as well. She could barely bring herself to look at me. I think she blamed herself for what happened, and I was just a reminder of what she'd lost.' Samantha shrugged then, cutting away from the old pain. 'She left about a month after the funeral. Just got in her car, drove off one night and didn't come back. I never saw her again.

'So that was it – it was just me and Dad from there on out. He'd lost pretty much everything, had his life fall down around his ears, and all he was left with was an angry, frightened eight-year-old kid to raise by himself.' She shook her head, as if she still couldn't comprehend what had transpired. 'A lot of guys would have lost it then, hit the bottle, gone off the rails, and I wouldn't blame a single one of them. But not him. He sat me down the morning after Mom left and said that it was going to be the two of us for a while, and that it wasn't going to be like before. We were a team now, we had to work together, and no matter what happened, he would never, ever leave me. And I believed him… maybe because I needed something to have faith in. But whatever the reason, he kept his word. It was like… the more pressure he was under, the calmer he got. I'll never understand how he did it, but somehow he got through it. He pulled us both through.'

Only then did she finally look at him, and he saw tears glistening in her eyes.

'When I said he was all I had left, I meant exactly that, Ryan. He was the only person who stuck around, never let me down, never gave up on me.' She swallowed, glancing up at the ceiling high above, now bathed in darkness. 'What we're doing here… it's a declaration of war. If Downfall fails, Cain will come after us with everything he's got, and he won't show any mercy. He'll target anyone close to us, including my dad. And I'm scared… scared that I'm going to lose him.'

Drake felt like the breath had been punched out of him. He couldn't believe Samantha had been carrying such a burden all this time, that she had never told him about the tragedy that had struck so early in her life or the struggles that had followed.

'Sam, why didn't you tell me? We could have gotten to him, found a safe—'

216

She shook her head. 'It's not that simple. My dad's old now, and sick. There's nowhere for him to go, and we'd have risked the whole group trying to protect him. I couldn't do that to them, to him... to you.'

Drake had moved close to her now, wanting to comfort her, wanting to somehow shield her from the grief and sadness that seemed to be closing in all around. But he couldn't. This was something that had been festering inside her for a long time. A few hastily spoken words wouldn't do anything to change that.

'I'm sorry I didn't tell you before, Ryan,' she said, tears streaking her cheeks. It was all coming out now; there was no stopping it. 'I'm sorry about a lot of things. I just... I didn't want to make things worse, didn't want to add to your problems. I tried to—'

He silenced her then, cupping her chin and tilting her head back, pressing his mouth against hers. Not hard or demanding, but slow and gentle, almost tentative, as if it were the first time he'd ever done it.

He didn't even know for sure why he did it. Every rational instinct in his body told him it was wrong, that it was dangerous and foolish to do such a thing at a moment like this, but he just couldn't help it. It felt right in a way that went far deeper than reason or rationality.

He felt a moment of tension, of hesitation at this sudden move. She hadn't expected this, hadn't been ready for it. Her full lips parted slightly as instinct and carefully repressed desire took over, and she let out a soft moan as he pulled her closer.

When he drew back, her eyes were staring into his, still shining with grief, the pupils dilated in the dim light. Her breathing was coming faster now, her body trembling beneath his touch as they held each other in that moment, bodies just inches apart.

'I'm sorry,' he said, feeling suddenly self-conscious over what he'd done. 'I shouldn't have—'

He didn't get a chance to say anything more as she kissed him again, and pretty soon he realized it no longer mattered. It was as if a dam had suddenly given way within her, and she wanted, needed nothing but him. Before he knew it, her arms were around his neck, her fingers running through his hair, her body pressed hard against his, her breath warm and close against his cheek.

Their kiss was no longer gentle or tentative as they fell to the floor together, fighting with each other's clothes, pulling and tearing at ties and belts, desperately seeking one another in the only way that mattered to either of them now.

'Now,' she whispered in his ear, yanking her trousers down. 'I need you now.'

She held him tight, her fingers digging painfully into his back as he entered her. This wasn't tender and careful lovemaking, and she didn't want it to be. That wasn't what she needed now. She closed her eyes and let out a low groan of pain and hunger, trying to keep from crying out as her body matched his, moving faster and harder with each thrust.

Images of her father, of Cain, of Drake and all the others whirled through her mind in a confusing kaleidoscope of memories and emotions, and she squeezed her eyes shut tighter to stop the tears coming. But even as they threatened to overwhelm her, she could feel them fading, burning away in the rising fire within her as the sensations rose to an unbearable peak.

And at last, she found the release she'd craved.

Nearby, Anya turned away from the scene, wishing she could cover her ears against the sounds of their lovemaking, wishing she could forget the sight of their straining bodies entwined.

She had lain awake, waiting until she was sure the others must be asleep before venturing out into the main warehouse to speak with Drake, hoping to find him alone, hoping to somehow make amends for what had happened earlier. She wasn't accustomed to apologizing to anyone, to admitting a bad decision or a lapse in judgement, but she'd been willing to do so tonight. After everything Drake had done, everything he'd sacrificed and lost because of her, she owed him that much.

And in truth, there was far more she wanted to say to him. It had been three years since they'd first met, yet their actual time together had been agonizingly brief. There had always been some new crisis brewing, some outside force pulling them apart. Never enough time to say what she needed to say.

Tonight she'd hoped to finally put that right. She'd been ready for it. Ready to open up, to take a risk, to put her trust in another.

The sound of muffled conversation as she'd approached had told her someone had beaten her to it, and curiosity had compelled her to listen in. Trained as she was to move unseen, it had been easy enough to slip silently through the shadows.

She hadn't been surprised to find McKnight there, but even she hadn't expected *this*. More than that, she hadn't expected the response it evoked in her.

She'd known it was happening between them of course. Living together as Drake and McKnight had, it was obvious what would happen. Even Anya had been young once, and knew all too well the power of such desires. She'd told herself it was a logical choice, that they made sense together, that Drake deserved someone who could offer him a normal life, a chance at a future.

Things she herself could never give him.

But actually seeing it with her own eyes, hearing the sounds of them coming together... that was something else entirely. That was when logic and common sense came undone, when her objectivity failed her. And that was when she felt an ache, an emptiness deep inside, as if some great gulf had been torn open.

Leaving as silently as she had come, she crept back to the derelict storage room that served as her sleeping quarters. A box of a room with crumbling plasterboard walls, measuring eight feet wide by ten feet long. She knew because she'd paced out the distance, just as she'd done every day in that freezing, squalid prison cell in Russia where she'd spent four years of her life.

As foolish as it seemed, that was still her standard of measure. Any room that worked out bigger was an improvement in her mind.

Lying down on the hard floor, she pulled the sleeping bag around her and drew her knees up to her chest, curling into a ball as if trying to protect herself from the pain. Another action she'd had a lot of chances to practice in her life.

She lay there, alone in the dark, hearing only the sound of her own breathing. She supposed she'd been alone most of her life, one way or the other, but never had she felt it more keenly than at that moment.

Angry at such thoughts of self-pity, Anya squeezed her eyes shut and tried to empty her mind, willing herself to surrender to sleep, though she knew it was a wasted effort. Sleep would be a long time coming tonight.

# Part III

# Culmination

In 2010, a report by the London School of Economics purported to have uncovered concrete evidence that the ISI was providing funding, training and sanctuary to the Taliban on a scale much larger than previously thought, even attending meetings with the Taliban's supreme council.

# Chapter 40

The new day dawned cloudy and indistinct in northern Pakistan, the sun visible only as a brightly luminous patch in the early morning haze that seemed to linger over the city of Rawalpindi. Whatever heat had bled off into space during the night soon returned with a vengeance as the temperature and humidity began to climb along with the sun.

It wasn't long before the streets began to fill with traffic and pedestrians as the population awoke from its slumber, millions of inhabitants heading out to work, to school, to shops and to the countless other places their daily lives took them. And all of them were oblivious to the events that were to play out tonight.

Drake and his team, however, had been awake long before that, already preparing themselves for the tasks that lay ahead. It was fair to say that none of them had enjoyed a particularly restful night; the combination of nervous tension, physical discomfort and growing anticipation conspiring to prevent all but the most fleeting snatches of sleep.

As a result, nobody was feeling very talkative as they ate a meagre breakfast of cereal bars and bottled water. Frost in particular looked abjectly miserable. She ate like a starving man most of the time, but on her own terms. As far as she was concerned, any breakfast that didn't contain large quantities of fried meat was a waste of space.

Still, they were here, they were awake, and they had a few hours left to finish their preparations for the house assault tonight.

'All right, to-do list,' Drake said, taking a gulp of water. 'Cole, you're on weapons and equipment detail. Give everything a final check, then get it stashed away in case any of our neighbours get curious about us.'

The warehouse was well surveilled by the cameras they had set up, but it was far from impregnable. And it was in the middle of a heavily used industrial district. The last thing they needed was for some curious local to poke his nose in and find tables of weapons and ammunition laid out for the world to see.

'Copy that.'

'Keira, stay in touch with Dan back at Langley. The minute Cain's plane hits the tarmac, I want to know about it.'

Frost gave a less than enthusiastic nod. 'I'm on it. What about you?'

He gave her a knowing smile. 'I'm going car shopping.'

The *Bukhanka* might have been sufficient to get them this far, but when it came time to make their escape from the safe house, they were going to need something fast, powerful and manoeuvrable. A 20-year-old panel van with an exhaust system held together by little more than patch welds and chewing gum just wasn't going to cut it.

Purchasing a vehicle at short notice with limited identification wasn't easy, but he was willing to bet there were dealers in this city prepared to part with their car for a healthy wad of cash, no questions asked. It was just a matter of finding them.

'I'll tag along, make sure you don't buy us a lemon,' McKnight ventured. 'I'm going to be driving the damn thing anyway.'

'No faith,' Drake said, feigning wounded pride.

'I've seen how you drive, Ryan. It isn't pretty.'

Things were different between the two of them this morning – easier, less fraught and strained. Maybe her admission last night had helped clear the air, or perhaps it was what had come afterwards that really made the difference. Whatever the reason, Drake wasn't complaining.

'Fair enough, you're in.' Then, seeing that she'd barely touched her food, he added, 'Might be a while before our next meal. You sure you don't want that?'

At this, her playful mood seemed to dissipate. She shrugged, trying to look casual about it. 'I'm not hungry right now.'

Drake frowned, surprised. Like the rest of them, she hadn't had a proper meal since leaving France, and that had been a good 24 hours ago. Was she feeling unwell? Looking closer, he couldn't help noticing her pale complexion…

'What about me?' Anya interjected. 'Where do you want me?'

'Why don't you keep an eye on the perimeter,' he suggested, trying to think of a way to keep her out of trouble. 'Make sure no one gets too close.'

He was expecting an argument on this, an insistence that she accompany Drake to find a suitable vehicle for tonight. So far on this operation, everything with her had been an argument, every decision contested, every point a struggle for control.

But to his surprise, the woman shrugged indifferently. 'Whatever you say.'

A moment of confounded silence descended on the room, as if no one was quite sure what to say or do. Each was harbouring similar thoughts to Drake, wondering why Anya had suddenly become compliant and accommodating. But sure enough, it was Frost who finally broke the deadlock in her own unique way.

'Well, shit,' she declared, flashing one of the crooked grins Drake had come to know so well. 'We've gotten through a whole meeting without an argument. Even I'm starting to believe this bullshit plan might actually work.'

'Thanks for that vote of confidence, Keira,' Drake said sarcastically. 'I'm all about supporting others.'

In truth, though, he was pleased to find the atmosphere a little less combative than yesterday. Napoleon's maxim that 'in war, morale is everything' had been true two centuries earlier, and it was no less so today.

Still, he was puzzled by Anya's change in demeanour. It was possible that she'd decided to heed his advice about learning to work with his team, but he wasn't convinced. Anya took advice like pop divas took criticism – badly. And there was something about the way she looked at him that suggested cooperation was the last thing on her mind.

Still, there was little to be gained by disrupting this new-found spirit of harmony, so he was content to let the matter rest for now. Standing up, he tossed his empty water bottle in the packing crate that served as their trash can, eager to get moving before someone found a reason to start an argument.

'Everyone has their assignments. Let's move like we know what we're doing.'

'That's a stretch,' Mason called after him as he headed for the exit.

'Wing it, mate,' Drake advised. 'It's what I always do.'

## Chapter 41

A few hours later, and Drake was behind the wheel of his brand new–third generation gunmetal-grey Range Rover. Well, not exactly brand new, but a mere five years old felt like cutting-edge vehicular luxury compared to the ancient transmission and steering mechanism he'd wrestled with in the *Bukhanka*.

After scouting out a few potential locations in the busy city, one or two of them suggested by local taxi drivers, he and McKnight had settled on a dealership on the southern edge of town that looked seedy enough to put through a cash sale with minimal paperwork, but also decent enough not to fob them off with a heap of scrap metal.

McKnight had argued in favour of a Honda SUV that she'd spotted, since Japanese cars seemed to be heavily represented in Pakistan, but Drake had been adamant about the Range Rover. It was bigger, more powerful and more durable than the Japanese car. And more importantly, he liked it.

The dealer had flashed him a knowing smile as the matter was settled and money exchanged, perhaps assuming McKnight to be a demanding wife who had just been put in her place. Drake was happy to let him think what he wanted as long as he signed over the car and let them go on their way.

Now here they were, on their way back to the warehouse with the air conditioner blasting cold air in their faces and Pakistan's answer to Beyoncé blaring through the speaker system while central Rawalpindi slid by outside the tinted windshield.

Not a bad way to get around, Drake had to admit. He felt a little like one of those rich arsehole footballers he used to see cruising down the King's Road in Chelsea, on his way to get a designer haircut or a spray tan or whatever the hell such people did with their spare time.

He couldn't help but smile at the notion. Driving, listening to the radio, thinking about normal everyday things. Simple pleasures that most people took for granted. But not him. Not ever again.

'Enjoying yourself?' Samantha asked, noticing his expression.

'I was just thinking.'

'Always a dangerous state of affairs.'

'Since we've started this op, we've flown in a private jet – with a disco ball, no less – blagged ourselves a free skydiving session, and now we're cruising in our own luxury car. If I'd known it was going to be like this, I'd have gone freelance years ago.'

She snorted in amusement. 'Yeah, I've been having the time of my life since we got here.'

Drake flashed her a sidelong grin. 'I was thinking about taking you out for dinner, maybe a couple of drinks afterwards. See where the evening takes us, you know?'

McKnight feigned a look of profound regret. 'Tempting, but I'm pretty sure we've got a prior engagement.'

'Killjoy.'

'Arrogant asshole,' she fired back. 'Don't think I'll forget you overruling me back at that dealership. That shit's not going to fly well.'

He shrugged, enjoying the banter all the same. 'Had to be done. It's about time you learned your place, woman.'

Forced to keep his grip on the wheel, he was unable to dodge aside as she thumped him soundly in the arm. It was a playful gesture, but delivered with enough sting to let him know she could still hurt him if she wanted to.

'Careful, Mr Drake. You're on dangerous ground.'

'Story of my life.'

Easing their way along the crowded street as cars, bikes and vans jostled for position all around them, Drake was afforded plenty of time to observe the situation outside. His impression of Rawalpindi when they'd arrived last night had been that of an ancient, chaotic city dragged uncomfortably into the twenty-first century, its old ramshackle buildings and winding back alleys standing in stark contrast to the neat efficiency of nearby Islamabad.

That impression was only heightened now that he saw it in the full light of day. If anything, the streets and roads were even more congested than before, the air thick with traffic fumes and smoke from outdoor kiosks cooking meat over open fires. Judging by the threadbare clothes and the gaunt, haggard faces, Drake guessed this was one of the less desirable districts. Nobody looked happy, nobody walked with energy or purpose, everyone was just plodding along, trying to get through another day.

It was the kids that put a dampener on his good mood, though. He was sadly familiar with their ilk after serving tours in Afghanistan. Any place there was poverty or conflict or deprivation, you saw them lurking in alleys, begging for food or money, or just wandering lost and alone. Ignored by most, pitied by some and preyed on by others.

And whatever their race or nationality, they all looked pretty much the same. The same skinny limbs, the same faces prematurely aged by the things they'd seen and done, the same hungry, desperate look in their eyes. The lucky or resourceful ones would band together into gangs for protection, constantly vying for the favour of a few ruthless leaders. As for the rest, they learned very quickly that only the strong survived.

McKnight could sense his change in mood.

'Saw plenty of them in Iraq,' she remarked quietly. 'Doesn't make it any easier.'

'No, it doesn't,' Drake agreed, pressing down on the accelerator, eager to get them away from this part of town. Eager to get those lost, desperate faces out of his mind.

The remainder of their journey passed in relative silence, each of them content to think their own thoughts as they left behind the dense urban sprawl and merged onto a main drag that would take them where they needed to go. It couldn't come fast enough for Drake, who was keen to rejoin his companions and complete the last of their preparations.

After driving halfway across the unfamiliar city, he almost felt like he was coming home as he turned into the run-down industrial estate and pulled to a stop in front of the rusting, neglected edifice that was their base of operations.

Knowing that Mason or Anya would spot their arrival on the security cameras, Drake sat there with the engine idling, waiting for the big double doors to slide open. But they didn't. No one emerged from the warehouse, and the doors remained firmly closed.

Exchanging an uneasy look with his passenger, Drake shut down the engine and yanked the keys from the ignition.

'They could just be changing shifts,' McKnight cautioned him, though her voice lacked conviction. 'Maybe they haven't seen us on the cameras.'

Honking their horn would of course settle the matter, but it would also alert anyone in there who wasn't supposed to be. He would rather keep quiet until he knew what was going on inside that building.

'Maybe.' Reaching behind him, Drake pulled out the Browning automatic that he'd kept with him all day, mostly to guard against carjackings. 'Maybe not.'

Bowing to the inevitable, McKnight armed herself in similar fashion and followed him outside as he eased his door open and stepped down. Straight away both of them felt the heat and humidity. It was approaching noon, the sun was high in the sky and the temperature had risen along with it.

Drake inhaled, the air hot and damp as a tropical jungle, and laced with the acrid scent of engine fumes and smoke from the industrial chimneys nearby. Almost immediately he could feel perspiration beading on his forehead and trickling down between his shoulder blades.

With McKnight covering him, he advanced towards the wicket gate set into the bigger set of sliding doors, making sure to keep his weapon out of sight in case they were spotted by a passer-by. Halting beside it, Drake leaned in close, pressing his ear against the metal.

Sure enough, he could hear raised voices echoing inside, though the acoustics combined with ambient noise and the closed door made it impossible to discern what was being said. One thing was clear, however – someone in there was not happy.

Had the rest of his team been ambushed and taken hostage? Were they being interrogated at this very moment, trying to make them give up Drake's whereabouts?

One way or another, he had to find out.

An experimental tug on the door handle confirmed it was still locked and secured, so whoever was in there hadn't made entry that way. Fortunately he'd made sure to take a spare key with them. Slipping it into the lock, he glanced up at McKnight and silently mouthed the countdown.

Three, two, one…

A single turn of the key allowed him to swing the door open and slip inside, with McKnight following close behind. As he crossed the threshold, he drew his weapon and brought it to bear with a single deft movement, his eyes sweeping the gloomy interior of the building as he tried to discern enemies from friendlies.

It didn't take him long to find them, though the scene that confronted him was so incongruous that he actually stopped in his tracks, uttering a single statement that perfectly summed up his reaction.

'Oh shit.'

# Chapter 42

Of all the sights and possibilities Drake's mind had conjured up in those anxious few moments before entering, this was not one of them.

First to catch his attention was Mason. The big specialist was standing near the parked *Bukhanka*, clutching his automatic as if ready for a fight. His shirt was ripped and bloodied by a long gash across the left side of his chest, as if someone had slashed at him with a knife. The wound was still oozing blood that gleamed dark in the wan light, though Mason himself was still very much in the game.

As for the perpetrator, that wasn't hard to guess.

A young boy was cowering on the floor by Mason's feet, his wrists and mouth bound by duct tape. He was trying to shrink away from the weapon in Mason's hand, trying to crawl beneath the van and hide, though the man's iron grip on his tattered shirt was more than enough to keep him in place.

This would have been unnerving enough, but it was the situation in the centre of the room that represented the greatest danger. Anya and Frost seemed to be locked in an armed stand-off against one another; Frost with one of the MP7s and Anya with her Colt .45 automatic. The younger woman had positioned herself between Anya and the boy, using herself as a human shield.

'Well, this doesn't look good,' McKnight said under her breath.

'Goddamn it, you put that fucking weapon down right now before I blow you in half!' Frost snarled, staring at Anya down the sights of the compact submachine gun. She hadn't even acknowledged Drake's return, so intent was she on facing down her enemy.

'You won't do it, Frost. You are not a killer,' Anya replied, her voice deceptively cold in contrast to her adversary's barely restrained fury. 'Stand aside.'

'Fuck you! I won't let you do it. Not again.'

'Both of you stop this shit!' Mason implored them, torn between keeping a grip on the youth at his feet and trying to intercede in what could prove to be a deadly battle of wills. 'This is out of control.'

'You don't know what she's capable of, Cole,' Frost shot back. 'She's a fucking murderer! I saw it with my own eyes last night.' She braced the weapon against her shoulder, tensing up to fire. 'Someone has to stop her before she gets us all killed.'

'And are you the one to do it, Keira Frost?' Anya challenged her.

Drake had heard enough. Whatever events had transpired in his absence, they could wait. He needed to end this situation now before one called the other's bluff.

'What the fuck is going on here?' he yelled, striding into the centre of the room and purposefully blocking their lines of fire. There was no thought of exercising restraint or diplomacy this time. He needed to be as loud and angry as possible, which suited him just fine. 'Put those guns down now! Both of you!'

'Stay out of this, Ryan,' Frost warned, trying to sidestep him and get a clean shot at her target. He made sure to match her movements. 'This is none of your business.'

'I'm making it my business,' he promised her. 'You've got exactly three seconds to lower your weapon, or I swear to God you'll have to shoot to stop me beating the shit out of you. One.'

Frost clenched her teeth. 'You know what she did last night. She's a killer; it's all she knows. She'll do it again if we don't stop her.'

'What's she talking about?' McKnight demanded.

Drake didn't answer. That was a conversation for another time.

'Two.' He took a step towards Frost, his fists clenched. He didn't want this to get physical, but if it came to it, he really would beat her down rather than see half his team wiped out in a needless friendly fire incident.

'You're fucking blind, Ryan. I'm not your enemy, *she* is!'

'Three...' Drake was moving towards her now, completely blocking her shot. If she wanted to hit Anya, she would have to kill him too.

'All right, goddamn it!' Frost snapped, lowering the gun and turning her back on him. 'Fucking Christ!'

Drake let out a barely perceptible breath. He hadn't really expected her to open fire, but in such a tense confrontation the chances of an accidental discharge were all too real.

'I did not need your help, Ryan,' Anya said from behind him.

Drake rounded on her, his anger and disappointment no less than it had been towards Frost. 'Don't say another word. Right now, I want to know what the hell's been going on here.' He jabbed a finger at the kid, who was still cowering at Mason's meet, mumbling something into his duct tape gag. 'Who's that little shithead, and what's he doing tied up?'

It was Mason, perhaps the most level headed of the three operatives by this point, who ventured to offer some explanation. 'Got ourselves a stowaway here. Anya found him crawling out through one of the rooftop ventilation ducts, with one of our tactical radios shoved inside his shirt. Fortunately she got to him before he made it out.'

Oh shit, Drake thought, looking at the boy and realising pretty quickly what he was about. He supposed it made sense – industrial lockups like this were probably rich pickings for street kids, filled with a wealth of goods or expensive equipment that could be stolen and sold on. He just hadn't expected one to find them so quickly or gain entrance so easily, especially with the security cameras they'd set up. It was a sobering realisation.

He glanced at his friend's chest wound again. 'You've got red on you, Cole.'

'Little bastard didn't go down without a fight.' Mason made a pained face, then reached into his pocket and produced what looked like a small home-made knife, its haft little more than strips of worn leather and duct tape wrapped around the steel blade. 'Tagged me pretty good. I'll live, though.'

If nothing else, Drake had to commend the kid on his bravery. It took balls to fight back against a man of Mason's size and strength. Then again, considering the world he was forced to survive in, fighting back was probably all he knew.

'The kid won't, if Anya has anything to do with it,' Frost interrupted, still bristling with anger. 'She wanted to take him out and kill him.'

'I did not say that,' Anya corrected her.

'You didn't have to. I know how people like you operate – you made that clear last night. Nobody gets in the way of the mission.'

'Will someone tell me what the hell happened last night?' McKnight demanded.

Drake was about to tell her to leave this one until later, but Frost beat him to it, no doubt feeling she'd kept it to herself long enough. 'We caught ourselves a couple of rent-a-cops during our recon trip. They tried to arrest us, but we disarmed them and took them out to the middle of nowhere. Ryan was all set to let them go, then Anya just pulled out a weapon and executed them. Cold-blooded, no hesitation. It was a fucking disgrace.'

McKnight let out a shocked breath and turned away, shaking her head. As she did so, she caught Drake's eye. The look that passed between them made it clear she didn't appreciate him keeping this to himself, and would likely have more to say on the matter when circumstances permitted it.

Meanwhile, Mason's attention turned to both Drake and Anya. Like McKnight, he too had been kept in the dark about her actions last night. 'This true?'

Anya didn't respond. She'd already said what she had to say on that matter.

'Why didn't you tell us, Ryan?' Mason demanded. McKnight might have been prepared to wait until later, but he wasn't.

Drake levelled an angry look at Frost. 'We've got enough problems as it is. I was trying to stop it getting worse.'

'He's covering for her, as always,' Frost spat, moving closer to the boy to protect him. 'Well, I'm not going to sit by and watch her murder a kid. You really will have to kill me first.'

Of all the people Drake had expected to demonstrate that kind of maternal protectiveness, Keira Frost would have been pretty near the end of the list. Not that he blamed her for taking a stand. There were lines even he wasn't willing to cross.

Unmoved by this display of self-sacrifice, Anya pointed to the youth at Mason's feet. 'Whether he is a child or not, he was old enough to infiltrate this warehouse, old enough to steal from us, and old enough to compromise us. He has seen everything; our weapons, our equipment, our radios. Even he must know this is no normal storage building. If we let him go now, there is no telling who he will talk to.'

'So you're suggesting we execute him?' Mason asked.

'Clearly we have to do something. We can't hand him over to the police, and we can't afford to let him go.' She shrugged. 'If you have a better idea, feel free to share it.'

Chewing his lip, Drake looked over at the boy. He'd stopped trying to crawl away from Mason and now sat in silence on the dusty concrete floor, eyes flicking from person to person, knowing they were talking about him and perhaps trying to decide how their debate was going to pan out.

'First things first,' he decided, tossing the keys for the Range Rover to McKnight. 'Bring the car inside before some arsehole nicks it. Keira, help her with the doors.'

'We need—' Frost began.

'No arguments,' Drake cut in. 'Just get it done. Now.'

As the two specialists strode off to open the warehouse doors, Drake turned his attention back to their prisoner. Holstering his weapon, he approached the boy and hunkered down in front of him to get a better look.

His age was hard to pin down because malnutrition had likely slowed his growth, but he guessed the kid had seen perhaps ten years. His small face made his eyes, deep brown and guarded, seem bigger than they were, while his shaggy mane of black hair looked like it had been hacked at with the same knife he'd used to attack Mason. Speaking of which, an angry discoloured bruise along his jawline stood as testimony to the fact he hadn't gone quietly.

All things considered, he was a thin, scrawny, bedraggled-looking kid. But as he'd already demonstrated, he was neither stupid nor cowardly. There was little fear in his eyes, but rather that same hungry, dangerous look Drake had come to know all too well.

'Nod if you understand what I'm saying,' Drake commanded.

Sure enough, he was rewarded with a reluctant nod, the kid's awkwardly shorn hair bobbing with the movement.

'I'm going to take your gag off now. If you try to scream or call out, you'll wish you hadn't. Nod again if you understand.'

Again he received a nod of affirmation.

Reaching out, Drake gripped the edge of the duct tape and tore it off with a single hard yank. The kid winced as the adhesive took away a layer of skin in the process, but to his credit managed not to cry out. Tough little bastard, Drake thought.

'What's your name?'

The boy stared back at him, saying nothing. The expression on his face suggested he'd understood the question; he simply didn't want to answer. Drake didn't blame him.

'What's your name?' Drake repeated. 'Answer, or we're finished here.'

He was smart enough to know when to capitulate. 'Yasin.'

A mechanical clanking from the warehouse entrance told him the doors were being hauled open. Moments later, he heard the sound of an engine starting up.

'Good. Yasin, I'm going to ask you a couple of questions. If you give me honest answers, everything will be fine. If you lie to me, I'll know about it,' he said, glancing at Anya. 'Now, are there other boys with you? Anyone expecting you back?'

Yasin's big liquid brown eyes flicked from Drake to the other members of the group, and the weapons they held. It wasn't hard to guess what was going through his head.

'Yes. I am in gang. Big gang, make big trouble for you, American.'

The Range Rover rolled to a stop beside the old Russian van, engine rumbling away at idle while Frost closed the warehouse doors behind, shielding them from the outside world.

'They come looking for me. They have guns, more guns than you,' the kid carried on, in full flow now. Some of his former bravado was returning as he sensed himself gaining the upper hand. 'They fuck you up big time unless you let me go.'

'Careful, dude,' Mason warned him. 'The only one who'll get fucked up is you.'

He sounded earnest and convincing enough, but Drake had an ace up his sleeve. He looked over his shoulder at Anya, who had been watching and listening. Her keen eyes took in every movement, every facial tic, every glance and change in posture. She shook her head, confirming Drake's suspicions.

'I suppose you weren't listening when I warned you not to lie to me, Yasin,' Drake chastised him. 'There's no one out there waiting for you, is there? You're on your own.'

Yasin's eyes flicked nervously back and forth, his new-found confidence evaporating as it became obvious he wasn't going to bluff his way out of this one.

'You kill me?' he asked, deciding to come right out with it. No sense beating around the bush, Drake supposed.

'That wasn't my first plan. Yasin, I—'

He was interrupted by the loud, jarring sound of a fist slamming against metal, and instinctively turned towards the main doors as the sound was repeated. Someone was trying to get in.

Someone had come for them.

# Chapter 43

Frost was over by the laptop within moments, quickly scanning the images projected by the outside cameras. It didn't take long to find what she was looking for.

'We've got company,' she hissed.

'No shit,' Drake replied, wondering for a moment whether Yasin had underplayed his hand. Perhaps he did have backup after all. 'What kind?'

'Two men in civvy clothes, one vehicle.'

Drake jumped to his feet, leaving the kid for now. 'Armed?'

'Can't tell, but they're both suited up. Look like government officials to me.'

The banging was repeated, louder this time. Whoever they were, they were clearly getting tired of waiting.

'Should we evac?' McKnight asked, checking the chamber on her weapon.

'We'd be inviting a car chase if we did,' Mason warned her.

It took Drake only a moment to make his decision. 'Clear the room. Weapons and equipment out of sight.'

'What about the kid?' Frost asked.

'Put him in the van,' Drake said, for lack of better options. 'Keira, get in there with him and keep him quiet, for Christ's sake.' He gave Yasin a hard look. 'If he moves, shoot him.'

'Let's go,' Frost said, replacing the duct tape on Yasin's mouth and hauling him into the *Bukhanka*. The boy knew better than to resist, either because he had no more love for the police than Drake and the others, or because he knew his life depended on it.

'Everyone else, be cool and follow my lead. Especially you,' he said, jabbing an accusing finger at Anya while the others quickly hid any incriminating weapons and equipment. Mason, remembering the bloodstain on his shirt, snatched up his jacket and threw it on.

As this frantic work was going on, Drake approached the doors, shoving the Browning automatic down the back of his jeans. No telling if he might need it in a hurry.

'Police! Open up!' a muffled voice called from outside.

'Coming,' Drake replied. 'Just a second.'

There was no time to check that the others were ready. All he could do was trust that they'd hidden the most incriminating evidence. Reaching the wicket door, he paused only a moment to compose himself, undid the latch and swung it open.

The two men he found himself facing were, as Frost had described, both dressed in civilian business suits, though neither looked like they'd seen a dry cleaner's or a clothes press for a while. Both men sported sunglasses and the kind of neatly trimmed moustaches that seemed to be regulation for any man over 30 in this part of the world, but that was pretty much where the similarities ended.

The man closest to Drake was the bigger of the two, standing a good four or five inches above his comrade. Grim faced and serious, everything about him seemed larger and more pronounced than it needed to be; his square chin jutted forward, his jaw as broad and heavy as a shovel, his nose long and high bridged, his brows thick and bushy. His skin was pockmarked and cratered, perhaps by teenage acne. Altogether, the impression conveyed was of a man one most definitely didn't want to fuck with.

The other man was shorter and lighter of build, his suit hanging loose on his slender frame. In contrast to his large and almost brutish companion, this man's features were soft and amiable, his greying hair combed over in a heroic but vain attempt to hide a growing bald patch. He had the sort of kindly, unthreatening face that reminded Drake of a Werther's Original commercial.

But despite his modest stature and less than intimidating visage, something about the smaller man seemed to hint at quiet authority and confidence. Drake had spent enough time in the military to know a ranking officer when he saw one.

'Can I help you?' Drake began, playing the innocent civilian card.

Sure enough, the smaller of the two men held up a badge just long enough for Drake to glimpse the insignia of the Punjab province police.

'Good afternoon, sir. I'm Detective Gondal, this is Detective Mahsud,' he began, his voice as soft and unassuming as his appearance. His English was impeccable. 'We are with the Punjab Police Department.'

'I see,' Drake said, hoping his expression didn't betray his wildly racing thoughts. 'What can I do for you?'

'Are you the owner of this building?' the big man, Mahsud, asked.

'Well, I'm renting it. It's just temporary storage space.'

'And how long have you been here?'

'Just got here yesterday, actually.'

'I see. Would you mind if we come inside, Mr...?' Gondal left the question hanging, expecting Drake to fill the gap.

'Douglas,' Drake replied, giving the name on his fake passport without hesitation. 'Robert Douglas.'

It was something of a cliché that fake identities should start with the same letters as real ones, but the logic was sound. The names rolled more easily off the tongue if they started with familiar letters, reducing the chance of the fatal pause that could give one away to experienced operators. Right now, Drake was undecided about just what kind of men he was up against.

'Douglas,' Gondal repeated. 'It's a hot day, Mr Douglas. May we come inside?'

'I'd rather know what brings you here first.' If he was too friendly or accommodating, they might wonder if he was trying to overcompensate for something.

'We only want to ask a few questions.' He looked almost apologetic for intruding on Drake's day. 'We won't keep you long, but we would appreciate your cooperation.'

Drake nodded, moving aside to let the two men in, Mahsud having to duck in through the small doorway. Straight away they took in the small gathering of people clustered near the collapsible tables. Drake couldn't help noticing Mahsud's hand straying towards his right hip, where there was no doubt a gun hidden beneath his suit jacket.

Drake's companions had stopped what they were pretending to be doing and turned towards the two detectives, their expressions ranging from surprise to wariness to thinly veiled hostility. Anya in particular looked like she was ready to shoot first and ask questions sometime next week.

'Guys, these men are from the Punjabi Police Department,' Drake explained as he led the two men across the warehouse floor, giving Anya a look that warned against any sudden moves. 'They've come to ask us a few questions.'

Both detectives exchanged glances as they approached the van. Clearly it meant something to them.

'This is your van?' Mahsud asked.

'For our sins.' Drake forced a pained smile. 'The old girl hasn't exactly distinguished herself. That's why we brought in the Rover. Something a bit more reliable, you know?'

'I'm afraid I wouldn't. A car like that is beyond the salary of a humble detective,' Gondal said with a faint chuckle. 'On that subject, what line of work are you in, Mr Douglas?'

'We're a freight company. Apex Deliveries.' Reaching into his pocket, Drake fished out a crumpled business card and proudly held it out, as if he relished the chance to represent his company. 'We're expanding into Pakistan, so they sent us as kind of an… advance team to lay the ground-work, set up warehousing, logistics, all the rest.'

Apex Deliveries was one of many front companies set up by the Agency as a convenient cover for clandestine operations. It was legitimate in the sense that it was a registered business which filed tax returns, kept financial records, contact details, even maintained its own website to create the illusion of a functioning business entity. Of course, it had never delivered a single piece of freight in its existence, and its 'corporate headquarters' was nothing more than a postal box in Milwaukee that was checked once a month, but that was unlikely to mean much to a pair of police officers half a world away.

Gondal looked around, taking in the meagre collection of empty tables, the decrepit van parked in the centre of the room. It didn't exactly look like the hub for a big delivery firm.

'You said you wanted to ask me some questions,' Drake prompted.

Mahsud turned to face him, removing his sunglasses to reveal a pair of dark, calculating eyes. 'Where were you between midnight and 2 a.m. last night?'

Drake knew right away what the man's agenda was. He was trying to catch him off guard with the sudden question, making him sweat and perhaps give away something critical.

'Well, right here,' Drake said, managing to look perplexed by the question. 'We'd only arrived yesterday evening.'

'All of you?' Mahsud persisted.

'Yeah, all of us.'

'And the night watchman will confirm this if we question him? Your van did not enter or leave during that time?'

He was trying to play hardball now. But Drake knew the night watchman didn't log vehicles entering or leaving. He'd had to specifically stop at the man's hut just to get his attention, and even then he'd acted put upon, disturbed from cricket match he'd been watching on a little portal TV.

'If he was doing his job, I'd imagine so.' He eyed the two men curiously. 'Look, I don't want to be difficult, but we have a lot of work ahead of us. Do you mind telling me what this is all about?'

'Forgive my companion, Mr Douglas. It has been a long day for both of us,' Gondal said, removing a handkerchief from his pocket and using it to wipe his brow. 'The truth is that two men disappeared last night from a residential district in Islamabad. Earlier today their bodies were found in shallow graves several miles outside the city. At the time of the abduction, witnesses reported seeing a grey panel van in the area matching the description of your vehicle, hearing the sounds of a scuffle and raised voices speaking in English.'

Fuck, fuck, *fuck*! his mind screamed at him. They obviously hadn't disposed of the two bodies as well as they'd thought last night. Perhaps the area in which they'd buried them was more heavily used than it appeared in the dead of night, or perhaps the scent had drawn predators to the area, which in turn sparked human interest.

Worse still, someone in a nearby building must have overheard the confrontation, perhaps even called those two security officers in the first place to investigate the van. And now the police were on the case.

This was a situation that could go downhill fast. If these men suspected them of wrongdoing, they could arrest them all on the spot. The result would be the total failure of their mission, and the end of any hopes they still held of taking out Cain.

A brief, fleeting glance at Anya told him she was harbouring similar thoughts, while her slight change in posture signalled her intention to take direct and violent action to remedy it. He was by now all too aware of how ruthless she could be when backed into a corner.

'So they've got you out questioning everyone in the district who owns a panel van?' Drake managed to chuckle in sympathy, shaking his head. 'You must have a lot of calls to make today, detective.'

The older man gave a rueful smile. 'You have no idea. But all the same, we have procedures to follow, so it must be done. Now, you say you were here in this warehouse last night. Can anyone corroborate that?'

'We all can,' Mason chimed in. 'We were here unpacking our stuff until pretty late. If anyone had tried to leave, we'd have seen them.'

'Unless you were all involved,' Mahsud reasoned, his tone dark and accusing.

Drake held his hands out in a gesture of helplessness. 'Look, I understand you have a job to do, but we're just delivery drivers — we're not in the business of murdering people.'

'I understand. Nobody is accusing you of anything, Mr Douglas. This is just standard procedure.' Gondal paused for a few seconds, considering the situation. 'May I see your passports?'

Drake looked over at Anya, wanting to remove her from the situation before she did something they all regretted. 'Anna, would you do me a favour and fetch them? They should be in the office at the back.'

'Anna' hesitated for a second, then reluctantly nodded. 'Of course.'

As she moved off to retrieve the fake IDs they'd brought, Drake did his best not to look like what he was — an extremely guilty man who was in very real danger of being discovered. His only hope at this moment was to try to bluff their way out. They certainly couldn't afford to leave any more dead bodies in their wake, especially not police officers who would soon be missed if they failed to report in.

It was at that moment that he happened to glance over at Mason, and felt his heart skip a beat. A small but noticeable stain had formed on his jacket, several small red patches beginning to show through the fabric across the left side of his chest. It wasn't too obvious yet, but he knew it would be soon enough.

If he could see it, then Gondal and Mahsud were likely to spot it at any moment. And when they saw a bloodstain on one of the very men they were questioning about an abduction and murder, it was safe to say they could kiss goodbye to any chance of talking their way out of this.

With no other way of getting his attention, Drake stared directly at Mason until the man sensed something was wrong and looked over. As soon as he had eye contact, Drake glanced purposefully down to Mason's chest. He couldn't say it out loud, but his meaning was plain.

*You're bleeding. Fucking do something before you give us all away!*

A sudden widening of his eyes and tightening in his friend's shoulders told Drake his message had been understood. Turning away nonchalantly, Mason reached for a plastic cup of coffee that had been sitting on the worktop since this morning, held it up and pretended to drink, only to fumble it and lose his grip at the last second.

'Aw, man. You've got to be kidding me,' he groaned as long-cold coffee slopped onto his jacket, neatly masking the blood stain. 'I just bought this damn thing.'

Mahsud watched with mild irritation as Mason picked up a rag that only hours before had been used for cleaning automatic weapons, and set about dabbing at the coffee stain.

Mercifully, Anya returned from her brief foray then, passports in hand. She turned them over to Gondal, who quickly leafed through them, comparing each person in the room to the picture laid out before him.

Each of them possessed several fake passports under various nationalities, obtained at no small cost from a forger in Berlin who had come highly recommended to Drake. They were unlikely to pass detailed technical examination, but he knew they were at least good enough to fool the naked eye.

Satisfied with what he saw, the detective laid them down on a nearby table. 'Well, these all look to be in order.' He reached into his jacket and produced a cell phone. 'You will not mind if I call your company to confirm what you told me?'

Drake resisted the urge to swallow. 'Of course not. Be my guest.'

Gondal had started dialling before he'd even replied.

–

Dan Franklin awoke with a start, jolted out of sleep by the buzz of his cell phone. Opening his eyes and forcing his head up from the pillow, he glanced with bleary eyes at his bedside clock – 3.12 a.m.

Who the hell was calling him at such an hour?

It took him a moment or two to realize the ringing wasn't coming from his work cell, which was charging on the floor beside his bed. It was his other phone. The burner. The one whose number was known only to one man – Ryan Drake.

The phone was hidden in the top drawer of his clothes bureau on the far side of the room. He could hear it buzzing again, the vibration slightly masked by the soft clothes it was nestled amongst.

If that phone was ringing, it meant Drake needed his help.

'Shit,' he said under his breath, swinging his legs over the edge of the bed as the ringing continued.

Gondal said nothing as he stood there with the phone to his ear, and indeed, all activity in the warehouse seemed to have ceased. Standing as close as he was, Drake could just hear the faint buzz as the line rang out.

The two detectives exchanged a look. The kind of look that can only pass between two people who have worked together for a long time and know each other well.

Taking it as a signal to be on his guard, Mahsud began pacing slowly around the *Bukhanka* like a shark circling its prey. As he passed the cab, he glanced inside the open driver's window, taking note of the grimy, worn interior, before heading towards the rear doors. His hand was at his hip again, ready to draw down at the first sign of trouble.

Drake knew he could do nothing to stop the man without arousing suspicion.

He could feel a pair of eyes on him, and guessed who it was. Looking over at Anya, he saw the woman make a small but purposeful nod towards the detective. He didn't need to be a mind reader to know exactly what she was thinking.

*If he opens those doors, you need to kill him.*

–

The phone was still ringing as Franklin worked frantically to heave himself out of bed. Weakened by spinal surgery that he was still recovering from, he was hardly light on his feet at the best of times, but the mornings were always the worst. It was as if his legs had to wake up independently of his brain.

And today was no day for sleeping in.

Gritting his teeth, he gripped his bedside table and used it to lever himself up into a standing position. His legs felt heavy and numb beneath him, like two lumps of dead flesh that weren't connected to his body, but he was upright.

Turning towards the source of the noise, he began to move, throwing one leg out in front and shifting his weight forward. Moving, one step at a time. The feeling was beginning to return now as the blood started pumping, the numbness gradually receding as if it were draining out through his feet.

Another step, and another. The phone was still ringing. How long had it been going? He didn't know.

Another step. He tried to kick his left leg out in front of him, tried to increase his pace, but his foot came down awkwardly and he went over on his ankle. Losing his balance, he pitched forward and fell, landing heavily on the wooden floor.

'Goddamn it!' he cried out in frustration.

Crouched down inside the rusting, dirty, oil-smelling cargo compartment, Keira Frost stared across the shadowy little enclosure at the young boy, bound and gagged, leaning against the opposite wall. His eyes were big and white in the gloom, staring right back at her, his chest rising and falling with short, rapid breaths.

No doubt he was well aware of the danger of discovery, and what it would mean for him. The automatic she had trained on him left him in no doubt about that.

Reaching up, Frost held a finger to her lips, imploring him to keep quiet. He couldn't cry out, but there were plenty of ways for one to make noise in such a small, metallic space. She could only hope he trusted the police even less than he trusted them, or that he knew what would happen to him if he tried to alert them.

Just outside, Drake watched with growing desperation as Mahsud closed in on the van's rear doors. It was clear now that the lack of response to Gondal's call was prompting him to search the vehicle, and that any protests would only fuel his suspicions.

At that moment, Gondal himself turned around to regard Drake. The look on his face had changed now, as if some subconscious switch had just been flicked. The amiable, kindly old man look had disappeared from his eyes, replaced by a shrewd, calculating intelligence that Drake knew had been lurking just beneath the surface the whole time.

It was clear Gondal now considered the call a waste of time, and the people in this warehouse had gone from being a routine line of enquiry to possible murder suspects. And any second, he would act on his suspicions.

There was no choice but to act first. They would have to take out the two police officers as quietly as possible, hide their bodies and just hope that they had completed their mission by the time the men's absence was noticed. It was a gamble, but it was all they had.

Two more needless deaths on his conscience.

Almost without being aware of it, Drake found himself reaching for the automatic hidden at the small of his back. Nearby, Anya did the same thing.

–

Franklin looked up at that bureau that seemed to tower over him like the summit of some indomitable mountain. He had landed hard on the cold, unyielding floor, and knew he'd be left with some telling bruises tomorrow, but none of that mattered now.

All that mattered was getting to the phone. Drake's life might well rest on what he did in the next few seconds.

Seized by a sudden surge of desperate energy, Franklin crawled forward the last couple of feet, then reached out and gripped the second drawer handle on the bureau, using it as leverage to pull himself up from the floor. His muscles were trembling from the exertion as he pulled himself higher, higher with each passing moment, managing to get one foot planted firmly on the floor.

Gripping the top drawer, he yanked it open and thrust his hand inside, managing to close his fingers around the cheap plastic body of the phone before slumping back down to the floor once again.

He didn't care now. Stabbing the accept call button, he held the phone to his ear, somehow forcing his breathing under control long enough to speak two words.

'Apex Deliveries.'

–

Half a world away, Detective Gondal froze on the spot, caught in the midst of lowering his phone to cancel the call. Holding his free hand out, he snapped his fingers to get his colleague's attention as he raised the device back up to his ear. Sure enough, Mahsud paused by the van's rear doors, waiting to see what would happen next.

Drake too had stopped just as he was reaching for his weapon, staring at the older man in tense, fraught silence. He wanted to punch the air in triumph, but knew it was far too early for celebrations. Even if Franklin had answered the call, there was no guarantee Gondal would buy what he was selling.

'Good morning, sir,' he began, assuming the same pleasant, amiable manner he'd used with Drake. 'My name is Detective Sajid Gondal with the Punjab Police Department. I'm calling about some of your employees based in Rawalpindi.'

'Police? Is everything all right?' Franklin gasped, managing to translate his physical discomfort and fatigue into shocked concern. 'Has something happened to them?'

'Not at all, sir. They're with me right now. I am actually following up on another matter, and was hoping to eliminate them from our enquiries.'

'I see…' Franklin allowed that statement to trail off. 'So how can I help you?'

'I have four of them here with me. I would appreciate it if you could name each of them in turn, and perhaps describe their appearance to me. That should be enough to confirm who they are.'

'Sure thing. Well, let's see… There's Bob Douglas, the team leader. He's late-thirties, tall, dark hair, green eyes. Then there's Carl Masterson. Big guy, shaved head, olive skin. Does a lot of heavy lifting. Sarah McCord is early thirties, with brownish hair and… freckles across her nose.'

Drake braced himself for what was coming. Already he could sense where Franklin's description was going to go off the rails, and this was it.

He could only hope his friend's ability to bullshit and improvise was as good as his memory.

'And the last one should be Kate Fisk. She's small, short dark hair and a piercing in her nose.'

Gondal frowned at this, glancing over at Anya. She was the odd one out. The only one whose appearance and passport didn't come close to matching Franklin's description.

'You are sure about that?' Gondal asked, and Drake winced inwardly.

'Well, I…' He trailed off, no doubt wondering what the hell was going on. He and Drake had agreed the cover story in advance, and Franklin had memorized the team's false identities just in case they encountered a situation like this where he had to vouch for them.

What he hadn't been prepared for was the change in their set-up. From his point of view, it was like trying to fight an opponent blind, with one hand tied behind his back.

Before Drake could say or do anything to intervene, Anya piped up. 'Kate was taken ill with the flu just before we left the States,' she said helpfully, speaking loud enough that Franklin could hear her voice down the line.

'Oh yeah, of course,' Franklin said, immediately grasping the situation and running with it like the pro he was. 'I'm sorry, detective, but it's early in the morning here and I haven't had nearly enough coffee. Kate had to bail out at the last minute. I can't remember the name of her replacement off the top of my head, but I know she was tall, with blonde hair and blue eyes. If you give me some time to check our personnel listings, I'm sure I can dig it out.'

'That won't be necessary, sir,' Gondal said, giving Drake a thoughtful, contemplative look. 'You've been very helpful. My office will be in touch if they need anything else.'

'Sure thing. You have a great day, sir,' Franklin added, playing his middle manager role to perfection. Drake could have kissed the man if he'd been within reach.

Ending the call, Gondal scooped up the passports and held them out to Drake. 'I am sorry to have troubled you, Mr Douglas. But I appreciate your cooperation.'

'No problem at all,' Drake lied as he took the documents.

'You will be here, if we have any follow-up questions?'

'Of course. Until the company pays for some decent accommodation, at least,' he added with a forced smile. 'Keep the card anyway. You can contact us through that number if you need anything else.'

'I will,' Gondal said, lingering a moment longer as if he intended to say something more. Instead, he released Drake from his gaze and slipped his sunglasses back on. 'In the meantime, I'm afraid we have a lot more calls to make before the day is out.'

With Mahsud accompanying him, he headed for the exit at a measured, unhurried pace, mercifully leaving Drake and the others alone.

'Oh, and one more thing, Mr Douglas,' he added, pausing by the door.

'What's that?'

He fixed Drake with a hard, direct stare. 'Stay out of trouble while you're in Pakistan.'

Somehow Drake managed an amused smile. 'I intend to.'

Nodding, the older man turned away and slipped through the wicket door, allowing it to swing shut behind him. Only when they heard the sound of a vehicle engine starting up outside did Mason risk opening the laptop linked to the outside security cameras.

'They're leaving,' he announced, lowering his head as the tension finally dissipated. 'We're good.'

McKnight let out a breath. 'Thank Christ for that.'

Approaching the van, Drake slapped the side a couple of times, signalling that it was safe to come out. Sure enough, the doors popped open immediately and Frost emerged from the darkened interior, clutching her weapon. Yasin was still sitting on the floor where she'd left him.

'You all right?' Mason asked as the young woman arched her back.

'Might need a new pair of underwear after that,' she observed drily. 'Jesus, talk about a close call. I thought we had Columbo on our asses back there.' She looked over at Drake, for once appearing genuinely impressed. 'Remind me to buy Dan a beer next time I see him. The guy earned it today.'

Drake only wished he could share their new-found sense of relief. 'I wouldn't break out the champagne any time soon.'

'What do you mean?'

'Those guys weren't Punjabi police – they were field operatives.'

That was enough to well and truly kill her buzz. 'Spooks?'

He nodded grimly, seeing Gondal for what he was. The crumpled, ill-fitting suit, the bumbling, affable mannerisms, the unassuming presence; all of it was a carefully cultivated facade intended to throw people off, to lower their guard and make mistakes. Mistakes he could exploit.

'How the hell can you—'

'Ryan is right,' Anya cut in, eyeing Drake with what might have been grudging approval. 'They were lying when they claimed to be police officers. My guess is they belong to the Pakistani Intelligence Service.'

Mason frowned, failing to see the connection. 'But why would the ISI care about two security guards going missing?'

Frost, however, had already connected the dots, even if she didn't like the picture they painted. 'Aw, Christ. Don't you get it, Cole?'

'They weren't security guards,' Drake finished for her.

Only now was he beginning to realize just how wrong he'd been last night. Those two men posing as neighbourhood security were, in all likelihood, ISI operatives themselves. Perhaps the Pakistanis already knew about the existence of the safe house, and were using field teams to covertly monitor the place. Or perhaps they had been given the location of the meeting in advance and were trying to scope it out.

Whatever the reason, Drake and Anya had wandered right into them last night. If he'd allowed them to go free, they would have returned to their masters and told them everything that had happened, blowing the entire operation out of the water. Only her swift and brutally pragmatic actions had prevented it.

He glanced over at Anya, meeting her gaze for a brief moment. He didn't have to say what he was thinking. She knew.

The rest of his team, however, didn't hesitate to voice their thoughts.

'Jesus, if the ISI's all over this, we're screwed,' Mason said.

'What if they've got us surrounded already?' McKnight wondered aloud.

Frost too was seeing the problems that seemed to be multiplying by the hour. 'First the Agency, then the Pakistanis? This is fucked. We'll be walking into a shitstorm tonight.'

'Then we need to cut and run now,' Mason concluded.

'All right, listen up! All of you,' Drake spoke up. 'Calm down. Nobody's surrounding us. If they knew for sure we were involved last night, we wouldn't even be having this conversation now.'

As frightening a notion as it was to contemplate, Drake knew the ISI wouldn't fuck around when it came to the deaths of their own operatives. Gondal would have come in here with an armed tactical team if he had any real evidence.

Frost shook her head. 'But they—'

'Obviously they know something's up,' he conceded. 'They suspected us enough to drive out here, but we're just one lead out of hundreds. They can't follow every single one, and by the time they figure out what we're really doing here, we'll be long gone.'

Frost folded her arms, eyeing him dubiously. 'So what are you suggesting?'

'We stick to the plan.'

It was a gamble to be sure, but then so was just about every aspect of this operation. Anyway, if Gondal had already allocated some kind of surveillance package to the warehouse, there could be few more incriminating sights than the entire team evacuating just minutes after his inspection. Their best option, as incongruous as it seemed, was to tough it out until it was time to leave.

Knowing he needed to get the others moving, he added, 'Cole, get yourself cleaned up. Sam, prep the van and load it up. Anya, take the kid into one of the offices at the back and make sure he's secured.'

'I'll take him,' Frost spoke up.

He shook his head. 'I need you to check everything's still in place with the Judas code. Anya, he's all yours.'

'Fine,' Anya replied, not looking happy about it.

She was about to clamber inside the van to retrieve their prisoner when Frost stepped into her path, defiant and protective even now. 'You're not going to kill him.'

One curious aspect of Anya's personality that Drake had come to understand was that she always held a certain respect for people who stuck by what they believed in, even if she didn't agree with it. She had never enjoyed a good relationship with Keira Frost – their personalities were too different for that – and yet he saw a glimmer of that same grudging respect now as she regarded the young technical specialist.

'That was our agreement,' she said at length.

Strangely, that seemed to satisfy Frost. Anya was many things, but one thing she'd never done was directly lie to any of them. Holding her gaze a moment longer, Frost stepped aside, allowing her to pass.

With yet another potential argument averted, Drake looked at his watch. 'All right, Cain's flight touches down within the hour. Finish up your weapon and equipment checks, and be ready to move out. Everyone understand?'

Nobody objected.

'Good. Let's go!'

# Chapter 44

As their car bumped along the rough, dusty road away from the industrial estate, Gondal was bent over his notebook in the passenger seat, neatly writing down a long series of numbers.

'What do you think?' Mahsud asked, his meaty hand on the wheel.

Gondal was quiet, concentrating on transcribing the passport number he'd memorized, plus the licence plates of the two vehicles. As fate would have it, he'd been endowed with a capacious memory, particularly when it came to numbers and written text. It was a gift that took a great deal of discipline to properly utilize, but it was one that had proven invaluable in his career as an intelligence operative.

Finishing his work, he laid the notepad in his lap and let out a breath, calming his mind while he replayed the encounter back at the warehouse. Every word spoken, every gesture, every movement and facial expression. Each of these factors were different elements in an equation that allowed him to make his judgement.

'The leader, Douglas… he is hiding something,' he decided at length. 'He was nervous around us, even if he hid it well.'

Of course, that could mean any number of things. Perhaps they were running some kind of illegal operation from that warehouse, perhaps one of the vehicles was stolen, in which case he had little interest in them. Petty crime or fraud meant nothing to Gondal. He had bigger concerns.

Two of their men were dead. That was something that couldn't go unanswered.

Mahsud grunted agreement. A naturally suspicious man, it was likely he harboured similar opinions, if less well informed.

'What do you want to do?'

That was the question. Sending in a field ops unit to apprehend them was heavy handed at best, while allocating a surveillance team would tie up valuable resources that were sorely needed elsewhere. He was reluctant to take either step based on gut instinct. He needed something more to work with.

'We do some digging,' he decided, reaching for his cell phone.

A background check on the licence plates, Douglas's passport, as well as Apex Deliveries that he claimed to work for, would tell him whether his suspicions were correct. And if so, he would come down on that man with everything he had.

Keira Frost was alone in one of the vacant offices when Drake found her. She had pulled up her T-shirt to expose the gunshot wound at her side, and was busy tending it. An old dressing, stained with patches of blood, lay on the table beside her. He heard a sharp intake of breath and saw her tense up as she pressed an antiseptic solution against the wound, though she wasn't being gentle or tentative about it. Her movements were rough, agitated, as if she wanted the discomfort.

He could guess what was eating her. It was the same reason he'd come here.

'You going to talk, or are you going to stand there eyeballing me?' she asked without turning around, having caught the sound of his approach.

Drake knew what he wanted to say. 'How long ago was it?'

'This ain't *Lord of the Rings*, Ryan. Stop speaking in riddles. How long ago was what?' Unrolling a fresh dressing, she pressed it against her side and reached for the surgical tape on the table in front of her.

He crossed his arms, knowing she wouldn't like the next question, knowing she probably wouldn't want to answer. But whether she wanted to or not, she needed to.

'That you were in the same situation as Yasin?'

Straight away he saw her tense up again, only this time it had nothing to do with pain. Her hand fumbled the tape just as she was picking it up, dropping it on the floor by her foot.

'Goddamn it,' she hissed, bending down stiffly to pick it up.

Drake was faster, and snatched it up before she could retrieve it. 'Give me that back,' she snapped, trying to pluck it from his grasp.

'I saw the way you stood up for him.'

'He was just a kid, for Christ's sake,' she said, though she couldn't hide the rush of colour that had risen to her cheeks.

'You've never acted that way before.'

'So what?' she demanded, bristling with anger. 'Christ, what does it matter?'

'It matters to me.' He didn't resist this time as she grabbed at the tape and pulled it angrily out of his hand. 'And I know this is going to eat away at you if you don't let it go.'

It hadn't been too hard to join the dots on this one. Frost had never spoken much about her life before the military and the Agency, and had always made it clear that was how she wanted it to stay. He'd always assumed she'd had a difficult upbringing that she wasn't keen to publicize, but even he hadn't expected something like this.

'Ancient history,' she mumbled. 'You don't want to know.'

'Try me.'

'I'd rather not.'

'I don't care.'

With a weary sigh, she laid the tape down on the table, her shoulders sagging in defeat. 'My dad – my real dad, I mean – didn't stick around long after I was born. Never even got a chance to meet the son of a bitch. But there were other guys... later. There were always other guys.' She flashed one of the crooked smiles he'd come to recognize when she was uncomfortable. 'Pick your sob story. Most of them didn't give a shit about me, some got real pissed off having me around. You think I'm a pain in the ass now? You should have seen me when I was ten.'

Drake didn't speak. He knew there was more coming.

'Then, I got a little older, I wasn't a kid any more... and one of them started taking a liking to me. That was all the reason I needed, so I bailed when I was 14, hitch-hiked to Chicago, where I figured I could disappear. Spent about a year living on the streets. Just like Yasin.'

She shrugged as if it was of no consequence to her now, but her eyes told a different story. 'You think you've had tough times, but you haven't. Not really. Not until your stomach's cramping up because you haven't eaten in two days, and you can't feel your feet because you've spent the night beneath an overpass in the middle of December. Chicago's got some real long winters, believe me. I didn't realize at first, but I learned. I learned a lot of things.'

Drake laid a hand on her shoulder, not really knowing what he hoped to achieve. Just wanting to give her something, to let her know he was there for her.

'I'm sorry, Keira.'

She smiled then. The kind of ironic, mocking smile he had come to know all too well. 'What the fuck are you sorry for? Everybody's got a sob story.'

'Including Yasin?'

The smile faded then. 'Give him a chance, Ryan. I know it's a risk, but... he doesn't deserve to be where he is. No kid does.'

Noble sentiments to be sure, but Drake was under no illusions about who and what this mission was about. They hadn't come to Pakistan to put the world to rights, to save or help anyone. They had a very different purpose here.

'Even if we let him go, it won't change anything,' Drake warned her. 'He won't be any better off than he was this morning.'

'But he'll be alive. That's a hell of a lot better than he could have ended up.'

She was right about that. Whatever their purpose here, however cold and ruthless they might have to be, they were still human beings. If they lost sight of that, then maybe they didn't deserve to survive tonight.

'Fair enough. I won't shoot him. How does that sound?'

A glimmer of a smile returned then. It wasn't much, but it was real.

'Sounds like progress.'

–

Yasin watched in silence as Anya carefully removed the rounds from the magazine on her Colt M1911 automatic and laid the brass cartridges in a line on the dusty floor. Taking the tension off the springs kept them from weakening, and helped ensure the weapon didn't jam at a crucial moment. And if nothing else, it gave her something to occupy herself with.

She sat cross-legged on the floor, her back against the wall, her eyes on the weapon. Even without the gun, she knew she had nothing to fear from the scrawny, untrained boy on the opposite side of the room.

Nonetheless, she could feel his eyes on her as she worked. It was distracting and irritating, and as much as she tried to ignore it, the feeling only intensified as the seconds crawled by. She had never been comfortable around children, perhaps because she'd had so little exposure to them in her adult life.

'If you have something to say, then speak,' she advised, speaking in Pashto. It wasn't often she felt the need to break the silence, but now was such a time.

She had removed his gag to make it easier to breathe, on the under-standing that if he screamed or cried out, she would take steps to ensure he never talked again. A graphic description of what was actually involved in removing a human tongue had been enough to get her point across.

'You know about guns.' It was more a statement than a question.

'I do.'

'Who taught you?'

'Lots of people.'

She could guess what was coming next.

'Have you ever killed anyone?'

She saw no need to lie to him. 'Yes.'

'How many?'

She glanced up at him then. 'Including young boys?'

'I'm not a boy,' he hit back, his pride stirred by her disparaging remark. 'I'll be 12 next month. Old enough to be a man.'

Anya couldn't quite hide a smile of amusement at such a futile display of masculine bravado, and turned her attention back to the weapon. 'There is more to being a man than getting older. You will learn that one day, if you live that long.'

'How would you know?'

She paused, in the midst of inspecting the weapon's feed mechanism. 'What?'

'How would you know?' he repeated. 'You're not a man.'

He had a point there, but she had no interest in being drawn into a philosophical debate with someone 30 years younger than herself.

'You talk too much,' she decided, resuming her work.

'Would you have killed me?' he asked suddenly, speaking with the frank honesty that only came with youth. 'If they hadn't stopped you?'

Forcing herself not to sigh in exasperation, she looked up at him once more. 'Would you like to find out?'

But for once, he didn't look intimidated by this implied threat. 'You won't do it now. You promised that other man you wouldn't. He's a good person, I think. You're not.'

Anya shrugged and turned her attention back to the weapon. Back to something she was comfortable with.

'Like I said, you talk too much.'

# Chapter 45

*Forward Operating Base 'Foxtail', Afghan–Pakistan border – 23 February 1986*

'No!' Anya snapped, bristling with indignation and defiance at the new orders Cain had just delivered. 'I will not do it.'

'It's not a matter of choice,' Cain reminded her. 'These are your instructions. You've been ordered to go back to Langley for debriefing.'

'Debriefing?' she repeated. 'Our mission here isn't over.'

'Yours is.'

Anya folded her arms, staring him down. She wasn't buying into this. 'So I am supposed to run back to Langley like a frightened dog, and leave the rest of the task force here? No.' She shook her head emphatically. 'I will not leave them.'

Cain was as annoyed as he was perplexed by her reaction. After months spent operating behind enemy lines, fighting and risking their lives in appalling conditions, most operatives would have jumped at the chance to return stateside. Why then was she so determined to stay here in this godforsaken place?

'You'll do what you're told,' he snapped, a harder edge in his voice now. 'What the hell's wrong with you, Anya?'

She took a step towards him, while outside the wind howled and the rain lashed against the side of the tent. 'You have no idea what we are doing here, what this means to me. I had to work twice as hard to get them to respect me, risk my life more times than I can remember. Now they do, finally, and you would have me turn and run like a coward? No!'

Overcome with frustration at her stubborn refusal to see sense, Cain slammed his fist down on the map table.

'Goddamn it, Anya! Do you know the strings I had to...' He trailed off, instantly wishing he could undo what he'd just said.

But it was too late. The damage was done.

Her vivid blue eyes narrowed. 'What do you mean by that, Marcus?'

'Forget it,' he said, turning away.

Moving forward, she clutched his arm, pulling him close and staring him hard in the eye. 'This was your doing, wasn't it? You were the one who made this happen. Why?'

'Because I'm afraid of losing you,' he snapped, finally admitting the truth he'd tried so hard to bury.' Because every day since you got on that flight, I've been thinking about you. Every night I've lain awake thinking about what you were *doing, wondering if you were safe... wishing I was with you. That's why I want you to come back, Anya. Because I don't want to go through that again.'*

*Anya took a step back, startled by what she'd just heard. Of course she was shocked, he thought angrily. How the hell had he expected her to react to such a confession from a man ten years older than her?*

*'Forget what you just heard,' he advised her, already trying to make excuses. He glanced away, unable to meet her gaze. 'It's been a long trip, and you don't need to hear this crap.'*

*That was when he heard her voice, thin and uncertain where before it had been defiant and angry. 'Marcus?'*

*'What?'*

*He looked up just as she moved closer, tilted her head back and pressed her lips against his, tentative and hesitant at first but soon with a growing confidence and desire. He was so surprised by the unexpected gesture that for a moment or two, he barely reacted.*

*Only when he felt her arms slip around his neck, and his own instinctively circle her waist, did he at last realize what was happening. That was when it all changed, when all his worries and fears and uncertainties seemed to melt away, as he felt the firm warmth of her body against his. He wanted her with an urgency, a need, a hunger he'd never experienced before, and somehow he knew it was the same for her. It always had been.*

*The two of them, so different in so many ways, had at last found what they both needed and wanted. Each other.*

–

*Benazir Bhutto International Airport, Pakistan – March 2010*

Travelling under diplomatic protection, Marcus Cain was able to breeze straight through the busy airport after disembarking his flight, circumventing security checkpoints and passport control as if he owned the place. Other men might have taken some measure of satisfaction in this exercise of power and privilege, but Cain had his mind on other matters.

As agreed, Hawkins and a contingent of security operatives were waiting to escort Cain to their two-vehicle convoy outside, his well-tailored suit standing in stark contrast to the fearsome appearance lent by his facial scarring. He would have to look into plastic surgery for that man, Cain thought absently as Hawkins fell in step beside him. It was just lucky for Hawkins that he was still useful enough to justify the investment.

'Where are we on security?' Cain asked right away. Hawkins knew better than to exchange greetings or enquire about his flight, most likely because the man didn't give a shit either way. Whatever the reason, it suited Cain just fine.

'Everything's set,' the field operative confirmed. 'The safe house is ready to go, and we have men standing by to cover all aspects of the op.'

'Reliable men, I assume?' Cain asked.

Hawkins gave him a sidelong glance, the scar twisting his smile into a disparaging sneer. 'Hand-picked them myself. Believe me, we've got the right guys for this kind of work.'

That was all he needed to know. Whatever his personal motivations, Cain was content to leave operational details in this man's hands.

Escorted by Hawkins, and with a pair of armed operatives in front and behind, Cain strode through the main terminal, the crowds of travellers parting with before him as he headed for the big automatic doors leading outside.

As soon as they were free from the cool, air-conditioned environment of the terminal building, the wall of heat hit him like a physical blow. The tropical air, heavy with moisture, seemed to raise beads of perspiration on his exposed skin almost immediately, while the sun beat down hard through a gap in the clouds.

Slipping on a pair of sunglasses, Cain glanced at the pair of black Audi SUVs with diplomatic plates waiting for them in the crowded pickup area. Cain and Hawkins went into the lead vehicle, eager to escape the oppressive heat, with most of the security detail taking the follow-up car.

'What was your read on Qalat?' Cain asked, loosening his tie. He'd once been well adapted to hot climates like this, but it had been a long time since he'd ventured out into the field. Too long, he realized now.

'He'll be at the meeting,' Hawkins concluded as their driver pulled away and the terminal building slid by outside.

'That's not what I asked.'

Hawkins shrugged. 'He's a hard-ass. Cool under pressure, not the kind to crack easily. I caught him off guard with the Black List, but I wouldn't count on that a second time.'

Cain most certainly wouldn't. He glanced at his watch as the convoy pulled out of the airport perimeter, joining the main drag leading into Islamabad. Just over four hours to go. Enough time to prepare himself for the task ahead. One way or another, it was sure to be a long day for both men, and he intended to be ready for it.

'A man like him isn't going to give up his best bargaining chip for nothing,' Hawkins went on. 'If he's going to play ball, he'll want something in return. Something big.'

He always did, Cain mused as he remembered the young Pakistani intelligence operative from two decades earlier. An upstart punching above his weight, testing his influence, always looking for a new play. He knew how to handle such men.

'I ever tell you about the first job I had?' he asked, leaning back in his seat as the traffic and tired looking travellers passed by outside. 'I was 15 years old, working in a T-shirt store joint down by San Clemente beach – the kind of place that does those shitty iron-on logos. Anyway, there was this older kid, college age I guess, named Billy Henderson; pretty much ran the place when the owner wasn't around. Kind of arrogant, full of himself, but man, you should have seen him sell. It was like watching a master artist at work. I mean, this kid could sell yellow snow to an Eskimo and make him feel good about it.'

Cain had always felt a certain admiration for people with that kind of self confidence. The kind who could just walk up to complete strangers and charm the money right out of their wallets. It took a special kind of guy to do that, and Billy had been one of the best.

'The only problem with young Billy was that he liked to put his hand in the till from time to time. Beer money, I guess, or maybe he just felt like he was owed. Now, I was an honest kid back then, believe it or not, so I told the store owner exactly what was going on. And you know what he said to me?' He smiled faintly at the memory. '*I know.* Can you believe that? He *knew* this kid was stealing from him all along, but he also knew the money Billy was bringing in was worth even more, so he let him get away with it. Mutually beneficial relationship.'

'So that's it?' Hawkins asked.

'Not quite. A month or two goes by. The summer season was over, young Billy was about to head back to college and stopped by to pick up his pay check. But he didn't get it. Instead he got a bill for all the money he'd stolen over the past couple of months, and a promise from the owner that he'd have Billy arrested if he didn't pay up. Turns out this old guy had been keeping real careful records of everything this kid had done, and was just waiting for the right time. With the season over, I guess he didn't need poor Billy to sell his shitty T-shirts any more.' Even now, he couldn't help but smirk in amusement at the look on that kid's face. 'I learned a pretty important lesson from that little punk. You can get away with a lot as long as you're useful, but it'll always catch up with you.'

Just like young Billy Henderson, Vizur Qalat might prove useful for the time being, but the summer season was going to end for him sooner or later.

'Once we have what we need, I might need you to present Qalat with my bill,' Cain decided. 'I don't want any loose ends left after this one.'

Hawkins smiled, the facial scar twisting his mouth into a cruel parody of a smile as he leaned back in his seat. Cain knew plenty of men who had become killers because circumstances or their profession demanded it, but Hawkins was of a different sort. He enjoyed it, sought it out, and never hesitated to do what was asked, no matter how abhorrent. That was what made him the perfect soldier for this new kind of war.

He supposed every great soldier was a product of their time, like a predator perfectly adapted to its hunting environment. Anya had certainly been a product of hers, but her war and her time were over now.

Cain would make sure of it.

# Chapter 46

Drake stood before the simple wooden table in the centre of the warehouse that had become the focus of the team's planning operation, and which was now strewn with laptops, cell phones, maps, printed pictures and design blueprints of the target building. A lot of work had been done in a very short space of time to put this all together. Only time would tell whether it was enough.

With no functioning air conditioning, the temperature inside the warehouse had risen steadily throughout the day. Even now he could feel beads of sweat trickling down his back, his shirt clinging uncomfortably to his damp skin.

Trying to push such thoughts aside, he looked up from the cluttered ops table, surveying the team that he'd called together to go over the plan one final time. His friends, his comrades; people he had fought and bled beside, who had risked their lives for his and who he had gladly done the same for in return. They were as much his family as the sister he had left back home, the mother he had lost only last year, and he was asking them to venture into the fray with him once more.

And standing slightly apart from the others, an ominous and intimidating presence, the woman who had started it all. Anya, the most lethal soldier he had ever known. He was asking her to go to war one last time, to risk everything on one final gamble.

All or nothing. Win or die. Only one side was getting out of this alive.

'All right, this is it,' he began. 'You've all been through this plan with me before, so I'll keep this brief. If anyone has anything to say, now's the time.'

The others nodded in silence as Drake turned his attention to the map of the target area laid out on the table.

'So, step one is neutralising the building's security systems. Keira, you'll approach to within transmission range and send the Judas code, hacking into the cameras and disabling the electronic door locks. Once we've confirmed Cain's presence and location, we move on to step two – the assault on the building.'

He pointed to the apartment block that he and Anya had scouted earlier. 'The assault team will take up position here, waiting for the go command. As soon as the cameras are down, we'll launch our grapple hooks, aiming for the satellite cluster on the roof here,' he added, holding up a printed picture of the satellite dish he'd snapped during the recon. 'When the hooks are in place, we zip-line across to the roof of the target building and take down any security teams outside.'

It sounded easy when described like that, but Drake was under no illusions. The assault team would be defenceless and utterly vulnerable while they were crossing the zip line. If they were spotted, they were as good as dead.

'Step three is to breach the safe house,' he pressed on. 'With Keira covering the cameras, the assault team moves quickly towards whichever room Cain is in, killing or incapacitating anyone in their way.' He turned his attention to the design blueprints. 'Judging by the building's layout, the most logical place for the meeting to be held is the upper storey lounge. It's a big open-plan conference room that can accommodate plenty of security personnel and guests, and it's got a straight line to the panic room in the event of an emergency. Our priority must be to seal off that line of escape. Assuming we've still got the element of surprise, we move in with stun grenades and take out Cain's security operatives.'

As he laid out their plan, he tried to picture how the breach would unfold. He imagined the thunderous booms of the flashbang grenades, imagined himself shoving his way through the door, weapon sweeping the room. He imagined the kick of the MP7 in his hands as he put a burst of automatic fire into anyone unlucky enough to stand against him.

That wasn't going to be an easy thing to do. There was a chance the men protecting Marcus Cain were simply operatives doing their job. Men with lives and families. Sons, fathers, brothers whose deaths would weigh heavily on Drake's conscience for a long time to come. But for now, they were enemies, threats that had to be dealt with in the harshest possible way, because they would show no mercy to him or his team.

'In the event that Cain makes it to the panic room, we go to our backup plan and use breaching charges to either compromise the security door, or kill him.' That wasn't his favoured outcome, but one way or another Cain would be taken care of.

'Will that work?' Anya asked.

'Each charge contains enough PE4 to breach 12 inches of hardened concrete,' Samantha explained. 'I rigged them myself. If they can't breach that panic room, nothing can.'

Anya eyed her dubiously. When it came to explosives, the margin for error was necessarily small. 'Do you know what you're doing?'

The specialist, far from being angered, instead gave her a patient smile. 'I worked in explosive ordnance disposal for five years. So yeah, I know what I'm doing.'

That was an understatement, Drake knew. What Samantha didn't know about bombs and explosives wasn't worth knowing.

Anya cocked her head, saying nothing. Her expression, however, suggested she was at least satisfied with McKnight's competence.

Drake cleared his throat, hoping to move on from that uncomfortable exchange. 'Anyway, that's a worst-case scenario. Assuming we make entry to the room and neutralize any operatives protecting him, Cain will be in our hands. Which brings us to the final step – extraction. Sam will be standing by with the Range Rover, and will move in to pick us up when we bring Cain outside. Keira will have disabled the gate security by that point, so she should be able to drive straight into the building's courtyard unopposed. The assault team will bundle Cain into the vehicle, and we'll exfiltrate from the area as quickly as possible.'

With his summary complete, Drake looked up at the others. 'Questions?'

Anya had one ready and waiting. 'Where will I be during the attack?'

'Here, on overwatch.' Drake pointed to the apartment block overlooking the safe house. 'Your job will be to cover the assault team as they go in, take out any hostiles that show themselves, and protect us as we pull out.'

'No,' she said immediately, shaking her head. 'I will lead the assault team.'

Mason, who had remained silent until now, exchanged a nervous glance with Drake. 'That's not the plan.'

'Then the plan isn't acceptable to me.'

Frost eyed the older woman irritably. 'Nobody asked if it was "acceptable" to you. This isn't a fucking democracy.'

Anya returned Frost's hostile look in equal measure. 'You were the ones who asked me to come. Which means you need my help.'

'We brought you here to help us, not to lead us,' Drake said, his tone guarded. He knew his team would never accept Anya as their leader, but he needed her to come to that realization by herself. 'You can help us best by covering our backs.'

'That's not your decision. I'm the most logical choice to lead the assault.'

'How do you figure?' Mason asked.

Anya raised her chin defiantly, eyes flashing with stubborn pride. 'I was doing this long before any of you. I have led more assaults like this than your whole team combined.'

'Hey Anya, reality check. Nobody gives a shit what you did 20 years ago,' Frost hit back, clearly in a far less diplomatic mood than Drake. 'That's ancient history, and so are you. We don't need some old has-been playing prima donna.'

In most circumstances, Anya viewed Frost's barbed remarks as somewhat akin to a mosquito bite; a minor irritation to be endured while one concentrated on more worthy matters. But those words seemed to cut through all that, striking a raw nerve.

Slowly she turned her head to regard the young specialist. 'Do you know something, Frost? I wasn't so different from you once. Confident, arrogant, convinced I knew it all. Ancient history, as you say. But I soon learned just how wrong I was. I hope for your sake that you don't have to learn as I did.'

Even Frost, despite her fiery temperament, looked momentarily taken aback. 'Spare me the lecture,' she said, though her words had lost some of their sting. 'It's getting old.'

At this, Anya shook her head and folded her arms – a gesture Drake always took to be a bad sign. 'I go in with the assault team, or I don't go at all. It's that simple.'

'Why?' Drake asked.

Her eyes swept across the group, taking in each member in turn, preparing herself for what was coming. 'Because I know your team has no intention of keeping to our agreement.'

Whatever reaction she might have expected from such a statement, Drake doubted it measured up to the vociferous and indignant protests that were suddenly aimed her way.

'Oh, fuck you,' Frost spat. 'Bringing you here was the biggest mistake we ever made.'

'Is this the person that's supposed to be helping us?' Mason demanded. 'This is bullshit, Ryan.'

'This is a goddamn waste of time,' McKnight said, turning away and running her hands through her hair, bristling with agitation.

Drake had heard more than enough. This situation was going downhill fast, and if he didn't get control of it now then their tentative alliance was over for good.

'All right, quiet down. Shut up! All of you!' he shouted, his angry voice rising above the others to echo around the warehouse.

Straight away his team lapsed into silence, though the simmering hostility towards Anya was almost palpable. The woman herself remained unfazed, however. She had endured far worse in her life than angry words and raised voices.

Exhaling slowly to compose himself, Drake turned his eyes on Anya. She was at the centre of this conflict, and one way or another he needed to bring her onside.

'Come with me,' he snapped, turning and striding off towards a side exit in the building's exterior wall. He didn't bother to look back. He knew she would follow him.

Hauling open the door, he found himself facing onto a wide service road that ran between their warehouse and a similar unit nearby. There was no sign of anyone else in the vicinity, which wasn't surprising given the neglected state of the area. Nonetheless, he could hear the rumble of traffic on the main drags nearby, accompanied by heavier machinery in some of the industrial units further off. The heat was, if anything, even more oppressive now that they were outside.

Already he was beginning to regret coming here, but he knew what they had to say to each other wasn't something to be done in front of the others.

'Say what you have to say, Ryan,' Anya prompted, slamming the door shut.

Keeping his back to her, Drake clenched his fists. 'What the hell's going on?'

'What do you mean?'

Drake rounded on her. 'You've been pushing at everyone since I brought you in, trying to provoke us, trying to break us apart. Why? Do you want this mission to fail? Because you seem to be doing everything you can to make that happen.'

Anya regarded him in terse silence. 'Are you finished?'

'No, I'm not. But *we are* unless I get some answers,' he promised her.

'You don't want answers.'

His eyes narrowed. 'Really? Then what do I want?'

'You want reassurance. You want to be told that everything is going to be all right, that we will all get through this if we work together.' She let out a faint sigh and shook her head. 'But we won't, Ryan. Make no mistake, people are going to die tonight. Maybe you, maybe me. Maybe all of us.'

He couldn't believe what he was hearing. 'If you really believe that, why do you want to lead the attack?'

To his surprise, she glanced away as if she couldn't meet his gaze. 'Like I said, you don't want answers.'

He could listen to this no more. Taking a step forward, Drake grabbed her by the shoulders and pushed her roughly against the side of the warehouse, the corrugated steel reverberating with the sound of the impact. Anya stared back at him, visibly surprised at his sudden, violent move.

'No more games,' he said, his face just inches from hers. 'Why are you doing this?'

'Because I'm afraid!' she shouted, losing her cool for the first time. 'Is that what you want to hear, Ryan? Well, there it is. There is my confession. I'm afraid!'

'Fuck that,' he said, refusing to buy it. In all the time he'd known her, he had never once seen Anya show even a hint of fear. She'd been through too much to feel such an emotion now. 'What could you possibly be afraid of now?'

He saw her swallow, saw the muscles in her throat tighten, saw the barriers start to break down. Her eyes were locked with his, and for once there was nothing masking what lay behind them, no steely resolve or calculating intelligence. He saw what truly lay at the core of her being, saw the fear and the regret for things left unsaid too long, the pain and sadness over what might have been, and the forlorn hope for what might still be.

'You,' she said, her voice wavering. 'I'm afraid of losing you.'

She was fighting hard to keep her composure, to hold her emotions in check as she'd always done, but this time it was different. This time she was losing the battle. The emotions she now faced were of a sort she hadn't allowed herself to feel for a long time.

Drake let out a breath, releasing his hold of her. He backed off a step as if he'd been struck by a physical blow. 'No,' he said, refusing to accept it. 'You're lying.'

That was when the rising tide finally became too much even for Anya to hold back. Launching herself forward as if to attack him, she seized Drake by his shirt and twisted him around, shoving him backward against the wall just as he'd done to her. She wasn't as big or as strong as him, but the sheer intensity and aggression of her actions were enough to overcome these physical limitations, and the thin steel wall shuddered as his heavy weight slammed into it.

'Look at me, Ryan. Look at me!' she hissed, her forearm pressed against his throat as if he were an enemy to be overcome. 'Tell me I'm lying.'

Anya had withheld things, kept secrets from him, but never had she intentionally lied to him. He knew she wouldn't start now, but that didn't make her words any easier to hear.

'No!' he snapped, angrily swatting her arm away. 'You almost got me a killed a dozen times over. You've put me and my team at risk every fucking time we've come close to you, and you've never shown the slightest regret about it, so don't start pretending my life means something to you now. We both know it doesn't.'

He hadn't wanted to go down this path, to dredge up old memories and resurrect old grudges, but if she insisted on trying to rewrite history then he was fully prepared to show her just how wrong she was. This was a confrontation that had been brewing since she'd left him to die in Iraq three years ago.

'If you gave a shit about me, you wouldn't have left me behind.'

He saw a flash of pain and anger in her eyes then, and knew that his words had cut deep. Deeper than he ever could have imagined in this distant, enigmatic woman. And the reaction they provoked was more intense than even he could have anticipated.

Her hands shot out, landing square in his chest to push him backward against the wall again. It was an instinctive action, driven by the need to lash out rather than a serious attempt to injure him.

'I did it to protect you, Ryan!' She was almost shaking with rage and long-buried frustration now as the two of them faced off. 'Don't you understand that? Or are you really too stupid to see the truth?'

He raised his arms to shove her away, and she responded the only way she knew how, grabbing his outstretched hands and trying to twist them aside. Drake, however, had come to know through painful experience just what she could do to people who tried to overpower her, and he was ready for it, exerting his considerable strength to stop her gaining the upper hand. Unable to prevail against him, she let out a sharp breath, reluctantly conceding that neither of them was going to win this fight.

'Leaving you behind was one of the hardest things I ever did,' she said, finally admitting the secret she had kept for so long. 'But I did it to protect you… from me, from the same thing that happens to everyone who gets close to me. You don't deserve that, because you are a good man. Better than this… better than me.'

Drake listened in stunned silence as she spoke, knowing she needed to get this out now that she'd started. Never before had she opened up like this, never had she allowed herself to show such vulnerability.

'I tried to stay away from you, hoping in time you would let it go, hoping you would let *me* go. But somehow, Ryan Drake… somehow you always draw me back. I knew it was wrong, it was dangerous for both of us, but I wanted it anyway. And that frightens me.' She swallowed hard, and he could have sworn he saw moisture glistening in her eyes. 'I'm afraid this time I'll lose you for good, and… I don't know if I could live with myself if that happened.'

A silence descended on them then, broken only by the strained gasps of their breath and the thump of their heartbeats as they stood locked together in the midst of their struggle, neither enemies nor friends but something else entirely. Standing this close to her, feeling the warmth of her body, seeing the anger and fear and vulnerability in her eyes, watching her lips part as she drew breath, Drake couldn't help but remember the only time he had seen her like this before.

The night the two of them had found each other, sharing their pain and grief in the flickering light of a campfire, finding release the only way they knew how. In that brief moment, he'd felt closer to her than he had with any other person in his entire life. Two souls, separated by a lifetime of different experiences, triumphs and tragedies, and yet they'd been drawn inexorably to each other, had accepted and understood each other without judgement or reservation.

It had been three long years since he had felt that same connection, but at last he felt a stirring of it again. And now that he did, he longed, ached with a desperate need to experience it again.

And, he realized then, so did she.

The moment was broken when the warehouse door swung open and Frost emerged, shielding her eyes against the late afternoon sun. Drake and Anya released their hold of each other, the woman backing away a step just as Frost turned her eyes on them.

'Sorry. I…didn't mean to interrupt,' she said, looking flustered and uncomfortable as it became clear that she'd interrupted something very personal indeed.

'What is it, Keira?' Drake demanded, regaining his composure with difficulty.

The young woman cleared her throat. 'I thought you ought to know, Cain's flight touched down a few minutes ago. My guess is he's en route to the US embassy by now.'

Drake let out a breath and nodded, forcing his mind back to the mission, forcing himself to block out everything else. The mission was what mattered now. It had to take priority over everything.

'Go on inside, pack everything up. We leave in ten minutes.'

Frost pulled the door open but hesitated before entering, perhaps thinking to say something about the confrontation she'd just witnessed.

'That's all, Keira,' Drake said firmly, pre-empting her.

As soon as she'd gone and closed the door behind her, Drake turned his attention back to Anya. There was much he still wanted to say to her, so many things they had to resolve, but now wasn't the time. They both knew that.

'We'll talk about this later,' he promised her. 'But right now, we need our heads in the game. Both of us.'

She said nothing. The moment of exposure, of vulnerability had passed, and she was herself again; calm and focussed and ruthless.

'And just so we're clear, *I'm* leading the assault team,' he said simply. Before she could protest, he held up his hand in an appeal for silence. 'We both know they won't follow you. So trust me, Anya. If everything you just said is true… then for once trust me to do this.'

She didn't say anything, but he saw her reluctant nod of acceptance. It was enough. Leaving her alone, Drake turned away and pulled open the door to rejoin the team.

Leaving her alone.

# Chapter 47

*Forward Operating Base 'Foxtail', Afghan–Pakistan border – 23 February 1986*

*Marcus Cain closed his eyes and exhaled, his body still warm from the afterglow of their fast, intense moment of passion. He'd imagined this moment more times than he could count, yet he'd scarcely believed it could ever be real. That he would ever live through it.*

*The young woman, naked as he was, stirred beside him and sat up. He opened his eyes to look at her then, just taking in the beauty of her, the sinewy lines of hard-won strength, the long graceful limbs, the soft curves of her breasts and hips. She made no attempt to cover or conceal herself, modesty being a trait she'd no doubt had to abandon after months in the field. Nonetheless, the effect was to render her even more compelling. Never had he seen a woman so completely at ease in her own body.*

*Sensing his eyes on her, she glanced at him. 'That was…' She trailed off, her face colouring with embarrassment. 'I did not mean to…'*

*'Do you regret it?' he asked, worried that he'd taken advantage of her.*

*She thought about it for a moment then shook her head. She was still blushing, but he saw a faint smile as well. And her eyes, so often daunting and intense, had a warmth in them now that left him in no doubt.*

*Leaning down, she kissed him again, slow and languid this time, but the brush of her naked skin against his made him wish he could do it all over again.*

*Reaching for her discarded trousers, Anya pulled them up over her hips. 'What you said to me before, Marcus… I understand why you did it,' she said, running her hands through her dishevelled hair. 'But I told you once that I did not want any favours, any special treatment. And I meant it.' She sighed and looked at him. 'It is your choice. If you order me home, I will go. But I would rather you didn't.'*

*He had a feeling she'd say that. Loyal to a fault as always.*

*'If you stay, what will you do?'*

*The young woman shrugged. 'Carry on, finish what we started.'*

*'You know, people are starting to take interest in you back at Langley. Your career in the Agency could anywhere you want. You could become an instructor; help train the next generation of female field operatives.'*

*'Next generation?' she repeated, looking almost amused. 'Am I already obsolete?'*

*'That's not what I meant.'*

*'I know,' she conceded. 'But I'm no leader, Marcus. I never wanted to be. This is what I want to do; what I was meant to do.'*

*He wondered about that. There was a magnetism about her, a charisma that one couldn't help but respond to, regardless of her age and gender. People would follow someone like her. He wondered if she herself even understood her potential.*

*'I can't change your mind?'* he asked without much hope.

*She looked at him, flashing a smile as she reached for her T-shirt. It was the smile of someone who knows they've won. 'When we're finished here in Afghanistan, I will take up your offer. I promise. But not yet.'*

*'I'll hold you to that.' Cain sighed, bowing to the inevitable. 'There's something else. Most field operatives are given a code name. The guys back at Langley were throwing around a couple of ideas, but I think I found one that suits you.'*

*She chuckled in amusement as she pulled the T-shirt over her head. 'This should be interesting. Tell me.'*

*'Maras.'*

*At this, she froze in the act of pulling on the garment.*

*'You said your mother used to tell you old myths and legends when you were a kid, so I did some digging. If I understand Lithuanian mythology right, Maras was a goddess of war.' He looked at her, partially dressed in her military fatigues and surrounded by the weapons of her profession. 'Pretty appropriate, don't you think?'*

*To his surprise, Anya turned away as if to hide her expression. 'Yes,' she said, her voice unusually heavy and serious at what was supposed to be a light-hearted conversation. 'Yes, it does, Marcus.'*

–

### US Embassy compound, Islamabad

Gasping as the ice-cold water splashed his face, banishing any lingering vestige of fatigue, Cain straightened up to regard the reflection staring back at him in the mirror.

You look old, he thought, noticing the lines around his eyes and mouth, the grey at his temples. One of the old men of Langley that he used to regard with such amusement.

Not a great prospect for one of the biggest meetings of his professional life, but he supposed it would have to do. The hour was almost upon them. Outside the windows of his temporary suite at the US embassy, the sun was descending towards the western horizon as afternoon gave way to evening.

Drying his face with a towel, he reached for his tie and carefully knotted it, making sure it was neatly centred. As if he were preparing for a job interview, he thought with a flash of dark humour. Pulling on his suit jacket, he ran his hands though his hair, then nodded to his reflection.

What was it Tennyson had once said about situations like this? *Made weak by time and fate, but strong in will.*

That would do.

Emerging from his suite a short time later, Cain was immediately joined by Hawkins, who had been standing guard outside. Together the two men advanced down the corridor, technicians and intelligence analysts parting before them like the sea before the prow of some mighty warship.

'Are we set?'

The formidable-looking operative nodded. 'Everything's in place. Say the word and we're good to go.'

Last chance to back out.

'Do it.'

Smiling that unique, sneering grin, Hawkins reached for his cell phone to make the call to the advance teams he'd already set up. As usual, his message was short and curt. 'Dalia is a go.'

Cain couldn't help but smile at that. Doubtless the code word for this operation meant nothing to a man like Hawkins, but if Anya had been here she would have appreciated its historical and spiritual significance. Dalia, the goddess of fate and destiny, who wove the threads of men's futures and wrote the stories of their lives.

Well, tonight he was about to write a new story.

Emerging into the larger office space that acted as the nerve centre of Agency operations in Islamabad, they were met by the station chief Hayden Quinn. In stark contrast to the confident and promising case officer Cain had personally promoted to station chief a year ago, the man now looked exhausted and worn out by the demands of the job, not to mention edgy and nervous now that Cain was before him.

'Deputy Director,' he began, trying to look genial and welcoming. 'Been a while since we spoke face to face. It's good to have you here.'

'Wouldn't get too used to me, Hayden,' Cain replied. 'I'm just here to tie up a few loose ends.'

It wasn't hard to guess the inferences Quinn was drawing from that. 'I see. Is there… anything I can help with?'

'Not at all. Everything's in hand.'

'Sir, if you're planning on going outside the embassy grounds, we need to at least brief our security teams—'

'Like I said, everything's in hand.' Taking a step closer, Cain laid a comforting hand on the younger man's shoulder. 'Don't worry, Hayden, you've been very helpful already.'

That much was certainly true. For better or worse, Quinn had played his part.

'You take care of yourself.'

Leaving the station chief to ponder just what the future held for him, Cain resumed his journey towards the parking garage, with Hawkins at his side.

Quinn waited until both men were well clear of the room before digging out his cell phone and hurriedly dialling a number back in DC.

'Yeah, Quinn?' Franklin began, his voice carrying an edge of tension now.

'It's happening now,' Quinn said. 'Cain's on the move.'

–

Leaning over the sink, Samantha spat out the last of the acrid-tasting mucus that had just risen from her stomach. Her abdomen ached from the painful muscle cramps it had just endured, and the lingering nausea that had prompted her sudden trip to the warehouse's primitive restroom did little to improve her mood.

'Not now,' she whispered, willing the sickness to abate as she stared at her reflection in the grimy mirror. '*Not now.*'

She couldn't afford to linger here for long. Drake and the others were ready to depart, both vehicles loaded and ready. If she kept them waiting, they were likely to get suspicious.

Just a couple of hours, she told herself. Hang in there for a couple more hours, and it would be done. It would be over.

'How long have you known?' a voice asked from the doorway.

Spinning around, Samantha felt the breath catch in her throat. Anya was standing there, arms folded, watching her with a shrewd and assessing stare.

'What are you talking about?'

'You know what I'm talking about, Samantha,' she said, using her first name for once. 'The others might not have noticed it, but I have. You have barely eaten since we got here, and when you do it usually leaves you in here.' Anya took a step towards her. 'They call it morning sickness, but morning or night it never really goes away. That feeling of tiredness that lingers no matter how much sleep you get… the nausea, like being trapped in a moving car. Believe me, I know.'

Samantha's eyes were wide as she stared at the older woman in the dim light. Someone who had been there long before her, who still carried the weight of what she'd lost.

'I will ask you again, how long have you known?'

Samantha let out a sigh, too weary to keep lying. It was useless with someone like Anya anyway. 'A week, maybe. When the sickness started.'

'And you intend to keep it?'

The briskness of the question felt like a punch in the gut, perhaps because it was something she barely had the courage to ask herself.

'I don't know.'

Anya looked her over for a long moment. 'You shouldn't be doing this. Where we are going is no place for a pregnant woman. People might die tonight. *You* might die tonight, and your child with you.'

Tell me something I don't know, Samantha thought grimly. Nonetheless, there was no way she was backing out now. 'It's my choice. I'm going.'

'And what would Ryan say if he knew?' She cocked an eyebrow. 'I assume you haven't told him yet.'

Samantha swallowed hard, forcing back the nausea as she took a step towards the veteran operative. 'Listen to me, Anya. You and I are never going to be friends. I know that, and so do you. But I'm asking you now, not to tell Ryan. I haven't told him because we need him focussed on the mission, not worrying about me, not thinking about the future or anything else. Tonight, the mission is all that matters. So I'm asking you not to tell him. I'm asking you to let me help. Please.'

Anya said nothing, but Samantha could see a change come over her as the words sank in. A pain and sadness, old and long buried, seemed to have resurfaced. And for once, she didn't look on her as a threat or an enemy.

'It is your choice,' she said at last, turning away. 'If you choose to go, I can't protect you.'

'I can protect myself.'

Anya paused for a moment or two in the doorway, about to say something more, then thinking better of it. Without looking at her again, she left, disappearing into the shadows of the hallway.

# Chapter 48

Agent Gondal had not long returned to his office after a long and wearisome afternoon spent following leads and tip-offs about vans matching the one reported last night. Most of them had led nowhere. He felt like he'd driven to every corner of the city in the course of the day, and was well and truly ready to end his shift.

At least, until Mahsud stormed into his office clutching several sheets of paper, his normally grim and serious face looking uncharacteristically excited.

'We have them,' he announced, slapping the papers down on Gondal's desk with his meaty hands. 'The results just came back from those numbers you asked me to run earlier today. It's fake – all of it. Those bastards lied to us.'

Frowning, Gondal snatched up the papers and hurriedly skim-read the results. Robert Douglas, according to his passport number, had never existed. There was no record of him in any of the UK databases they were able to covertly access.

Not only that, but Apex Deliveries didn't appear to be a functioning business entity, despite the call he'd made to 'Douglas's' superior earlier in the day. And to top it all off, the van whose licence plate he'd quietly memorized had been reported stolen from a depot in Peshawar last month.

He'd seen enough.

'Get a tactical team together,' he said quickly. 'Tell them to converge on that warehouse immediately.'

Mahsud's smile was almost feral. 'I already have.'

–

Located about 2,500 feet above sea level at the edge of the Margalla mountains, the hilltop viewing point known as Daman-e-Koh, literally meaning *foot hills* in ancient Persian, was where Drake and his team had chosen to stop after leaving the warehouse. It was a popular spot for tourists during the day, offering an unspoiled, panoramic view over central Islamabad to the south, and the impressive peaks of the mountains behind.

From an operational point of view, this place was an ideal stop-off point. They were barely a mile from the United States embassy here, and not much further from the safe house they would soon be assaulting. It was, in effect, their final staging area. A place to make their last preparations and gear up for the attack.

With the onset of evening, most of the sightseers and tourists had packed up for the day, leaving just a few stragglers making their way back to their cars from the long hike up to the peak of the mighty Pir Sohawa. Having stopped both their van and the Range Rover in a quiet corner of the parking lot, the team were able to go about their work with little fear of discovery.

A short distance away from this last-minute work, on a grassy outcrop facing the setting sun, Anya gently lowered herself to her knees. Closing her eyes, she inhaled deeply, tasting the scent of grass and wild flowers in the air, then bent forward and lightly brushed her fingertips across the coarse, springy grass beneath her.

Though the gathering rain clouds overhead had yet to truly open up, a light drizzle had fallen over the city during their drive here, and the grass was still damp from the brief shower.

Keeping her eyes closed and her back bent, she drew her wet hands across her face, exhaling as she did so. She could feel the faint breeze caressing her damp skin, the last rays of the setting sun playing across her face as she raised it up to the sky.

Taught to her by her mother, Anya had performed this simple ritual of purification and preparation more times than she could hope to remember, always before going into battle. Once it had made her an object of curiosity and even ridicule amongst her comrades, but she did it all the same. It helped, and it allowed her to hold on to some tiny fragment of who she had once been.

'Never took you for the religious type.'

Anya opened her eyes, disturbed from her reverie, and glanced around. Frost was standing nearby, having approached while she'd been occupied with the ritual. The young woman nodded off to her left as if to emphasize her point.

Anya followed her line of sight. Directly beneath them, situated at the end of a wide tree-lined avenue running straight through the heart of the city, lay the great multifaceted structure of the Faisal Mosque; an immense building of Islamic worship able to accommodate over 10,000 people in its main prayer hall alone. Its four minaret towers, each 260 feet tall, rose up into the evening sky like the tips of gigantic spears turned towards the heavens.

'I was not praying,' she said, realizing Frost had mistaken her actions for an Islamic ritual. Anya had experienced a great deal of that religion in her life, mostly through its followers. There was much about its teachings that she found admirable, but in truth no religion had ever held much appeal for her. No matter how noble their ideals or how humane their principles, they were all too easy for bitter, angry, vengeful men to twist into weapons.

'What was it, then?'

Anya could feel the colour rising to her cheeks. This wasn't an aspect of her life she was comfortable discussing, especially with someone like Keira Frost. The woman already hated her – the last thing she needed was to give her reason to mock her.

'Preparation.' She rose to her feet with the graceful ease born from long years of practice. 'Nothing more.'

That was when Frost said a name Anya hadn't expected to hear again. 'Maras.'

Anya felt herself tense up. 'What?'

'That was your code name, wasn't it? The one Cain gave you when you worked for the Agency,' she explained. 'Ryan had me look it up, back when we were first handed our mission to break you out of jail. Maras – it's a legend from Baltic paganism. A goddess of war. That's what Cain thought you were.' She gave Anya a curious look then, caught somewhere between mockery and, inexplicable as it seemed, respect. 'Must have been quite something back in the day.'

Anya smiled at that notion, but there was no humour or warmth in it. It was a sad, reflective smile. 'It's funny, that you should make the same mistake he did.'

'What do you mean?'

'Maras. She was not a goddess of war, but of death and misery.'

'Same difference, isn't it?'

Anya shook her head sadly. 'There is honour in war. At least, there is supposed to be. But Maras… she was a bringer of death in any form. Her fate was to love mortal men, and to watch them die for her. All who came close to her met the same end, no matter what she did to stop it. That was her fate… and mine. Maybe Cain wasn't so wrong after all.'

For once, Frost said nothing in response. But Anya could sense the wheels turning in her mind, the pieces of the puzzle coming together to form a single conclusion. She didn't say what she was thinking, because she didn't have to.

'Why did you come looking for me, Frost?' Anya asked, quickly changing the subject.

'Actually, I came to apologize.'

It was Anya's turn to be surprised. 'Apologize?'

The young woman sighed and looked out across the city below. She had the look of someone psyching themselves up for an unpleasant, difficult task. 'I'm not in the habit of doing this kind of thing, so don't expect it to happen again. Ever. But for what it's worth… I'm sorry for some of the things I said to you. *Some*, but not all,' she hastened to add.

Truly that was a first. Never had Frost apologized to her for anything.

'Why tell me this now?'

'Well, fuck it, we might be dead by this time tomorrow. Not like I'll get another chance.' She shrugged, glancing sidelong at Anya, her usual brusque demeanour softening just a little. 'And... well, I get that you've been through some tough times, okay? I don't pretend to know the gory details, and to be honest I don't want to know. I've got a hard enough time sleeping at night. But I guess what I'm trying to say is... I understand why you are the way you are. I don't always like it, and, to be honest, your people skills could use some real work, but I can't exactly blame you for being a paranoid sociopath.'

Anya genuinely didn't know what to say to that. She hadn't prepared herself for a conversation like this, and for a moment wondered if Frost was simply trying to make fun of her. Yet she had detected no hint of mockery in the woman's tone or expression. One way or another, she'd meant what she said.

'Thank you. I think.'

'Well, that wasn't awkward at all.' It was then that she saw a smile of amusement light up the younger woman's face. 'Doesn't mean we're friends or anything, though.'

That much was true, and Anya supposed it had always been that way. Her life hadn't afforded many opportunities to form female relationships, and in truth she'd come to prefer the company of men after a while. That wasn't to say they didn't have their own flaws, but the dynamics of their relationships were simpler, easier to understand. The friendships women forged were, in her mind at least, based on subtle inference, shades of meaning, veiled remarks and constant evaluation of one another. For one easily able to sense deception or misdirection, it had often proven to be a difficult and frustrating experience, and eventually she'd begun to distance herself from her own sex.

And yet, there were rare moments where she caught herself questioning the path she'd taken, wondering what she might have missed out on. As inexplicable as it seemed, given who she was standing with, this was one such moment.

'I would not dream of it,' she said quietly.

She said nothing more, and neither did Frost. Each was content merely to share the silence. And for once, Anya didn't mind the young woman's presence.

Nearby, Drake unlatched the rear doors of the decrepit old van that had somehow made it up the steep winding road to their hilltop rally point. Swinging them open, he found himself confronted by the slender face and big dark eyes of Yasin. They had untied him and removed his gag, content to keep him contained within the van while they decided what to do with him.

Now it was time to get it over with.

'Here,' Drake said, tossing him a pair of jeans, trainers and a fresh shirt. They had picked them up on the way here for practically nothing at one of the countless outdoor markets that littered the streets of Rawalpindi. 'Put these on.'

The boy eyed him suspiciously, saying and doing nothing.

'You've got 30 seconds,' Drake advised him. 'After that, you're leaving this van one way or another.'

He closed the door again, counting out the time on his watch. Sure enough, he could hear the sound of hurried movement within the van. When he opened the door again, Yasin was dressed in the new clothes, his old ones lying in a crumpled, dirty heap beside him.

The new shirt hung loosely on his spare frame, and the jeans had been turned up at the ankles to make them fit, but overall he looked much improved from his previous appearance. He could still use a trip to a barber's, though.

'Out,' Drake said, beckoning him forward.

Yasin crept forward, his movements deliberate and wary, as if he feared this might all be some cruel joke. As if Drake might have a last-minute change of heart and kill him after all. Nonetheless, he did finally clamber down onto the tarmac in front of Drake, drawing himself up to his full if modest height.

Reaching into his pocket, Drake pulled out what little cash remained to him and unrolled about a hundred dollars' worth of local currency. Yasin's eyes seemed to light up at the sight of what must have been a small fortune to him.

Drake held out the small wad of notes. 'Take this. It's not much, but it should buy you food and a place to stay for a while.'

That was when the wonder and avarice quickly turned to suspicion and borderline hostility. Doubtless he was no stranger to older men offering young homeless boys cash in exchange for favours of a different sort.

'Why you give me this?'

'Relax. I don't want anything in return,' Drake said, guessing his thoughts. 'Just take the money and piss off.'

The kid frowned at that. 'That is it?'

'That's it. I'd suggest you stay away from your old neighbourhood, though. At least as long as the money lasts.'

Drake knew all too well how these things worked, having witnessed for himself the brutality that such kids were capable of in the name of survival. Yasin was part of the food chain in his old stomping ground. He was known there, and if any of his street-dwelling rivals got even a hint that he had money on him, they would tear him to shreds to get it, until they in turn lost it to bigger, tougher, more ruthless kids. Money filtered up the ladder – that was how it always worked.

'Oh, and I'd appreciate it if you didn't mention us to anyone,' Drake added. 'We prefer not to make a fuss, and I'm guessing you feel the same.'

Somehow he couldn't see this kid reporting them to the police, since doing so would certainly mean parting with the money Drake had given him, but it didn't hurt to reiterate this.

Yasin looked torn, desperate to reach out for the money that could sustain him for weeks if used carefully, but unable to let go of the wariness that had kept him alive far longer.

'You do not answer my question. Why do you help me? I steal from you. I hurt one of your friends.'

Drake shrugged, though for a moment he glanced over at Frost, who had just returned from a grassy area beyond the parking lot. 'A friend of mine... well, she's all about second chances. Maybe it's rubbed off on me. So take it before I change my mind.'

Reaching out, Yasin snatched the money out of Drake's hand, quickly withdrawing as if he expected Drake to attack him for such impudence. When it became obvious the man had no intention of harming him, he seemed to relax and lower his guard a little.

'It's a long walk back into town,' Drake said, nodding back down the road. 'Better get going if you want to be there before nightfall.'

'Take me with you,' Yasin said then, blurting it out so fast that the words seemed to merge into one.

'Excuse me?'

'Take me with you. I can fight. I can help you.'

Drake might have laughed at such an offer were it not for the earnest, almost desperate look in the young boy's eyes. He'd meant every word he'd just said, which made this all the more difficult.

Drake was under no illusions about what would happen to Yasin when the money eventually ran out. It might make him more comfortable for a while, but it couldn't alter the course of his life. Drake could sense what the future held for him, and the countless others like him in places like Rawalpindi – absolutely nothing.

Doubtless Yasin sensed it too, and perhaps saw Drake and the others as a way out, a window into another world. A dangerous and uncertain world perhaps, but anything was a step up from the misery and grinding poverty of his own existence.

'Trust me, you don't want to go where we're going,' Drake promised him. 'You're better off here.'

'I will die here.' There was no anger, fear or hope in his voice when he said that. Just the sad acceptance of something known beyond all doubt.

He felt like shit for pushing Yasin away. But as things stood, he'd be lucky if he and his own team made it through this alive, never mind taking in every waif and stray they encountered along the way. He certainly couldn't offer protection or a new life to this kid, and pretending otherwise was worse than the alternative.

Better to be straight with him than build a false hope.

'That's not up to me, mate. But for what it's worth, I hope you make it.' He pointed towards the road again. 'Go on. Get moving, and for fuck's sake stay away from warehouses in future. The next group might not be as forgiving as us.'

Hesitating, Yasin finally turned away and started to walk, slowly at first, but gathering pace as his natural wariness took hold once more. He turned back only once, a thin and forlorn figure in his ill-fitting clothes, and then was gone.

Drake let out a breath, putting aside the lingering guilt and forcing his thoughts back to matters closer at hand. He closed the van up, slamming the doors a little harder than necessary, then turned towards the others who seemed to have congregated by the guard railing at the edge of the parking lot.

'Yo, Ryan. Come take a look at this,' Mason called over.

He knew they had little time for sightseeing, but nonetheless walked over to join them. As soon as he reached the hilltop observation point and saw what they saw, he stopped in his tracks, staring in silent awe at the view that confronted him.

All of Islamabad seemed to stretch out beneath them, the steel and glass skin of new skyscrapers gleaming, the tiny headlight beams of thousands of vehicles forming thin ribbons of light, like blood pumping through the arteries of the city. Overhead, the sky seemed to be aglow with orange, golds and deep reds.

It was a breathtaking, awe-inspiring vista, and for a few seconds not a single one of them uttered a word. It was enough just to be there, to share the moment together.

Drake felt a hand reach for his, and glanced around at Samantha. In response, he squeezed her hand, wanting to pull her to him. He saw a gentle trace of a smile; a silent acknowledgement of his intent.

'Never waste time doing anything important when there's a sunset you could be sitting under,' Mason said, breaking the silence. He was smiling at the remark, but there was a wistful, pensive look in his eyes. 'Something my old man used to say when I was a kid. Never really got it until now.'

'I think your old man was on to something,' McKnight agreed.

'No argument here,' Frost added, looking unusually quiet and reflective now.

Anya voiced neither agreement or objection. But Drake sensed from her expression that Mason's words had struck a chord in her as well.

This was a moment, he knew then. A moment that would remain with him for the rest of his life, no matter how long that might be. The last sunset, the last moment of calm before the storm, before they went into battle against the most dangerous adversary they had ever faced. The last chance to say what he had to.

'I don't pretend to know how things are going to play out tonight,' Drake began. 'But I know what it took to get us here, how far we've had to go. Each of us. And I know how much we've had to leave behind along the way. Well, we're not losing anything more, we're not leaving anything else behind. I told you when this all started that Downfall isn't just another mission, it's the end of the line for all of us. We do this right, and it's over. All of it. Tonight we finish this.'

He felt Samantha's grip tighten then, felt the closeness of her presence. And more than just that, he felt the rest of the group around him, the reassurance of their presence. Five different people from vastly different lives, united behind a single purpose.

Ready to go to war.

# Chapter 49

Vizur Qalat once more found himself in the back seat of his plush Mercedes SUV, watching the grand buildings that faced out onto Jinnah Avenue glide past beyond the bulletproof, tinted window. Night had fallen by now, and the traffic along the city's main arteries had begun to ease off as the rush hour abated.

The site for their meeting was located deep within the city's western residential district. The kind of well-to-do area that belonged to doctors, lawyers, successful government ministers, or just those who were good at skimming a little off the top without getting caught. That was where he would finally meet his old CIA contact.

Marcus Cain – a man he hadn't spoken to face to face in over 20 years. How both of their lives had changed in that time, he reflected. Both had risen through the ranks of their respective organizations, through fair means and foul, and both had proven themselves worthy adversaries. And here they were, each with something the other wanted, about to step into the ring once more.

'How long?' he called to his driver, Baloch, up front.

His two bodyguards were up there, with three more following in a second car about 40 yards behind. He doubted Cain would go to this much trouble just to stage an assassination, but that didn't mean he was prepared to walk into this meeting without protection.

'Five minutes, sir,' the big, heavily built man replied over his shoulder. His already sizeable frame was bulked out by the body armour he wore beneath his suit.

Qalat nodded, easing back into his seat. Staring off to the north, he caught sight of the four massive minaret towers of Faisal Mosque jutting up into the night sky, illuminated from below by powerful floodlights. A modern design intended to evoke Islamabad's own melding of past and future, of tradition and progress, it was, in Qalat's view, a decadent and ugly piece of engineering.

If he'd been a devout Muslim, he supposed he might have said a prayer as he passed it, invoking Mohammed's help in his work tonight, but he had little need of such spiritual props. A real man shaped his own destiny with courage, willpower and intelligence. He had enough to have made it this far, and he didn't intend to fail now.

He was ready for Marcus Cain.

–

'This is it. Stop up here,' Drake said, pointing to a narrow side street just off the main road. The safe house wasn't far from here, and it was time to disembark.

Turning off the road, Samantha manoeuvred the Range Rover into the street and brought them to a halt, keeping the engine running so she could move off as soon as the assault group were out.

Closing his eyes for a moment to calm his mind, Drake nodded to himself and reached for his door. 'This is it. Get yourselves into position and stay on comms. We'll radio when we're in position.'

Frost twisted around in her seat to look at him, no doubt wishing she were going with them. Unfortunately she had other tasks to perform tonight. 'Kick some ass out there, you hear me?'

Mason grinned at her. 'Wouldn't have it any other way.'

Disembarking, Mason and Anya circled around to the rear of the vehicle and popped the trunk to retrieve their weapons, tactical gear and the grapple launchers. All of it was stowed away inside heavy canvas bags that they'd have to carry up to the rooftop. No doubt the sight of three people hauling such conspicuous loads would arouse suspicion if they were seen in broad daylight, but fortunately the darkness would mask them somewhat.

Drake too was about to leave when Samantha turned around. 'Ryan?'

'Yeah?'

She held out hand to him. He could tell from the look in her eyes that there was much she wanted to say, but they both knew she couldn't. Time was a luxury they no longer had. Instead, Drake reached out and clasped her hand. Her grip was strong, knuckles standing out hard and white against the skin, as if she never wanted to let go.

'We'll be back soon,' he promised. 'Keep the seats warm for us, okay?'

She smiled then, but there was nothing light hearted about it. It was a sad, bittersweet smile, full of regrets. 'Come back soon. Or I'll kick your ass myself.'

'Ryan, we have to go now,' Anya said, leaning in his doorway with a heavy satchel slung over one shoulder. He couldn't help notice her gaze flick momentarily to Samantha, and caught himself wondering what secrets lay between those two.

But now wasn't the time. Releasing Samantha's hand, Drake ducked out onto the sidewalk and swung the door shut behind him, slapping the roof to signal they were good to go.

Samantha wasted no time backing out onto the road and accelerating away. Within moments the Rover was lost amongst other traffic, leaving the three operatives alone.

Drake's eyes turned towards the apartment building that lay nearby. They were on site, but they still had to reach the roof.

'Let's go,' he said quietly, hoisting the satchel up onto his shoulder.

–

At an industrial estate on the southern edge of Rawalpindi, the night watchman jumped up in shock as several black SUVs came roaring through the main entrance, heading deep into the maze of warehouses and factories at top speed.

The small convoy came to a screeching halt outside one warehouse in particular: a small, decrepit, rusting edifice that looked like it was being held up by sheer willpower. No sooner had the SUVs stopped than black-clad tactical operatives poured out, converging on the warehouse from all sides, submachine guns up at their shoulders.

Urgent orders and updates flashed across the radio net as they took up position at key access points, ready to storm in as soon as the command was issued.

Meanwhile, ten miles away in neighbouring Islamabad, Gondal was seated in one of the ISI's many situation rooms, watching shaky, green-tinted footage being transmitted live from a couple of the operatives' helmet-mounted cameras.

'The strike team leader reports they are in position,' Mahsud said, a phone cradled against his sizeable chest. 'Waiting for go command.'

Gondal let out a breath. 'Go.'

A blur of movement, the muted boom of shotgun blasts obliterating door locks, and suddenly he found himself looking at the familiar interior of the warehouse. This time, however, there was no Range Rover, no dilapidated old Russian van, and most importantly no sign of the building's occupants.

Clenching his fists, Gondal leaned back in his seat as the tactical team, doing their duty, carried out a search of the small network of offices and storage rooms at the rear of the warehouse. He already knew they wouldn't find anything.

'Robert Douglas' and his cohorts were way ahead of them.

He looked up at Mahsud, whose grim and unhappy expression mirrored his own. 'Put out a city-wide alert on both vehicles, and start circulating those facial composites I had drafted up. I want them found!'

Those people, whoever they were and whatever their purpose in Pakistan, had murdered two of his field agents. He would see to it they answered for their crime.

–

At the top of the apartment building overlooking the safe house, Drake eased open the stairwell door half an inch, then knelt down and felt around the doorjamb for the tell he'd left there – a broken fragment of matchstick. It was still in place.

Gripping his silenced Browning automatic tightly, he pushed the door open further and advanced out onto the roof, sweeping the area. Mason was right behind him, clutching a pistol in one hand and his heavy canvas equipment bag in the other. Anya brought up the rear, similarly armed and weighed down.

'Clear,' Drake hissed, lowering the weapon and easing the door closed.

Straight away Anya went to work. Dumping her satchel on the ground, she knelt down and unzipped it, quickly removing the dismantled sniper rifle she'd brought with her. She worked with calm, expert efficiency, her fingers quick and nimble as she slotted the bolt and firing assembly together, before inserting the barrel and clipping it into place.

Mason too was busy unpacking his own bag, carefully lifting out the two MP7 submachine guns, followed by eight 40-round box magazines – four apiece. They could perhaps have carried more, but both men agreed there was little to be gained by it. If there was a situation that 320 rounds of automatic gunfire couldn't get them out of, they were dead anyway.

As his two comrades went about their allocated tasks, Drake hurried over to the building's parapet, keeping low to avoid being seen from the ground.

Raising himself just high enough to look out over the edge, Drake lifted a pair of binoculars to his eyes and focussed in on the safe house. As he'd expected, the internal lights were on and the blinds closed. There was no sign of any activity on the rooftop terrace or in the courtyard below, which meant any operatives on site had to be inside.

Hearing the light crunch of boots on gravel, Drake turned just as Anya crept over beside him, the sniper rifle cradled in her arms. Laying the heavy weapon down, she raised herself up, quickly surveying their target.

'Looks quiet,' she remarked.

It was no surprise. Armed guards patrolling the courtyard or the building's rooftop would have attracted attention from the police, local security patrols, even curious neighbours. All of which was exactly what Cain was no doubt hoping to avoid.

'We'll soon change that,' Drake assured her, reaching for his tactical radio. 'Alpha One to Bravo One. We're at the rally point. What's your sitrep?'

'Bravo One is in position. Comms pack is green. Standing by to patch in now.'

'Copy that. Wait for my command.' Clicking his radio off, Drake crept over to where Mason had unpacked their weapons and other gear.

'We good?' the assault specialist asked, his voice hushed.

'So far, at least.' Unzipping his jacket to expose the dark T-shirt beneath, Drake picked up the body armour that Mason had laid on the ground and pulled it over his head, quickly locking the clips into place and tightening the straps until it was good and secure.

The spare magazines went into a series of pouches fixed to the right side of the vest. Since Drake was right handed and therefore used his left to reload, it would have been awkward and cumbersome to have to reach anywhere else. Mason, however, favoured his left hand, and so his vest had been adjusted accordingly.

The stun and smoke grenades went into a pair of sealed Velcro pouches across his chest. Hollywood might show soldiers with grenades dangling from their body armour by their pins, but Drake had never seen it happen in real life. Not unless the soldier in question had some kind of deep-seated grudge against his own body.

Last of all came the breaching charges. Both Drake and Mason were carrying one shaped plastic explosive charge each, in a special pouch wrapped around their thigh. The charges could blast through pretty much anything, from a reinforced door to the hinges on a bank vault. They could be triggered remotely if necessary, but such a set-up took time, and Drake preferred to keep it simple. Thus Samantha had rigged a basic grenade fuse set to a five-second delay for them.

Mason had also removed and assembled the two Plumett grapple launchers. Gripping the big cumbersome guns by their carry handles, he carried them over to the far edge of the roof and laid them down beside Anya. When the time came, that was where they would launch their hooks from.

'Both guns are primed and loaded,' Mason said as soon as he returned.

Drake nodded acknowledgement.

His comrade hesitated then. 'You know there's no spare hooks or line reels.'

'I know.'

'If we miss…'

Drake gave him a sharp look. 'We won't.'

The Plumetts were fitted with fairly primitive iron sights, allowing them to be adjusted up to their maximum range of 100 yards, but they were hardly precision weapons at the best of times. The heavy steel grapple hook along with its trailing line of cable was about as aerodynamic as a brick hurled from a catapult, forcing the two men to fall back on their years of experience and training in weapons handling, plus a dose of luck.

Drake's best-case scenario was that both hooks would find their target, allowing the two men to slide down their lines simultaneously for maximum surprise, but failing that, he knew one high-tensile line could support both of them at a pinch. That was part of the reason they were wearing lighter body armour and carrying smaller, more compact weapons to keep their combined weight down.

Of course, there was always a chance that both hooks would fail, in which case their assault was over before it began. Drake preferred not to think about that.

'I know, Ryan.' Mason eyed his friend for a second or two before turning his attention back to his prep work. With his armour fixed in place and his spare ammunition loaded, he pulled on a pair of leather climbing gloves that would aid them during their fast rope descent, tensing and flexing his fingers several times to get a feel for them.

Drake looked him over. Mason was a big man, his body hardened and well muscled by an active career and supplemented with regular weight training. A descent by fast rope should have been easy for a man with such upper body strength, but Mason was nursing an old gunshot injury to the shoulder. Surgery and rehab had done their part, but the wound still gave him problems. Drake could guess what was going through his mind.

'Hey,' he said, tapping him on the arm with his own gloved hand. 'You've got this. The descent's the easy part.'

Mason nodded slowly, chewing his lip.

'Just try not to land your fat arse on someone's flower bed, yeah?'

That at last prompted a reaction. 'When this is over, remind me to drag you into a boxing ring sometime,' Mason said, eyes flashing with pride and defiance. 'Then we'll see who's out of shape.'

Drake grinned. When all else failed, taking the piss out of someone was usually the best course of action. It had worked in the military, and it still worked now.

He was about to respond to his friend's challenge when he felt something land on his cheek. Reaching up, he touched at it and found his glove glistening with moisture.

The droplet of rain was followed by another, and another. Drake could hear them pattering on the gravel-covered roof all around them. And then, as if someone had turned a shower head on, the heavens suddenly opened. Crouched out in the open as they were, the two men could do little but watch as the rain shower quickly turned into a soaking, hammering deluge.

Pakistan and Afghanistan might have entered the popular consciousness as mountainous, desert countries, baked by scorching hot summers and chilled by bitterly cold winters, but Islamabad enjoyed a tropical continental climate. And tropical weather meant monsoons. It seemed the dark rain clouds that had been gathering throughout the day had chosen this moment to drop their load on Drake and his companions.

'Well, I'll take this as a good omen,' Mason said, trying to shield himself from the onslaught. His clothes were already soaked through, as were Drake's. 'Like having a seagull shit on you.'

Sure enough, Drake's earpiece crackled into life. 'Might want to grab your ponchos, Alpha Team,' Frost advised, speaking from the perfectly dry confines of the Range Rover. He could hear water droplets hammering on the roof, even over the radio net. 'Looks like rain.'

'No shit, Bravo,' Drake replied tersely. 'We'd barely noticed.'

On the plus side, bad weather meant fewer people on the streets, less activity and less chance of being spotted. And the sound of the rain itself might well provide some useful ambient noise that would help mask their attack.

On the other hand, it meant sitting here in darkness, soaked to the skin while they waited for their targets to arrive. That was nobody's idea of a good time.

'This ain't going to do our comms equipment much good,' Mason pointed out.

'Try to shield it as best you can.' Their tactical radios were designed to survive inclement weather, but no electronic device was entirely immune to moisture, and they had no spare units available. Anyone whose radio failed was effectively cut off.

'Heads-up,' Anya called out, speaking over the radio net to make sure she had everyone's attention. 'I have a vehicle approaching the safe house. One SUV, black. Late model Mercedes.'

Drake was over by the wall within moments, his binoculars trained on the target building. Sure enough, a vehicle matching Anya's description had pulled to a stop in front of the automatic security gates. He saw a window roll down, saw the driver lean out to speak into the gate's radio intercom, holding his arm up to shield himself from the downpour.

And a few moments later, the gates began to trundle open as electric motors worked to draw them back along their runners.

Swapping an excited look with Anya, Drake keyed his radio. 'All units, look sharp. We have one vehicle making entry to the compound. This could be it.'

# Chapter 50

As his vehicle pulled to a halt by the main entrance of the grand, lavishly designed residence, Vizur Qalat couldn't help but feel impressed. And perhaps a little envious. He had to hand it to Marcus Cain; the man certainly did things in style.

The chosen place for their meeting was a luxurious two-storey private villa, set within a walled and gated compound that was no doubt covered from every angle by cameras and motion sensors. The building itself was a little too modern for his tastes – all sharp uncompromising angles, grey concrete and big sheet-glass windows – but its sheer ambition and dominance held a certain appeal for him.

It was particularly impressive given that this safe house was now effectively burned. He now knew of its existence, which rendered its function useless after tonight. It was a powerful statement of how much Cain could afford to give up just to make a simple meeting happen. This fact was not lost on Qalat.

Braving the heavy onslaught of rain, Qalat's driver circled around to his door and opened it for him. He carried no umbrella, and his suit was already glistening with damp.

Taking a deep breath, Qalat rose from his seat and strode directly for the building's front entrance, moving at a brisk but measured pace. He didn't run despite the rain. Nor did he glance around as his two bodyguards hurried to flank him.

As he'd expected, the door opened just as he approached, revealing a tall, well-built man in his mid-thirties, who smiled in welcome. He was wearing an expensive suit, but his short practical haircut combined with his age and build suggested a military background.

Qalat could almost feel his two protectors tensing up as they approached.

'Mr Qalat. Please, come in,' he said, moving aside so that Qalat and his entourage could pass. 'My name's Wilkins.'

Qalat paid him little heed, concentrating instead on quickly taking in and assessing his surroundings. Given their situation, it was plain that this man's name wasn't Wilkins, and that he was simply one of Cain's lackeys.

As he'd expected, the interior of the building was very much in keeping with its outward appearance. A lot of modernist concrete and exposed steelwork, some sparse furniture further down the hall in what he presumed was a living area. The floor was covered by polished marble tiles, their edges so perfectly aligned that he imagined a man could run his fingertips across the join without feeling a thing.

'I'm sorry about the weather this evening,' the American went on. 'There's a restroom just down the hall if you'd like?'

Qalat ran a hand through his hair. Though damp, it had avoided the worst of the downpour outside and seemed to have kept its style. And his suit jacket, spotted with droplets, wasn't wet enough to need replacing.

His two bodyguards were another matter, but one that didn't concern him. They were being paid well enough; they could endure a little soaking.

'That will not be necessary,' he assured the younger man

Wilkins nodded. 'Excellent. Then can I ask all of you to switch off any cell phones or recording devices you may be carrying, and remove the batteries.'

One of Qalat's bodyguards began to voice his objection, but Qalat himself raised a hand to stop him. 'Of course,' he replied tersely. 'We would be happy to.'

It was a standard precaution for a meeting like this. Qalat would have done the same in Cain's position. After removing the battery from his phone and handing it over to Wilkins, and checking that his two operatives had done likewise, he drew himself up to his full height, regarding the younger man with an impatient look.

'You have what you wanted, Mr Wilkins. Now, I'm a busy man. I would like to speak with Cain now.'

He saw a flicker of something in Wilkins's eyes. Not mockery or amusement as such, but a certain suggestion that he knew Qalat was bluffing. This wasn't some minor inconvenience to be dealt with as a matter of course. It was perhaps the most important meeting of his life, and they both knew it.

'Of course. This way, Mr Qalat.'

–

As the party from the car quickly entered the building and the door closed behind them, Drake turned to Anya. With the sniper rifle's powerful magnified scope at her disposal, she had likely seen things better than he.

'You get an ID on Cain?'

The woman shook her head, loose tendrils of damp blonde hair swinging in front of her face. 'It was too dark to make anyone out.'

He'd guessed as much. Fortunately he didn't need to see from up here.

'Alpha One to Bravo One,' he spoke into his radio. 'Possible sighting. Fire it up.'

'Copy that, Alpha. Bravo's on it.'

–

Half a mile away, Keira Frost was in the front passenger seat of the Range Rover, oblivious to the dull hammering of the rain on the roof as she concentrated on the laptop in front of her.

'Come on, come on. Talk to me,' she mumbled as her portable satellite uplink tried to establish a connection with the host security program. 'Don't play hard to get.'

Beside her, McKnight was anxiously glancing around, a silenced automatic resting on the floor beneath her seat. The heavy rain had had the beneficial effect of limiting pedestrian traffic in the area, but that did little to assuage her fraught nerves now that they were so close to their goal. The anxiety was only adding to the lingering sense of nausea that refused to leave her, further adding to her discomfort.

'How long is this going to take?' she asked impatiently.

'Chill, Sam. I'm on it.'

'Ryan and Cole's lives depend on this, Keira. Don't tell me to—'

'I said I'm on it,' Frost bit back, giving her a sharp look. Before she could say anything more, she looked back down at the screen as a new dialogue window popped up, notifying her that a connection had been established.

Reaching up, Frost hit her radio transmitter. 'Bravo One, we have an uplink. Inputting the Judas code now.'

The dialogue window flickered a couple of times as her computer tried to wrest control of the building's security system, a digital battle was playing out within its coded circuits. Both women tensed up, waiting in anxious silence to see how it would end.

Then suddenly the window changed, replaced by a selection of different video feeds, showing various views from both the interior and exterior of the house. Live shots from the security cameras positioned throughout the building.

'Yes! We're in,' Frost exclaimed, grinning with excitement.

'What you got?' McKnight asked, eager to know more.

'Cameras, alarms, gate controls. I've got it all.' Reaching up, she keyed her radio. 'Bravo to all units. We're online.'

'Do you have eyes on Tempest?' Drake asked right away.

Tempest was their code word for Cain. Not entirely inappropriate either considering the chaos and destruction he'd brought about in his time.

'Working on it now.'

# Chapter 51

After being conducted to the building's upper level, Qalat found two more operatives standing guard at the entrance to what he presumed was a lounge or seating area of some kind. The door behind them was closed, and the two men's presence made it impossible to get past.

'I'm afraid I'll have to ask your security personnel to remain here,' Wilkins said, managing to sound almost apologetic. His two companions had other ideas, somehow making themselves even bigger.

'You can't go in there without protection, sir,' Baloch, his chief body-guard whispered urgently in Pashto. 'There's no telling what—'

'I can assure you, it's perfectly safe,' Wilkins cut in, speaking the same language with flawless precision and taking a small measure of satisfaction in the surprise it evoked. 'No harm will come to you while you're in this building. That's why we're here.'

Qalat thought on it for a moment. It went against his instincts to go into a situation like this blind and defenceless, but once again he recognized that if all Cain wanted was to see him dead, there were easier ways to do it. And to back out now would be a great show of weakness.

'It's fine,' he said at last, motioning Baloch to stand down. He gave Wilkins a sour look before adding, 'After all, we are all friends here.'

This time Wilkins did smile, but there was no warmth in it.

'Thank you, sir. Could you raise your arms, please?'

Qalat did as he asked. Moving forward, Wilkins quickly and efficiently frisked him for hidden weapons. Finding none, he took a step back and nodded to the two operatives guarding the door, who stepped neatly aside, one of them opening the door to reveal a wide, open-plan sitting area beyond.

'Deputy Director Cain is waiting for you inside, sir,' he said, gesturing for Qalat to go on ahead. 'Please go in.'

Giving his two men a meaningful glance, Qalat straightened his back, raised his chin and walked onward to meet his adversary.

–

On the rooftop overlooking the safe house, the atmosphere was growing increasingly tense as the seconds crawled by without word from Frost. Every moment they delayed increased the chance they might be spotted, or lose their window to strike.

'We're exposed out here, Ryan,' Mason hissed, eager to get moving. 'I say we go now, while we still can.'

'No,' Drake decided. 'Not until we have eyes on Cain.'

'We will not get another chance at this, Mason,' Anya added, looking up from her weapon to regard the two men. 'Be patient.'

'Easy for you to say.'

The look she gave him then offered a glimpse into the years of lies and betrayals she had experienced because of Cain, the lifetime she had given up in service of hopeless causes, the suffering and pain she had endured. It was only a glimpse, but it was enough.

'It is not easy for me,' she promised him.

–

The expansive sitting room was, like the rest of the house, of ultra-modern design, with bare concrete walls and exposed steelwork. The full-length windows probably offered an impressive view over the city, but all of them had been blocked by thick blinds to shield the interior from prying eyes. The floor was expensive hardwood, unlike the marble tiles downstairs, but polished to a mirror sheen.

A pair of white leather couches sat in the centre of the room, on opposite sides of a glass-topped coffee table. Cups and a pot of coffee had already been laid out. It was on the furthest couch that Marcus Cain was reclining in apparent ease, as a man might relax after a hard day at work.

Seeing Qalat's arrival, he smiled and rose from his seat. There was no warmth in that smile, however, and despite his outward show of hospitality he had the look of a fighter making his way to the ring.

'Vizur, good to see you. It's been a long time,' he said, rounding the coffee table and approaching with his hand outstretched.

Qalat shook hands with him, noting the power of the man's grip. Typical American, trying to assert strength in a situation that demanded wits and intelligence.

'Indeed it has,' Qalat agreed, quickly comparing the man before him to the one he'd met in Afghanistan two decades earlier. His hair was greying at the sides, his face a little more lined and careworn than before, but all things considered he seemed to have weathered the years quite well. 'You have an impressive place here.'

Cain shrugged, as if it were a matter of no importance. 'The Agency isn't short on money these days.' Then, remembering his manners, he gestured to the couch closest to them. 'Please, make yourself comfortable. We've got a lot to talk about.'

'Holy shit! We've got him!' Frost cried out, punching the car dashboard in her excitement.

Sure enough, the video window in front of her showed Cain, along with a second man in the building's living room, just where they predicted the meeting would take place.

McKnight, her hand trembling, reached for her radio transmitter. 'Bravo Two to all units. We have a confirmed sighting of Tempest. Repeat, Tempest is on site.'

'Copy that,' Drake replied, the tension in his voice evident even over the radio net. 'What's his location?'

'He's in the upper-floor living room. Right where we expected. I see one other tango with him. Male, Asian, mid-forties, likely of Pakistani origin.'

'No one else?'

'Negative. Two other Pakistani men are waiting outside in the upper corridor, along with three white males in suits. They look like bodyguards to me.'

'Understood. Focus on Tempest for now. What's his situation?'

'He's seated at a coffee table in the centre of the room, talking with his Pakistani contact.'

'Can you patch through the audio?' Drake asked quickly.

'Stand by, Alpha. I'm on it,' she replied, going to work.

Qalat settled himself on the couch opposite the deputy director, surveying him calmly across the expanse of polished glass.

'Would you like a cup of coffee?' Cain asked, reaching for the pot and pouring himself a cup. 'I understand you're partial to it.'

Qalat felt his pulse quicken a little at that remark, Cain subtly reminding him how easily his man had been able to slip past Qalat's bodyguards several days ago. They'd been able to get to him once. They could do so again if need be.

'Thank you,' Qalat replied, his tone even.

'Before we get started, I wanted to thank you for meeting with me tonight,' Cain went on, steaming hot black liquid tumbling from the pot into the cup. The aroma of freshly ground coffee filled the air around them. 'Not every man would have taken a leap of faith like this, but I had a feeling you were different. After all, that's how men like us get ahead in this business. By taking risks.'

'Marcus, we have known each other a long time. Too long to play these games. So, as they say at times like these, let's dispense with the pleasantries. We are both here because we want something, and we both have something to offer. Why don't we get down to business?'

Cain, in the midst of pouring Qalat's coffee, glanced up from his task. His expression betrayed no anger or irritation, but something akin to relief.

'You know something, Vizur? You're right about that.'

Out in the corridor, Baloch paced anxiously back and forth across the wide hallway. With the door closed and securely barred by the two CIA operatives, he had no idea what was going on in the room beyond. No idea what his boss was discussing, or even if he was safe.

His comrade Kassar had taken a seat on an expensive-looking oak chair about halfway along the corridor, his sodden clothes dripping water on the tiled floor. His jaw was clenched tight, fingers tensing and relaxing as if he were trying to expel the nervous tension that filled him.

This situation felt all wrong. He couldn't pin it down to anything specific – by any normal standard their American hosts had been perfectly polite and accommodating – but on some deeper level he sensed it. An almost palpable aura of menace and foreboding seemed to linger about this place, despite all assurances to the contrary, and it was only growing stronger.

He felt edgy, confined, trapped. His damp suit clung uncomfortably to his skin, his swollen tie felt tight around his neck. Reaching up, he loosened it, then reached into his suit jacket for a pack of cigarettes he always kept there. Some men drank, some sought comfort in women or other distractions, but for him it was always nicotine.

Straight away the two American guards tensed up, no doubt suspecting the worst, but they relaxed slightly as he withdrew the pack.

'I'll have to ask you not to smoke in here, sir,' the man named Wilkins warned as he tapped one out and placed it between his lips.

'Why?' Baloch asked, turning away to light it. 'Worried it will kill you?'

'Not exactly.'

Baloch started at the familiar muted thump of a silenced weapon discharging. Catching a sudden rush of red off to his left, he instinctively turned towards it, just in time to see Kassar slumping sideways and toppling off the expensive oak chair. A wide spray of blood and brain matter coated the concrete wall behind him.

'Contact!' he yelled out instinctively in Pashto, reaching for his concealed weapon. A second thump, and an explosion of darkness told him he was already too late.

–

'Holy shit!' Frost cried out over the radio net.

Instantly Drake felt his heart rate soar, all thoughts of the rain still sluicing down on them forgotten now. Though they were listening in on the audio patched through from the safe house, neither he nor his two companions could see a thing. Only Frost and McKnight knew the full picture.

'Bravo, say again your last? What's your sitrep?'

'The two Pakistani bodyguards are dead.'

Drake's eyes met with Anya's. Her look reflected the same shock and disbelief he felt. 'What happened, Bravo?'

'Cain's men just fucking killed them both,' she said, abandoning radio protocol in her haste to explain what she'd witnessed.

Neither Drake nor Anya said a word, because they were both thinking the same thing. What the hell was going on in that building?

–

Qalat jumped to his feet at the panicked cry from outside, as well as the distinctive thud of silenced weapons discharging.

'Sit down please, Vizur,' Cain said calmly, laying down the coffee pot.

Qalat's heart was pounding now, his eyes dark and accusing. 'What the hell was that?'

'That? That was the sound of your men being executed,' the deputy director replied, as if nothing of any great interest had transpired. 'Now, do you take milk or sugar in your coffee?'

Qalat felt the bile rising in his throat, as well as a growing fury that Cain had staged such an elaborate ruse just to murder him. It had all been a lie. The clandestine contact, the promise of mutual assistance, of negotiation. All of it had been done to get him to come here, to expose himself.

'You bastard!' he snarled, fists clenched in rage. 'How dare you? I came here in good faith!'

Cain shrugged. 'This is one of those give and take scenarios. You took something from me when one of your men blew himself up at Camp Chapman, so I took something back today. Be thankful I haven't taken more. Yet.'

'Your man promised we would not be harmed.'

'No, he promised *you* wouldn't be harmed. And you won't, provided you cooperate.' He leaned back in his seat, cup of coffee in hand. 'So sit down. Now.'

The veneer of polite courtesy had been cast aside, exposing the man that lay behind it. The cold, calculating, ruthless intellect that had engineered everything leading up to this moment.

Slowly Qalat lowered himself back onto the couch, his eyes blazing with hatred.

'Better,' Cain allowed. 'Now, you might not think it to look at me, but I'm a lot like Father Christmas. I make it my business to know when people have been naughty or nice. And you've been a very naughty boy, Vizur. I know you've been actively working against our hunt for senior al-Qaeda commanders on both sides of the Afghan border. I know you were behind the suicide attack at Camp Chapman, and that al-Balawi was an ISI double agent operating under your orders.'

Qalat said nothing to this, didn't waste time trying to refute the accusations, because he knew it was futile. Cain would not have gone to this kind of trouble without proof.

'I know your men were active in Turkey last year, that you were part of a failed attempt to steal a classified Agency computer file known as the Black List. You did this because you wanted an intimate knowledge of our covert operations here, you wanted to know whether we were nearing our goal. So you could stop us before we got too close.'

Qalat couldn't believe how much this man knew, how many pieces he'd managed to put together, how many seemingly unrelated events he'd assembled into a coherent narrative. He felt like he were trying to play chess against a man who had foreseen every move, countered every strategy, thwarted every advance. He was being outmanoeuvred, outplayed, outmatched in every way imaginable.

'You seem to know a lot, Marcus,' he said, somehow managing to retain his icy composure. 'Very impressive, but I presume there is a reason I am still alive. Tell me what you want.'

'You know what I want. Or rather, who I want.' Cain took a sip of his coffee and laid it down on the table, keeping his eyes focussed on Qalat the whole time. 'I want Osama Bin Laden, and you're going to give him to me.'

–

'Jesus Christ, I don't believe what I'm hearing,' Mason gasped, listening in on the conversation as it played out over the radio net. 'This isn't happening.'

'Bravo, tell me you're recording this,' Drake hissed, stunned by the conversation playing out in that safe house. With only an audio feed to listen to, he couldn't actually see what was going on, but he didn't have to. The words alone were enough to chill him to the core.

'Every word, Alpha,' Frost confirmed.

'Good. Stand by to kill the external cameras on my mark. We're going in.'

Regardless of whatever shady deal might be on the agenda in there tonight, Drake hadn't forgotten their true purpose here. Cain was on site and vulnerable, and they were unlikely to get a better chance at taking him down. This was it.

'Wait,' Mason interrupted suddenly. 'Not yet.'

Drake looked at him. 'What do you mean?'

'This isn't some pissant arms deal we've stumbled on here. He's talking about taking down the world's most wanted man, for Christ's sake.'

'He's talking about a lot of things,' Drake reminded him. 'Doesn't make them real.'

'Suppose you're wrong? Suppose Cain can actually make this happen? We interrupt this thing, and we might be killing our only chance to stop that raghead son of a bitch.'

'Bravo is standing by. What are your orders?'

'Wait one, Bravo,' Drake replied quickly, turning his attention back to Mason. Whatever they were hearing over the radio net could be disinformation, speculation or even outright lies. 'We didn't come here to deal in chances. Cain's our target, Cole. We stick to the plan.'

'Plans change.'

'Not this one.'

'Especially this one,' he hissed. 'Don't you get it? You have any idea how many thousands, tens of thousands of people have died because of that *one man*, how many thousands more might die if he's allowed to live? You want all those deaths on your conscience? Because they will be if we go in there now.'

Drake had no answer for that. Mason was asking him to make an impossible choice – the life of one enemy against the possibility of killing another. The chance to protect the people he cared most about in this world, set against countless other innocents whose deaths could perhaps be averted.

Perhaps.

–

Qalat regarded this adversary in thoughtful silence for several moments. So they had finally gotten down it. This was Cain's endgame; the thread on which both their fates now hung. The death of the world's most wanted man. The decapitation of the terrorist network that had spread years of fear and destruction across the globe.

'An ambitious goal,' he remarked coolly, giving nothing away. 'And one that many others have set for themselves. Assuming for a moment—'

'No more assumptions,' Cain interrupted. 'No more lies, no more suggestions, no more bullshit. I didn't fly halfway around the world to your shithole of a country on an *assumption*, Vizur. We both know the ISI has been protecting him and probably most of al-Qaeda's top commanders at least since the invasion. And we both know you're one of the men who can lead us to him. So let's not talk about what we *assume*, let's talk about what you *know*.'

–

'Are you hearing this, Alpha?' Frost cut in over the radio net, her tinny voice resonating in Drake's ear. 'Jesus Christ, I think the son of a bitch is about to break.'

Drake made his decision in that moment. A rain-soaked rooftop seconds before they were about to go into combat was no place for such philosophical musings, and he knew that if they delayed much longer they would lose their window of opportunity.

One way or another, Cain was going down tonight.

'We don't have time for this—'

He was silenced when Mason reached out and grabbed him by the forearm, his grip tightening like a vice. 'It wasn't *your* country that got hit by those bastards, Ryan,' he said, eyes alight now with the kind of fire Drake had never seen before. 'Cain's a lowlife piece of shit, but I'm not going to let you—'

It was Mason's turn to fall silent as he felt something cold and metallic pressed against the side of his head. It was the long, chunky barrel of a silenced Colt M1911 automatic.

'We came here for one reason,' Anya said, thumbing back the hammer. 'The mission is all that matters now. If you can't see that, you are no good to us.'

Far from looking frightened or angry at this show of force, Mason flashed a twisted, ironic smile. 'So that's where we're at, huh? You going to let this bitch shoot me, Ryan?'

Drake gave Anya a look warning her to back down, though whether she would was anyone's guess. 'I'd rather you came with me so we can finish this together.'

'You know what's at stake here.'

'I do,' he assured his friend.

'You know we can't sacrifice thousands of innocent lives just to save our own asses.' He shook his head. 'If you're asking me to live with that, you'd better pull the trigger now.'

Reaching out, Drake gripped his friend's arm and leaned in close. 'It's not going to come to that. I swear to God, if the deal in there is real, we'll find a way to make it happen. Even if we have to grab that ISI agent and beat the truth out of him ourselves.' His gaze switched to Anya, who still held the weapon at the ready. 'Right?'

'I am here for Cain,' she said, not taking her eyes off the man she was covering. 'This war is no longer my concern.'

'I'll take that as a yes,' Drake said, looking at Mason again. 'Cole, I need you, mate. I need you to trust me, one last time. Please.'

The man was torn. It was written on his face as plain as day. But he trusted Drake about as much as anyone on the face of the earth, and in the end, trust won out.

'All right, goddamn it. All right.'

Drake released his hold. 'Lower the gun, Anya.'

A moment's hesitation, then the weapon was withdrawn, though the woman continued to watch Mason warily.

Drake was reaching up for his radio transmitter when Mason gripped him by the shoulder, leaning in close. 'For all our sakes, I hope to Christ you're right about this one, Ryan.'

Drake said nothing to this, and after a moment of simmering tension Mason withdrew to ready his Plumett grapple gun.

Drawing a deep breath, Drake hit his radio transmitter. 'Alpha to all units. Downfall is a go. I say again, Downfall is a go. Prepare to cut external cameras on my mark.'

'Copy that, Alpha. Bravo is ready.'

Anya returned to her sniping position, bringing her rifle to bear. 'Charlie is ready,' she said, her voice low and steady.

Stooping down, Drake seized the heavy grapple gun by its carry handle and hoisted it up to his shoulder, swinging the long ungainly barrel towards the target building.

# Chapter 52

Qalat was taken aback by Cain's abrupt change in tone, the almost brutish way he'd made his play. The facade of courtesy and civility had slipped aside, and not through choice. Cain's barely restrained aggression spoke of years of pent-up frustration, disappointments and failures.

That was when he realized the truth – his adversary had staged this meeting not out of cold, ruthless calculation, but out of desperation. He needed what Qalat had.

That gave him an edge.

'Very well,' Qalat said at length, deciding to give the man what he wanted. To a point, at least. 'You're right, of course. Since you seem to value plain speaking, here it is. We *have* been protecting senior leaders of the global jihad, we *have* undermined the CIA's efforts to track them down, and we've been doing it for some time. Successfully, I might add.'

–

Ignoring the rain still lashing down around him, Drake stared down the grapple gun's primitive iron sight at the communications dish mounted on a steel frame at one corner of the building's roof about 70 yards away. A difficult enough mark to hit under ideal conditions, never mind in darkness with rain weighing down the cable and interfering with his vision.

All he could do was take his best shot, and hope.

Beside him, he could make out the dark shape of Mason crouched low, weapon similarly trained on the target. Two chances to make the hit.

And no more time to waste.

'On my mark, Bravo,' he said, flexing his trigger finger. 'Three, two, one… mark.'

A couple of hundred yards away, Frost enabled a single pre-prepared command on her laptop, killing power to all external cameras. An instant later, their feeds went blank on her screen as they shut down.

'Cameras down, Alpha. I say again, they're blind.'

Making one last fractional adjustment to his aim, Drake let out a barely audible breath and pulled the trigger.

There was no deafening crack or boom as with a conventional firearm. His first impression was of a sudden, powerful *whoosh* as the Plumett's compressed air cartridge discharged, sending the steel grapple hook and its attached cable arching over 70 yards of open air.

The kinetic energy of the blast caused the weapon to kick back against his shoulder, but Drake was oblivious to it now. All his attention was focussed on his hook as it rocketed through the air towards the communications array, joined an instant later by a second projectile from Mason's weapon.

Both hooks raced towards their objective, angling slowly downwards as their velocity slowed and gravity began to take hold, high-tensile cable spooling out of their reels like fishing rods that had just hooked a prime catch.

Then suddenly Mason's gun jerked forward, nearly torn from his grasp. His hook instantly came to a halt and dropped straight to the ground as if it had collided with some invisible wall.

'Shit! Fuck!' the man snarled in frustration, looking down at the kink in the cable that had snagged on his reel as it was unspooling, jamming it.

Drake paid the malfunction no heed. There was nothing that could be done about it now. Instead he watched as his own hook arched downwards, plunging towards its target like some ungainly projectile hurled from an ancient siege engine.

'Come on, come on,' he whispered, praying that his aim had been true. Contact.

He had aimed high, he realized with sickening dismay, his hook missing the solid steel framework that the dish was mounted on, and instead striking the dish surface itself.

Drake winced, waiting for it to simply bounce off the metal surface and fall uselessly onto the roof below, where there was nothing that it could conceivably hook onto.

Instead, to his amazement, the barbed projectile punched straight through the thin metal mesh that made up the dish skin, swinging freely on the other side where one of the three prongs caught on the dish mounting arm below.

'I don't believe it,' he gasped.

A hinged metal bracket, easily an inch thick and designed to not only support the dish's weight but also keep it in position even if it was being buffeted by bad weather, the mounting arm was about as good a grapple point as he could have hoped to hit. It should, in theory at least, be enough to support the weight of a man.

He would find out in a few seconds.

Dropping the gun, he gripped the trailing cable in his gloved hands and pulled it as taut as his strength would allow, locking it into place at the anchor point placed there during yesterday's recon trip.

'Alpha has one firm lock,' he spoke over the radio, notifying the others of the situation. 'Preparing to move in. Any sign of activity, Bravo?'

'Nothing yet, Alpha,' Frost replied, her voice as taut as the cable trailing off into the night. It seemed the sound of the hook's impact hadn't been noticed.

As Drake picked up the simple handheld pulley used for his descent down the zip line, Mason sprinted over to him. 'Fucking cable jam,' he growled under his breath as he removed his own pulley from his harness.

'Not your fault, mate,' Drake replied quickly. Such things could, and unfortunately did, happen to the best of them. 'I'm up first. Give me three seconds to get clear, then come down after me.'

Mason eyed the single line doubtfully. 'Will it take our weight?'

That was the golden question. In theory the line had a tensile strength of over 500 pounds; slightly more than the combined weight of the two men plus their gear. But the unexpected jam in Mason's line might be indicative of badly maintained or flawed cables, either of which could result in a fast one-way trip to the ground. Drake could only hope the two sets had come from different manufacturing batches.

'We'll find out in a minute,' he said, snapping his pulley into place and locking it in. 'Get ready. Three seconds. Yeah?'

'Yeah.'

Taking a breath, Drake gripped the line tight and braced one foot against the parapet running along the edge of the building.

'Ryan?'

Surprised, Drake glanced down at Anya. The woman had briefly taken her eyes off the rifle scope to look at him. She said nothing, but he could sense her struggling to find the words, straining to say something that would encapsulate everything she was feeling at that moment.

Knowing that was one battle she couldn't win, he took the lead for her.

'I'll see you again,' he promised, giving her a wink.

With that, he rocked back once to gain a little momentum, tightened his grip on the pulley and launched himself towards the distant building.

–

For several seconds, not a sound could be heard in that expansive living room. Cain stared at Qalat across the table, as if struggling to believe that the man had so openly admitted to something of this scale, that he would so brazenly flaunt the fact that his own agency was working to protect the most wanted man in the world.

'Well, aren't you going to ask me?' Qalat said, breaking the silence.

'Ask you what?'

A flicker of a smile. 'Why, of course? Is that not what every man in your position wants; to know why his supposed allies would betray him? To understand his adversary?'

It was Cain's turn to smile. 'No, Vizur. I'm not going to ask, because I honestly don't care. Maybe it's religious ideology, maybe it's intimidation, maybe it's part of some regional power play. Hell, maybe it's something as simple as money.' He shrugged, dismissing it all. 'Makes no difference to me.'

Reaching down, Cain carefully picked up his coffee cup and took a sip of the steaming black liquid.

'Let me tell you something – I've been playing this little game of deception for 30 years. I've persuaded Soviet generals to defect; manipulated tribal leaders out to settle blood feuds; made alliances with warlords in every shithole from Afghanistan to Africa; bribed, assassinated and blackmailed government officials, and worked with *and* against intelligence operatives from pretty much every agency on the face of the earth. You know what I learned? All of them are the same, when you get right down to it. All of them do what's in their own best interests at any given moment. And right now, what's in your best interest – and I can't stress this enough – is to tell me where he is.'

–

Drake clenched his teeth, his arms and shoulders straining as his full weight settled on them, the cable flexing and bouncing but holding firm. Within moments, the apartment building had receded behind him as he accelerated down the zip line, rain and wind whipping into his face and rooftops flying past below. The pulley on which his fate now rested screamed with increasing speed as the cable raced through it.

There was no going back now, no way to stop what was coming, no means of protecting himself. If a guard appeared on the rooftop terrace he was aiming for, Drake couldn't hope to bring his weapon to bear. He'd just have to trust that Anya's sniping skills were at their best tonight.

For now, all he could do was hang on tight, take the strain and brace himself for the landing as the target building hurtled towards him.

A second jolting flex on the line told him that Mason too had begun his descent. Once more he tensed up, waiting with bated breath for that sudden ping, that loss of tension that would tell him the line had failed.

But it never came. Despite the increased weight, the single cable held firm.

The target building was approaching fast out of the night now, its external security lights putting him in mind of car headlamps hurtling towards him. Drake tried not to think of himself as a deer about to be turned into roadkill as he brought his legs up, ready to take the impact as he approached the upper wall.

If he came in too fast, it wouldn't matter how well the descent had gone – he'd still break bones, which would put him out of action for good. But to his relief, his descent was slowing, the angle of the line growing shallow due to the natural flex of a cable stretched out over such a long distance. He glanced down at the glass-topped perimeter wall as it passed beneath him, wary of enemies but finding none.

The upper terrace wall loomed out of the darkness right in front of him. Bringing his legs into position, Drake braced himself. A thump and scrape as both boots slammed into the wet concrete wall, followed by a jarring impact that travelled up his legs as if his bones were reverberating with the hit. Drake bent his knees, softening the impact, then let out a breath as he finally came to a halt.

He'd made it.

Relief at this momentary success surged through him, but it was quickly tempered by the realization that he needed to move. Undoing the quick release strap on his wrist, Drake slipped free of the pulley and ducked aside just as Mason arrived.

The older man's touch down was more graceful than his own. A seasoned army ranger, Mason was no stranger to house assaults like this, and knew how best to position his body so that he landed with maximum efficiency.

In a matter of seconds he had released himself from his pulley, drawn his weapon and scurried over to join Drake, who was positioned by the door leading inside, covering the entrance.

A single curt nod confirmed he was good to go, and Drake reached for his radio. 'Alpha team's in position,' he whispered. 'Standing by to move in.'

'Copy that. I see you, Alpha,' Anya confirmed. 'No targets in sight.'

The rooftop door was secured with an electronic combination lock, a single red indicator light burning in silent defiance, confirming it was locked.

'Bravo, kill the door lock.'

A second or so later, the light turned green, followed by a metallic click as the lock disengaged. The way ahead was open.

'Wish we'd had this shit in Iraq a few years ago,' Mason remarked as Drake reached for the door handle.

'Hard part's still to come,' Drake warned him. 'Alpha team's moving in.'

A single turn of the handle, and the door swung open. With Drake leading the way, the two men advanced inside.

–

'Suppose for a moment this all works out exactly as you hope. You kill Bin Laden and decapitate al-Qaeda,' Qalat began. 'Do you really believe it will make any difference? You and I both know how hard his followers are prepared to fight. We should – we trained many of them ourselves. A fact you may have found it politically convenient to forget.'

'I haven't forgotten a single thing we did,' Cain assured him.

'Then you know that killing one of their leaders will not stop them. These men are fighting a holy war on behalf of Allah Himself. Any one of them would gladly lay down their life in His name.'

'Would you?'

Qalat shifted position. 'I am not afraid of death, if that is what you mean.'

Cain's eyes glittered. 'There are worse things than death, Vizur. Much, much worse. Believe me, you don't want to find out what I'm capable of.'

–

Drake descended the steel steps leading from the rooftop terrace outside, his wet boots making only the faintest clang against the metal with each step. The MP7 was up at his shoulder, its bulky silencer fixed on the open doorway below as they approached. Mason was only a few steps behind, covering him. The faint drip of water from their soaked clothes was the only other sound in that cramped stairwell.

Having studied the building's design blueprints and committed them to memory, Drake knew every inch of this safe house as if it were his childhood home. Beyond the doorway below lay the upper floor hallway, leading to the living room at the far end. That was where they would find Cain and his mysterious contact.

Unlike the building's exterior which projected an image of sophisticated modernity, the stairwell was plain and starkly utilitarian by comparison. The walls were simple plasterboard, unmarked save for a couple of handwritten notations scrawled across their surface, likely left by the builders during construction. Illumination came via a single bare light bulb in the ceiling. No effort had been put into finishing or decorating this area, because it was never intended to be lived in.

'Alpha's in the stairwell, approaching first-floor hallway,' he said, his voice barely audible over the pounding of his own heartbeat. 'Bravo, what's the sitrep? How many tangos ahead?'

–

In the passenger seat of the Range Rover a couple of hundred yards away, Frost switched the video feed to the hallway cameras, searching for a good angle on Cain's bodyguards.

'Bravo has – shit,' she gasped as the feeds suddenly cut out, leaving her staring at nothing more than a series of blank test screens. 'Stand by, Alpha.'

She could feel her heart beating faster as she frantically sought the source of the problem. Don't panic yet, she told herself. It could just be a glitch.

'What the fuck's going on?' McKnight demanded, leaning in closer.

'I'm working on it,' Frost hissed, fear and concern making her defensive.

McKnight glared at her. 'Well work faster, for Christ's sake. Cole and Ryan are sitting ducks in there!'

–

Crouching down in the stairwell and forcing calm into his voice, Drake hit his transmitter again. 'What's the sitrep, Bravo?'

He heard a muttered curse. 'Bravo is in the dark,' Frost reported, unable to hide the fear in her voice. 'We have no visuals inside the building.'

The breath caught in his throat. 'Can you get them back?'

'The whole thing's dead, I don't have control here,' she admitted. 'Repeat, Bravo does not have control.'

'Christ,' Mason growled, tensing up and eyeing the doorway with his weapon raised. 'We're blind.'

'I don't like this, Alpha,' McKnight's voice echoed in his ear. 'Recommend you fall back *now*.'

'No,' Drake insisted.

'We're *locked out*. We have to abort.'

'We abort now, we'll lose him.' He could feel the anger, the impatience, the desperation mounting with each passing second. They had travelled halfway around the world, risked everything to get this far, and now Marcus Cain was sitting no more than 10 yards away. 'And this was all for nothing.'

'I know how bad you want this, but use your head, Alpha,' she pleaded with him. 'This isn't worth dying for.'

Drake already knew what he was going to do, but he needed to know Mason was with him. Taking his eyes off the doorway for a moment, Drake glanced at his teammate, the two men sharing a look born from years of serving together on missions just like this, of risking their lives and placing their trust in each other.

'We go all the way,' he said quietly.

Mason nodded. 'Damn right we do.'

Sparing his friend a brief smile of gratitude, Drake reached for his radio. 'All units, stand by. Alpha is going in.'

With Mason right behind him, he vaulted down the last couple of steps at the bottom of the stairwell, through the doorway and into the pristine marble corridor beyond. His silenced weapon's tritium sight swept left and right, eagerly seeking a target and finding none. The hallway was empty.

No targets, no bloodstains from the two supposedly dead ISI operatives. Had they been killed on the ground floor? Had their murderers already cleaned up the crime scene and moved to dispose of the bodies?

'Clear left,' he whispered.

Mason, covering his back, similarly found no enemies. 'Clear right.'

The doorway leading to the living room was directly ahead. No guards stood in their way. Beyond lay Marcus Cain. He had to be there. There was only one way in or out of that room, and he couldn't possibly have escaped without them seeing him.

He was there, and Drake was coming for him.

# Chapter 53

On the rooftop of the apartment building overlooking the safe house, Anya was still crouched by the parapet, her eye to the powerful magnified scope, oblivious to the rain that was still hammering down around her. The long barrel of her rifle tracked slowly back and forth across the building's exterior, searching for a target and finding none.

No sign of any security presence at all, in fact.

Something about this assault wasn't right. She couldn't explain it rationally, but her gut instinct told her something was afoot. In the course of her long career she'd taken part in operations that, for one reason or another, had proven less challenging than anticipated. But this was something else. It was simply too easy.

It was as if they were being led inside...

Eyes opening wide as the disparate pieces suddenly coalesced into a single chilling possibility, Anya reached for her radio transmitter.

'Charlie to Alpha. Bravo is right, this is a trap. Fall back now. I repeat, fall back!'

–

But Drake wasn't hearing her. He was already committed to the attack, the blood pounding in his ears as his heartbeat went into overtime.

Sprinting down the short length of hallway, his boots leaving wet prints on the marble tiles, he halted in front of the door, weapon raised, safety off. Mason closed in beside him, ready to cover his every move.

They had rehearsed this final step of the attack countless times. Each had their own sectors of the room to cover, their own fields of fire. When they breached the door, Drake would go right, Mason left, advancing quickly to put some space between them, and killing anything that pointed a weapon in their direction.

Once they had Cain and his ISI contact in their sights, they would subdue both men and prep them for transport. Drake almost hoped that Cain tried to resist. He wouldn't kill him – yet – but a 4.6 x 30mm round through the kneecap was unlikely to be fatal.

He briefly thought about using the breaching charge to make entry, but dismissed the idea after a quick inspection of the door barring their way.

This was no hardened, reinforced security barricade, but a simple internal door set within a standard wooden frame. No explosives would be needed to get it open.

Glancing one last time at his companion to check that he was ready, Drake nodded once, raised his boot and planted a single, powerful kick just beneath the lock. Straight away the door flew open, yielding to the force of the impact with the crunch of splintering wood, revealing the big open-plan living room beyond.

Both men were moving instantly, Mason going in first because Drake's kick had interrupted his momentum for half a second. As planned, Drake fanned out right while his companion moved left, both sweeping the room for targets.

Drake's eyes and weapon were a blur of adrenaline-fuelled movement, taking in every detail of his surroundings as he advanced. The room was large, its sparse furnishings serving to emphasize its proportions. The blinds were drawn over the windows, obscuring their view of the city outside. A pair of leather couches sat on either side of a coffee table in the centre of the room. A couple of book cases stood against the far wall, both empty.

A big, mostly empty room. No Cain. No ISI agent.

Nothing.

'Clear!' he called out, lowering his weapon.

'Clear!' came Mason's reply from the other side of the room. 'What the fuck? There's nothing here.'

A hundred questions were whirling through his mind in that moment, but all of them were silenced by the deep knot of fear and apprehension that had suddenly tightened in his stomach.

'This is all wrong,' he said under his breath.

Mason turned towards him, his expression one of utter disbelief. 'This is impossible. Frost had eyes on him, and there was no way he could have slipped by us. He was in this goddamn room!'

Only then did an idea stir in Drake's mind. A possibility, seemingly remote and unlikely yet the only one that fit with what they knew. The only explanation for what had just happened.

'No he wasn't,' Drake gasped. 'It was fake.'

'What?'

'It wasn't real! What Keira saw on her monitor was happening some-where else. It was all staged to lead us here!'

Somehow Cain had known of their plan in advance. Somehow the bastard had been one step ahead yet again. He couldn't explain how it had happened, couldn't rationalize how his plan had suddenly unravelled in such horrifying fashion, but those were questions for another time.

For now, getting out of this place was the priority. Disbelief and shock instantly gave way to an urgent, overwhelming urge to escape.

'On me!' he hissed, raising his weapon and striding towards the door. As he did so, he reached up and clicked his radio transmitter. 'Alpha to all units, Downfall is blown. I repeat, we're compromised. Fall back to—'

He winced at the sudden high-pitched electrical screech that suddenly pulsed through his comms unit, and hurriedly tore the earpiece out before the noise deafened him. Judging by Mason's own growl of pain and similar reaction, he had just experienced the same thing.

'Ow! Goddamn it. What the fuck was that?' Mason demanded.

Before Drake could reply, the building's internal lights suddenly went out, plunging the room and the two men inside it into darkness. They were alone, cut off from support, unable to communicate, unable even to see.

An instant of shock, and Drake's brain immediately switched from thoughts of evacuation to simple survival. Killing the lights in the building could only be a prelude to one thing, and this terrible realization was confirmed by the sound of footsteps in the corridor outside.

'Down!' he yelled, turning and throwing himself behind the nearest couch just as a burst of silenced gunfire erupted from the doorway.

–

In the Range Rover not far away, Frost looked up from her laptop, her face screwed up in pain as she wrenched the radio transmitter from her ear. 'Shit, we're being jammed!' she warned, recognizing the distinctive static distortion all too well. 'Ryan and Cole are cut off. What the fuck do we do?'

McKnight had heard enough. Abandoning her vigil over the technical specialist, she slipped back into her seat behind the wheel and turned over the ignition key. The engine fired first time, rumbling back into loud, urgent life like some ancient beast awoken from its slumber.

'Hang on,' she advised, throwing the big vehicle into gear.

–

Drake barely cleared the couch with his desperate leap, landing hard on the marble tiles beyond and pulling the heavy piece of furniture down on top of himself just as the shooter in the doorway opened fire. The first burst arced just over his head, the rounds passing so close that he could feel the subsonic change in air pressure as they whizzed by.

There was little noise beyond the low-pitched thump of the weapon's suppressor and the click of the feed mechanism at work, allowing him to hear the distinctive crunch of glass as some of them embedded in the big windows beyond.

Adjusting his aim, the shooter opened fire on full automatic, spraying the upturned couch with silenced rounds. Unable to respond in the face of such murderous fire, Drake was forced to flatten himself against the floor as shots tore through his meagre cover, showering him with torn shreds of fabric, foam padding and fragments of shattered wood. The muzzle flare of each discharge illuminated his surroundings like lightning bursts, drawing his sparse surroundings in stark, cordite-lit relief.

He had no idea where Mason was, or what kind of situation he was in. From his position behind the bulky couch, he could only see a small portion of the room, but that alone was enough to tell him they were deep in the shit.

Sooner or later the gunman in the doorway would run dry, but there was every chance that one of his companions was waiting right there beside him, ready to take over. They could be moving into the room at this very moment under his covering fire, no doubt using night-vision equipment to let them operate with ease while their opponents were blinded. Cornered, outnumbered and outgunned, this was one fight he and Mason could never hope to win.

Twisting around, he brought his own weapon to bear and opened fire on full automatic, spraying his shots straight though the couch just as his enemy had done. There was no thought of aiming or controlling his ammunition usage; he just wanted to put as many rounds in that bastard's direction as possible.

The MP7 kicked back hard against his shoulder, spent shell casings pattering against the floor all around him. The couch, already damaged by his opponent's fire, was virtually shredded under the onslaught. Drake felt something zip past his arm from the other side, leaving a hot, uncomfortable trail as it passed, but paid little attention to such a minor irritation.

Switching to firing the compact submachine gun one handed, he reached into his webbing with his free hand, yanked one of the stun grenades free and hooked his thumb into the pin. A single hard pull was enough to snap it free. Releasing his fingers to let the fly-off handle detach, he hurled the grenade over the top of the couch in what he hoped was the direction of the doorway and put his hands over his ears.

'Cole, bang out!' he screamed, an instant before the grenade detonated.

The couch protected his eyes from the searingly intense flash. Vaguely he detected a muffled cry of pain over near the doorway, and urgent commands spoken by at least two men.

'Infra-red's blown.'

'Fall back. Cover! Cover!'

More movement, rapid footsteps thumping against the marble tiles. They were moving, falling back from the bottleneck of the doorway, trying to regain their cohesion after having their night vision knocked out by the flashbang.

He expected a flurry of gunfire in retaliation, but what he heard instead was a series of dull pops, too loud for a silenced weapon but too muted to be a conventional firearm. He felt a moment of confusion, wondering what form this fresh assault would take.

However, his questions were answered an instant later when he felt something heavy and solid hit the other side of the couch, followed by a metallic *thunk* as the same object rebounded onto the floor. A second later there was a second dull thump as something hit the window nearby, falling to the floor in similar fashion.

He knew exactly what was causing the noise now. Someone out there was using a Milkor MGL (Multiple Grenade Launcher) to fire low-velocity grenades into the room. Resembling a giant revolver pistol that fired 40mm grenades instead of bullets, the MGL was a devastating infantry weapon capable of laying down a carpet of high-explosive ordnance on a target area.

But there was no explosion this time, no deadly hail of shrapnel; just a loud continuous hiss as the chemicals inside the grenades went to work, spewing out ghostly white smoke. For a moment he wondered if they were simply laying down a smoke screen to cover a renewed attacked, but the instant Drake felt the stinging vapour reach his eyes, he realized their strategy was far more insidious.

'Cole! Tear gas!' he shouted, scrambling away from the source of the choking cloud that was quickly enveloping the room.

–

On the roof of the apartment building overlooking the safe house, the fire escape door suddenly flew open from inside and a team of black-clad operatives rushed out, fanning out in different directions to cover the open space, with M4 assault rifles up at their shoulders.

Three of them converged on Anya's rooftop sniper position, knowing exactly where to look for her. Two were armed like the rest of the assault team, the other carrying a handheld taser intended to stun and incapacitate – they had orders to bring her in alive and unharmed if possible. But instead of catching the would-be sniper at her most vulnerable, they found the position vacant, the unused rifle resting on the ground.

'Clear!' came a call from the far side of the roof.

Beside the rifle, a single rope snaked over the edge of the building, trailing all the way down to ground level. Enough for someone to rappel quickly down if they suspected their position was compromised. The taser operative exchanged a glance with his two companions, reached up and hit his radio transmitter.

'Team Two. Rooftop secure. No sign of Maras. Repeat, Maras is not on site. Looks like she fast-roped out of here.'

The reply, when it came, was characteristically abrupt. 'She's close. She won't leave without Drake. Find her.'

The operative knew better than to argue. 'Copy that.'

# Chapter 54

Ejecting the spent magazine from his weapon, Drake fished a fresh one from his webbing, pushed it home and tapped it hard to make sure it was locked in place. The air around him already reeked of burned cordite, magnesium from the stun grenade and, most worryingly, the acrid stench of CS gas.

Shutting his eyes, Drake dove for the closest grenade, which was spewing a steady stream of toxic smoke into the air. He was grateful for the leather climbing gloves as he closed his hand around the projectile; the reaction within it was exothermic, leaving the casing red hot to the touch.

Even with this extra protection, he let out a growl of pain as the heat seared his skin, before launching the missile towards the far end of the room and ducking aside to get clear of the worst of the gas. He'd bought himself a little time, but seconds only. The CS gas canisters would fill up a room of this size within moments, creating a suffocating cloud they could neither resist nor escape.

And Drake knew from experience how ruthlessly effective such gas could be. Already his eyes felt like they were on fire, tears streaming down his cheeks, while his throat seemed to be closing up, making breathing difficult. If he was heavily exposed, he'd be blinded and incapacitated within seconds.

'Cole. Sound off, mate!' he ordered, pulling back the cocking lever to chamber the first round. If Mason was here, the last thing he wanted was to open fire on him by mistake.

No response. Drake felt his heart skip a beat.

'Cole! Where are you?'

Hearing footsteps heading right for him, Drake raised his weapon just as a dark figure leapt over the couch, landing heavily beside him.

'Goddamn it, give it a rest,' Mason hissed, backing up against the meagre cover. 'You're worse than Keira.'

'You all right?' Drake asked, raising his weapon up over the edge of the couch and sending a short burst of suppressed fire whizzing out into the hallway, encouraging their enemies to keep their heads down.

'Can't hear too good,' he admitted. Like Drake, his eyes were streaming from exposure to the CS. 'What's our situation?'

'We're bone here.'

Mason frowned at the British military term. 'Huh?'

'Shit. FUBAR. Not altogether good,' Drake hurriedly explained. 'They're just going to wait us out until the gas takes us down.'

'Then we need an exit, fast. Preferably one that involves not dying.'

Drake wasn't about to argue. Twisting around, he turned his weapon towards the nearest full-length window that looked out over the driveway below, and squeezed off a five-round burst.

He was expecting to hear the musical tinkle of shattering glass as the window disintegrated under the impacts, but instead was rewarded with nothing but a series of heavy thuds as the rounds ricocheted off the flat surface, making no impression whatsoever. A second burst, fired more in frustration than hope, yielded the same result.

'Fucking bulletproof glass,' Drake said in disbelief, lowering the gun. Their attackers had thought of everything. No wonder they weren't rushing in to storm the room – with their targets trapped in here, time was on their side.

Only then did the full weight of his folly settle on him. 'I walked us right into a trap, Cole,' he said, almost in shock. 'Didn't even see it coming.'

Hearing movement in the smoke-filled corridor, Mason raised himself up and sprayed a burst of fire into the hallway, prompting a muffled shout and an answering flurry of suppressed gunfire that was similarly inaccurate.

'Beat yourself up later. In fact, I'll do it myself once we're out of here,' he promised, ducking back down. 'Right now, focus on staying alive. Get us an exit!'

The ominous gas cloud was rolling in around them, like the fingers of some great ghostly hand seeking to strangle the life out of them. They couldn't break the windows with their weapons, and they were too close to set off a breaching charge without being killed in the resulting blast. The only way out was through the house, and the armed operatives barring their way.

It was a battle they were unlikely to win, but anything was better than suffocating to death in here.

'Cole, give me your breaching charge,' he said, holding out his hand.

'What the hell for?'

'Just give it to me,' Drake demanded. With no grenades left to clear the corridor, he had no choice but to improvise.

Swearing under his breath, Mason dug into the pouch at his thigh and handed over a block of olive green plastic with a simple grenade-like pin fuse mounted in the centre.

Removing the second breaching charge from his own pouch, Drake looked up at his companion. 'Cover me.'

'I oughta shoot you myself,' Mason growled, nonetheless rising up to his knees and training his weapon on the hallway. 'Go!'

Clutching both charges, Drake yanked the pins out to activate the five-second fuses as Mason started firing in short bursts, spraying rounds randomly into the corridor while trying to conserve ammunition.

Four seconds.

Rising up just far enough to take a rough bearing on the doorway, Drake hurled the first breaching charge out into the corridor. If he missed and the device landed in the room with them, it was likely to be the last mistake he ever made.

Three seconds.

The first one was out. He could hear muffled shouts from further away, possibly from one of the enemy operatives who had spotted the breaching charge. He could only hope none of them were brave enough to try to throw it back into the room.

Two seconds.

Gripping the second device, Drake threw it just as the cloud of gas swept in around them. Too late to go back now, he grabbed Mason by a strap on his webbing and pulled him down, clapping his hands over his ears and opening his mouth in the hopes it would offer some protection against the pressure wave that was about to engulf them both.

'Cover! Cover!' he screamed.

One second.

—

Skidding around a street corner not far away, wheels screeching as they clawed for purchase against the rain-slicked road, the Range Rover with its high centre of gravity leaned perilously to one side, threatening to tip. Only a frantic wrench on the wheel by McKnight was enough to bring the wildly fishtailing vehicle back under control.

'There it is!' Frost cried out, pointing towards the safe house about 50 yards up ahead. 'Right there!'

'Got it.' McKnight stamped on the gas, and the powerful engine growled in response.

'Great. You got a plan?'

'Go in, get Ryan and Cole, kill any fucker that stands in our way. Not necessarily in that order. Questions?'

She didn't need to look at Frost to tell the young woman had just flashed one of her fierce, predatory grins. 'My kind of plan. You'd better—'

She fell silent as a sudden bright orange flash in front of them cast the street into hideously sharp relief, the glare throwing long shadows across the soaking ground. Looking instinctively towards the safe house, both women stared in shock as the upper-floor windows suddenly blasted outwards in a spray of fire, smoke and shattered glass, the detonation accompanied by a thunderous boom loud enough to blow out windows in nearby houses.

'Shit!' she cried, jamming on the brakes as pieces of shrapnel and flaming debris rained down on the road in front of them.

Skidding wildly in the appalling driving conditions, the Range Rover screeched to a halt just short of the debris field. Too stunned by what they'd just seen to react further, they both stared in awe and horror at the ragged, smoke-filled hole that had just been blasted in the upper floor of the safe house.

'Ryan!' McKnight gasped.

–

He was alive.

His body ached like he'd been locked inside the world's biggest washing machine with a dozen bricks for company, the world around him had been reduced to darkness and a high-pitched buzz that seemed to blot out all other noise, but he was alive.

Shaking the dust from his head, Drake opened his eyes and looked around, his blurry surroundings slowly resolving themselves into something approaching normal visibility

One look was enough to confirm that the breaching charges had done their work, and then some. Likely the second charge had been close enough to produce a sympathetic detonation when the first went off, effectively doubling the explosive yield.

Light from the street lamps and other buildings outside now streamed through the smoke and flames, allowing him to make out the rest of the room. Both couches and the coffee table that had once sat in the middle of the room had been hurled aside like children's toys by the force of the explosion, ending up in crumpled, broken heaps.

At least the blast had served to disperse the worst of the CS gas, and what remained was drifting outside.

Movement nearby told him his comrade was still alive. Drake watched as the broken couch shifted, then suddenly overturned, revealing a battered and bruised-looking Mason who sat up and shook his head. Like Drake, he was covered in dust from the blast, and bleeding from several small lacerations where pieces of broken glass had cut him, but otherwise seemed to be in working order.

'Cole!' he called out, relieved to see his friend alive, though not exactly unhurt. 'You okay?'

'I'll be a lot fucking better once we're clear of here.' He gestured towards the shattered windows. Rain from the deluge outside had served to damp down whatever fires had been started by the blast, but the air was still thick with smoke. 'Nice work, by the way. Subtle.'

'Thank me later. Come on, move!' Drake replied, dragging himself to his feet. Their enemies might have been disoriented and driven back by the blast, but they would soon recover and retaliate at any moment. Their only chance of surviving was to strike first.

The windows might have offered a way out had this room been on the ground floor. The thirty foot drop was as likely to break bones as to offer an escape route.

Snatching up their fallen weapons, both men advanced into the corridor beyond. What greeted them was a scene of utter devastation. Clearly Drake had underestimated the explosive potential of the two devices, because the combined blasts had blown a hole right through the floor into the lower level. Chunks of smoking rubble lay everywhere, intermingled with bloody chunks of flesh and shredded of uniforms.

It seemed not everyone had made it to cover before the charges went off.

'Go, mate,' Drake urged his companion, leaping over the ragged hole blown in the floor. The air was thick with cordite smoke, and something else that Drake had come to grimly recognize during his military career. The smell of charred flesh.

'Contact!' Mason called out beside him.

Sure enough, a figure in combat armour had emerged from the smoke up ahead, staggering against the wall as if drunk. Likely the detonation had destroyed his sense of balance.

Either way, they weren't taking any chances. Both men raised their weapons and opened fire, spraying twin bursts into him. The dull wet thumps as they slammed into body armour and tore through flesh was accompanied by a grunt of pain and surprise, and the man slumped backwards, collapsing in a pool of blood amidst the rubble.

Drake and Mason were on their way before he'd even stopped moving, stumbling past him with smoke stinging their eyes, their weapons up and ready as they hurried towards the stairwell that lay at the end of the corridor. Once they made it down to the lower level, Drake knew they could break out into the courtyard and try to find a way...

His thoughts were dismissed in an instant as a pair of operatives appeared at the top of the stairwell, weapons already swinging towards them.

'Contact!' he cried, bringing his weapon up to fire.

His finger was already tightening on the trigger when something slammed hard into the centre of his chest, throwing him backwards and punching the air from his lungs. Loosing an unaimed burst of automatic fire, he let out a grunt of pain and fell, struggling to draw breath.

Through blurred vision he watched as the two enemies advanced towards him, twin muzzle flashes from their weapons illuminating the gloom. His body armour might have stopped the first round from killing him outright, but at any second he expected another to tear through him.

Then suddenly another figure had appeared behind them. More flashes lit the darkness like lightning bursts, and he stared in disbelief as the two men crumpled and fell to the ground.

'I don't believe it,' Mason gasped as a figure emerged from the smoke. A woman, armed only with a handgun. A woman with blonde hair.

'Are you all right, Ryan?' Anya asked, crouching down beside him. Smoke still trailed from the barrel of her weapon.

Drake coughed, struggling to get air back in his lungs. 'Having a great time,' he rasped. 'I thought you were supposed to be covering us?'

She must have descended the zip line by herself when they lost radio contact, knowing she could be of little use from her distant vantage point.

Nevertheless, she could scarcely have timed her arrival better, and he saw a grim smile light her face. 'I am.'

Drake might have laughed at that, had their situation been less dire. As it was, he gave her a smile of gratitude that was more profound than any words he could have summoned up.

She held a gloved hand out to him. 'Now get up.'

He gripped her hand as she hauled him to his feet. Managing to get one foot planted firmly on the ground, Drake forced himself up, clutching at the wall for support. Something warm and wet was dripping down his arm, and with a strange sense of detached curiosity he saw blood running from a long straight wound across his forearm. He hadn't even noticed it until now, but he dimly recalled the faint sting as something zipped past him during the fire fight in the living room earlier. Apparently it had come a little closer than he'd thought.

'Can you make it?' Anya asked, for once sounding concerned.

'I'm fine. I'm fine,' he said, waving her away as he snatched up his weapon, ejecting the spent magazine to insert a new one.

'Then let's get the fuck out before more of them show up,' Mason urged, hurrying towards the stairwell. Drake and Anya followed close behind, weapons sweeping left and right.

Descending the stairs, they crossed the expansive reception area downstairs, halting beside the main door.

'Ready?' Drake asked, clutching the handle with bloodied fingers.

Mason and Anya nodded in silence, and with a single turn of the handle, Drake threw the door open to reveal a wide empty courtyard beyond. No cover presented itself. If they were caught out in the open while trying to evacuate, they would have nothing to do but die.

'Smoke out,' Mason hissed, popping the smoke grenade and hurling it into the centre of the open compound. The area was already strewn with smoking debris, but a smoke screen might just save their lives as they made a run for it. Straight away a plume of bright red smoke began to rise from the device.

–

'There! What's that?' Frost called out, pointing towards the sudden cloud of red smoke that had begun to drift through the air from inside the courtyard.

McKnight's eyes lit up with sudden, wild hope. No explosion or fire could produce smoke of that colour, and it seemed unlikely that whoever had tried to ambush their team would have triggered a smoke bomb. It could only have come from one of their own smoke grenades.

'It's them!' she cried, throwing the 4 x 4 into gear. 'We're going in. Hold on, Keira.'

Scarcely had she delivered her warning before her boot stomped down on the accelerator, pressing it all the way to the floor.

–

'Incoming vehicle!' Mason called, pointing to the 4 x 4 rocketing towards the main gate that still blocked the entrance to the compound.

Drake could hardly believe what he was seeing. 'It's Sam,' he gasped, realizing she must have seen the red smoke. 'Get ready to move.'

The gate itself was constructed of thick steel bars welded together and supported by heavier cross beams, designed to retract automatically when the correct code was entered on the keypad entry system beside it.

McKnight had no intention of waiting that long. Drake almost winced at the thump and crunch as the vehicle's bumper and grille took the brunt of the impact, shattering and buckling. But the gate fared little better, unable to resist the force of two tonnes of 4 x 4 moving at high speed, and immediately broke free of its hinges before collapsing across the hood and windshield.

McKnight jammed on the brakes, the sudden change in momentum causing the broken frame of the gate to slide off the front of the Range Rover, clattering to the ground in a heap of twisted metal. The vehicle's nose had been reduced to a mass of shattered fibreglass, broken headlights and buckled bodywork, but the engine still roared with defiant power.

'Go! Get them in here!' she screamed, pointing to Frost.

The young woman needed no encouragement, drawing her automatic and throwing her door open to venture out and retrieve their two comrades. However, no sooner had her foot touched the ground than a burst of gunfire tore into the tarmac driveway right in front of her, peppering the vehicle's interior with fragments of broken rock.

'Shit! Incoming!' she cried, ducking down into the footwell.

McKnight scarcely had time to throw herself down between the seats before another burst tore a line of ragged holes in the windshield, several bullets punching right through to embed themselves in her seat. She let out a cry of pain and fear as fragments of glass rained down on her.

Outside, Drake started at the sound of automatic gunfire from some-where up above, and watched in horror as rounds slammed into the ground around the Range Rover, many tearing into the vehicle itself. McKnight and Frost seemed to have taken cover, and the swirling smoke screen created by the grenade was helping to obscure them to a degree, but it was only a matter of time before the erratic bombardment found a target.

'Defilade above!' Mason called out, craning his weapon upwards in search of the shooter, only to find his line of sight blocked by the overhang of the upper-floor terrace. 'I can't get a shot!'

'I'll go,' Anya decided. 'Get ready to move when the firing stops.'

She had barely taken two steps before Drake seized her arm. 'We're not splitting up.'

'No time to argue.' Anya yanked her arm from the man's grasp. 'Your friends need you here, Ryan. Let me do this.'

The look of fierce, iron determination in her eyes told him she wouldn't be dissuaded. As she always had, Anya made her own decisions, and she had chosen to cover their escape. And yet, he felt the significance of this moment press down on him like a physical weight.

'You be right behind us when we leave,' he said, unable to shake the feeling that she wouldn't be.

Anya gave him a simple nod of acknowledgement and turned to go, but hesitated for a moment. 'Look after Samantha. She is… she will need you when this is over, Ryan.'

Before Drake could say anything further, she had turned and sprinted back into the house, leaving the two operatives alone.

High above them, on the terrace they had zip-lined down only minutes earlier, a pair of black-clothed operatives were perched on the edge, their M4 carbines trained on the vehicle just visible through the swirling smoke below. One was concentrating on keeping the occupants pinned down, hoping to kill or incapacitate the driver, while the other focussed his fire on the engine block to the cripple the vehicle and prevent an escape.

It was no easy task with the smoke masking their target, but both men were battle-hardened professionals, and from their elevated position were able to fire into the courtyard with impunity. Rarely did soldiers like themselves enjoy such overwhelming tactical superiority.

After loosing one last shot, the first operative felt the charging handle on his weapon fly back and lock in place, signalling that the chamber was empty.

'Changing mags,' he warned, ejecting the spent clip and hurriedly slipping a fresh one into place.

With his focus momentarily shifted to the weapon in his hands, he didn't notice the figure creeping through the shadows near the wall behind him, didn't hear the faint splash of boots on wet concrete.

The first hint of danger was pretty much the last thing he felt, as his head was grabbed and yanked back violently, exposing his throat. He saw the momentary gleam of a blade, and let out a gurgling moan of agony as the knife was plunged into his neck, severing arteries and his windpipe.

He was powerless to resist as the carbine was yanked from his grip and he was turned towards his companion by his unseen killer. His fellow operative had reacted to the sudden scuffle by swinging his rifle towards the source of the noise, perhaps sensing they'd been outflanked and attacked. Seeing his dying comrade being used as a human shield, he opened fire, aiming for the barely visible figure behind, but most of the 5.56mm rounds flattened against the man's body armour.

A cry of pain and a spray of crimson told him at least one round had found its target, but it was too little too late. The answering burst, fired one-handed, was aimed at his head. It was a clumsy way to fire an assault rifle, and although several rounds went wide, at such close range at least one found its mark. He grunted almost in surprise as the round entered through his left eye socket, destroying one half of his vision before blasting out through the back of his head.

Spun around by the force of the impact, he toppled over the edge of the terrace in his death throes, plunging to the ground below.

Below, Drake and Mason jumped back in shock as the dead operative slammed into the ground mere feet away from them, blood and brain matter from his gory head wound already pooling in the puddles around him.

'Jesus Christ!' Mason gasped, looking up.

Realizing that the firing overhead had ceased, Drake immediately understood what had happened. 'She did it,' he said, eyes widening at the realisation. 'This is our chance. Go, Cole!'

Mason needed no encouragement, sprinting towards the Range Rover and hauling the passenger door open to reveal Frost still crouched in the footwell.

'You okay?' he asked, his usual bravado deserting him as he surveyed the two women, looking for gunshot wounds.

'Never better.' Frost flashed him a crooked grin. 'What took you so long?'

'Sightseeing.' Raising his weapon, he turned it towards the building in case more operatives appeared to fire down on them. 'Ryan, you're covered. Let's go!'

Shaking fragments of glass from her hair, McKnight clambered back into the driver's seat. 'We need to be somewhere else. Now!'

Drake arrived a moment later. Yanking the rear door open, he hesitated for only a second, his eyes turned upwards to the terrace where the two operatives had been laying down their murderous suppressing fire only seconds before.

Sure enough, even in the darkness and rain, he was able to discern a lone figure standing up there. A woman, her clothes and blonde hair soaked by the deluge. Anya.

She might well have saved their lives, but at what cost? She couldn't jump from such a height without killing or seriously injuring herself, and making her way down through the interior of the house would take precious time they didn't have. This car was a bullet magnet that his injured and depleted team couldn't hope to defend, and if it was destroyed then they could kiss goodbye to any hope of escape.

Their eyes met for a brief moment, and she nodded to him. It was a nod of acceptance, and of encouragement. She knew the situation as well as he did; she'd known it the moment she volunteered to go. She was telling him to leave her behind.

'Damn it, Anya,' he whispered, turning away and throwing himself into the vehicle's rear seat. 'Get in, Cole! We have to go!'

Abandoning his position, Mason clambered in and slammed the door shut.

'What about Anya?' Frost asked as McKnight threw the Range Rover into reverse. 'We can't just—'

'We can't wait for her!' the driver interrupted, trembling with anger as she twisted around in her seat. 'We stay here, we all die!'

As much as he hated to admit it, Drake knew their only chance was to fall back and try to rendezvous with Anya once they were clear. The woman was, if nothing else, a survivor. If anyone could make it out, she could.

Drake caught Samantha's eye in the rear-view mirror. 'Do it, Sam.'

Unwilling to debate the issue further, she hit the accelerator. The engine, though battered by the impact with the gate and possibly damaged by gunfire, still had some grunt left in it, and the vehicle rocketed backwards, bumping over pieces of debris.

Clearing the destroyed remains of the compound entrance, McKnight twisted the wheel hard, sending them into a skidding left turn. No sooner had the nose swung around to face the roadway opposite than she engaged first gear and floored it once again, sending them screaming forward in a spray of water.

On the terrace high above, Anya watched the vehicle go with a sense of heartfelt relief. The others had made it out of the trap Cain had set for them. That much at least she could feel good about.

As the rain continued to lash down, she glanced at the blood seeping from the gunshot wound at her side. One of the rounds fired at point-blank range must have punched through a weak point in her body armour, cracking a rib as it did so. It hurt just to breathe, and she knew the injury would slow her down severely.

That was why she'd told Drake to go. She never would have made it to the waiting car in time, and all of this would have been for nothing.

Groaning in pain, she pushed herself away from the terrace railing and stumbled back inside. One way or another, she was on her own now.

'This whole thing was a set-up,' Frost said as the safe house receded into the distance. 'All of it. The override code, the meeting, the surveillance footage... Cain was just trying to draw us out. He knew everything we were planning.'

McKnight spared the young woman a brief, uncomfortable glance, but quickly refocused her attention on the road ahead.

'He set a trap. We never had a chance,' Mason replied, shoulders slumped in defeat.

Frost closed her eyes, breathing hard, muscles locked rigid. Then suddenly she slammed her fist into the dashboard in front of her, striking it hard enough to crack the plastic.

'Motherfucker!' she screamed, punching it again in her frustration. 'We did all of this for nothing!'

'Stop it, Keira. Stop it!' Drake snapped. 'We're all thinking the same thing. Screaming about it isn't going to change anything.'

McKnight was about to weigh into the burgeoning argument, only for movement on the road up ahead to divert her attention. A single figure had walked right onto the road, blocking their path.

For an instant she wondered if it were some oblivious pedestrian on their way home. Only when they turned towards the car and raised what they were holding in their right hand did she realize what it truly was.

'Oh no,' she gasped, jamming on the brakes and swinging the wheel over, desperately trying to take evasive action.

A single flash from the metal tube told her she was too late. Her last act was to turn towards Drake to yell a warning of what was coming, then the 40mm grenade impacted against the vehicle's front left wheel and detonated.

# Chapter 55

The time had come to make his play.

'Very well,' Qalat conceded at last. 'I can get him for you.'

Cain leaned back a little on the couch, though he remained as icy and focussed as before. 'All right. Talk.'

'I have some conditions first, obviously.'

At this, Cain cocked an eyebrow. 'Still trying to overplay your hand, huh? Explain to me why I should negotiate, when I could take you somewhere very far off the map and torture it out of you?'

He didn't doubt it. Cain was more than capable of running his own black sites, far beyond the knowledge of the US government or even the rest of the CIA. Not to mention the ISI, who would likely never learn what had become of him.

'Because I don't *have* the information you need.' Qalat raised a hand. 'Not yet, at least. But I can get it for you.'

'Keep going,' Cain prompted.

'The ISI is much like your own agency. Everything is compartmentalized, hidden away, known only to a few key personnel to guard against precisely the situation we now find ourselves in.'

'And you're not one of them.'

'No,' he conceded. 'But I know how to get in.'

He heard the slow exhalation of breath as Cain prepared himself for what his adversary was about to ask. 'And how exactly can the CIA help with that?'

Qalat smiled. 'I'm going to need you to kill someone for me.'

–

Hawkins smiled in satisfaction as the wreck of the Range Rover came to rest about 20 yards away, lying on its roof now, the impact of the high-explosive round having flipped it over as the driver tried to evade him. All useless – he'd been prepared for every eventuality.

Slinging the M203 grenade launcher over his shoulder by its carry strap, he reached up and keyed his radio as he walked towards the ruined vehicle at a slow, leisurely pace.

'All units, we have them,' he said calmly, drawing the USP .45 automatic holstered at his hip. 'Move in and look for survivors.'

Half a dozen of his operatives converged on the upturned wreck as he approached, hammering and wrenching the buckled doors open. He saw one young woman dragged out from the front, her body limp and sagging; unconscious or dead, he didn't care much either way.

A man was next, big and powerfully built, and still with enough fight in him to lash out at his captors despite the hopeless odds. One or two wild punches struck home, but a rifle butt to the back of his neck was enough to drop him, silencing his feeble attempts at resistance.

And then, at last, Hawkins saw him.

Ryan Drake, pulled semi-conscious from the wreckage, bloodied and bruised but still alive. Tough son of a bitch to survive a wreck like that. He looked up with bleary eyes as Hawkins approached, struggling to see as rainwater pelted him.

'Hello, Ryan,' Hawkins said, relishing the moment he'd been awaiting for seven long years. He was pleased to find Drake alive. For now, at least. 'It's been a long time.'

That was when he saw the shock and fear and horror dawning in Drake's eyes. The disbelief, the anguish as long-buried memories resurfaced. Hawkins caught himself wondering how much Drake truly remembered of their time together.

Well, he would find out before he was done. He would find out everything Drake knew. Then he would kill him.

'I'm looking forward to getting to know you again,' he said, then hunkered down beside him. 'But first, do your old pal a favour and tell me something. Where's Anya?'

Hatred and defiance blazed in Drake's vivid green eyes. In a sudden blur of movement, his right hand reached down and drew something from a hidden sheath at his waist. Steel flashed, and one of the operatives restraining him cried out in pain and stumbled aside, blood spurting from a gory knife wound to his neck.

A heartbeat later, Drake swept the knife around at Hawkins, aiming for his chest, only for the blade to jerk to a halt mere inches short of its target. Tightening his iron grip on Drake's wrist, Hawkins suddenly wrenched the extended limb back against itself, eliciting a satisfying growl of pain and fury. Tendons and ligaments stretching beyond their limits, Drake's grip on the knife slackened and the blade fell away, clattering to the ground.

Hawkins couldn't help but smile at the man's valiant but futile attempt to take him out. A little faster, and he might well have succeeded.

'Oh, buddy, I can't begin to tell you how much you're going to regret that. But first, I've got some things to take care of here.' Rising to his feet, he turned to the operatives around him. 'Secure them for transport. We don't have long before the police get here.'

Needless to say, such a violent and explosive confrontation had drawn considerable attention from the local residents. Many, fearing a terrorist attack, had taken shelter deep inside their homes, cowering in basements or in some cases panic rooms. Others had emerged onto the street to gawp in shock at the upturned vehicle, and the armed men in tactical gear swarming around it.

Already they could hear the distant wail of sirens. Straight away Hawkins' men went to work, dragging the injured survivors into a van that had just pulled up nearby.

Catching one of his subordinates by the arm, Hawkins moved in close; a dark and menacing presence looming over the man. 'Give me some good news about Anya or find yourself a new job.'

'We picked up a blood trail leading from the house, and we've got men on it now. Looks like she's injured. She won't get far.'

'Find her!' he snapped, anger showing for the first time.

The man seemed to wilt visibly under such barely restrained fury, and hurried off with one hand already on the transmitter of his radio.

–

A few hundred yards away, Anya stumbled along a narrow back alley, struggling to breathe as her cracked rib seemed to press against her lungs. She could hear shouts and voices behind, all in English, and even caught the glare of flashlight beams bounding off the rippling puddles as she ran.

'Got more blood here!' one called out.

'I'm on it,' another replied. 'Look sharp!'

Cain's men were closing in on her. There was nothing she could do to fight them off; not by herself. And she couldn't hope to outrun them. Her pace slowed as the gravity of her situation began to sink in.

Rather than exit through the destroyed gate and risk being seen, she had made her escape from the compound by vaulting one of the perimeter walls, using her combat vest to cover the glass shards embedded in the cement on top. Even with this precaution, she'd sustained several deep lacerations, warm blood soaking into her clothes. She barely felt the pain now, however.

It was nothing compared to the agony that had ripped through her as she'd watched the Rover take the brunt of that grenade impact, as she'd seen the vehicle flip right over and come to a crashing halt on its roof. As she'd seen Drake and his companions hauled from the wreckage.

It was all over. Everything they had planned, all of their strategies and schemes now lay in ruins. Once again, Cain had defeated them. Had defeated her.

Bumping into a rough brick wall, Anya slid down it until she was sitting in a pool of fetid rainwater, oblivious to the deluge that continued around her.

'She can't be far!' she heard a call echo from around a turn in the alley. 'We've got her.'

Indeed they had. But if they were intending to capture her alive, they were to be disappointed. She still had the M1911, with a few rounds left in the mag, the last of which she would use on herself. She'd spent enough of her life in captivity to know she'd never endure it again.

If this was where she was to make her last stand, then so be it. She'd cheated death enough times in her life, she supposed the odds were bound to catch up with her eventually. And she wasn't afraid of what was coming.

Her biggest regret was that she would never get to face Cain, never find the answers she needed.

That was when she heard it. A voice.

'Anya!'

Frowning, she looked around, seeking its source, wondering for a fleeting moment if one of the team had somehow escaped the wreck and had made it here to rendezvous with her.

'Anya!' the voice called out again. Not a man's voice, but a boy's.

Looking to her right, Anya stared in disbelief as one of the heavy steel doors facing out into the alley swung open a crack, revealing the slender face and dark eyes of a boy she'd never expected to see again.

'Yasin?' she said, hardly believing what she was seeing. 'What are you—'

'Hurry!' the boy urged, beckoning her towards him. 'To me! Now!'

With the sound of footsteps splashing through puddles now clearly audible, Anya reacted instinctively, pushing herself off the wall and stumbling across the alley. Slipping through the doorway, she practically collapsed on the floor beyond as the door clicked shut and the lock was engaged.

As shouts echoed from outside and the footsteps sprinted past, Anya sat there in darkness for a second or two, hearing only the sound of her own laboured breathing. Then a flame leapt up from a few feet away, a simple flint lighter, revealing the young lad they had abandoned earlier in the day.

He stared at her for several seconds, noting her pained expression, her soaking hair, the blood on her clothes.

'How did you find me?' she asked, barely able to remember the right words.

She saw a flicker of a smile. 'I followed you. I saw the house, the explosion, the shooting. I knew they were chasing you, so I broke in here and waited until you passed.'

'What is this place?' The light illuminated little more than a few feet of plain concrete flooring and breeze block walls.

'A clothes store, I think. Easy to pick the locks on a place like this.'

Anya simply didn't know what to say. As far as resourcefulness went, this mere boy put a lot of professional operatives to shame.

One thing, however, still escaped her. 'Why are you helping me? I was ready to kill you today.'

The boy's eyes glimmered in the light of the flame. 'What did your friend Ryan say? I am all about second chances.'

Anya reached up and pushed her soaking hair out of her eyes. The wound at her side was paining her more with each passing minute. It would need treatment soon before it became a real problem, assuming she made it that far.

'We must leave here soon,' Yasin went on. 'They have lost your trail, but it won't take them long to find it again.'

What was the point, she wondered in a moment of brutal honesty. It wouldn't change what had happened tonight. Drake and the others would still be gone.

Then a thought occurred to her; something she hadn't had time to consider in the frantic rush to escape. Drake and the others had been pulled alive from the wreckage, not executed on the spot as she might have expected. They would no doubt make a fine prize for Cain, but they weren't the real objective.

She was.

As long as she remained at large, Cain wouldn't kill them. He would keep them as leverage, because he knew they could be used against her. And in that respect, he was right. She couldn't fight, and she couldn't remain here, therefore the only logical course of action was to retreat.

She hated it, but there it was. Fight and die for nothing, or run and live. And perhaps find a way to turn this around.

She looked at Yasin again, remembering the boy's choice of pronoun. 'You said we,' she remarked. 'What do you mean?'

'I want to go with you,' he explained. 'I can help you escape, but only if you take me.'

Anya said nothing to this, knowing that where she was going was no place for a mere child. Then again, life here didn't seem to be a bed of roses either. And if he was right, he might just be able to help her. A distant shout, accompanied by the wail of police sirens, forced the issue.

'Time to decide,' Yasin prompted. 'Because I'm leaving with or without you.'

'All right,' Anya finally conceded, having to force the words out through clenched teeth. 'I will help you, but first you must get me out of here.'

Vowing that both Cain and Hawkins would pay for tonight's events, Anya dragged herself to her feet and followed Yasin deeper into the building.

# Chapter 56

'Who do you want dead, exactly?' Cain asked, mildly curious.

Pausing a moment, Qalat told him the name. And to his credit, Cain managed to maintain his poker face.

'That's a big ask.'

'And it will get big results,' Qalat assured him. 'We both know the current ISI director is a fundamentalist sympathizer, and one of the biggest obstacles to cooperation between us. He has many friends in parliament and elsewhere. But once he is... handled, it will leave a power vacuum that has to be filled. I will see to it that I am appointed as interim director. Once I have control and access to his security clearance, you will have all the information you need to kill Bin Laden.'

'And you'll be in charge of the ISI,' Cain reminded him.

'What is it your people say about clouds and silver linings?' A flicker of a smile. 'Think of this as an opportunity, Marcus. An opportunity not just to kill one man, but to bring about a new era of trust and cooperation between our two agencies, maybe our two countries. Imagine what you could accomplish in this part of the world with the ISI firmly on your side. We could permanently change the balance of power in central Asia.'

'Those are grand words,' Cain remarked cynically. 'But you're asking a lot without any guarantee of a return. If I come through for you, what's to stop you reneging on our deal?'

Qalat gestured around him. He didn't need to see the microphones and cameras to know they were there. 'Only a foolish man would have failed to record every word spoken in this room tonight. Our agreement is what binds us – both of us. If one betrays the other, both will fall. Personally, I would rather work with you than against you.' He shrugged. 'Or, you could set to work with your torture chambers and see which of us is proven right.'

He took another sip of coffee, managing to hide the slight tremor in his hand. Outwardly he might have projected the image of a man calm and in control of the situation, but inside he was acutely aware that Cain could well make good on his threat. It was clear now that he was facing a very different man from the one he'd know 20 years ago.

'If you fail me, it won't matter how high you rise in the ISI,' Cain said at last. 'It won't matter how far you run, or how well you hide. Sooner or later, I will find you, and the exposure of your agreement will be the last thing you need to worry about.'

The sincerity of those words was chillingly real, but nonetheless Qalat sensed victory. 'So we have a deal.'

'I have a condition of my own,' Cain chipped in. 'There's an operation going on tonight across town, in parallel to our meeting here. It doesn't involve Pakistani citizens; it's more of a… house-clearing exercise for us. But I'd appreciate it if you kept your people out of the way. We wouldn't want any… uncomfortable situations for either of us.'

Qalat eyed him curiously, but nonetheless nodded. 'Very well. You have my word.'

Putting down his coffee, Cain rose stiffly from the couch and gestured towards the door. 'My associates outside will make sure you get home safely. And don't worry, we'll take care of your two friends.'

Of that, he had no doubt. Taking Cain's formal dismissal as tacit acceptance of their agreement, Qalat nodded and turned to leave. He was just reaching for the door handle when Cain added one last parting remark.

'You know, Billy Henderson would have liked you.'

Qalat frowned and glanced back over his shoulder. 'Who?'

'Doesn't matter,' Cain said, waving it off. 'Have a safe trip, Vizur.'

After an uncomfortable pause, Qalat turned and left.

–

'What's the status on those tactical teams?' Gondal demanded, pacing the room like a cornered animal while he waited for an update.

Ten minutes earlier, reports had begun to filter through to him of explosions and gunfire in a residential district on the west side of the city. Not far from where the two ISI agents were known to have disappeared the previous night.

It hadn't taken much to put two and two together, and come up with a probable location for 'Robert Douglas' and his team of operatives. Reacting immediately, Gondal had directed all available tactical units to that location, hoping to interrupt whatever terrorist plot Douglas had set in motion.

However, Mahsud didn't reply to his query. Looking over at the big man, Gondal found him hunched over his phone, his thick brows drawn together in a frown.

'Damn it, what's happening?' Gondal snapped in an uncharacteristic display of frustration.

Slowly Mahsud turned to look at him. 'The tactical teams are standing down.'

'What?' Gondal stammered, wondering if he'd misheard his colleague. 'On whose authority?'

Mahsud laid the phone down. 'This one came from the top. We're to stand down and hand over all files relating to Douglas and his team. Apparently this one is going to be handled "quietly".'

'You mean we're being locked out?'

Mahsud said nothing. There was no need. Both men knew an official sanction when they saw it. The question was, where had it come from?

–

Cain's phone was ringing. Knowing who was calling, he snatched up the device and hit the button to take the call.

'Report,' he said, his voice tight with anticipation.

Hawkins was in a moving vehicle judging by the background sound of an engine that seemed close to redline. 'Drake and the others took the bait just like we planned. We got them. We're en route to the rally point now.'

'What about Anya?' Cain demanded. Drake and the others were of little interest compared to her.

A pause. 'We're working on it.'

Cain closed his eyes, breathing deep to summon some inner reserve of calm and patience. 'You're working on it,' he repeated. 'You understand that if she gets away, everything we've accomplished will have been for nothing!'

'She won't get away,' Hawkins promised him, though some of his usual confidence seemed to have faded. 'Not while we have Drake. He's still the key to finding her, and now he's all ours.'

That at least Cain knew to be true. 'What's his status?'

'He's alive. Hurt, but alive.'

'Make sure he stays that way,' Cain instructed, knowing Hawkins' penchant for torture and summary executions. 'What about McKnight? She make it?'

'Yeah, more or less. Want me to change that?'

All in good time, he thought to himself. With Drake taken care of, there were still a few loose ends to tie up. Starting with Samantha.

'No, bring her to me. It's time we had ourselves a debriefing.'

## Chapter 57

Drake couldn't move. He was secured to a chair, hands cuffed behind his back.

He had no idea where he was, only that it had been a good few hours since the failed assault on the safe house. He remembered the jolting, painful journey here, gagged and blindfolded, unable to move as the circulation in his hands was slowly cut off by the plasticuffs digging into his wrists.

Then at last the journey had come to an end. And here he was, tied up in some dingy underground room that smelled of damp and decay, lit by a single bare bulb in the ceiling.

A door swung open on rusted hinges behind him. Footsteps on the dirty floor.

A figure moved into view, eyes on him the whole time.

Jason Hawkins. A man he'd once known all too well. A man who had once been his commanding officer.

He hadn't changed much since the last time Drake had seen him. Same tall, powerful frame, same short dark hair, same strong, arrogant features. Only the big scar bisecting one side of his face was a new addition. Drake hoped the person who'd given it to him went on to live a long and happy life.

'Well, Ryan, here we are,' Hawkins said, folding his arms across his broad chest. 'Sorry this isn't exactly the Hilton, but let's face it, we've both bedded down in worse, right?'

His tone was almost jovial, as if they truly were old friends catching up.

'You're probably feeling pretty pissed right about now,' Hawkins went on. 'I know I would be. Shit, all that work, all that planning and effort, to see it all come to nothing. It's enough to drive a man to distraction. If I were you, I'd probably be wondering how we did it. How did we know? Did we use satellite tracking? Drones? Digital surveillance?'

He let out a sympathetic sigh. 'Afraid not. The answer was a little closer to home. Real close, in your case.'

In that instant, an image of Samantha flashed before Drake's eyes. Samantha, who he'd first met in Afghanistan two years ago, who had become an integral part of his team in the months following, who had always been so reliable, so dependable, so willing to put others before herself. Samantha, who become far more to him than just another team-mate.

'No,' he gasped, appalled by what he was hearing. It was trick, he told himself. Just a trick to mess with his head. 'No, you're lying.'

'Am I? How much do you really know about her? Her service record, her history...'

She had never been much inclined to talk about herself or her past, but then plenty of people were like that. That didn't make her a traitor.

'She was vetted by the Agency.'

'Faked, good buddy. Rubber-stamped by Cain himself. She was brought in to do a job, keep tabs on you, make sure you never got too close. The Samantha McKnight you think you know... well, she never really existed. And now she never will.'

'Bollocks. I don't believe you,' he snarled, still desperately clinging to the hope that the man was lying. Refusing to believe that the woman he loved would do such a thing.

'Thought you might say that.' Hawkins smiled with malicious glee as he removed a cell phone from his pocket, held it up and enabled the audio playback feature.

*'Don't tell me to calm down. They almost died,'* a voice hissed, filled with anger and recrimination. A woman's voice.

Samantha's voice.

*'And what if they had?'* This voice was male, deep in tone, smooth and polished like its owner. Marcus Cain.

*'This wasn't our deal, Marcus. I didn't sign up for this.'*

Drake could barely bring himself to listen, but Hawkins increased the audio volume, making sure he heard every word. He was relishing the torment being inflicted on his prisoner, far more effective than any physical damage he could do.

*'And what exactly did you sign up for, Samantha? To keep Drake out of trouble? To tell me his favourite movies? What about fucking him? Was that part of our agreement?'*

Oh Christ, no. Drake could feel the bile rising in his throat as the pieces suddenly came together. Samantha, always cautioning against taking direct action against Cain, always trying to dissuade them from confrontation. It hadn't just been natural prudence driving her actions; she'd been actively trying to protect her true master.

–

*'You asked me to gain his trust. I did what I had to do.'*

That last remark came out as a plaintive admission, filled with guilt and regret. It was clear she'd taken no pleasure in her actions, but that couldn't undo the betrayal she had inflicted on him. On all of them.

There could be no denying it now. Samantha, the woman he'd trusted with his life, had been working against them the whole time.

'No...' Drake said through clenched teeth, looking down at the floor to avoid Hawkins's triumphant smile.

'Women, huh? Never can trust them,' Hawkins said as he slipped the phone back into his pocket. 'Anyway, now we've got that out of the way, you and I have other business to attend to.'

Drake's head rose up, hardly daring to imagine what else this man had in store for him. 'What business?'

Hawkins gave him a look of patient, sympathetic understanding. 'Here's the problem, Ryan. A lot of my men are dead after last night, mostly because of you. Hell, you even took a swipe at me. That's the sort of thing I can't allow to go unpunished. You understand, don't you? The boys are just baying for blood. Your blood, and they won't be happy until they get it. Fortunately for you, Cain wants you alive, but that puts me in a tricky spot. So... what's a man to do?'

Drake could feel his pulse rising by the second. Knowing Hawkins as he did, he sensed something terrible coming. But nothing could prepare him for what the man did next.

'Bring them in!' he called out.

The door opened again, and Drake heard scuffling footsteps, muttered curses and struggling. Nonetheless, two of Hawkins's men appeared a moment later, their faces obscured by masks, each with a bound prisoner in front of them.

'Take a seat, guys,' Hawkins said, nodding to them.

A kick to the back of the legs dropped Mason and Frost to their knees in front of Drake. Both had their hands bound behind their backs, both were battered and bruised by the crash and, he suspected, rough handling by their captors. But they were alive, and they were looking to him. He saw fear in their eyes, matching his own.

'Great, now that we're all here, it's time I explained the situation,' Hawkins carried on, clearly enjoying every second of this. 'I've been ordered to bring you guys in. I'm cool with that, but wouldn't you know it? I've only got space for two.' Drake watched in horror as he drew a big square-looking automatic from the holster at his waist. 'But I'm a reasonable man, and I want this to be a fair process. So, I'm going to let Ryan here decide which one gets to come along, and which one... well, doesn't.'

Oh God, Drake's mind screamed at him. Hawkins was going to make him choose which one of his teammates was to be executed.

'No!' Drake cried out, straining against his bonds. 'No! You take me. You kill me, and you leave them alone, you fuck!'

He didn't see the blow coming from behind, but the sudden explosion of light and pain inside his head told him one of Hawkins's operatives had struck him across the back of the head. Not hard enough to render him unconscious, but enough to silence him and leave stars flickering across his eyes.

'Next time you interrupt like that, I'll kill them both,' Hawkins promised him. 'Now, it's pretty simple. You've got to the count of five to decide which one to save. You can't take one for the team on this, so forget about nominating yourself. If you refuse to pick one, I'm just going to have to go ahead and kill them both. And we don't want that, do we?'

'Don't give this piece of shit the pleasure,' Frost spat, glaring up at Hawkins.

He grinned in amusement. 'She's a little wildcat, this one. That the kind of person you want to keep around a little longer?'

Mason, who had remained silent until now, swallowed and raised his chin in defiance. 'I'll do it, Ryan,' he said calmly. 'I'm ready. I'm not afraid of this asshole.'

'Shut the fuck up, Cole!' Frost hit back, though her eyes were shining with tears. 'Ryan, if one of us has to go, pick me. No way I could live with that shit otherwise.'

'Wow, noble stuff,' Hawkins remarked, impressed. 'All this self-sacrifice is bringing a tear to my eye.' His comment was met with a few chuckles from the other operatives in the room. 'But time's marching on. Let's get this done, shall we? One.'

'Don't do this,' Drake pleaded, staring at both his friends. How could he possibly make such a choice?

Hawkins ignored him as he readied his weapon. 'Two.'

'Ryan, I swear to God, you'd better save Cole!' Frost implored him, fury and fear vying for control of her. 'I'll kill you myself if you don't.'

'Three.'

Mason ignored her, concentrating on Drake. 'Ryan, listen to me. Just do it, man. Pick me. Don't pussy out now! Fucking choose me!'

'Four.'

Drake closed his eyes, tears trickling down his cheeks as the shouts, the threats and pleas blended together into background noise, and all that remained was the countdown. One final second to save a friend's life, and condemn another.

'Five. Time's up, Ryan.'

Drake opened his eyes then, staring straight at Hawkins. The word came out almost before he knew it. 'Keira,' he said quietly. 'I save Keira.'

'Good man, Ryan.' Hawkins smiled, satisfied. 'Now, you might think I'd pull some dickish move, like killing her just to fuck with your head, but I'm not going to do that. I want you to know that what happens next is all on you, Ryan.'

With that, he pressed the gun against Mason's head. Drake's eyes met them in that final instant, seeing not fear but acceptance. And gratitude.

'No!' Frost screamed as he pulled the trigger.

The single thunderous shot echoed around the room, drowning out Drake's cry of grief and agony as his friend slumped to the floor at Hawkins's feet.

Drake could feel himself trembling, the breath frozen in his throat, shock setting in as he stared at Mason's body. He was gone. He was dead.

'There, that wasn't too hard now, was it?' Hawkins said, holstering the automatic.

Drake looked up at him, burning with utter hatred. 'You're going to die for this. And the last thing you're going to see is my face.'

'Keep telling yourself that, buddy. It might make what happens in the next few days… easier.' With this chilling warning delivered, he glanced at his fellow operatives, then pointed to the body. 'Dispose of that, would you? And get the other two ready to move. Time's-a-wasting, boys.'

Drake was no longer hearing him. His head was bowed, eyes closed as utter anguish swept over him like an endless wave.

# Chapter 58

Samantha winced as the hood was yanked off her head, revealing a bleak landscape of rocky mountains and arid, windswept plains. The sun was just rising above the horizon, spilling its orange glow across the scorched land beneath.

The van she'd been brought here in was idling nearby, its driver and her two guards smoking, weapons slung over their shoulders. A second vehicle was parked close to it. A big Mercedes SUV – the kind used for ferrying executives and high-ranking Agency personnel around.

'I'm disappointed in you, Samantha.'

Swallowing, she turned around to find Marcus Cain standing just a few feet away. He was still dressed in the kind of expensive suit she'd come to know him for, but he looked a little less crisp and perfect today. It had been a long night for both of them, and his mildly dishevelled appearance gave her a perverted sense of satisfaction.

She didn't care to imagine what she must look like.

'You let me down,' he carried on. 'I put a lot of faith in you. Trusted you to be my eyes and ears. I thought we understood each other.'

'I'm happy to disappoint you. Where are my friends?' she demanded.

This brought a chuckle of amusement. 'Your friends? That's funny, still calling them your friends after what you did. Well, you can bet your ass they don't think of *you* as a friend any more.' His expression turned more serious then; sombre and grave. 'I wish I'd been there, you know. When they told Drake exactly what you were, what you'd done. I understand that was what finally broke the man.'

His words were like a knife driven into her guts, twisting and tearing with each passing moment, but somehow she forced herself not to show the agony she felt. She wouldn't give him the satisfaction of knowing how deeply she cared.

And yet, even as she stood there, part of her still couldn't understand how he'd beaten them, how he had known where they would be and what they were planning. She had severed her ties with Cain after the raid on their villa, gone dark and dedicated herself to bringing about his destruction.

'You're wondering how we found you. How I beat you,' he said, guessing her thoughts. 'There's no shame in it. I'd want to know if I was in your shoes.'

Samantha said nothing.

'It was your dad,' Cain said quietly, looking almost sympathetic. 'The burner phone you always insisted he keep with him. It took one of our people in the hospital about two days to find and bug it.'

She should have felt furious that he'd seen through her attempt at deception so easily, that she hadn't anticipated he would have spies in the hospital where her father was being treated. She should have, but she couldn't summon up that feeling now. All she felt was an abiding sadness.

'As soon as you called to check in on him, we had your number,' Cain explained. 'We could trace you anywhere on the planet; all the way to Islamabad. That's how I knew Drake had taken the bait. And you were in it with him. Like I said, I'm disappointed in you. It didn't have to come to this.'

'Cut the bullshit, Marcus. We both know what happened last night. It's over, *we're* over.' She was under no illusions about why they'd brought her out to such a remote place. It was pretty obvious she wasn't going to walk away from this one.

She let out a breath and looked around, taking in the snow-capped peaks and the clear blue sky. There was a beauty in the absolute starkness of it that appealed to her. All things considered, it wasn't a bad place to meet one's end.

With a fleeting feeling of sadness and regret, she absently touched at her abdomen. She knew she would never get to feel the baby kick, to sense its tiny movements within her, to hold it in her arms and look into its eyes. Would it have blue eyes like her, or vivid green like Drake? Such stupid thoughts to entertain, she realized then. She didn't even know if it was a boy or girl.

Perhaps it was better not to know, she thought. It would only make what was coming harder to bear.

'So this is where it's going to happen.' It was phrased as a statement, not a question. 'Got a nice spot picked out for me, I suppose. Well, you might as well get it over with. Just do me the courtesy of making it quick, and spare me your shitty victory speech.'

'You mean kill you?' He sounded almost offended by the suggestion. 'Why would I do that? No, Samantha, I'm not going to kill you. I'm going to make sure you live a long life filled with plenty of time to think about your choices. You're going back to prison where I found you. Well, more or less,' he added. 'The place you'll be calling home from now on is a little more... basic than you're used to.'

Those words sent a chill down her spine.

'Speaking of which,' Cain went on. 'Every prisoner's entitled to a phone call. Hope you don't mind, but I took the liberty of making yours.' He held out a cell phone to her that already had an active call connected. 'Go ahead, take it. There's someone who wants to talk to you.'

Oh God, she silently cried. Please don't let it be him.

Unable to stop her hand from trembling, she reached out and took the phone, raising it to her ear. 'Who's there?'

A pause. She held her breath.

'Sam.'

Something died within her in that moment, and she felt herself crumbling from the inside. She knew her father's voice instantly.

Cupping a hand over the phone, she glared at Cain with pure hatred. 'You fucking—'

Instantly a trio of weapons were pointed her way.

'Careful,' he warned, gesturing to the operatives who now had her covered, and wouldn't hesitate to shoot if she made a wrong move. 'Time's ticking, Sam. If I were you, I'd make use of it.'

Forcing herself to be calm, she returned to the phone. 'Dad. I'm...'

'There are people here, Sam. Men with guns. I don't know how they tracked me down out here, but they did.' There was no fear in his voice. Then again, a man dying of cancer had little left in this world to fear. 'I'm sorry, kid. I let you down.'

Samantha squeezed her eyes shut as tears silently streamed down her cheeks. If only he knew how easily Cain had been able to find him.

'I'm the one who should apologize, Dad. I...wasn't there for you, when you needed me. This was all my fault. I'm...' Her voice was breaking with the strain. 'I didn't want it to turn out like this.'

'You're wrong about that,' he cut in then, his voice taking on a harder, commanding edge. A father to the end. 'It was you, Sam. Don't you see? When Liam died, when your mom left... You were the one who kept me going. You gave me a reason to go on. Every day, you were what I fought for, what I worked for, what I lived for. That was all I ever needed.'

She heard him sigh then. A wistful, peaceful sigh.

'I'm standing by the lake, Sam. Where we used to fish. I'm looking at the most amazing view. I wish you could be here to see it.'

'So do I, Dad.' She had to tell him. She had to tell him now. 'I lo—'

She jumped as the harsh crack of a single gunshot resounded down the line, letting out a cry of shock and grief and anguish all mingled together as the call was disconnected. Dropping the phone, she fell to her knees, shoulders slumped in utter defeat, tears streaming down her face.

'It's hard, isn't it?' Cain said, sounding almost compassionate for a moment. 'Losing someone you love.'

'My father never hurt anyone,' she managed to say. 'You didn't have to kill him.'

She saw a knowing look in his eyes. 'Since you're so fond of my speeches, let me tell you a story about my own father. He was a different generation from your old man, served in the Pacific during the war. Fighter pilot; pretty decent one too, until he got himself shot down and captured at Guadalcanal.

Like most men in that situation, he ended up in a Japanese POW camp. Now, you can probably imagine what the conditions were like there, and it didn't take long before he started thinking about escape. Took a while, but he finally made it out through the wire during the night and vanished into the jungle, managed to stay on the run for two days before they caught up with him. They didn't kill him, though. Instead they brought him back in front of the whole camp, picked out two of his buddies from the crowd and beheaded them both right in front of him.' He shrugged. 'No more escape attempts. See, it's not the impact we have on our own lives that deters us – it's what happens to the people we care about. They're the ones who pay the price for our mistakes. And it's their suffering that keeps us from sleeping at night. Believe me… I know.'

Samantha couldn't summon a response to that. She should have been furious at him for what he'd done, should have hurled herself at him despite the armed guards, should have torn his throat out or gouged his eyes with her fingernails, but instead she just sat there on her knees doing nothing. Because deep down she knew Cain wasn't really to blame for this.

She was.

'Would you have honoured our agreement, if I'd come through for you? Would you have left us alone?' she asked, not even sure why she wanted to know, why she'd chosen to torment herself with the question.

He thought about it for a long moment. 'Yeah,' he finally admitted. 'Yeah, I would have.' He allowed those words to sink in before speaking again. 'You're going to have a long time to think about that.'

He gestured to the nearby operatives. Two of them moved forward and seized her by the arms, lifting her to her feet so they could lead her towards the waiting van.

'This is where we part ways, Samantha,' Cain said, turning away. 'You and I are headed in different directions, and I don't imagine we'll be seeing each other again.'

'Wait,' she pleaded, turning to Cain in desperation. 'Just tell me one thing. What about Ryan? Is he alive?'

The look in Cain's eyes was maddeningly, terrifyingly impossible to fathom. And she knew that was exactly what he wanted her to see, because he knew that unanswered question would torment her for the rest of her days.

'Get her out of here,' he ordered, turning and striding back towards the SUV.

The last thing Samantha saw before the doors slammed shut was Marcus Cain slipping on a pair of sunglasses as he entered the luxury vehicle, then with a clang the world outside vanished, leaving her alone in the darkness.

# Epilogue

*Krakow, Poland – three days later*

Careful to keep his face a blank mask devoid of expression, Alex Yates glanced down at the cards in his hand, silently contemplating them once again in the dim light cast by the single bulb positioned over the table.

Three queens, a ten and a two. Three of a kind – hardly a winning hand by any stretch of the imagination. The only question was whether it was better than his opponent's. Only the two of them were left in the game, the others having folded as the stakes were progressively raised.

Based on the hands that had been dealt and revealed so far, and the pattern of shuffling used by the dealer, Alex estimated about a 60 per cent probability that his own hand was superior. A different man would have been forced to go on gut instinct, making a judgement call based on little more than his belief in his own hand and whatever he could discern from his opponent. Alex was of another sort.

His mind, and the photographic memory that recorded the most minis-cule detail with perfect clarity, were new and unique weapons that his fellow players were unlikely to match.

Of all the ways he'd imagined his life playing out, this hadn't been one of them. About a year ago, armed only with a fake passport and a rucksack full of cash from his exploits trying to steal classified computer files from the CIA, he'd been forced to go on the run from the authorities.

He'd almost welcomed the release from his former existence of boredom and drudgery at the time, viewing a life on the run as an almost romantic, adventurous affair, his overactive imagination conjuring up visions of James Bond-style tuxedos, cocktails and high-stakes card games in opulent casinos.

Well, he'd gotten the last one, after a fashion. But there were no tuxedos to be seen in this underground gambling den hidden beneath the medieval streets of Krakow, and the shot of cheap vodka sitting before him wouldn't have done much to impress Mr Bond.

*If only my friends could see me now,* he thought with a sardonic smile.

'All in,' he judged at last, pushing all of his remaining money into the centre of the table. What the hell – of he was to screw this up, he'd rather do it in spectacular fashion.

His opponent was a lean-faced man in his thirties with a broken nose, his loosely buttoned shirt exposing a chest tattoo of Stalin's severed head lying in a basket that Alex was too scared to ask about; the kind of man Alex would normally have been happy to stay at least two time zones away from, fearing for his life if he said or did the wrong thing. But he was lucky enough to know the owner of this gambling club, having helped him track down a couple of men who'd tried to blackmail him over the internet. Alex had no idea what had happened to them after they'd been located, but he did know one thing for sure – while he was here, no harm would come to him.

Chewing slowly on the gum that had been in his mouth for the past two hours, his opponent's eyes rose slowly from the pile of money to Alex's face, searching for a tell.

Alex stared right back at him, giving him nothing.

'*Skurwysyn!*' he growled at last – loosely translated as 'son of a bitch' – as he laid his cards face down on the table.

Forcing himself not to smile, or to give into the urge to yell in relief that he now had enough money to live for another month, Alex reached out to collect his winnings as the other players dispersed in search of more drinks.

'Fuck it. When in Rome,' he decided, downing his shot of vodka. He'd earned it today.

Such was his preoccupation with his success, he almost didn't notice the sleek-looking blonde woman slide into a chair beside him.

'This is not quite how I pictured you using the money I gave you, Alex,' she chided him.

Alex froze in the midst of folding the Polish notes, closing his eyes as memories of last year suddenly came rushing back to him. Memories of being pursued, interrogated, almost murdered. Memories of watching friends die. Memories of a woman with blonde hair at the centre of it all.

'Anya,' he said, turning slowly to regard her. He could feel a chill running down his spine at the sight of that hard, cruelly beautiful face. 'Do I even want to know how you found me?'

'You are not as hard to track down as you think,' she explained. 'Especially when you make connections in the Polish underworld.'

That was enough to raise his ire. 'If you're here to deliver a lecture, spare me. There aren't a lot of job opportunities for guys with no employment history and a dodgy ID.'

'I did not come here to lecture you,' she said sharply, though her expression softened a little before she carried on. 'I came here to ask for your help.'

'My help?' he repeated, taken aback by her admission. 'What help can a retired computer hacker be to you?'

'Exactly the kind I need.'

She looked at him for a long moment, as if mentally sizing him up for the task that lay ahead, trying to decide whether or not he had what it took. It was a good couple of seconds later, but sure enough she made her decision.

'I need you to find someone for me.'

# Acknowledgements

Working as I have on the Ryan Drake series these past few years, I've come to understand that as an author, any book series really comes down to two things – patience and reward. Patience in setting up confrontations, characters and motivations; and reward in finally turning them loose on each other and letting the drama unfold. *Ghost Target* is, for me at least, the reward for several years of preparation and patience, and it has genuinely been one of the most enjoyable books I've ever written.

That said, it didn't come together just through my writing, but through the combined efforts of many people behind the scenes. First and foremost, I'd like to thank my editor Iain Millar for his insightful and professional guidance in shaping this book, and his ability to see straight to the heart of the story. My thanks as well go to all the staff at Canelo for their support and expertise, and to Dan Mogford for his excellent cover designs. And as always, my gratitude to my agent Diane Banks for her continued encouragement and guidance.